Amarjit Kaur Pannu is a biotech-scientist-turned-writer. She has been honored by several literary organizations in India and Canada for her captivating storytelling style. Her collection of stories and a science fiction in Punjabi was very well-received. Her novel, *Splintered Waters: Tryst with Destiny*, is an engaging saga of an intense desire for freedom, sacrifice, and healing power of love set during the British Rule in India.

Amarjit is a mother of two daughters and lives in California in a small town named Pinole, surrounded by lush green hills near San Francisco. She enjoys being in nature and loves morning walks in the hills.

To my daughters, Kiranjit and Jasmeet; son-in-law, Scott Hayes; grandsons, Mahaan and Mohkam; granddaughters, Layla, Kira, and Talia. Because of you all, my life is beautiful and worth living every moment of it.

Amarjit Kaur Pannu

SPLINTERED WATERS: TRYST WITH DESTINY

AUSTIN MACAULEY PUBLISHERS™

LONDON ∗ CAMBRIDGE ∗ NEW YORK ∗ SHARJAH

Ordering Information
Quantity sales: Special discounts are available on quantity purchases by corporations, associations, and others. For details, contact the publisher at the address below.

Publisher's Cataloging-in-Publication data
Pannu, Amarjit Kaur
Splintered Waters: Tryst with Destiny

ISBN 9781647501501 (Paperback)
ISBN 9781647501495 (Hardback)
ISBN 9781647501518 (ePub e-book)

Library of Congress Control Number: 2021901849

www.austinmacauley.com/us

First Published (2021)
Austin Macauley Publishers LLC
40 Wall Street, 33rd Floor, Suite 3302
New York, NY 10005
USA

mail-usa@austinmacauley.com
+1 (646) 5125767

I am indebted to the members of Berkeley Writers Circle for their constructive criticism and support. My special thanks to Alon Shalev, Madelin Wolf, Sheila Kogan, and John Putnam. I am thankful to Prof. Karamjit Singh Gill. Without his help, I could not have grasped the immensity and horrors of the biggest forced migration in the history of mankind during the partition of India and Pakistan. I would also like to acknowledge my brother, Amrik Singh, whose fatherly support kept my spirits up when I felt down and overwhelmed.

Table of Contents

Introduction

Ancient India, the land of gems and minerals, tea and spices, mysticism, and sophisticated prehistoric civilization has intrigued the world since time immemorial. The Indus Valley civilization, in 3000 BC, consisted of cities of Harappa and Mohenjo-Daro with multistory stone buildings, bathing pools, and sewage systems. The world's very first university, Takshila, was established in 700 BC and Nalanda University in 400 BC. Number zero and decimal points were created by a man named Aryabhatta who also discovered that the earth revolves around the sun and the moon orbits the earth. Albert Einstein once said, "We owe a lot to the Indians, who taught us how to count, without which no worthwhile scientific discovery could have been made."

Allured by India's wealth and prosperity the invaders plundered it time and again and returned with the loot along with slaves, elephants, and horses. The British came to India as The East India Trading Company and tactically subjugated the country by strategic ploys of treaties with the local maharajas. The systematic pillage of India's resources began that lasted almost two centuries. A well-known economist, Utsa Patnaik, in a research paper recently published by Columbia University Press estimated that Britain drained over $45 trillion from India.

Thousands of Indian Sikhs had come to the west coast of America in the 1890s and worked as farmers. Many of them leased the land and farmed with a great success. At the same time, a number of Indian students studied at the University of California, Berkeley. The Indians met constant resistance from European and American laborers, calling it a 'Brown Invasion.' In their own homeland, depressed and demoralized due to draining of resources by the British causing famines and disease, they had come to America for a better future but what they faced was hatred.

While the British ruled with an iron fist, the struggle for independence continued in one form or another throughout the Raj. The world knows about Gandhi, but very few know about the martyrs of The Ghadar Party

(Revolutionary Party) founded in San Francisco in 1913 by Sohan Singh as its president and Har Dayal a lecturer at Stanford University, with an aim to go back and free their country from the British. Soon the party grew to great numbers with branches in Europe, Northern Africa, and the Middle East.

A young man named Kartar Singh was sent by his parents to study at UC Berkeley in 1912 at the age of 17. He was aghast and humiliated, being called 'Damn Hindu' by the whites. But at the same time, his young mind was mesmerized by the free lives of the Americans. He quit school to join the Revolutionary Party to overthrow the British who treated Indians as inferiors in their own homeland while guzzling their natural resources. The Ghadar Party started printing a paper, Ghadar di Goonj (Echoes of revolution), which was published in Punjabi, Hindi, Urdu, and Bengali languages. The printing operation was run by Kartar Singh Sarabha by a hand-operated machine. He wrote patriotic poetry and articles to expose the atrocities being committed on Indians by the British government. The paper included articles about the drainage of grain and raw materials, leaving people hungry and destitute. The paper was sent to Indians living in many countries of the world.

Kartar gave passionate talks to Indians in the United States urging them to join and fund the Ghadar Party whose aim was to go back and infiltrate the army to revolt and liberate India from the British. He explained to them how death was a thousand times better than a life of slavery filled with humiliation.

A British man W. C. Hopkinson, born and raised in India, knew the language and he set up a network of spies. As the members of the Ghadar Party left the United States in batches, Kartar Singh was among the largest group of sixty men to leave San Francisco by a steamship on August 29, 1914. He visited various British garrisons to organize discontented Indian soldiers in support of the revolution. But before they could carry out their planned uprising on February 21, 1915, they were betrayed by Kirpal, a police informer. In the coming days, thousands were arrested and the local soldiers disarmed.

Kartar Singh Sarabha was executed at age 19, by the British on November 16, 1915, along with 42 of his companions. Another 8000 were incarcerated or exiled for life.

The execution of Kartar created a tornado of emotions in the young minds and they vowed to walk in his footsteps. Although the uprising failed it had laid a foundation stone for future revolutionary movements. Kartar Singh

Sarabha was a hero to many including Bhagat Singh whose execution on March 23rd, 1931 at the age of 23, shook the core of the mighty British Empire.

The novel Splintered Waters: Tryst with Destiny is the story of those who walked in Kartar's footsteps including my grandfathers Lal Singh and Hakam Singh, to remove the yoke of slavery from India's neck.

The party headquarters at 5 Wood Street, San Francisco, is now a memorial to the Ghadar Party where festivities are held in their memories and their sacrifices are celebrated. A Ghadar Party Trust was established in Stockton to preserve the relics and memories of the martyrs.

Part-I
The Obedient Son

Chapter 1

Loud thumping, the door shuddered. Thunderous shouts of "open the door" and frantic barking of stray dogs made them jump out of their cozy beds. "It's the police!" Jinder whispered. They ran upstairs and jumped from the roof behind the house, first Jinder, then Hakam. The ground shook beneath their panicked strides and the wind smacked their faces as they ran barefoot to the limit of their breath.

The yelling and pounding on the door faded behind them as they reached the outer boundary of the village. Soon, they could not hear anything other than their own hammering heartbeats. Out of breath, they entered into the maize fields.

The maize crop on both sides of the unpaved road, not far from the village, was the best hiding place they could find, for now. The long dried-out leaves of the ready-to-harvest crop made a rustling sound with the slightest movement. The two friends sat still with their eyes and ears wide open.

They shivered in their flimsy undershirts in the mid-November cold night. The time seemed to have frozen as did their fingers and toes. Sitting on the frosty hard ground what felt like forever, they heard the clip-clop sound of hoofbeats and men talking. They could see the shadowy figures through the maize stalks. A man jogged next to two British officers on horseback, trying to keep up.

Hakam pressed Jinder's elbow. Holding their breath, they listened.

"You wasted our time, you filthy Indian hog!" shouted one of the officers in a throaty voice.

"Sahib... Sir, I saw them with my own eyes, last evening," the voice sounded familiar.

"Then why didn't you inform us at that time?"

"Sahib, I didn't think they would leave during the night."

"You didn't think...?"

"These Indian idiots don't think!" the officer with the thick voice howled. "Go back, you animal, or I will arrest *you*, instead!"

Jinder and Hakam huddled trying not to breathe loudly. Shielded by the maize plants they heard every word. After the officers left, the familiar-sounding man stood still for a few moments and then turned towards the village.

"You will not be paid anything. Do you understand?" the police officer shouted over his shoulder as he trotted away.

"It is Karim!" Hakam whispered.

"He's selling us out." Jinder shook with rage. "It must've been him behind Jaydev's arrest."

They waited a while longer to make sure Karim would have reached his home. Teeth chattering and the wind whipping, they started homeward. The village was dark and quiet as if nothing had happened.

Jinder's mother clung to him as they entered the house through the broken door, "They said they'll be back," she wept. "I didn't know where you were."

"They won't be back tonight, Ma, they're gone." Jinder walked her to her cot, trying to calm her down.

"We should be leaving now." Hakam shifted his weight from one leg to the other.

"Don't you think it will be safe here for a while?" Jinder picked up two blankets from the cot, giving one to Hakam and wrapped the other around him, "And Karim needs a visit from us."

Hakam nodded. "He does."

They sat in their cots waiting for daybreak. When a yellowish glow appeared on the Eastern horizon, Jinder said to his mother, "It's time to leave, Ma."

She looked at him. Tears started flowing again.

In the misty light of the morning, he saw a red circular mark on her forehead and cried out, "What happened?"

"They pushed a gun into my forehead." Her left cheek was swollen with a handprint on it that Jinder had not seen at night.

"Feringhee bastards…!" Grinding his teeth, he threw a fist into the air. "Your days are numbered!"

"They kept asking where you were."

"They will hear from us, soon." He gave her a quick hug. "Take care of yourself, Ma."

She buried her head into his chest. "How can I let you go when the police are roaming like rabid dogs?"

"Ma, listen, we were sleeping lions and they woke us up. We are Singh, the lions, and we are not afraid of dogs!" He bent down to touch her feet for motherly respect.

"Let's go!" he turned to Hakam.

They walked out the door towards Karim's house. Jinder stopped in front of a house about two streets down, "This is the one," he said.

Hakam knocked.

Karim turned pale like a lemon as he opened the door. He gasped as if he saw a cobra at the door.

"Aren't you happy to see us?" Hakam stared into his eyes.

"When…when did you come?" Karim stuttered.

"Last night," Jinder and Hakam said, simultaneously.

"Since we didn't see you at the last meeting, we thought we should update you," Jinder said.

"Let's go for a walk. We'll talk on the way." Hakam held his arm and the three of them headed towards the maize fields. Karim moved forward but his feet seemed to drag backward. An unnatural silence between the three was unsettling.

They stopped by the maize crops, where they had heard Karim and the police at night. The first rays of the sun struggled to pierce through the gray haze. Last night's harsh wind had come to a standstill but a chill lingered in the air. A flock of noisy sparrows landed next to them in a frenzy of chirping and hopping. The very next moment they flew away creating a momentary silence, broken by a rabbit running across the dirt road. Jinder's eyes followed the rabbit, *we were like this rabbit last night, running away from dogs, and this traitor is one of them.* Jinder fumed inside.

"So, making money these days?" Hakam asked.

"How would I make money?" Karim's brows joined at the base of his nose.

Jinder lunged at him. "You want to know?" He held him by the neck and started choking. "How about selling out Jaydev? How about selling all of us to the British?"

Karim's eyes bulged and arms flailed.

"Let go of his neck, Jinder!" Hakam yelled. "Have you lost your mind?" Jinder pushed Karim away.

"I swear. It wasn't me." Karim coughed massaging his neck.

"It wasn't you even last night? You son of a bitch, traitor!" Jinder trembled vehemently.

"I don't know what you are talking about!"

"I tell you what I'm talking about."

Jinder pounced on him again and grabbed his hand twisting his index finger. "Is this the finger you pointed at us?" he sneered. "We heard you last night."

"Stop this madness, Jinder!" Hakam yelled.

"You're asking me to stop the madness, after what he did?"

"We cannot become the torturers!" Hakam shouted.

Jinder gazed at Hakam as if he had snapped out of a spell. The maize plants stood tall, studded with corncobs containing sweetness in their bosom, oblivious to the bitterness that was all around them. The bitterness of betrayal between the friends who had sworn to fight for a common cause, a cause for restoring the dignity of a nation, a cause for rebuilding the honor of the downtrodden, a cause for removing the yoke of slavery to bring freedom.

"You broke the pledge we made holding hands." Jinder sounded more hurt than angry. "You betrayed the spirit of Kartar's martyrdom." Overcome by emotions he stepped away but seconds later turned back like a whirlwind. Eyes bloodshot he towered over Karim, "they hanged him. He was 19. Do you hear me? He had just returned from America! San Francisco! And this tyrannical British government executed him."

"I will never do it again, I swear." Karim fell on his knees, begging.

Hakam sat next to Karim on the ground, "Listen, the informers don't last long. If one of us doesn't kill you, the police will. Their policy of 'divide and rule' has worked for them because of despicable traitors like you."

"I am sorry." Karim sounded as if speaking from inside a cave.

"You're sorry because you were caught." Jinder still seethed in anger. "How can we ever trust you?"

"I will prove it to you."

"Prove to us? How?"

"Sever my arm if I do it again." Karim looked at Jinder, in tears.

A contemptuous smile appeared on Jinder's face. "I will sever your head next time," he scowled. The three walked back towards the village.

The village had woken up with the roosters crowing and the sound of churning milk for making butter was coming from almost every house. The melody of the tinkling bells around the bullock's necks announced the farmers going to their fields, to start the day with plowing, harvesting, or tending to cattle.

As Karim split to go home, Jinder held his arm, "Never again!"

"Never!" Karim mouthed.

He's going to betray us again. Hakam is too trusting. Jinder could not stop worrying as they walked towards the bus stop.

Chapter 2

They arrested Jinder! The words kept ringing in his ears. My son could be next. Pacing in the room, Rattan Singh felt a wave of terror passing through his body and he leaned against the door. They could hang him or exile him to Kala Pani forever. We could lose our farm, our house, cattle. Our horses! They will confiscate everything and turn us into beggars. Rattan Singh shook his head trying to shake off the thought.

These college boys don't understand the power of the British. How stupid it is to go against the mighty empire and jeopardize your whole life!

"Lal has to come home! No more college!" he blurted out.

"What is it, Sardar ji? Are you alright?" Bhani's steps froze as she looked at his pallid face.

"I'm leaving for Lahore."

"Now? For what?" her questions matched the two creases that suddenly appeared on her forehead. She squinted.

"Lal has to come home."

"Why?"

"I'll tell you later. Pack a few clothes for me." Rattan Singh stomped out of the room. Bhani followed.

"Tell me what's going on, Sardar ji!"

"He has gotten himself into a very risky situation, I hear. He has to come home."

"What risky situation?"

"Stop pestering me, Bhani!" Rattan Singh bellowed, "I said, I will tell you everything when I bring him home." He hurried to the outer courtyard.

"Kaku, get the horse ready!" he hollered.

"What has happened to him?" Bhani muttered stuffing a few clothes in a bag.

The servant quickly saddled the horse, "Where to, Sardar ji?" he asked.

Taking the reins from him Rattan Singh mounted the horse.

22

"Hop on!" he said. Kaku hesitated for a moment and then hoisted himself up, behind him.

Bhani hurried through the courtyard carrying a small bag, "Sardar ji's clothes." She handed the bag to Kaku.

As soon as they were out of the village, the horse broke into a gallop. The station master was locking the door when they arrived at the one-room countryside railway station.

"You folks are just a few minutes late," he said.

"Oh, no! When is the next train?" Rattan Singh asked.

"In two hours. But it doesn't stop here." He got on his bicycle and paddled away.

"When is the one that stops here?" Rattan Singh called after him.

"Tomorrow morning at seven," the station master said without looking back and kept going.

"What now?" Rattan Singh looked at the horse. She was panting and frothing at the mouth. Sweat had lathered up around her ears and chest.

"Get her some water, Kaku." He pointed to the hand pump nearby.

The horse limped as Kaku walked her to the pump.

"What happened?" Rattan Singh dashed towards her. He examined the hooves one by one but could not find anything wrong. "Maybe she's just tired."

Kaku filled the dented iron trough lying under the waterspout. The horse drank like she had been thirsty forever. He splashed her head and chest. Her breathing returned to normal but the limp stayed. Letting her rest another hour did not help.

"It might be a sprained ankle," Rattan Singh said to Kaku. "Go back and take her to the doctor if she still limps. I'm staying here for the night."

"There's no place to sleep here, Sardar ji." Kaku stared at the locked room.

"I'll be fine. Two people would be hard on the horse." Rattan Singh looked at the dusty wooden bench outside the locked room. "Also, remind Hafiz to plow the field next to the water well tomorrow morning."

"Yes, Sardar ji." Kaku nodded holding the reins.

The late evening was hot and humid. Not a leaf stirred. The *tahli* trees near the water pump and the *deks* growing across the train track stood motionless. Sweat trickled down Rattan Singh's spine giving him an itchy quiver. He fanned himself with a towel Bhani had packed along with an extra shirt, a *churidar,* and a turban.

23

The rural railway station, built not long ago, consisted of only a small brick room by the side of a single track. The station master lazily dozed all day except when a train in the morning and another in the evening stopped to pick up an occasional passenger. A slightly raised unpaved area cleared of the vegetation, stretching about twenty feet on either side of the room, served as the platform.

Rattan Singh recalled when the neighboring villagers had protested, though unsuccessfully, when the train track was built right through their crops, a few years ago. Only the freight trains passed carrying grain and cotton from Punjab to be transported to England. Later a passenger train was added that stopped once in the morning and again in the evening, anyone hardly used. Slowly people put their grievances behind and went on with their lives. An occasional traveler took the train to Lahore.

Rattan Singh anxiously walked back and forth on the platform, avoiding the muddy puddles left by last night's downpour. "They arrested Jinder too!" He sighed noisily. "These boys have lost their way. They don't know what they're getting into." He quickened his steps as if he could reach Lahore by some magic carpet on the platform. The next moment he stepped into a puddle and the mud flew in all directions including his face and clothes.

"Son of a bitch!" he yelled wiping his beard and forehead. The brown sludge on his white shirt got worse when he tried to wipe it off. Embarrassed he looked around, "good, no one's here to see me like this." Tall and burly Rattan Singh smiled coyly like a young woman.

He washed his face from the hand pump and opened the bag to change, but chose not to. Tomorrow morning, he decided. Never know what the night may bring, or he made another stupid mistake.

The freight train loaded with grain whooshed by like a bullet and shook the platform and the trees nearby. Rattan Singh held on to his turban from flying away and ran toward the bench away from the platform.

A light breeze picked up from the east helping to dry his clothes. He lay down on the hard bench using his bag as a pillow, but could hardly close his eyes. Staring at the cloudless night sky studded with millions of shimmering diamonds put him in awe. Without blinking he kept looking at the sky. "So many stars!" he whispered. For the moment all the worries of the world evaporated.

Chirping crickets and the wind swirling through the leaves produced a symphony he had never paid attention to before. The branches of the *tahli* tree moved like a synchronized slow dance in response to the music of the wind. Rattan Singh felt like a participant in the miraculous show nature had put forth. He smiled ecstatically. He did not know how long he was in that elated state when a jackal howled nearby and brought him back to the uncomfortable wooden bench. Another jackal joined in and the opus of nature was turned into a kind of dirge.

"Huh, the spoilers never fail!" Rattan Singh chuckled.

The breeze lulled him into a slumber and he woke up before the sunrise to the sound of birds twittering and bathing in the trough by the hand pump. The train arrived soon after he cleaned up and changed.

Fears about his son's future popped up in his mind the moment he settled on the cushionless seat. Memories of execution of Kartar Singh along with many of his comrades, who had returned from America with a dream to free their country from the British, became fresh on his mind. The ruthless massacre of more than a thousand men, women, and children, celebrating the holy festival of *Baisakhi* near the Golden Temple, Amritsar, was chafed on his heart like a permanent blister that erupted every time he heard the word *revolution* against the British Raj.

Rattan Singh jolted out of his thoughts by the shrilly voices of hawkers selling peanuts and bananas and handkerchiefs, on the platform as the train stopped. Ignoring all the hustle and bustle he walked out of the railway station.

******

"Is everything alright, *Bapu ji*?" Lal leaped out of the chair when his father unexpectedly showed up at his college dorm room.

"No, everything is not alright, Lal!"

"Why? Is Ma okay?"

"She is fine for now," Rattan Singh said looking around the room, "but may not be for long."

"What is it, *Bapu ji*? What's wrong?"

"I want you to come home with me."

"Why?"

"You don't need any more college education."

"You're not making any sense."

"I am not making any sense and you are? The road you and your friends have taken will lead to nothing but destruction!"

"What road are you talking about? I am studying here."

"There are more important things than books."

Lal looked at his father, *have you lost your mind?* He wanted to say. But the words came out differently. "What could be more important than my studies?"

"Your life! Your mother's and mine." Rattan Singh's assertive voice reverberated in the room.

"But, *Bapu ji…*"

"Do you know what they will do to you if you're caught? You boys don't realize the power they have over us."

"That's why we…"

"Pack up, we have to leave now." Rattan Singh gave his ultimatum.

"No, I cannot."

"You cannot? Do you not have any respect left in your head, for your elders? I am your father!" Rattan Singh roared and jumped up from the chair. Face red, his hands shook with anger.

"*Bapu ji*, please calm down," Lal said. *What is it with him? I've never seen him like this.*

"I cannot calm down until we leave this place." Rattan Singh's voice suddenly was much calmer as he sat back.

An uncomfortable silence hung in the room. Both sat awkwardly trying to avoid each other's eyes.

"Listen, Son, I want you to come home. We need to talk, your mother, you, and me," Rattan Singh said softly.

"Okay, but only for a few days."

"That's my son!" Rattan Singh heaved a sigh of relief.

"But I have to take care of something. I'll be back soon." Lal left before Rattan Singh could say anything.

Hakam had not arrived yet but two of their associates waited in the library. Lal told them to let Hakam know, he'll be back in a few days.

On his way back, Lal wondered, how his father found out his association with the revolutionaries. Maybe, Jinder's much-advertised arrest a few days ago had alarmed him.

Rattan Singh had already packed most of his clothes when Lal returned. "Let's go," he said slinging the bag over his shoulder.

Lal looked at the bookshelves that Rattan Singh had not touched. Better leave them here. A reason to come back, he thought.

Many rickshaw pullers hurried towards them as they walked out of the college gate.

"Bus station," Rattan Singh said getting into the rickshaw.

Lal looked back and kept looking until the rickshaw made a turn.

They reached home late at night. Bhani clung to Lal, "I will never let you out of my sight ever again, Lali!" His shoulder felt wet with her tears.

"What are you saying, Ma? I'm not going anywhere," he said wiping her tears with the heels of his hands. "We'll talk in the morning."

Lal spent the night tossing and turning, "*Bapu ji* does not understand our cause."

Chapter 3

The midday sun shone high up in the sky. Hakam looked at his dwarfed shadow walking beside him.

"Did you notice something?" he said to Harjit.

"Notice what?" She looked to her left and then right.

"Our shadows! That's what the British have done to us. Dwarfed our thinking, squeezed our strength out, and reduced the masses into beggars." Hakam stopped walking.

Harjit stood next to him looking at her own stunted shadow. "That's exactly what they've done to us, enslaved our intellect."

"What we were and what they turned us into." Hakam's sneer turned into a serious grunt, "We have to bring pride back into the minds of our people!"

"I doubt if the British even know how advanced our civilization was when the Europeans still lived in caves," Harjit said, "And now they are the masters and we, their servants."

"You know, Aryabhatta, one of the ancient scientists, calculated the value of 'pi' and added a decimal point to mathematics in the fifth century," Hakam said. "He also accurately calculated the distance between the earth and the sun and explained how the eclipses happen."

"But for us, an eternal eclipse has fallen over our land. The perpetual darkness blurred our vision and tarnished our thinking." Harjit looked down on her shadow again.

"They even devised the numerals from one to nine before 500 BC. The Arabs later adopted them and hundreds of years later did the Westerns. And let's not forget, we are the descendants of the great minds and we still have it within us."

"I'm sure we do. We're getting late for your speech and you seem to be making it here, without the audience." Harjit laughed looking at her wristwatch.

"Oh, I am?" he chuckled, wrapping his arm around her shoulders.

They hurried towards the college mathematics department. "Maybe you should talk to them about the geniuses of India in your speech today," Harjit said.

"Good idea, my genius! I will."

The room resonated with whispers, as they entered. "That's his wife, Harjit, with him," someone said.

"They got married?"

"Yes, they did."

The large room with a high ceiling looked almost empty with about fifteen men and four women sitting on metallic chairs. They stood up, folding hands as the customary greetings.

Hakam and Harjit did the same in reciprocation. Harjit walked to the women and took a chair beside them. Hakam's chair had been placed in front of the room facing the group. He closed the door behind him before taking his seat. He looked around the room. A few of the young men and a woman were newcomers. They introduced themselves. The tall and slim man was Teja Singh and he was a third-year college student. Another man told his name Ram Singh, also in the third year and his younger sister Raji, a first-year student.

"I'm Hakam Singh. I graduated last year from this college," he said shaking hands. "My wife, Harjit," he pointed to her.

The atmosphere in the room was rather somber.

"You might have already heard about Jinder," Hakam said pulling his chair a little forward.

"How did it happen?" Surjit asked, "First Jaydev, now Jinder."

"Karim betrayed them both." Hakam's hands curled into fists as he tried to control his anger and squirmed in his chair.

"Karim was an informer?" Surjit gasped.

Soon muffled voices engulfed the room. Their lips moved, but words were inaudible. They shook heads in disbelief and they looked at each other with eyeballs about to pop out.

"What a shame!" A man in the back stood up shouting.

"They arrested Karim too, yesterday," Hakam said loud enough to draw their attention. And a round of loud voices began.

"That's what they do to the moles. Use them for a while and then get rid of them."

"Karim deserved it!"

"The informers sell their soul for a few coins."

"That's how the British have ruled us for centuries."

Hakam stood up and pushed the chair to the side, "We are members of *Punjab Naujawan Sabha*, The Punjab Youngmans Association, started by our leader, Sardar Bhagat Singh. We will crush the traitors and their masters!" he roared. The veins in his neck became taut and his eyes bloody red. He clenched his teeth and waved his fist into the air.

"The British have ears but they do not hear," Hakam shouted. "Their eyes look around, but only for gold. Their hearts beat in their chest but they have no empathy." His voice was heavy with the weight of afflictions of bondage, but his head was held high with the spirit of self-confidence.

People in the room gazed at him. Some nodded and some seemed in a trance, just staring at him.

"This is our land, our home and they swindled it by guns and ghastly tactics. They trounced upon our natural resources and filled the Londoners' pockets."

Every word from Hakam's mouth came out like a thunderbolt, colliding with the hearts and minds of his listeners.

"They bleed our country's veins by taking more than a hundred crore rupees to England every year. They not only loot the gold and silver, but they also ship our wheat and rice to England as well, or sell it to other countries for profit, while our people go hungry and beg on the streets. The fruit of our back-breaking labor becomes their wine and lavish dinners, while India's poor face famines and disease."

After a moment of silence, he shouted, "We will force open the ruler's deaf ears so that they hear the voices of revolt. As our leader, Sardar Bhagat Singh says, 'If the deaf is to hear, the sound has to be very loud.'

"We will remove the blinders from their eyes so that they find their way back to their island. That's our goal, no more Feringhee rule!"

The room exploded with clapping as if a sudden hailstorm fell on to the tin roof.

They all stood up, "No more Feringhee rule!" the room echoed.

"Shame, shame! Down with the Raj!" they shouted, waving fists.

Hakam stood calmly waiting for the commotion to go down. The stillness that followed was poignant yet satisfying.

"Let me share a word or two about Gandhi. He goes around preaching non-violence. The question is what happens after he leaves?" Hakam's gaze glided over the young men and women listening to his every word and sat as if wonder struck.

"Not long ago, he scolded the Hindus for being cowards and the Muslims for being bullies. Let me repeat his exact words." Hakam took out a newspaper cutting from his pocket and unfolded it,

"Gandhi says, 'There is no doubt in my mind that in most of the quarrels the Hindus come out second best. But my own experience confirms the opinion that the *Musalman* as rule is a bully and Hindu as a rule is a coward.'"

An ocean deep silence fell in the room. "Gandhi further says, 'I, as a Hindu, am more ashamed of Hindu cowardice than I am angry at the *Musalman* bullying.'"

Hakam looked at the audience sarcastically shaking his head, "Tell me something, won't this kind of remarks infuriate both sides and create more violence instead? Won't this kind of message divide the people more than uniting them?" Hakam's voice thundered.

Angry voices erupted in the room like someone had thrown a firecracker into the crowd. Most of them stood up shouting.

"Gandhi and his non-violence double standards. What a hypocrite!"

"No wonder violence breaks out as soon as he leaves the gathering."

"I think he's kind of a cunning genius."

"He incites hostilities and calls it non-violence?"

"Please, sit down!" Hakam shouted. "You can read the whole piece in Gandhi's May 29th, 1924, Young India journal." Hakam waved the paper as everyone took their seats.

"Listen, everyone," Hakam shouted, "Our goal is not to create divisions. Our goal is to make people understand what slavery has done to our nation, regardless if they are Hindu, Sikh, or Muslims. Our goal is not to beg, but to stand up for our motherland's independence."

Hakam stood in the front of the room, tall and strong. His eyes radiated confidence and his gestures conveyed determination. "On the other hand, in Gandhi's opinion, India is not ready for independence. He has said it many times."

"What a shame!" someone stood up.

"We are ready. If not now, when?" Another person hollered louder than the first.

"Lastly," Hakam gestured them to sit down, "I urge you to never forget the martyrs who gave their life for freedom. They hanged Kartar Singh Sarabha only 19 years old. Today we are all Kartar Singhs. Hundreds of more will take his place. I will read one of his poems from the magazine, 'Echoes of Freedom' the *Ghadar Party* published in San Francisco, America." Harjit handed him a piece of paper.

"Kartar's family had sent him to study at the University of California, Berkeley. But he quit his studies and joined the Revolutionary Party founded by Sohan Singh and Har Dayal, a visiting professor at Stanford University. Thousands of men joined in and the party aspired to organize themselves and come back to India to end the tyrannical British Raj.

Here's what Kartar wrote,

If they ask who we are
Tell them, our name is fearless
Tell them, our duty is to end the tyranny
Our profession is to launch revolution

Hakam's voice echoed in the room as he recited the poem. The young men stood up clapping, repeating the lines, 'Our duty is to end the tyranny.' Hakam waited for them to settle down before reciting the rest of the poem,

Tell them
That is our religion and our prayer
Our Guru, our worship
This is our only Allah, our only Rama
This is our only God
To end the tyranny of the Raj.

"End the tyranny of the Raj!" they sang and clapped at the end of the poem.

"Kartar Singh Sarabha!" Hakam shouted.

"Lives forever!" the rest of the men answered.

"We will continue what the Ghadar Party started in San Francisco. Each of us can inspire another ten, and so on. One day we will break the manacles of slavery and end the perpetual eclipse that has gloomed our very existence." Hakam ended the speech to the chants of,

'Long live revolution'

'Down with the Raj'

He left the room, Harjit followed. "We will talk about India's contributions to Math and Science next time. It's too big a subject to cover quickly." Hakam held her hand.

She nodded, "Well, there's always a next time. Your speech was great!"

Chapter 4

"What is it *Bapu ji*, that you brought me home for?" Lal Singh asked his father, the next morning, while having breakfast of *Aloo Parotha* and *Lassi*. "What's the emergency you were so worried about?"

"I wasn't worried about nothing, Lali. There *is* an emergency!" Rattan Singh tilted the glass over his mouth taking the last sip of *Lassi*. "Let's walk to the farm and we'll talk."

It had been a while since they had walked together to the farm. Whenever Lal came back from college, he went around the farm on horseback or he walked with Kaku. On the way, Kaku updated him about everything that had happened in the village and at the farm while he was away. Which one of their old friends was getting married and who had a fight with whom and who had won the *Kabbadi* match and so on? Kaku had worked in their house since he was a boy, and his father before him. Being about the same age, he was more like a friend to Lal than a servant.

Walking with his father that morning, Lal felt a strange uneasiness between them. The sun peeked through a thin feathery layer of clouds. The morning breeze was cool and refreshing, but Lal's mind was occupied by disquieting thoughts about his strained relationship with his father. They reached the farm without saying much to each other. Kaku had spread a quilted coverlet on the wooden divan under the mulberry tree by the *Tindan Wala Khooh,* (The bucket irrigation well.) Rattan Singh ignored the divan and kept walking to the fields. Lal close by his side.

"Look," Rattan Singh pointed to the wheat fields.

The young green wheat crops stretched as far as the eye could see. The delicate wheat shoots waved in the breeze in unison. A few acres of cattle fodder and sugarcane crops to the other side also looked healthy and vibrant. Lal felt a refreshed connection with the place that had been slowly fading from his mind since he had gone to college. Although he went around the farm every time he came home, it was more like a casual visit. Lal looked at the crops and could not keep his eyes off of it. He was mesmerized by the stretches of luscious and healthy wheat plants, slowly waving and dancing in the gentle morning wind.

"Looks like, we'll have a robust yield this year, *Bapu ji*," Lal said.

"Yes, certainly looks like it," Rattan Singh said glancing back at the crops, "the maize harvest did very well this year too."

They walked back to the irrigation well and settled on the divan. After a long uneasy silence, Rattan Singh said, "I think you have enough education needed to run a farm and a household. No one in our village has even gone to high school and you have almost two years of college."

"What you mean *Bapu ji*?" Lal stared at him.

"I mean you don't need to find a job and work for someone else when you have your own fertile land."

"You're asking me to quit college and come home?"

"No Lal, I'm telling you to come home and take care of your farm!"

"Didn't you and Ma felt proud of me going to college? And now you want me to leave everything and come home?"

"Yes, we did, but that was until you lost your way and got into the risky business."

"What did I do wrong?" Lal said louder than usual, raising his arms in the air.

"You're asking me? Don't you know how dangerous it is to go against the law and the government?" Rattan Singh got up from the divan, glaring, "I know all about you and Hakam."

"You call it a government? It's a rule of tyranny. Don't you see how they are filling up the prisons?"

"And pretty soon you will end up in a prison too. What will then happen to your revolution and the 'people' you say you want to help?" Rattan Singh trembled. "You could be exiled for life, or even sent to the gallows!"

"Guru Gobind Singh sacrificed his whole family, including his four sons fighting against the unjust Mughal rulers." Lal tried to reason.

"I am not Guru Gobind Singh! Do you hear me?" Rattan Singh stomped away.

"But, *Bapu ji*…" Lal sat with his hands in his lap. The apprehension of the turmoil that could change his and his parent's life forever was overwhelming. *No argument can convince him now.* Lal looked at his father taking long determined strides towards the men chopping fodder for cattle. *Either I defy everything he says and leave, never to return. That will certainly kill Ma and maybe him too. Or just wait a few days and let him cool down, which may not happen. I might end up being a farmer forever.*

Wrestling his tumultuous thoughts he got up from the divan but sat down soon after. A little later got up again but could not take more than a few steps towards the wheat fields and turned back. Hissing a noisy sigh he sat perhaps unintentionally, where his father was sitting a few minutes ago. He rested his face in his palms while the thoughts arose and ebbed like a twig in the whirlpool of a flooded river. Hearing footsteps he looked up.

"Lal," Kaku said and sat by him quietly. Lal felt the comforting calmness of his friend's presence.

"I'm okay," Lal said after a while.

Kaku gave him a light pat on the arm and walked to the irrigation well. The sound of water falling from the buckets one after the other onto the gutter and the *tik, tik, tik* sound of the wheel stopper attracted Lal's attention. He was always captivated by the simple but brilliant mechanism of the well. A blindfolded bullock harnessed to a horizontal wooden pole turns two iron wheels with gears. The vertical wheel is connected to a heavy chain running over a pulley above the well. Several iron *Tindan* (buckets) attached to the chain work in a vertical circle, going down into the well to fill up and empty out onto a gutter above the well, before going down to fill up again. The gutter carries the water up to the ground channels reaching the fields for irrigation.

Who would have invented this simple but brilliant system of pulley and the buckets for irrigation? Lal wondered every time he saw the *Khooh* working. For the moment he was absorbed in the beauty of the growing crops and the chorus of gushing water and twittering birds. He felt a weight gradually lifting from his mind. He closed his eyes and pulled in a deep breath, letting it out slowly.

"Lal, Son," he felt his father's hand over his shoulder and opened his eyes. Rattan Singh wrapped his arm around him and sat quietly for a while.

"Son," he began in a soft and caring tone, "you know you are the life of this place. You are our life, mine, and your mother's. If something happened to you, we will not have any purpose in this world or desire to live any longer."

"I will never do anything to hurt you or Ma or anyone else, *Bapu ji*," Lal said.

"You are a compassionate man and you want to improve people's lives, I know that. But the route you've chosen will hurt you and the very people you want to help." Rattan Singh tightened his fatherly embrace.

No matter what I say now, it's not going to make any difference. Lal kept quiet for the want of right words.

"Do you see all those poor children running around naked in summer and shiver in the freezing winters? I think giving them clothes and helping them is patriotic enough."

Rattan Singh waited for Lal's reaction but there was none. He continued, "Grow more crops, Lali! Give work to more people. Our village depends on us."

Lal looked at his father with eyes wide open as if he was seeing something for the first time. *That makes sense. But how can I just give up everything and come home to become a farmer?*

"A farmer's land is the breadbasket for so many, and we have been farmers for generations." Rattan Singh seemed to have read his mind. "We take pride in being farmers, Lali, and you should too!"

That was the end of conversation. His father got up from the divan and walked towards the men working in the fields.

Lal stood up and looked at the wheat crops. "Looks good," he said.

Chapter 5

I turned my back on them. The thought haunted him day and night. Every time he sat to write to Hakam, the words would not go beyond 'Dear Hakam.' His hand shook and the pen refused to go on. The blank paper stared back at his frustrated face. A little while later the crumpled up unwritten letter joined the others in the wastebasket.

Lal looked at the pile of crunched up paper balls, "What's wrong with me?" A muted screech shook him to the core. "Tomorrow, the letter!" he said and went out the gate towards the farm.

Daily rounds of the farm and watching the crops grow was comforting and took the feeling of remorse away for the time being. But the solace was short-lived and the feeling of guilt trounced his mind as soon as he was alone. He felt a sinkhole swallowing him inch by inch and he flailed his arms and legs for a tether to hang on to the solid ground.

Bhani sat by him one evening. "What's wrong, Son? You never smile, you never laugh as you used to." She fixed her eyes on his face as if trying to read something written in a foreign language. "What has the college done to you?"

"Nothing's wrong, Ma," Lal said without looking at her.

"Maybe you're lonely. I'm going to find a beautiful bride for you." She smiled taking his face in her palms, "my handsome boy!"

"I don't want to get married, Ma, and I am not lonely."

"Everyone gets married," Bhani said. "So many families have approached us with their daughter's marriage proposals. But we haven't said yes to anyone yet."

"Ma, let's not talk about this." Lal stood up from the cot and walked away.

"What has happened to my son?" Bhani mumbled, letting out a sigh.

Lal turned back looking at her worried face. "Don't worry, Ma. I'm fine," he said wrapping his arms around her, "I will tell you when I'm ready to get married."

"Promise?" she asked.

"I promise! Sleep well, Ma."

The days and nights flew by like there was a contest between the two, which one of them runs faster. Lal felt a competition going on between the guilt of abandoning his friends and redress of being a dutiful son. The time of day decided which one of the two had the upper hand.

I will definitely write to Hakam today and mail it. A feeling of resolve and contentment came over him. *Today!* He looked at the basket that had been emptied out by one of the household helpers. He grinned.

On his way to the farm, he stroked his pocket to make sure he had the pen and paper with him.

"You look a bit happy today!" Kaku said as he cleared the fallen leaves from the divan.

"I'm always happy, Kaku. Who says I am not?" Lal helped clear the leaves.

"I think most of the time your eyes and sometimes the whole of you shouts, *I'm sad!*" Kaku said gazing at him.

Lal laughed, "You are…something Kaku!" He smacked him with a friendly punch.

"Do you have a woman?" Kaku asked looking intently at his face.

"No, I don't."

"You need one. That's why you're sad."

"I'm not sad, Kaku, I'm just…"

"You are a good man, Lal," Kaku said. "You, Sardar Lal Singh, are a good man."

"Okay Kaku, okay! You're a good man too and a good friend."

After Kaku left to tend to the cattle, Lal straightened the folds from the paper and wrote, Dear Hakam, I am sorry I haven't written to you sooner, but I…

What next? He sat with the end of the pen between his teeth. His right knee shook up and down in a jittery rhythm. Minutes passed. The paper stayed blank. *How can you explain things like this in a letter? It's just not possible!* Lal folded the paper and closed the pen. "I have to go there myself," he suddenly felt a little better and went to check the irrigation channels for any leakage. Everything looked good. No leaks. Satisfied he turned back towards the well.

"Is that Hakam?" Lal gasped in disbelief when he saw someone talking to Kaku by the Mulberry tree.

He hurried back, "What a wonderful surprise Hakam!" Lal called out taking Hakam in a tight embrace. Hakam instead picked him up from the ground and spun around twice, laughing his lungs out. Lal's feet dangled a few feet above the ground, even though he was taller than Hakam. Their eyes watered laughing.

They sat on the divan, where Lal and his father had, about a month and a half ago. They sat where Lal's future was decided, and where Lal like a good son had accepted what his father wanted him to do, and that's where Lal had felt guilty and dutiful at the same time.

"I'm so happy to see you," Lal said with the biggest smile.

"And you, Lal, worried me to death! You said you'll be back in a few days." Hakam said, "But I'm glad to see, you're okay."

"I am okay, Hakam." Lal struggled to find words to explain the things to him. He turned to Kaku, "Go home and get some tea for us, Kaku."

"You missed the exams, I was told. That worried me about you and your family."

"I've decided to stay home and help *Bapu ji* with the farming."

"Does he really need your help at the farm, or is there some other reason?" Hakam looked into Lal's eyes.

"I think *Bapu ji* needs me more than I need college. Anyway, I don't need a college degree to run the farm. And how's Harjit?"

"Don't try to change the subject! Tell me what the real reason is. I doubt Rattan Singh *Chacha ji* would want you quit college without a solid reason."

"*Bapu ji* found out about our activities and thinks I will end up in prison." Lal felt like he was stabbing his friend in the stomach, whom he had looked up to as an elder brother. "He's worried about you too."

"I cannot ask you to go against your father, but I believe our 'cause' is more important than our own lives." Hakam's voice suddenly turned a bit feeble.

"I am ashamed of myself. I wish I was like you, strong and determined. I could not go against *Bapu ji's* reasoning. And you don't need cowards like me. But I will keep helping our cause financially though. I promise!"

"Calm down, Lal! You're a sincere warm person who is lucky to have loving parents. Do you know, every time I met them, I wished I had parents like yours?"

Lal looked at him numbed, not knowing what to say.

"I was brought up by my father's cousin and his wife, who could not have resented my presence more in the house." Hakam held Lal's arm as he spoke, "I was an orphan at five and was forced upon them by the village elders, but they just wanted my father's land and not me."

"I am so sorry, I didn't know." Lal looked at Hakam.

"I never told anyone. I shivered in cold nights under a flimsy sheet while my stomach growled with hunger. Somehow I survived."

"Why did the elders decide for your father's distant cousin?"

"My parents did not have any siblings. Some died in infancy and some perished in the plague."

"Oh!" Lal let out sigh.

"Later on Baba Budh Singh took me in and sent me to school and college. He also helped me to get my father's land back, but only a part of it. The rest my uncle had already sold."

"Where are they now?"

"Both passed away, but their son is not a bad person." Hakam's eyes moistened, "I have not shared it with anyone except Harjit and you."

Lal wiped his eyes and wrapped his arm around Hakam. "How's Harjit?" he asked.

"She's great!" Hakam's saddened eyes lit up with a blissful smile. "She..." He caressed his belly over the shirt.

"Really?" It was Lal's turn to pick Hakam up and swirl him around. "I'm going to be *Chacha ji* for a niece or a nephew." He laughed and sang that sounded more like shouting than singing.

The melancholic atmosphere of a little while ago was permeated with joy and excitement. Kaku joined them with a pot of hot tea along with spicy *pakoras* and sweet *laddoos*, a perfect fit for a celebration. The three of them laughed and joked, enjoying the moment to the fullest.

The time for Hakam to leave approached, mercilessly interrupting the festivity. They both took off their turbans and exchanged with each other. After tying the swapped turbans they held hands, saying, "Brothers till the end." They wiped tears of joy hugging and patting each other's shoulders. They whispered 'good lucks' and teary good-byes.

Chapter 6

The wheat harvest was bountiful. The workers had been paid, and Rattan Singh was pleased how Lal handled the farm responsibilities. As they walked home from the farm one day, Rattan Singh said to Lal, "You know, Son, harvesting is the most important and toughest job in a farmer's life and you managed it well. Now it's time for you to bring home a bride." A jovial smile played on Rattan Singh's face. "Sardar Sham Singh's daughter will make a perfect wife for you."

"What? What did you say, *Bapu ji?*" Mouth agape, Lal looked at his father as if he woke up from sleepwalking.

"I say, Sham Singh is well respected in the area and the union between our two families will make us stronger." Rattan Singh's excitement overflowed as he continued, "And he has personally approached me about his daughter."

"What you mean 'make us stronger? Aren't we strong enough?"

"Strength is in the numbers, Lali. The large families help each other in times of need. Sham Singh has two sons, one a bit older than you and one younger. His daughter is the youngest of the children. And you know they're even bigger landlords than we are."

"You want me to marry someone because her father owns more land than us and she has two brothers?" Lal frowned. "What are you talking about?"

Rattan Singh's brisk steps slowed. His head lugged slightly backward; *I shouldn't have said that.* He looked at Lal's disappointed face.

"It's not about the land, Son. It's that they'd be overjoyed to have you as their son-in-law. And their land is not more than ours by far anyway."

"But I know nothing about her. The girl you want me to marry."

"We know everything about the family, we need to know. Sham Singh is well known in the area and their village is not too far from here, only three villages in between."

"It's not Sham Singh I'm talking about, *Bapu ji,* it's the girl. I don't care if they have one acre of land or a thousand. I want to meet her before making any decision."

"Did you say you want to meet her?" Taken aback, Rattan Singh froze for a moment then jerkily looked at Lal, "that's the most ridiculous thing I've ever heard! We cannot go around looking at girls, examining them like we are buying a cow or a goat."

"I'm not buying a cow or a goat. I just want to meet the girl you want me to marry." Lal's lips contorted as he let out a nervous laugh.

"You want me to go to Sham Singh's house and tell him that my son wants to inspect and test out his daughter? Won't happen! It's not the custom!"

By this time they had reached home. Rattan Singh extended his arm to open the gate and then decided against it. They stood outside the front gate of the house.

"I will not blindly follow the customs that shut out our minds and smother our judgment."

Rattan Singh felt like stung by a swarm of bees. Blood rushed to his face and head. He stomped his foot, "Did I send you to college and paid fees for you to behave like this? Disrespect the customs and your elders!" He trembled in a fit of temper.

"You sent me to college because I was good at studies and then you pulled me out because *you* wanted me to quit and come home," Lal shouted.

The sun was going down the western horizon as if trying to run away from the fury of father and son arguing like never before. Layers of feathery clouds swayed, turning orange to gray and from gray to orange by the fiery glow of the sun. An aroma of *daal tarka* and *tandoori roti* floated in the air. A flock of crows flew overhead crowing loudly.

For a moment Rattan Singh could not hear what Lal was saying.

"Now, you listen to me. You *are* going to marry this girl! I've already given my word to Sham Singh and I will not back out on my word." He lowered his voice as he saw Bhani walking towards them through the courtyard.

"How can you give your word to someone about my life without even telling me?" Lal also softened his voice as his mother came closer.

"What are you two talking about?" Bhani said looking at Lal and then her eyes shifted to Rattan Singh. "Is it about our future daughter-in-law?"

"Yes, but your son is being a bit unreasonable." Rattan Singh's gruffy voice of a few seconds ago suddenly softened.

"It's not unreasonable to ask—"

"I never saw your mother before marriage and look at her. Isn't she perfect?" Rattan Singh interrupted Lal and impishly winked at Bhani. "But you on the other hand…" he looked at Lal and forgot what he wanted to say.

"You're always criticizing him, Sardar ji! Come inside. The dinner's getting cold!" Bhani held Lal's hand and walked towards the house.

"I'm not criticizing him. I am just trying to tell him about our customs, but he is being totally irrational."

"Why don't we wait till we come back from my niece's wedding? It's only a few weeks away." Bhani looked back at Rattan Singh, who seemed to have agreed even before taking another step through the courtyard.

"Your father wants the best for you, Lali," Bhani whispered still holding Lal's hand. "I know…"

"I heard that!" Rattan Singh laughed. "Oh, you mother and son!" Rattan Singh's anger melted like butter as he walked close behind them. He wedged himself between the two and wrapped his arms around both of them.

Chapter 7

The preparations to attend Bhani's niece's wedding had already begun. Rolls of silk and cotton fabrics, some printed, some solid colors had been bought from a reputable shop in the city. A tailor was sent for. He came with an assistant, a sewing machine, needles, threads, buttons, measuring tape, scissors, and a worn-out notebook with imprints of embroidery designs. The tailor took the measurements and the assistant wrote them down. He sewed the clothes on the machine and the assistant did the hemming and attached the buttons.

Lal's mother meticulously selected the intricate embroidery designs from the notebook. The tailor embroidered her silk *duppatas* (long scarves) with different color threads to match with her *salwar kameez* sets. She also asked him to embroider and stitch two sets of pricey silk *salwar kameez* sets for her niece, the bride-to-be.

The tailor sewed special occasion *achkans* and *churidars* for Rattan Singh and Lal to their measurements. The permanent employees of the farm were equally excited. It was the family tradition to provide new clothes to the workers on special occasions, and every year at the start of the winter.

The tailor and his assistant stayed many days sewing, hemming, and doing the embroidery. Their every need for food and rest was taken care of as special guests. They left happy being generously compensated.

"Don't forget to hire us for your son's wedding," the tailor said to Bhani, before leaving.

"Sure, we will hire you when he gets married." Bhani looked at Lal with a beaming smile, "you might have to bring two helpers with you. There's going to be a lot more work than this."

"I will be happy to work for you again," the tailor said, loading the sacks of grain he received as compensation, on to the mule cart.

While Bhani was busy at home packing and preparing for her niece's wedding, Rattan Singh and Lal kept their routine taking rounds of the farm as if the argument between the two never happened.

The day to leave for the wedding was approaching fast. Kaku and another worker cleaned the canopy and the floor of the horse buggy that had not been used for a while. They removed the cushions and shook off the dust by thumping them with hands. They rubbed and polished the buggy shafts and the metal rims of the wheels. They groomed the horse and braided her mane with a red ribbon. The buggy was ready to show off at the wedding.

The oxen-pulled cart was also decorated with bows of multi-stranded red and orange cotton yarn. The oxen's foreheads were painted and tinkling bells tied around their necks, which sounded like wind chimes when they walked. The cart was loaded with house gifts for the bride and the groom and for many other relatives.

The much-awaited day to go to the wedding arrived. Lal accompanied his parents in the buggy that took about four hours to get to his aunt's village. Kaku and two other servants rode the oxen-pulled cart and reached late at night.

Bhani's sister was overjoyed and greeted them at the front gate. The house was decorated with ornate bannerets and streamers. The whole courtyard looked like a big kitchen with dug-in wood-burning furnaces. Several cooks were busy preparing the wedding feast. They talked loudly and walked fast, carrying kitchen utensils and trays of cooked food. The head cook ran around shouting and giving instructions, "That's not done yet, Jindoo! You need to cook it longer with more *garam masala,* for the goat curry!"

"Haven't you learned how to make the proper consistency sugar syrup for *jalebis?*" he yelled at another cook before helping him with the syrup. His shouts were unending and the cooks meekly followed the orders. "The guests are staying for several days, I'm told. You have to be well-organized to cook for more than three hundred people." He exaggerated the number of guests.

The whole atmosphere was festive, filled with color, noisy guests, and the aroma of food. Lal suddenly felt hungry. His stomach growled. Embarrassed, he looked around. Everyone seemed too busy to hear his rumbling belly. He smiled and kept walking behind his parents and aunt through the courtyard toward the main house.

As soon as they settled in the front room, Lal's aunt called out to the maid, "Namo, tell the cook to make fresh tea and *pakore* for the guests. In the meanwhile bring some sweets for them." She walked to Lal and kissed his forehead. "My nephew has grown into such a handsome young man! We have to find a beautiful bride for him," she said looking at Bhani and Rattan Singh.

"We already have Sardar Sham Singh's daughter in mind. I'm sure she's very pretty since both her parents are good looking," Bhani replied. "Her name is Rupi, which means beautiful!"

"I'm glad to hear that. It's hard to find good looking girls who also have a virtue of modesty in them, these days."

"Sham Singh himself came to our house asking for his daughter's hand in marriage to our son." Bhani straightened herself in the chair. Her *duppatta* slid from her neck revealing her eye-catching necklace. Her eyes twinkled proudly and her lips stretched into a self-assured smile.

The conversation between the sisters shifted from modesty and beautiful girls to commenting and admiring each other's clothes and jewelry.

Lal sat looking nowhere as if the conversation had nothing to do with him. His father and uncle were busy talking to each other, about what, he did not know. He just waited for food. The aroma was turning his stomach into an uprising rebellion.

A young woman carrying a tray of *jalebis* came into the room. "The tea and *pakore* will be ready soon," she said placing the tray on the center table.

"Namo, tell the cook to hurry up," Lal's aunt said to her.

"Yes, Bibi ji," she said and quickly walked out of the room.

Lal looked at the *jalebis* and his mouth watered like a rivulet. Namo came back with a stack of plates and filled them with *jalebis* from the tray. She handed one to Rattan Singh and turned to Lal. He casually glanced at her and froze. *Who is she?* Dazed he looked at her and forgot to breathe. *How do I know her?* He felt deep in his heart that he was connected to her in some way. How? He was dying to know.

Awestruck he gazed at her without realizing that she was holding a plate for him. "Take the plate, Sardar ji," she said. Her voice sounded like a heavenly melody.

"Huh, yes..." Lal took the plate. His heart leaped out of his chest as his fingers touched hers.

Their eyes met. Vibes like a gentle spring breeze emanated from her dark brown eyes. It quickly changed into a glimpse of a wilting bud in a desert, thirsty for a drop of love and kindness. She lowered her eyes and turned towards the table. A twinge shook him to the core and he could not take his eyes off of her.

"Namo, bring tea. It must be ready by now." Lal's aunt's voice came like a tempest that blew away the petals of a newly blossomed flower.

"Yes, Bibi ji." Namo's feet quickened towards the door.

Lal felt his heart being pulled by an invisible string towards her as she walked out of the room. A typhoon of strange feelings engulfed him. *It's not possible! Don't be foolish!* He scolded himself. The plate shook in his hands. He tried to sit straight but his knee kept tapping uncontrollably. He placed the plate back on the table.

"Have a *jalebi*, son. The cook we hired is famous for his delicious delicacies," his aunt said picking up Lal's plate.

"Thanks, I'm not hungry," he said trying to be polite, "I will eat later."

"Namo, Is the tea ready?" she hollered looking out the door.

"Yes, Bibi ji." Namo hurried in carrying a tray of *pakoras,* followed by a male servant with a tea kettle and cups. He quickly filled the cups with steaming hot tea and served the *pakoras.*

"Leave mine on the table, please," Lal said as the servant offered him a cup of tea. His appetite had vanished.

"You didn't eat anything, Son," Bhani said taking a bite of the spicy pakora.

"Ma, I'm not hungry." Lal sounded agitated.

He felt Namo's presence in the room but dared not look at her again. His heart hammered his chest like the hoofs of a galloping horse. Beads of sweat trickled on his forehead.

"I'm going for a walk." He got up and walked out the door.

"Don't be long, Lali," his aunt said. "There're many people who want to meet you."

"I'll be back soon." He walked through the courtyard ignoring the hubbub of the cooks and the aroma of chicken curry. He roamed the village streets aimlessly trying to shake off the feeling that was simultaneously aching and exhilarating. The more he tried to escape, the more he felt tangled in it. He wanted to force out the pain of longing, her momentary glance had given him. But he knew it was ingrained on his mind permanently.

He wandered around until dark. The courtyard was empty and quiet when he came back. The guests had gone to bed, tired from travel and partying.

Bhani met him by the door. She was the only one still awake, "Where've you been, Lal? I was worried sick."

"I'm a grown man, Ma. Stop worrying."

"I understand, but…"

"You must be tired. Go to sleep."

"You're back. Now I can sleep peacefully," she said walking to her bedroom.

The *Baraat* (groom's party) came the next day with great pomp and show. They rode decorated horses and camels in a big procession. A band playing loud music with trumpets and clarinets walked in front of the procession. The groom, dressed in princely clothes, rode a magnificent black horse trotting behind the band followed by the groomsmen and the rest of the wedding party.

For a moment Lal imagined dressed in groom's clothes riding his own white horse and arriving at Namo's house, to marry her. *That's not possible Lal!* He reminded himself. *It is going to create havoc in the family, 'Sardar Rattan Singh's only son marrying a servant!' Bapu ji will never agree to this.*

The whole village gathered in the open space in front of the house to receive the *Baraat*. The bride and her friends went upstairs onto the flat roof of the house. They looked at the groom and his party through the lattice paling that surrounded the edges of the roof. They joked and teased the bride who just had the first glimpse of her soon-to-be husband. The groom would not be able to see her until after the wedding ceremony.

The band stopped playing while the parents of the bride and the groom formally met and hugged each other.

"Oh, the groom's so handsome! I could die for him," one of the girls shouted. The guests and the wedding party looked up. The girls giggled and hid behind the paling.

An older woman shouted at the girls, "Be sensible! Have you lost all your manners?"

The girls went quiet for a moment and then giggled even louder. The groom smiled, staring towards the roof of the house.

The groom's party and the guests stayed for four days and the festivities went on uninterrupted. So much wine, meat, and sweets, so much laughter and dancing, and the servants ran around frantically serving food and cleaning up after the guests. The bride's father carrying a hurried look and a forced smile made every effort for things to go smoothly.

While everyone was absorbed in the celebrations, Lal ached inside out. He tried to avoid Namo at all costs but felt her presence even when she was not there. He could not look at her when she served food to the guests and to him as well. He could not bear the sight of her holding a heavy tray filled with delicacies, going from one guest to another. They took the food without paying any attention to her. Dressed in a simple cotton *Salwar kameez,* she looked more beautiful than any of the other women wearing expensive silk clothes and dazzling jewelry.

He wanted to take her to a faraway place where it was just him and Namo. He watched her helplessly and suffered quietly. *I will not survive without her and my parents will not survive without me.* The anguish of longing was terrifying.

Finally, the wedding ceremony took place. The bride and groom went around *Guru Granth Sahib*, the Sikh Holy Book, four times, while the priest read the wedding hymns from it.

Then it was time for the departure. The bridal palanquin was brought in. The happy atmosphere quickly changed into a somber one. The bride's parents, her uncles, and aunts, her cousins, and friends all hugged her one after the other, crying and sobbing. The bride also cried her heart out. Leaving her father's house to live at her in-laws' house forever was heartrending. Leaving her friends behind, and the places where she played tic-tac-toe and hide-n-seek with friends, was just unbearable.

The groom's father walked to the father of the bride, "Sardar Sahib, I know how hard it is to send your child away. My own daughter's wedding was last year. I know how you feel. From now on your daughter is our daughter and we will treat her as one."

The bride's dowry and the gifts were loaded onto the buggies to take them to her in-laws' house. Since a daughter did not have any right to her father's land or other property, it was the customary way of making up to her by giving her dowry in the form of jewelry, housewares, even horses and buggies to settle in her in-laws home. Generally, more the dowry a bride brought in, more the respect she received at her in-laws. And Lal Singh's cousin was loaded with a dowry to take it to her husband's home.

The bearers, four of them supported the palanquin on their shoulders and started walking as soon as the bride settled in it, still wiping her tears.

The moment the groom's party left, Lal was ready to go home.

"Lali, why don't you stay a few more days? We can go back together in a day or two," his mother said.

"I need to go back and take care of the farm," Lal said. But inside he knew his feelings for Namo, would create big problems. He wanted to get away and forget everything.

Rattan Singh proudly patted his shoulder, "See how responsible my son is, going back home right away to take care of the farm. Kaku can stay back with us to help out with the aftermath of the big event."

Lal came back home and tried to busy himself in the farm work but found it impossible. His heartache for Namo was unbearable. Running away from her did not help, rather intensified the longing. He fell on his bed and did not want to get up. The day and night went by quietly without making any difference. His parents came back on the third day.

"What happened?" Bhani screamed, holding her chest when she saw him lying in the bed. "Are you sick? Do you have fever?" She touched his forehead that was rather cold.

"What's the matter?" Rattan Singh walked in.

"He doesn't look well! I don't know what's wrong…"

Rattan Singh looked at Lal's listless face and ran out of the room, "Kaku, get the doctor!" he shouted and came back staring at Lal.

"You don't need to send for the doctor. I'm fine," Lal protested.

"You don't look fine to me." Rattan Singh shifted his weight from one leg to the other.

The village doctor, who lived not very far, came within a few minutes. He examined Lal's pulse, felt his belly gently pressing it with his fingers. He told him to open his mouth and examined his tongue and throat and asked, "What did you eat, son, and how long ago?"

"Listen, Doctor, I'll be all right. I don't need…" Lal said dryly.

"Yes Lali, tell us what you ate?" Bhani asked staring at Lal's face.

"I'm not sick. Would you please leave me alone, all of you?" Lal turned facing the wall.

Rattan Singh and Bhani looked at each other and then at the doctor, as if asking 'what now?'

"Give him something to drink. Maybe a little bit of warm milk," the doctor said. "I will check on him again tomorrow morning."

He shook hands with Rattan Singh, "Don't worry, Sardar ji. It's nothing serious."

Kaku walked the doctor to the outer gate.

The doctor had not studied medicine himself but had worked with a doctor for many years in the city. Then he opened his own little clinic and treated the villagers for many of their ailments and had gained their respect and trust.

Bhani quickly brought a glass of milk filled to the rim.

"Ma, I'm not hungry."

"Take a few sips, Lali!" she begged, caressing his broad shoulders.

Lal took a sip and grimaced returning the glass to her.

"What's going on, Lal? Normally, you'd have gulped it down in no time," Rattan Singh said.

"I would have if I was hungry, and I am not," Lal mumbled.

The next few days the doctor stopped by twice daily. Checked his belly and throat each time and recommended light food, simple *dal,* and *roti.*

Lal started eating, but he wanted to be left alone all the time. Kaku tried to talk him out of his room, "There is a *Kabaddi* match next week, Lal. Why don't we get our team ready? We haven't practiced for a while."

"Not now, Kaku. We'll talk later," was Lal's usual answer. He hardly left the house, let alone play cricket or *Kabaddi*, which they used to do, almost every evening. The handsome Lal lost the glow from his face. His gleaming eyes were becoming dull. His joyful radiant smile had disappeared from his lips, and his lovestruck heart ached constantly.

The more he convinced himself to stop thinking about Namo, the more he was consumed by it. He remembered the sadness in her eyes. She was a mesmerizing picture of perfection and at the same time a bruised image of an abandoned wasteland. He wanted to shower the deserts of her heart with fountains of love. He wanted to replace the despair with hope and joys of life. At night he talked to her in his dreams and flew over the river and above the clouds toward the brightest of the stars. During the day he anguished about losing the one whom he never had.

Does she even know how I feel about her? He wondered. The very next moment he relived the vibes of love that had radiated from her dark brown eyes. It filled him with bliss that changed into melancholy soon after, as the dark of the night replaces the light of the day.

One morning, Bhani sat by his side and took his hand in hers, "It feels like only yesterday, when these were soft little baby hands and now, look at these strong manly hands. How quickly time has flown by." A gentle sigh escaped her lips. "I know you are lonely. Your father is going to send for Sardar Sham Singh today, when he comes back from the farm."

"No!" Lal pulled his hand away. He stood up and moved away from her.

"The company of a young woman will be the best healing remedy for you, Lali," Bhani said. Startled by his reaction, she followed him.

Unable to hide his obsession for Namo, he erupted like a volcano and could not contain the lava of his emotions any longer.

"I'm not going to marry Sham Singh's daughter. Are you listening, Ma?"

"Why?"

"Because…"

"Because what?"

"Because I want to marry Namo."

"Namo? Who is she?" Bhani stared at him as if he were a stranger. "You mean my sister's servant?"

Lal nodded and sat back on the cot.

Bhani's jaw dropped. "Do you even know what you are saying?"

"Yes, Ma. Now I do."

"Your father is not going to shame himself by backing out on his word he gave to Sham Singh." Bhani's lips trembled. Her eyes darted towards the door and then again at Lal.

"He shouldn't have done that, without talking to me." Lal looked rather composed after his initial outburst.

"That's not how things are done, Son." Bhani's voice cracked.

"How are they done, Ma?"

Bhani looked around. She could not look into her son's eyes and answer the question.

An eerie silence settled into the room waiting for the bigger storm when Rattan Singh heard about it. Bhani sat by Lal's side quietly, still holding his hand.

"I will talk to your father," she said after an infinitely long pause and quickly went out the room.

A little later, Lal heard his parents argue in the adjacent room.

"Marry a servant? Have you lost your mind, woman?" Rattan Singh sounded like a tornado, demolishing everything in its way. "You've spoiled him rotten."

"I spoiled him? Go and see Sham Singh's sons. Then you would know what 'spoiled' really means." Bhani's voice was equally angry.

Rattan Singh stomped his foot and turned to go out of the room. "Let me teach him how the sons of respectable families are supposed to behave!"

Bhani ran to the door and stood firmly in front of him, blocking his way out.

"Get out of my way and stop bad-mouthing Sham Singh." He shook with rage.

"No, Sardar ji, you listen to me," Bhani shouted. "Didn't we hear a while ago that his sons had beaten him up when he refused to give them money? Also, those boys, someone told me, go shamelessly around the village, mistreating poor women, as if it's just a fun game."

"What are you saying, Bhani? They can't be that bad." His voice softened a little. "Now move!" He tried to push her away. Bhani held on to the frame of the door and stood strong like a tree in front of him.

"I will not let you hurt my son. You have to bury me first…" She looked at him like a lioness protecting her cub. "And what makes you think that his daughter would be any better?" she added.

"Don't be foolish, Bhani, I'm not going to hurt him. He is my son too. And stop talking about them," he shouted.

Lal squirmed and fidgeted hearing his parents fight and walked to them. "*Bapu ji,* Ma, please don't fight over this. I… I will…" he said, awkwardly looking at them.

"Lali, you don't have to say anything. I'm not going to bring Sham Singh's spoiled brat into my home as my daughter-in-law," Bhani said still holding the door.

"And you want to bring a low-level miserable servant as your daughter-in-law, instead?" Rattan sneered.

"Oh, you have not seen her, Sardar ji, or paid any attention to her!" Bhani said looking straight into his eyes. "She has the beauty of a princess! And you know what, her manners are better than the highest of the high class."

Rattan Singh's flash flood of anger was receding quickly, "I did pay attention, Bhani, but the problem is…" Calmness replaced the wrath of the storm.

"There's no problem that you have not handled before, Sardar ji." Bhani held his hand. The glower in her eyes faded and she was back to being her normal self, a caring wife.

Lal stood dumbfounded looking at his parents. *How easily they made up with each other.* He was filled with awe and admiration for them.

"The rumors about Sham Singh's family may be true," Rattan Singh said. "If there's smoke, there is fire for sure."

"It's not just a little fire. From what I've heard, it could blow into an inferno anytime."

Lal left them talking to each other and headed to the farm that he had avoided going to for a while.

Chapter 8

Rattan Singh had agreed to his son's marriage to Namo, but there was still a battle going on in his mind. *My son wants to marry a girl who has no eminence in society and whose family we know nothing about. The only thing we know is that she's my sister-in-law's servant and my son is in love with her. How did this all happen?* He was rattled by an internal turmoil.

Sham Singh would be very unhappy about this because I gave him my word. Walking by the cotton crops, he was tangled in thoughts. *But could I ever sacrifice my own son's happiness for this?* A voice inside him bellowed, *No!* His body shuddered when he remembered that Sham Singh was assaulted by his own sons. The news had spread like summer fire! *His sons are hooligans, intoxicated by wealth and alcohol. Why did I ever agree to link my son's life to theirs?* Rattan scowled.

"We *are* doing the right thing," he said out loud as if trying to convince himself. A dim painting of a sweet, innocent-looking, young woman, serving food to the guests appeared on the canvas of his mind. He *had* paid attention to her in a dream-like state wishing for a daughter, he never had. *Namo will be the perfect wife for Lal!* A feeling of calmness surged in him as he looked around. The crops were healthy, the cattle were strong and sturdy, the workers seemed to be contented and his land was productive. *Most of all, my son is a gentle and selfless man! What more can I ask for?* He asked, looking upwards with folded hands. A surprising realization of triumph filled his heart and he walked home as if a mountain of weight had been lifted off of his chest.

"We should send a message to your sister to come here, soon," Rattan Singh said as the family sat for dinner. Bhani nodded, "Yes, we should. But wouldn't it be better if we go there instead?"

"Even better if we go tomorrow morning, why wait?" he said.

Rattan Singh patted Lal's shoulder. "Tell Kaku to get the buggy ready, early morning."

A shy smile appeared on Lal's lips as he walked to the courtyard looking for Kaku. They left the next morning to talk to Bhani's sister.

"Is everything all right?" she asked with an alarmed look by their unexpected visit.

"Don't panic big sister, everything is fine," Bhani said, following her into the front room of the house.

"First things first, we're here to talk about Namo. Where is she?" Rattan Singh asked.

"Talk about Namo? What for? Did she do anything wrong while you were here?" Bhani's sister stood still. Her mouth half-open as if some kind of unpleasant news was on its way. Her husband walked in equally surprised to see them and shook hands with Rattan Singh.

"We want to take Namo as our daughter-in-law," Bhani said bursting with an exuberant smile.

"What?" Her sister's jaw dropped and looked like it may never go back to its normal position. "Can't we find a family that has some status?"

"The person is more important for us than the status." Rattan Singh cut in. "Where is she, anyway?" Bhani wiggled in her chair.

"Oh, I sent her to run some errands. But I don't understand why you want Lal to marry her. What about Sham Singh's daughter you were talking about? He has good standing in the area, equal to our families, and why you want to bring home a girl with no social standing?" her questions shot out of her mouth nonstop. She stared at Bhani and Rattan Singh waiting for an explanation.

"Our son wants to marry her and we support him," Bhani said with firmness in her voice. Her looks conveyed a message to her sister to stop asking any more questions. "And to let you know, we're not interested in Sham Singh's family."

"Well, if Lal wants to marry her and you're okay with it, what objection could I have?" Bhani's sister looked at her husband who had not said a word so far. He nodded.

"Tell us about her parents. Does she have any siblings?" Rattan Singh asked.

Bhani's sister recovering from the initial shock told them that at one point Namo's father did own some land but he was addicted to opium and wasteful living. He sold the land piece by piece to keep the lifestyle he was hooked on. He died of an overdose or someone killed him, no one knows, since he had made many enemies. The family was left penniless after his death. Her mother died soon after, while Namo was still a baby.

"Oh, poor Namo!" Bhani sighed, "How old is she?"

"Sixteen, maybe seventeen."

"Does she have any brother or sister?" Rattan Singh asked.

"Her elder brother Banta is married and works at seasonal odd jobs. His wife Jeeto comes every month to collect Namo's wages. They have two young sons."

"At this point, I think we should talk to Namo's brother," Rattan Singh said.

"Here she comes!" Bhani said excitedly, as she saw Namo walking through the courtyard.

"Namo, come here," Bhani's sister hollered.

"Coming, Bibi ji," Namo froze at the door when she saw Lal's parents. She bowed folding her hands to pay respect.

"Do you remember them? They were here at the wedding."

"Yes, Bibi ji, they had stayed back to help out after the wedding," Namo said.

"Their son, Lal Singh was here too. Remember him?"

Namo's already rosy cheeks turned crimson and her eyelids dropped momentarily as if she wanted to hide herself behind them. "Yes," she whispered.

"Well, you are the luckiest girl on the earth, Namo! He's madly in love with you," she said, in a conspiratorial voice.

"Huh…?" Namo stood motionless, eyes dazed, looking nowhere.

"So you like him too!" Lal's aunt said to her.

She nodded. Tears started flowing down her cheeks.

Bhani got up and took Namo in her arms. "We're going to talk to your brother," she said. A messenger was sent and Banta Singh and his wife Jeeto arrived the next day.

"My sister is going to be Sardar Rattan Singh's daughter-in-law! Could it be true?" he said in disbelief when told about it.

"Yes, she is going to be our daughter-in-law." Bhani took off her gold bangles and put them on Namo's wrists as a gesture of love and beginning of the new relationship. "You are the most beautiful girl I've ever seen. No wonder my son was smitten."

Namo smiled for the first time since Lal's parents had come.

The wedding date was fixed for a Wednesday, a month and a half later. They laughed and congratulated each other. Rattan Singh hugged Banta as an equal.

"Take care of my daughter until the wedding," Bhani said to her sister, giving a snug hug to Namo before leaving.

"I've always treated her as a daughter, Bhani. And now she's ours for real."

******

The day of the wedding was approaching fast. Rattan Singh and Lal's uncle were on their way to Banta's village to discuss the wedding ceremony. Banta's house was at the end of a narrow street. The open-drain sludge in the street filled the air with a kind of nauseating stench. Lal's uncle instinctively raised his hand to his nose and grimaced. "It's not that bad," Rattan Singh looked at him and smiled.

The one-room mudbrick house with a low thatched roof was surrounded by similar houses. A low mud wall encircled the yard separating it from the street. As soon as Banta saw the guests approaching, he spread a printed bed sheet over a cot in the yard for them to sit. Banta sat facing them on the one without the cover sheet.

A scrawny cow sat at the far side of the yard, lazily chewing, and regurgitating the cud. On the other side, close to the main room of the house, was an open-air kitchen. Dried cow dung cakes burned in the hearth, and layers of thick smoke swirled around, before dissipating into the air. Steam rose from the blackened metal pot over the hearth making the lid rattle.

Rattan Singh looked around. He had always dreamed about a glorious procession of the *Baraat*, (grooms party), for his only son's wedding, with not only decorated horses and camels but also elephants. In his mind's eye, he had seen his son dressed like a prince, riding a magnificent elephant with a canopy on the top, embellished with brocades and garlands. He saw the rest of the *Baraat* men following him on horses and camels arriving at the bride's village with a glorious show of pageantry. He had imagined hiring the most extravagant band and dancers, the villagers had ever seen. He had hoped to build a new relationship with a well-heeled family of equal status or better but the dream had ended abruptly. *Everything has changed now,* he thought. *But it's all for my son's happiness*, he consoled himself.

"Banta Singh, you do not have to worry about making any arrangements. We are not going to bring a *Baraat.*" Rattan Singh said, "Only four of us will come. It's just because of the custom that the ceremony is done at the bride's house, so we'll have the wedding ceremony at your village."

Banta nodded.

As they talked, Jeeto brought tea in metal tumblers and sat next to Banta. Her clothes were wrinkled as if she had hurriedly changed into them. Fixing her *dupatta* over her head she asked Rattan Singh how Lal and his mother were doing.

"They're fine, can't wait for Namo to become part of our family," Rattan Singh said, taking a sip of the tea.

A few women and children gathered outside the house peeking over the low mud wall. The women whispered to each other covering the sides of their faces with their *dupattas*. They seemed surprised to see the Sardars visiting Banta's house. Jeeto sat straight, evidently feeling proud and superior to the women standing outside of her house. She glanced at them every now and then with a smug smile.

"We will have a simple ceremony in your village *Gurdwara* (Sikh temple)," Rattan Singh continued, "Also, we'll arrange for the bridal palanquin and the bearers ourselves. We do not want you to feel any burden of the wedding."

"It is our good fortune that my sister will become your daughter-in-law, Sardar Sahib." Banta's voice was heavy with humility.

"We're going to have the celebrations at our house after the wedding. You and your wife are invited as our special guests."

Jeeto smiled, nodding her head rather too vigorously.

As they stood up to leave, Banta accompanied them to the outer periphery of his village where Kaku had been waiting with their horses. A few of the children in rags walked behind them, giggling, and pushing each other into the stinky water puddles. Stray dogs and cats strolled around oblivious to the surroundings. Once or twice a dog lazily barked at them and then disappeared around the street corner.

Chapter 9

Rattan Singh's house was full of activity, making arrangements to throw a lavish party for Lal's wedding to Namo. The spacious house was repainted and redecorated. Cooks were hired and cooking hearths dug in the outer courtyard.

Sleeping arrangements for more than a hundred invited guests was an enormous undertaking. The inner rooms of the house were prepared for women and small children, while the verandah and the greater *dalaan* by the side of the house were readied for the men. A number of tents were also put in the playground, not far from the house. Rattan Singh employed additional workers to handle the fodder and water needs of the guest's horses and camels and to park their buggies.

Bhani and Lal had selected several sets of gold jewelry for Namo, from the reputed jewelers in the city. Expensive clothes were embroidered and tailored to her measurements. A big carved wood *sandook,* embellished with brass motifs and mirrors was bought. The inside of the *sandook* had many compartments within the compartments that concealed jewelry boxes. A two-step ladder was needed to reach the uppermost compartment.

In the midst of all the hustle and bustle, two days before the wedding, Banta and Jeeto showed up unannounced. After they were offered tea and sweets and asked about their wellbeing, the atmosphere turned tense and awkward. Banta sat quietly next to Jeeto with his head down and his right hand clenched into a tight fist, while the left hand shook visibly. Rattan Singh and Bhani stared at him, puzzled. After long moments of uneasy silence, Jeeto lightly elbowed him. Banta looked up as if he had just woken up from a nap. Jeeto elbowed him again, a little firmly this time.

Banta's lips moved, "Sardar ji, I have only one sister…and…and you know…" He fell silent again.

Jeeto shot an angry look at him and blurted out, "Listen, Sardar ji, Namo is going to marry your son and will not be working at your relative's house anymore. We will not get paid from her work, as before." Jeeto did not look at

Rattan Singh or Bhani while they stared at her. "We want something in exchange. You are wealthy and it's not going to make any difference to you if you give us a bit of money…"

"In exchange?" Rattan Singh jumped up like a tightly wound spring had suddenly gone loose, "you lowest of the low, son of a bitch! You think your sister is a goat and you want to sell her?" he roared looking straight into Banta's eyes. "Get out of my house, before I make pulp of your head."

Jeeto, not expecting the turn of events, sheepishly tried to pacify the situation. "We didn't mean to…"

Rattan Singh ignored Jeeto and kept yelling at Banta, "I would have given you some financial help if you had asked. But you are demanding money as if you are selling your sister. It is a crime I will not forgive you for. Get out of my house!" Rattan Singh stomped his foot. "Now!"

Banta wiped the sweat from his forehead. His voice trembled. "Please, Sardar ji…"

"There's no greater sin than selling your sister or daughter. I was going to consider you part of my family. But you have severed yourself by your wickedness."

Jeeto held Banta by the arm. "Let's go!" she mumbled. "We don't have to marry Namo to his son."

"You listen to me," Rattan Singh glared at Jeeto, "we do not need your or anybody else's permission for the wedding. Now get out!"

Banta turned, hands folded, "Sardar ji, I am ashamed beyond words…" Jeeto yanked his arm and started walking towards the gate.

"What just happened?" Bhani stood dumbfounded, looking at Banta and Jeeto walking out the gate.

"I'm sure it was Jeeto's scheme to extort money and that dense headed Banta went along with it," Rattan Singh said. "Bhani, do not tell Namo or Lal about it. It's good that Lal was not home when they came."

"You're quite right. It would hurt them immensely if they found out." Bhani was still in shock. "I think Jeeto is jealous of Namo. You should've seen her contorted face when she saw the bangles, I had put on Namo's arms, that day."

"Let's put it behind us and not be bothered by it. We don't have to follow the custom of the wedding at the bride's house. We'll do the ceremony here, at our house."

"It makes me feel so much better," Bhani said, "Since we have ignored so many other customs, why not one more," she said, giving a gentle push to Rattan Singh. He chuckled.

Two days later the guests started arriving. Hakam Singh and Harjit came with their eighteen-month-old son, Baldev, who attracted everyone's attention with his cute baby talk. Bhani's sister came with her family and brought Namo along with her. Since the bride-to-be was not to be seen by the guests before the ceremony, she stayed mostly inside. Harjit and Baldev kept her company while Hakam Singh helped with the preparations.

"Give your *Chachi ji* a big hug," Harjit said to Baldev. He shyly walked to Namo with his finger in-between his baby teeth. She took him in her arms and kissed his round chubby cheeks. Baldev giggled and ran back to his mother.

"Come," Namo extended her arms again. He walked to her, not very shy this time. She lifted him up kissing his forehead and his fat baby hands. She tickled his belly and he squirmed and laughed. Soon, it became a game, Baldev running and giggling between Namo and Harjit. It brought the two women close as if they had always known each other.

"Do you know, Namo, how we are related?" Harjit asked.

Namo shook her head.

"My husband Hakam Singh and your about-to-be husband, Lal Singh, became brothers by exchanging their turbans. So, we're sisters-in-law."

Harjit reached over and hugged Namo. Baldev pushed himself between the two. The three laughed squeezing each other in a group hug.

While the jangle and jingle of the arriving guests and their buggies went on outside, Harjit and Namo sat in the room like long lost sisters had found each other. A bond had instantly formed between the two.

Banta and Jeeto showed up uninvited, late in the evening. "We're not going to make a scene," Rattan Singh said to Bhani. "Just ignore them."

Early morning on the day of the wedding, Hakam Singh and Kaku set up the courtyard for the ceremony. A day earlier a temporary wooden platform with a canopy on the top had been erected in the inner courtyard where the Sikh holy book, Guru Granth Sahib would be placed for the wedding ceremony. They spread a quilt on the platform and placed the Guru Granth Sahib on it. They covered the brick floor in front of the platform with thick layers of soft paddy straw and spread rugs over it, for the guests to sit.

Bhani and Harjit helped Namo into her wedding clothes, a red silk *kameez salwar,* intricately embroidered with gold threads. They made her long dark hair into a bun. Bhani spread the matching see-through *dupatta* over her head and pulled it down to her chin. Harjit unfolded a heavy shawl to cover her head as well as her face, following the tradition. "You're too beautiful to hide your face behind this," she said.

"You read my mind. Let's wrap it around her shoulders instead of covering her face." Bhani smiled looking at Namo. And that's what they did, an unheard-of deviation from the social custom.

As the guests settled on the rugs and the Sikh priest took his place behind Guru Granth Sahib, Lal Singh wearing a princely *achkan* and an orangey-red turban, sat on the rug in front of the Holy Book.

"It's time!" Bhani looked out the window. Namo's hands shook nervously.

"Don't worry, Namo. Just keep your head high and you do not have to look at anyone," Harjit said, massaging her hands.

As Namo walked in with Bhani and Harjit on either side, the air filled with gasps and murmurs. Some gasped seeing a bride without a thick veil and others, seeing her stunning beauty behind the see-through *dupatta*. Some of the men looked at her and lowered their eyes and some stared with eyes widened to the limit.

"No veil? Only a *dupatta*?" an older woman said, loudly.

"She's sooo pretty!" another whispered.

"She looks so delicate."

"But her steps are confident."

Women talked in hushed voices.

"No wonder they didn't care about her family status."

"I heard Lal almost starved himself to death until Rattan Singh agreed to the marriage."

"I heard that too," the woman next to her said.

Lal looked at Namo and was smitten all over again.

Namo kept walking with her head high but her eyes lowered. A natural soft smile on her face glowed with grace. Murmurs continued until Namo sat next to Lal in front of the Guru Granth Sahib and the priest started reading the wedding hymns.

The four stanzas of the wedding hymns contain instructions for performing the daily duties of married life. The couple should stay humble and pray on

God's name every day. At the end of each stanza, Lal and Namo walked around the holy book, as their submission to God and commitment to each other.

After the ceremony, the wedding celebrations began that would continue for the next four days. The guests ate and drank, danced, and laughed, all through the sumptuous party. Dressed in elegant clothes, Namo's beauty caught everyone's eye. The women admired her clothes and stunning jewelry. They also gossiped and whispered about her background and Bhani's absurdity for not veiling her face.

Chapter 10

As was the custom, the newlyweds would play a game for everyone's enjoyment and fun. Namo and Lal were asked to sit on low stools, facing each other, surrounded by the guests, mostly women. A shallow trough placed in front of them was filled with water. Lal's mother poured milk in it until it was opaque, and a coin was dropped into the trough. The newlyweds were asked to retrieve the coin. The myth behind the game was, whosoever grabbed the coin first would be the domineering partner. But it was almost always the man who grabbed the coin or maybe the women willingly or unwillingly let it go.

Half the guests cheered for Namo and the other half for Lal. Namo looked at her brother's wife Jeeto. *Why is she looking so tight faced and grim?* She wondered. *But she doesn't talk to me much anyway, other than when she picks up my earnings from work!* She had no idea about their encounter with Lal's parents.

"Okay, get set!" one of the women guests announced. Lal and Namo dipped their hands in the water. "One, two, three, go!"

Namo and Lal moved their fingers in the milky water searching for the coin.

"Go Lal!" someone said.

"Get the coin, Namo!" another one shouted.

The crowd laughed and cheered, trying to guess who would be the winner.

I am not going to grab the coin. I will let him have it. Namo just kept her hands in the milky water without trying to search for the coin.

Lal's hands moved around for a little while and soon had the coin under his fingers. He dragged it towards Namo and pushed it under her palm. He tenderly caressed her hands concealed behind the veil of milky water. Namo looked at him. Lal returned the look and gently nodded. She slightly moved her head in a 'no' gesture, 'I want you to have it' she told him without words.

"Who has the coin?" someone asked.

"It is Lal!"

"No, I think Namo has it."

Unaffected by the noise and shouting they kept looking at each other.

"They don't seem to care about the coin. They're struck by the lightning of love!" There were giggles and laughs and loud sighs in the crowd.

Lal squinted asking Namo to take her hands out and show the coin to the crowd. And she did! The crowd cheered. Women hugged Namo one after the other who were on her side.

They laughed and joked, "O, poor Lal!" A woman, who cheered for Namo, pinched his cheek.

"It's only a superstition," said another woman who had been cheering for Lal. "It doesn't matter who won!" She gave him a tight hug. The fun went on for a long while.

The couples always try to snatch the coin from each other, but Lal slipped it right into my hands. Namo was amazed. *There cannot be anyone nicer than him!* The thought filled her with admiration for her husband. Every time she recalled the gentle touch of his hands in the milky trough, she felt a pleasant current through her body. She wanted him to hold her in his arms. But the guests were all around them, eating and dancing and shouting and laughing and singing! There was not much difference between the day and the night for them.

It was shameful to show affection in front of people. *When are they going to leave?* Namo felt restless. They had not talked freely or even held hands so far, other than the coin game. They were not supposed to get together while the guests were still there. *Does Lal feel the same as I do?* A look at Lal conveyed a message that filled her with torrents of joyful reassurance.

The guests took their time to leave. Finally, the last one was gone.

Namo lay in the bed, satin sheets wrapped around her. Every few seconds she sighed with a feeling of elation, mixed with nervousness. She stretched impulsively and yawned repeatedly.

She heard a soft knock at the door and turned her head. Lal stood by the door smiling. Her heart nearly jumped out of her chest. She tried to pull herself to sit. Lal stretched his arms and took her henna-painted hands to help. Namo's bangles tinkled and the soft satin sheets made a subtle swishing sound. Lal sat by the side of the bed and gently pulled her towards him. Her head on his chest, Namo felt the rhythm of his heart. A soft, blissful sigh escaped her lips. Gently cupping the jawline of her face in his strong hands, Lal looked into her eyes, "There's no one as beautiful as you, Namo!" he whispered.

She blushed and turned her gaze away for a split second. Looking back into his eyes she said in a barely audible voice, "How could I be so fortunate to be your wife!" Her eyes and lips, both smiled. Their breath mingled. Namo smelled the scent of cardamom and cinnamon. Their hearts beating as one, they stayed in a gentle embrace.

Lal caressed her face. He fondled her neck and stroked her soft full lips with his index finger. He leaned over and their lips touched tenderly and softly, increasing in passion and strength with each passing moment. He gently laid her on the bed and removed her clothes and his own, one by one. She felt his hands roaming about her body, caressing it, pressing and feeling it. She wiggled with inexplicable joy, letting out a string of moans and sighs. The very next moment Namo cowered. Her face like a frightened doe, she looked at him. "Please forgive me!"

"Shhh, I'll be gentle!" Lal whispered in her ear, kissing the peaks of her breasts. A few moments later Namo felt a thrust, a brief sharp pain, a ripple of ecstatic spasm, and then there was pleasure, only the pleasure, as if a slice of heaven had descended onto the earth. Lal looked at Namo. She appeared like a newly blossomed flower. With their body and soul wrapped around each other, they slipped into a peaceful slumber.

Chapter 11

Rattan Singh, who had resisted Lal's marriage to Namo in the beginning, loved her as the daughter he always wished he had. Bhani talked about her daughter-in-law proudly to everyone. Namo had quickly picked up the household duties while Lal managed the farm. He went around the farm twice daily. In the morning he went by himself or accompanied by Kaku. But the evenings were special when he took Namo along. She sat behind him on horseback with her arms tightly wrapped around his waist.

Rattan Singh and Bhani stood by the gate watching them go. Bhani would cross her arms on her chest praying for their safety and wellbeing. At the farm Lal and Namo walked holding hands, that was quite unusual, but they were loved by everyone. Lal gave instructions to the workers while Namo listened.

Life was good in the household until one evening, about a month and a half after the wedding. They had just finished having dinner, when they heard a loud pounding on the gate and shouts of obscenities.

"Laloo, bastard! You married a servant and belittled my sister...!" Someone yelled.

"Come out and face me, you coward! I'm going to smash your head..."

"O, Namo! Come out and clean my horse's shit..." the other one shouted.

Rattan Singh quickly took down the sword from the wall and drew it from the scabbard. He ran towards the gate followed by Lal and Kaku holding bamboo truncheons.

It didn't take long to discover that they were Sham Singh's sons, Pinta and Babbu, heavily drunk. Lal and Kaku easily yanked them down from their horses.

"I can chop off your heads right now, you sons of a bitch," Rattan Singh shouted. "Lock them up and send a message to their father in the morning."

"How dare you..." Lal punched Pinta, the older brother. Kaku slapped the younger one and they dragged them into one of the servant's rooms and put a padlock on the door. They tied their horses in the yard. The brothers shouted and squirmed, and kicked the floor for a while but soon the alcohol sent them to sleep.

"What a disgrace to have sons like these loathsome animals!" Rattan Singh heard them snore and shook his head in disgust.

The next morning, Rattan Singh assembled the village *panchayat* (council of elders) and sent a messenger for Sham Singh to come immediately. The elders and the villagers gathered in the outer courtyard. The brothers, tied together with a sturdy rope, sat on the floor. As soon as Sham Singh arrived, he started yelling, "You both are going to get killed one of these days, you thick-headed animals! And that would be the day I heave a sigh of relief." He gnashed his teeth and jumped towards them waving his fists. People intervened and held Sham Singh back.

"Sardar Sahib do not lose temper. We need to solve the problem with cool heads so that it does not happen again," the council head Sardar Puran Singh said.

"How many times will you two degrade the family name?" Sham Singh trembled with rage. "I'm ashamed to even call you my sons."

The villagers had heard his sons howling profanities at the family, the night before. They looked at Sham Singh and then at his sons. Some shook their heads and some inaudibly whispered to each other.

"Do you have anything in mind about how to handle the situation?" the council head asked Rattan Singh.

"Whatever you collectively decide would be acceptable to me," Rattan Singh answered. The council members discussed and debated about the appropriate punishment.

After a while, Sardar Puran Singh addressed the boys, "You have a choice, either we hand you over to the police or we try to discipline you here." The brothers looked at each other and nodded in favor of the second option.

"Alright then, you will bend on your knees and beg for pardon from Rattan Singh and Lal Singh, and promise never to come near their house or their farm ever again."

"Secondly, you will strike each other with your own shoes, fifteen times. Five times on the head and ten on the back and buttocks." People gathered there grinned and chuckled. Many laughed out loud.

"It is not a laughing matter!" Puran Singh scolded them.

Silence followed.

"If you tried to be soft to each other, you will each get fifteen more. From me," Puran Singh continued. "Not with a shoe, but with a heavy stick."

"That's what they need! Beat each other, instead of going around beating other people!" Someone shouted.

"Remember, do not repeat this kind of behavior again, or you will be punished here first and then handed over to the police."

The brothers were not soft with each other for the shoe beating. The council punished them but was unable to wipe the angry, implacable expressions from their face.

"Sham Singh, I advise you to tighten the rein, to keep them under control. Otherwise, they can put you in bigger trouble than this one," Puran Singh said.

Sham Singh nodded with his head down in embarrassment. "You're right," he said with humility in his voice.

Some people looked at Sham Singh with sympathy and some stared at his sons and shook their heads.

After the incident, they did not come to Lal Singh's village or bothered the family again, but talks about their misconduct were frequently heard. People talked about them and were afraid of them because they carried pistols and showed off wearing them over their clothes. Sham Singh was powerless to do anything because they threatened him too.

Chapter 12

The trees stood still. Not a single leaf moved as if an unknown ghastly power had overpowered their movement and they froze in fear. The sun pounded the earth with angry rays of heat. Blurry waves of hot air rose from the surface of the earth swaying upwards as if asking for mercy from *sooraj devta,* the Sun God.

The stillness of the midday was pierced by Namo's deafening screams, which were increasing in intensity and frequency. Each wave of excruciating pain accompanied by Namo's shriek sent an arrow of agony through Lal's chest. Pacing in the verandah outside the room he felt helpless. Every time the midwife or her assistant came out of the room, he asked, "How much longer?"

"Any time now," they had told him multiple times.

Rattan Singh and Bhani could not bear Namo's painful shrieks. They went to another room and waited. Bhani sat with hands folded praying while Rattan Singh paced restlessly.

Finally, after a gut-wrenching scream, there was silence. And then a baby cried. Lal slumped on a chair in the verandah as if he was exhausted and exhaled loudly.

The midwife came out. "You have a daughter, *Chhote* Sardar ji."

"How's Namo?" he asked impatiently.

"She is weak but okay. Your daughter gave her much trouble," she said.

Lal ran into the room and held Namo in his arms. Drained of strength, she pointed to the baby, "Your daughter!" she whispered. Her lips parted into a weak smile and a breath of relief left her tired lungs. Lal looked at the baby and could not take his eyes off her. She was the most beautiful little thing he had ever seen. *Is it a doll or a real person!* He kept staring in awe.

Rattan Singh and Bhani could not contain their excitement at becoming grandparents. "Kaku get ten sacks of wheat grain from the godown for the midwife," he hollered.

Bhani opened her jewelry box and took out a ruby studded gold ring. "Here, keep it for your daughter's wedding," she said.

The midwife's jaw dropped looking at the ring. "You are too generous, Bibi ji. May God bless you with a grandson next time." She left the house happy and astonished at their generosity. Kaku carried the grain to her house in a cart.

Rattan Singh saw the little girl smiling in her sleep and his heart melted, "O, my little *rajkumari*, my princess!" He picked her up in his arms. "We are going to name her Pali," he said.

"Don't disturb her sleep, Sardar ji!" Bhani scolded.

Ignoring the rebuke, he kept looking at her, while she slept undisturbed in his arms, breathing softly and peacefully.

"She got the best of both parents!" Bhani remarked and tried to take her back from Rattan Singh. He quickly turned his back to her and did not let her take the baby away from him.

"Don't disturb her sleep, Bhani!" he mocked.

The next few days, Bhani donated food and clothes to the poor as customarily done for the birth of a son, and as a gesture of thankfulness to God. More people heard about it and flooded to their house.

The mystics and the fortunetellers came, asking for alms. They begged to take one brief look at the baby to be able to tell, what her future holds. Bhani brought the baby out, wrapped in soft voile summer clothes with a small black dot on the left side of her forehead, to protect her from the evil eye.

"Your granddaughter is a very blessed child. She will marry a prince and enjoy great wealth and fortune," they said.

The gypsy women sang the praises of the family and good luck songs for the baby. They danced in their gaudy clothes and tinkling bells tied around their ankles and wrists. They laughed and winked and clapped with their hardened palms, while their glitzy, glittery makeup ran down their faces mixed with sweat. Lal Singh and Namo stood in the verandah watching the dance with big smiles on their face.

One of the gypsy women wanted to hold the baby to tell her future and she stretched her arms to Bhani to take the baby.

"Do not touch my granddaughter!" Rattan Singh yelled entering the courtyard. "Give them some grain and get rid of them," he said.

Bhani gave them grain and clothes. But they sounded dissatisfied. "Is this what we get from the rich Sardars? Even the poor ones give us more than this!" Then the haggling began about the money.

Rattan Singh took out a bill from his pocket and handed it to them. "Now get going," he said with a gesture towards the gate.

"Rattan's head screw seems a little loose!" Gossip also went around the village. "It is the son who carries the name of the family, but he is celebrating the birth of a girl like a son!" People had never seen anyone celebrating the birth of a daughter. Normally there would have been a sense of sadness in the family and everyone would be quiet and praying for a son next time.

"When a son is born, the foundation of the house trembles with fear and uncertainty, whether he will strengthen it or pull it apart into pieces when he grows up. But, when a daughter is born, the foundation of the house heaves a sigh of relief because a daughter is always selfless and compassionate towards her parent's home," Rattan said sitting at the men's gatherings.

"Rightly said," men nodded, mostly agreeing with him.

People started calling Lal Singh *'Chhote Sardar ji,'* the younger landlord. His status seemed to have risen after becoming a father. And Rattan Singh was now the *'Waddhe Sardar ji,'* the elder landlord.

Chapter 13

Young and old, villagers and college students, Hindu, Sikh, and Muslims, marched in a procession towards the Lahore Railway Station to protest the arrival of the Simon Commission. The air reverberated with the slogans.

"Simon Commission!"

"Go Back. Go back!"

A seven-member committee had arrived from England headed by Sir John Simon, to decide the future of India's political policies. None of the committee members had ever been to India. And not a single Indian member was included in the committee. It enraged people all over the country. As the commission arrived in Bombay, it was greeted with black flags and shouts of, 'Go back, Simon.' It had met the same response at Calcutta and Lucknow before coming to Lahore.

When Simon and his party reached Lahore, the capital of Punjab, hundreds of people carrying placards and flags gathered, to protest. Lala Lajpat Rai was in the front leading the demonstration.

Hakam Singh stood next to Teja Singh, a student from the Lahore National College, holding a placard. A few teenage boys stood in front of them, shouting excitedly, "Simon, Go Back." The police stood like a wall in front of the crowd. The police superintendent, James Scott looked on, standing next to the deputy superintendent, John Saunders.

"Charge!" the superintendent ordered. The deputy, Suanders looked at him. "Charge!" James Scott repeated.

The police pounced on the crowd beating them with batons and truncheons. Deputy Suanders headed the assault. People ran whichever way they could. A peaceful demonstration turned into a frenzy of shouts and screams. Hakam, pulled two of the boys by the arms, "Run!" he shouted. They darted back pushing through the crowd and turned into a side street. Teja followed right behind taking another young boy to safety. They kept running until the noise faded behind them.

"Are you alright?" Hakam asked the frightened out of breath boys. They nodded. "Go home," he told them, "take the back streets."

Hakam and Teja ran back to where the attack had happened. Hakam felt intense pain in his left hand. The upper side was swollen black and blue. He had not realized he was hit by a baton while trying to protect the boys. He slowed down.

"What is it?" Teja asked slowing down with him, "your hand!"

"It could've been my head," Hakam felt relieved and kept walking to the rally. The crowd had scattered and the place was littered with shoes, turbans, and eyeglasses. Here and there the ground was stained with blood. The police had retreated and the commission members had been taken away in protected vehicles.

Lajpat Rai lay on the ground surrounded by people. His skull was fractured and blood flowed from his head onto his face and chest. Though badly injured he addressed the crowd around him that, every strike of the baton on his head was another nail hammered into the coffin of the British Rule.

"Lajpat Rai, *Zindabad*!" Long live Lajpat Rai!

"Simon, go back!" the crowd chanted again.

An ambulance took him to the hospital. Hakam and Teja followed along with a large crowd and waited outside, some prayed and some angrily chanted.

While the demonstrations against the Simon Commission and demand for total independence were in force, Gandhi insisted to ask for a Dominion Status under the British Crown. Many leaders opposed but caved under his influence. If they did not get the Dominion Status within a year, they would demand complete independence, Gandhi told them.

Subhash Chandar spoke against it. Why did Gandhi still want to stay under the British? Why not demand complete independence now?

Gandhi rebuked, "You may take the name of independence on your lips, but all your muttering will be an empty formula if there is no honor behind it. If you are not prepared to stand by your words, where will the independence be?"

Bhagat Singh and his young revolutionary companions were irritated by Gandhi's desire to stay in the British dominion. "Why wait another year? Why not now?" Bhagat Singh asked Nehru, but got no answer.

The feeling of betrayal by Gandhi about seven years ago was still fresh on many minds when he had aroused the nation for a Non-Cooperation Movement and then suddenly decided to withdraw from it. He had urged people to boycott the British sponsored schools and police and the English made goods. Many teachers and lawyers resigned from their jobs. The shops and schools were closed. The office workers refused to work and many returned the honors and titles given to them by the British.

Over forty thousand men and women were arrested all over the country. Peaceful demonstrators were beaten and dragged by the legs while their faces bumped and bled onto the ground. Sikhs were pulled by their long beards and some were tied to each other by their long hair. All through the arrests, people stayed non-violent and did not resist, no matter how badly they were beaten. The injured were thrown in prisons without any medical help. Many were crippled for life due to beatings and scores lost their jobs as teachers, lawyers, and civil servants.

And then Gandhi suddenly withdrew the movement. Then he went on hunger strike for three weeks demanding people to suspend the boycott. His argument, 'India was not ready for independence.' It angered and disappointed the public who had blindly followed him.

Now after seven years Gandhi still wanted to ask for dominion from the commission rather than independence. The revolutionaries, who were ready to pay with their lives for freedom, felt betrayed and were infuriated.

A few days after the beating, Lajpat Rai succumbed to his injuries in the hospital. His death infused a cyclone of vengeance into the hearts of many.

The Naujawan Sabha and the Hindustan Socialist Republican Association (HSRA) founded by Bhagat Singh, of which Hakam and Teja and many other young men were members, wanted revenge.

A month after Lajpat Rai's death, the deputy police superintendent, John Saunders was gunned down in broad daylight, and pamphlets about revenge were hurled.

23-year-old Bhagat Singh and his equally young associates Rajguru and Sukhdev were executed in Lahore jail by the British. They were hanged to death on March 23, 1931, a day before the set date.

"This is the highest award for patriots and I am proud that I am going to get it," Bhagat Singh had said. "They may kill me, but they cannot kill my ideas. They may crush my body, but they will not be able to crush my spirits. My ideas will haunt the British like a curse until they are forced to run away from here."

"After I am hanged the fragrance of my revolutionary ideas will permeate the atmosphere of this beautiful land of ours. It will intoxicate the youth and (prepare them) for freedom and revolution, and that would bring the doom of British imperialists nearer," with full passion, he had said.

As the news of Bhagat Singh's execution spread, the nation went into mourning. There were processions throughout the country. Many went without food that day. People wore black badges and shut down their businesses in grief. It generated a flood of young men and women in Punjab and elsewhere who wowed to sacrifice their lives for the sake of freedom from the brutal foreign rulers.

Bhagat Singh had appeared on the sky of revolution like a bright star. He was rather like a shooting star that had shined on the horizon for a very short time, but it awakened millions of people from the slumber of slavery forever. Many more revolutionary groups popped up by the day. Hakam and scores of others were their dedicated members. At the same time, the government was equally bent upon crushing the movement by imparting harshest punishments for the slightest offenses. Many more were being executed or exiled to the Andaman and Nicobar Island prison.

Chapter 14

Rupi walked briskly along the outer courtyard wall of her house towards the cornfield. The night was dark and windy. She wrapped her *duppatta* tightly around her body. Hearing muted footsteps behind, she quickened her pace. Her heart hammered in her chest. A strong hand covered her mouth preventing her from screaming and the other arm wrapped around her waist holding her tight. Her heart sank with fear. She felt a face close to her own and recognized Daulat.

"Shhhhh, it's me," he whispered, "we'll go to the grove tonight. The cornfield is too close to your house." He held her arm and started walking quickly.

"It's too far," Rupi whispered.

"It's not too far. The place is obscured by trees and shrubs," Daulat said, "I cleared up a space for us today."

They hurried towards the grove.

It had all started about two months ago, when Rupi laid her eyes on Daulat. The first clouds of the monsoon were gathering in the sky. The air suddenly became heavy and moist and a thunderclap burst through the sky. The scorching midday sun seemed to have retracted its rays, pushed up by the billowing clouds.

Rupi stood by the upstairs window looking at the clouds. She felt a storm gathering in her chest. She wanted to fly away with the clouds and become the lightning of the thunder that was getting louder and more frequent by the minute. Her parents and both her brothers, Pinta and Babbu had gone to the city for the day and she was home alone.

Daulat, feeding the buffalos in the outer courtyard caught her eye. He had moved the cows and the calves into the shed and was quickly filling up their feeding troughs with fodder. *He is so handsome! But working with cattle all day long makes him look dirty and smell like cow dung.* A sigh escaped her chest. Her body tightened with yearning for strong arms to hold her tight. She felt thirsty with a burning desire. Every teaching of her mother was overpowered by her craving body.

She came downstairs and walked to him. A mischievous smile playing on her lips, she called out, "Hey Daulat!"

"Yes, *Chhote Bibi ji,*" he said, keeping his eyes down.

"Hey, look at me! Is the dirty, dung covered floor prettier than me?" He nervously looked up. A strange wave of fear and excitement flushed his face. He had never looked straight at her before. "No, *Bibi ji!*"

"No, *Bibi ji*, what? Go wash your face and hands," she ordered. "Wash the whole of you," and he did. His light skin and bluish eyes appeared as if a thick layer of mud had been removed from his face. She held him by the arm and pulled him inside the house.

That was the day, she made him feel special. Since then they had been meeting in the maize field. He would take a bath as soon as he finished his work and wait for the night.

Daulat had been working at Sham Singh's house for a while, mostly taking care of the cattle. His very light skin and bluish eyes were the reason of a rumor that a *ferringhee* had had his way with his mother. She was one of the maids of a Maharaja of another state. He was famous for throwing lavish parties and inviting rich merchants and British officers. They would drink and smoke and laugh all night long. One of the British officers entered the servant quarters and had forced himself on her. When her husband retaliated, he was killed. Whether it was true or not, no one knew, but people had stopped paying attention to his light skin and bluish eyes.

In the beginning of the forbidden romance, Daulat would fearfully ask Rupi, "What will happen if we were caught?"

"Nothing!" Rupi answered, "*Bapu ji*, my father, never says 'no' to me, whatever I ask for."

"But this is different," Daulat said.

"Why different? Didn't Lal marry a servant?"

"I'm not the same caste as you. That's why it's different."

"*Bapu ji* would understand."

"What about your brothers, Pinta and Babbu?"

Rupi unable to answer about her brothers would tighten her embrace around him, "My *Bapu ji* listens to me." Daulat would heave a sigh of relief, taking her into his arms.

Tonight, they were going to the grove.

They entered into the thicket of the grove through brush and shrubs. Daulat retrieved a quilt hidden behind a bush and spread it over the soft bed he had made during the day, by piling up layers of grass. They kissed passionately, oblivious to the waving tree branches and the fluttering of leaves in the wind. They were unaware of the chirping crickets and occasional hooting of owls. They satiated their hunger with each other's bodies.

******

"Hey, wake up!" Pinta whispered, shaking Babbu's shoulder.

"What?" Babbu said rubbing his eyes.

"You know what. We have to catch that bastard."

"Did Rupi leave?"

"Yes." Pinta pulled Babbu by the arm.

They stealthily took their horses from the stable and went out into the night.

"Rupi would never have become what she has if Lal had married her," Babbu said.

"I agree. We need to teach him a lesson," Pinta said.

"Don't you think his father is the one needing to be set right more than Lal?" Babbu asked.

"Maybe both!" Pinta answered, turning the horse towards the grove.

"Where're you going?" Babbu asked following him.

"I'm sure they're at the grove."

"How do you know?"

"I saw that son of a bitch, Daulat, going towards it, during the day. I've been watching him." The horses picked up speed. Soon they were at the grove.

"There!" Pinta shouted.

Rupi screamed and Daulat shook like an autumn leaf about to fall from the tree.

"You dirty immoral bitch. What are you doing with this low caste bastard?" Babbu caught her by the hair dragging her away from Daulat.

Pinta took out his pistol and fired at Daulat, but missed.

"Please don't kill him, please...please, brother!" Rupi dropped on the ground. Clinging on to her brother's leg, she begged.

Pinta violently kicked, shaking her off like a little animal. "Next is your turn, bitch!" Pinta was a mad bull.

Daulat fell backward with the sound of bang, bang. A bullet pierced through his forehead and another entered his chest. A shrill out of his throat stopped half-way and his left leg writhed for a moment before becoming still.

Rupi darted towards him. Her cries muted by shock and horror; she fell on his chest. The very next moment she got up and ran back to Pinta, "You killed him!" she yelled, hitting him with fists.

Pinta pushed her. She fell. She got up again and rammed into him, digging her teeth into his arm again like a wild animal.

Another bang. Her body fell near Daulat's stretched out arm.

"Why did you kill her?" Babbu shouted.

"Do you want to be called the brother of a whore? Fucked by a low caste bastard, our servant, who lives on our shit?" Pinta vomited fire with his words.

"But why kill her?" Babbu turned and pushed Pinta.

"You want to join them?" Pinta stood boorishly staring at the bodies.

Babbu stepped back. "What are we going to do now?" he asked panicking.

"Let the vultures feast on them," Pinta said, kicking Daulat's lifeless body.

"We cannot leave them here."

"Okay then, wrap them up tight in the quilt and load them on your horse," Pinta said, wiping the blood oozing from two semicircular wounds, where Rupi had bitten him.

Babbu did as told. He loaded both bodies in front and mounted the horse. As they neared the village, Pinta turned his horse towards the road, away from home.

"Where're you going?" Babbu asked.

"You want to go home? You fool!" Pinta retorted.

Babbu followed. They rode quietly for a while. Then Pinta heard Babbu sobbing.

"Stop crying! I didn't want to kill her," Pinta said.

"Then why did you?"

"She bit me like a dog."

"Her bite was not going to kill you. And you didn't say you were going to kill Daulat either."

"And what did you think we were going to do?" Pinta asked.

"You said we were going to catch him."

"Catch him and then what? Make that son-of-a-whore, our brother-in-law?"

"But why kill Rupi?" Babbu said between sobs.

"In a way, it's Lal who's responsible for Rupi's death," Pinta tried shifting the guilt. "Don't worry Babbu, we'll take revenge soon."

"Don't talk to me!" Babbu yelled.

"Keep your voice down. You want to get caught?"

Chapter 15

Sham Singh and his wife Jeet Kaur stood in the verandah, worrying to death.

"Where the hell have they gone?" Sham Singh said looking out, over the courtyard wall. "They've been gone for a month."

"My heart is sinking. Something bad has happened," Jeet Kaur said holding her chest. Her face turned pallid and she sat down on a stool as if her legs were too weak to bear her weight.

"I see a cloud of dust. Looks like, some sort of a vehicle is coming this way," Sham Singh squinted.

Jeet Kaur joined him, "A car?"

A dusty old blue car stopped in front of the house. Babbu got out and opened the gate. Pinta drove it into the courtyard.

Sham Singh and Jeet Kaur ran towards them.

"Where've you been all this time?" Sham Singh shouted. "Where is Rupi?" their mother asked.

"We left her at your sister's house!" Pinta said. Babbu lowered his eyes.

"You are lying!" she cried.

"We sent a message to her sister, only yesterday, and you were never there." Sham Singh gnashed his teeth.

"Do not lie to me."

"Tell me, Pintu, what did you do to her? Where *is* Rupi?" Jeet Kaur pulled him by the shirt.

"We don't know!" Pinta yelled.

"You've done something to her. My heart tells me. Why, Pintu…? We could have married her off!" Her hands went limp and she let go of his shirt. Sobbing uncontrollably, she slipped on to the floor.

"I'm going to cut your throats, you…you…!" Sham Singh picked up a sickle, threatening them.

"Have you not a shred of honor left in your gut, you old faggot!" Pinta touched his pocket holding the pistol.

"I should have put poison into your mouth, when you were born, instead of feeding you milk!" Jeet Kaur jumped in front of Sham Singh.

"Go ahead, shoot me!" Sham Singh pushed his wife away and stepped towards Pinta.

"I'm not going to kill you! Not a word to anyone!" Pinta said starting the car. "Get in," he said to Babbu. Soon they were out of sight, leaving behind a thick cloud of dust.

Sham Singh and Jeet Kaur mourned in silence, not knowing what happened to their daughter.

Sham Singh fell ill and the village doctor was unable to bring him back to health. He was getting weaker by the day but refused to go to the city hospital.

******

Pinta and Babbu would come and go as they pleased. People shied away from them when they saw their car and pistols. No one knew where they got the car from.

Daulat's mother looked for her son everywhere. She asked everyone, including Pinta and Babbu.

"Sardar ji, please help me find my son!" she begged Pinta.

"Get out of here woman! You yourself are hiding that slothful son of yours somewhere. That lazy bum never wanted to work hard." Pinta yelled.

A few days later she came back, "Sardar ji, he worked for you day and night. What happened to him? Where did he go?"

"I am going to feed you to my dogs if you come back here."

Pinta, yelled, "I don't know anything about him." Clenching his fists, he rushed towards her.

She fell backward and did not dare to come near him again. The rumors continued in the village that the brothers had done something to Daulat and Rupi, but no one dared say anything.

Chapter 16

"Come here, princess!" Lal stretched out his arms. A big smile on her face, Pali got up from the floor. With her chubby, little feet she straggled towards him.

"My turn, walk to Ma, Pali!" Namo sitting on the other side of the room clapped, to attract her attention. She started her wobbly journey from Lal to Namo and back to Lal.

Pali took her first steps a few days before her first birthday. Suddenly she had left Namo's lap to have a taste of freedom. With her tiny legs and unsteady footsteps, she would fall on her pudgy butt but would not cry. She'd pull herself up and walk a few steps before falling again. It became a game that went on until she needed a nap or was hungry.

The preparations for her first birthday party were in full swing. Word-of-mouth invitations had been sent to many families in the neighboring villages. Rattan Singh and Bhani went to the city to shop for the party items.

When they did not return till dark, Lal worriedly said to Namo, "What's taking them so long?"

"Even if they took the last bus, they should've been here hours ago," Namo said, carrying Pali on her hip. "It'll be dark soon. We should go look for them."

Lal and Kaku rode their horses to the bus stop a few miles away. No sign of them.

"Should we go to the train station?" Kaku asked as they turned homeward.

"We could, but the passenger train runs this way only in the morning, that too every other day. Also, the train station is too far for them to walk," Lal said and turned the horse towards the train station anyway. The night was almost over when they returned without a clue.

Rattan Singh and Bhani did not come back the next day or the day after that. Lal sent messengers to all relatives asking if anyone had any information about them.

"Where could they have gone? What could have happened to them?" Lal asked himself again and again. The police wrote the missing person report but did nothing to find them. Frantic searches did not reveal a single clue and they were out of options looking for them. The birthday celebrations never happened.

"Do you think Hakam Singh might be able to help in any way?" Namo asked Lal.

"We definitely need to inform him!" Lal felt he was drowning and Hakam may come as a wisp of straw to hold on to, to keep him afloat.

Hakam and Harjit came the very next day and brought along their four-year-old son Baldev.

The friends embraced, teary-eyed, and heavy-hearted. "Where could they have gone?" Hakam asked the question that had been churning over in Lal's mind.

While they talked, Baldev saw little Pali sitting on the floor and ran to her. She giggled, clapping her baby hands. Baldev held her arm helping her to get up. The two walked around the room holding hands, Pali with her shaky unstable legs and Baldev with his four-year-old steady secure steps. Hearing their children's joyful shrieks the parents forgot their worries for a few moments.

However, the atmosphere turned somber again rather quickly.

"There was a protest march in the main bazaar the same day in support of Gandhi and the police had used truncheons and batons to disperse the crowd," Hakam said. "Many people were injured and many more arrested that day."

"But why would they go to the protest? They had gone to shop for Pali's birthday."

"They might have been in the wrong place at the wrong time," Hakam said.

Lal and Hakam immediately left for the city, praying for a miracle. They checked all the hospitals. They enquired at the police station if they had been arrested by mistake. But no one knew anything about them.

Hakam and Harjit left a few days later, promising to come back soon. Every relative, distant or close, came to help in any way they could. Hakam Singh came back several times giving Lal much needed mental and moral support.

Days turned into weeks and the weeks into months. "Any news?" people would ask Lal, even though they knew there *was* no news and his raw wounds of grief would start oozing again.

Two grown people in their fifties had disappeared without a trace as if the earth had swallowed them. The depth of despair was taking its toll on Lal. As the time passed, dark circles appeared around his eyes. The nightmares would not let him sleep and his stomach frequently refused to retain any food.

The only bright spot in life was Pali's chirpy giggles that brought a smile on his gloomy face. She would run towards him, shouting, "Maaa!" as soon as she saw him entering the house.

"I'm your *Bapu ji*, princess, not Ma," Lal said every time, picking her up. She'd shake her head, "No, Ma!" and wrap her little arms around his neck, laughing playfully. It had become a game for her. Lal pressed her against his chest and laughed. It took the anguish out of his mind for a while, and Namo's support kept him going.

And then it occurred to him. Could it be Pinta and Babbu? The thought sent a bloodcurdling feeling through his body. *Didn't they threaten to teach my family a lesson, for not marrying their sister?* He felt dizzy.

He had not paid any attention to the scandalous tittle-tattle about the brothers. Rumors had been floating around that they had killed their own sister and her lover. People talked about them abducting young women from the southern states and selling them at Hira Mandy, the red-light district at Lahore. Their father Sham Singh had fallen sick and their farm was in shambles.

The next morning, Lal filed a complaint with the police. Pinta and Babbu were taken into custody for questioning and were let go within a few days.

No evidence. End of case.

Was that the end of an era? The thought gave Lal a sickening feeling. People had already started calling him Sardar ji instead of *Chhotte,* the younger Sardar ji. The most hurtful feeling was, not knowing what had happened to his parents.

Chapter 17

The evening sky turned orangey-red with alternating layers of gray. The birds were returning to their nests, flying low, crowing in barely audible tunes. Lal rode his horse homeward at a leisurely pace while planning the wheat harvest in his mind. The crop was ready and the slightest rain or wind could destroy the dried-out wheat awns filled with grain. He would have to hire several temporary workers.

The evening breeze felt good on his face. *Grow more crops, Lali! Give work to more people.* His father's voice echoed in his ears. Lal looked at the darkening sky and let the horse pick up speed.

A car coming from behind jerked to a stop in front of him with a screechy loud noise. Clouds of dust flew up from the dirt road and the horse panicked. Her front legs up in the air, she almost threw Lal off her back.

"Easy, easy," Lal tried to control the horse. He looked at the two men in the car. *Is it Pinta and Babbu?*

Pinta stuck his head out the driver's side window, "Hey, Laloo, did you find your old man yet?" A devilish smile playing on his face, he looked at Lal.

"Feel sorry for you, friend," he said, twisting his mustache between his index finger and thumb. His mouth said 'sorry' but the action of twirling his mustache conveyed a threatening message.

Babbu opened the passenger side door and waved a gun pointing upwards. "There!" he said.

Lal looked at him in horror. His mouth dried and his tongue felt glued to his palate. *Is he going to kill me?* Pali and Namo's faces flashed in his mind. The earth whooshed around him instantaneously and his body quivered.

Looking at Lal's frightened face, Babbu winked at him and laughed.

"Close the door, Babbu," Pinta said pressing the accelerator.

The car turned around and sped away leaving behind dust and the smell of petrol. *What are they doing here, near our village? Did Babbu mean that they had killed his parents, or was it they wanted to kill him? They could have killed me right then!* His shaky hands folded instinctively and he looked up towards the sky. "Thank you!" he whispered.

Heading home, anger replaced the fear. *I have to stop them. No more insults from these criminals!* His jaws tightened and he heard the sound of his teeth, gnashing spontaneously. I too have men on my side, and I too have money, maybe more than them! A feeling of courage restored in his gut, and he felt a newly found strength, he did not know he had.

"What is it, Lal?" Namo gazed at him, wide-eyed.

Lal held Namo and Pali in his arms and hugged them tightly.

"Nothing!" he said, tightening his hold around Namo's waist.

That night he talked to Kaku. "We need a couple of guns."

"Yes, we do!" Kaku answered.

Chapter 18

"I've been wanting to see that chicken-hearted coward's face for a while," Pinta said, driving full speed on the uneven dirt road. The car spewed thick smoke from the tailpipe that mixed with clouds of dust. As they entered the village, people leaped out of the way. Children stopped playing and stared at them zooming by.

"Laloo shivered like a wet kitten!" Babbu laughed.

"He looked as if he just saw his dead mother's face!" Pinta pouted his lips and puckered his eyebrows as if he was about to cry, then burst into a maniacal laughter.

"He shook like this," Babbu mimicked Lal, shaking his hand bent at the wrist.

"I know," Pinta said, parking the car at the back of their house.

"Why aren't you parking in the courtyard?" Babbu asked.

"We'll be leaving soon."

"It's already getting dark. I don't want to go anywhere tonight."

"We won't get paid unless we make another delivery. We have to go to Calcutta again."

"I don't want to do it anymore," Babbu said, as they entered the house through the backdoor.

"Okay, only one more, maybe two at the most," Pinta said coaxingly.

"I told you, I don't want to go anywhere. We just got back after so long."

"They're going to take the car back if we don't make any more deliveries."

"No, Pintu! I feel bad for the women, we take to Lahore."

"I said only one more. We're out of money. And father has none left either."

"Why did you come home if father has no money?"

"Ma has a lot of gold jewelry, stupid!"

"You want to sell Ma's jewelry?" Babbu glared at Pinta walking towards the verandah.

"Who is she going to keep it for? Rupi isn't there anymore." Pinta stopped in the courtyard.

Hearing Rupi's name, Babbu turned back shouting, "You killed Rupi and I am going to kill you," he pointed the gun at Pinta.

Startled, Pinta quickly took out his gun. "Have you lost your mind, you brainless maggot!"

Babbu had always followed his elder brother and did whatever he was told. Since Pinta had killed Rupi, Babbu hated him deeply but was scared to confront him. Now his long bottled-up anger blew off its top and he was ready to meet his big brother head-on.

"I'm going to tell everyone what you did."

"No, you won't. How dare you challenge me?" Pinta yelled.

Hearing the noise, Sham Singh limped out of his room, aided by a walking stick.

"What's going on out here?"

The explosive sound of gunshots cut through the twilight of the evening. Sham Singh fell with a thud. Blood gushed out of his mouth and chest like a fountain. A flock of frightened sparrows chirping noisily flew out of the mulberry tree in the courtyard.

And then a ghastly silence ensued that froze the time and halted the wind. But the short-lived stillness was tattered by Babbu's scream,

"Look what you've done!"

"No, you did it!" Pinta yelled back.

Both ran towards Sham Singh.

Babbu lifted his lifeless arm and softly let it fall to the ground.

Their mother, Jeet Kaur ran out of the room, screaming and wailing. She slumped on Sham Singh's body. Her clothes drenched with thick sticky blood.

She got up, raised her arms above her head, and then slapped her thighs with all the strength she had in her scrawny body. She kept beating herself, again and again, letting out earth-shattering screams. Pinta and Babbu stood dumbfounded.

"We didn't mean to…" Pinta said, turning towards her.

She leaped at him like a lioness, beating him with her fists and then fell down writhing. A few moments later she went silent.

A sickle-shaped moon emerged above the mulberry tree. Its feeble glow turned them into blackened shadows. The warm summer night warped into a bone-chilling, horrific night and the stray dogs howled in the streets.

******

Hearing blood-curdling shrieks, Nand Singh's steps froze as if glued to the ground but his 70-year-old heart sped like a startled stallion. He stood still for a few moments and then hurried towards Sham Singh's house where the wailing was coming from. The screams stopped as he came close to the house. "Something terrible has happened," he said picking up pace.

"You killed them?" Nand Singh yelled as he saw Sham Singh and Jeet Kaur on the floor, "your own father? And mother?" He glared at Pinta and Babbu standing nearby, still holding guns.

The whole village had been stirred up hearing gunshots and Jeet Kaur's screams. Men and women swarmed towards Sham Singh's crumbling house that was once a glorious mansion. Some carried kerosene oil lanterns, others came holding bamboo batons. Women ran towards Jeet Kaur while the men stood around Sham Singh's blood-soaked body.

"She is alive!" a woman shouted.

The village women helped her from the floor to a cot where she collapsed again. They sprinkled water on her face. She opened her eyes and started wailing.

While people gathered around Sham Singh and Jeet Kaur, Pinta tried escaping through the backdoor they had entered the house earlier. Some of the men jumped on him.

"Where do you think you're going?" one of them punched him in the stomach.

Babbu stood paralyzed. Only his eyeballs moved from Sham Singh to Jeet Kaur and back to Sham Singh.

"Tie them up!" Nand Singh said.

They bound their hands and ankles with chains used for cows.

People whispered to each other, "It was bound to happen one day. They've been terrorizing the whole area."

"And now they killed their own father."

"What had been smoldering for a long time was destined to go up in flames. And finally, it did."

Nand Singh's eyes scanned the crowd and he pointed at Gian and Teg Singh, "You two, go get your horses and leave for the city immediately. We have to report to the police," he said. "Take two more men with you," he hollered, as Gian and Teg left.

Most of the villagers stayed at Sham Singh's house, waiting for the police. Some stared at the tied-up brothers and some at Sham Singh's body lying in the courtyard. A few of the women went home and came back with food for the people gathered and some stayed back trying to console the inconsolable Jeet Kaur. Nand Singh told a young man to spread a few sheets on the floor in the verandah for people to sit, while some sat on the cots. They talked in hushed voices and waited for the police. They dozed off in-between Jeet Kaur's sighs and hysterical sobs, but none of them got up to go home.

The police arrived around midmorning the next day. By the time they examined Sham Singh's body, finished inquiries and paperwork, it was late afternoon. They took Pinta and Babbu in custody along with their guns. Pinta defiantly glared at the police and the villagers while Babbu squirmed and cried, "I didn't do anything, I swear…" One of the officers slapped him and pushed him into the police van. Soon they were out of sight.

Sham Singh's body lay in the courtyard under the sweltering sun. Nand Singh looked at the people gathered saying, "Now it's our duty to cremate him before the body starts decomposing due to heat."

"Yes, yes," a few voices came simultaneously.

"Get the funeral pyre ready as soon as possible," Nand Singh said.

"I will arrange for the wood," Gian said. Several men got up and left with him to help with the pyre.

As they lifted Sham Singh's body onto a bier for taking it to the cremation grounds, Jeet Kaur fainted again. No water sprinkling on her face worked. She took a few labored breaths and was gone. Dead.

People stood bewildered, looking at her. Nand Singh lowered himself onto a cot as if his old bones suddenly defeated him. After a long while, he said, "We'll cremate them both at the same pyre."

They loaded the bodies on two separate biers and carried to the cremation grounds. The villagers walked in a somber procession.

"What a shameful tragedy! It is the sons who carry their parent's bier on their shoulders to the cremation grounds, but here the sons are the killers," Nand Singh said to the man walking next to him.

The man nodded, "Poor Sham Singh!"

"They say that a sage once said, *your enemies from the past life will be born as your children in this life to take revenge*," Nand Singh said, "I always made fun of this aphorism. But in this case, it seems so very true." He let out a long breath, moving his head side to side.

They laid both bodies side by side onto the pyre and ignited it. The flames leaped towards the sky, as the dry wood crackled like firecrackers. A dynasty once rich and powerful now turned into ashes and merged with the dust of the earth.

Chapter 19

"It was an unfortunate accident. They did not mean to kill him," the lawyers claimed Pinta and Babbu's innocence.

"The evidence is right in front of your eyes that Sham Singh was hit by both brothers from the opposite directions. One of the bullets hit him in the face, and the other pierced through the back making its way out the chest, killing him on the spot," the prosecutor argued.

Pinta and Babbu were both found guilty of Sham Singh's murder but were acquitted for their mother's death.

Then the trial about Rupi and Daulat's disappearance began. The prosecutors brought in a low cast man, Chhajju who had been working at Sham Singh's farm along with Daulat.

"I saw them killing Rupi and Daulat with my own eyes," he said.

The translator interpreted the Punjabi-speaking witness's testimony into English for the British judge.

"Daulat told me that he had been meeting Rupi in the cornfields for a while, and that night he was taking her to the grove," Chhaju's voice shook. "I did not believe him, so I hid in the bushes at the grove. Rupi and Daulat came around midnight."

Chhaju went quiet for a moment as if struggling for words.

"What happened next?" the prosecutor asked.

"They lay on the sheet Daulat had spread on the grass."

"Then what did you see?" The prosecutor walked close to Chhaju.

"Pinta and Babbu showed up a little later and yelled at them. Then Pinta shot them."

"Did you see him shoot?"

Chhaju nodded. "Pinta killed Daulat and then he shot Rupi." His dark brown face turned pale as he spoke.

"Then what happened?"

"They loaded the bodies on the horse and left."

"Why didn't you say anything at that time or tell anyone?" the lawyer asked.

"I was scared. They would have killed me if I told anyone."

People murmured as if a swarm of bumblebees had been set free in the room.

"Three murders."

"Maybe even five!"

"They might have killed Rattan Singh and Bhani too. They both disappeared without a trace."

"Silence in the court!" the judge shouted. His white skin momentarily glowed like red, hot coal, and he looked around the courtroom over the top of his glasses, which had fallen on to his nose.

People hushed.

The prosecutors brought Daulat's mother, barefooted and dressed in rags to testify.

"I am a poor widow," she said. "Daulat, my son, was everything to me. He was the one I lived for." She shifted her weight from one leg to the other as if her scrawny body was too heavy for her swollen feet and cracked heels.

"Now I ask for death every day, but it is not coming to me!" She stared around the room with empty eyes as if looking for something but not finding it. Soon tears flowed down her bony cheeks.

"Okay, I have heard enough. I will see that you are fairly compensated," the judge said waving his hand. "Take her out of here," he said to the orderly.

The workers, who had not been paid and the ones beaten by the brothers for asking for payment, appeared before the judge one by one. The translator tried to convert every word of Punjabi into English for the judge.

Pinta and Babbu confessed abducting four young women from the state of Bengal and selling them into prostitution at Hira Mandi, Lahore.

At the end of the testimonies, the judge ordered Sham Singh's land, whatever was left of it, to be auctioned off. He ordered Daulat's mother two hundred rupees compensation and the farmworkers paid from the auction proceedings.

In exchange for sparing him the gallows, Pinta confessed to killing Rupi and Daulat.

The judge announced Pinta's sentence looking straight at him. "You will grow old and die in the prison for the horrific crimes you have committed. You will be transported to *Kala Pani,* the Black Waters Cellular Prison in the Andaman and Nicobar Islands, where you will spend the rest of your life."

The judge sentenced Babbu to 15 years imprisonment that he would complete at one of the mainland Indian prisons.

Chapter 20

"I know in my heart, Pinta and Babbu did something to Ma and *Bapu ji*," Lal said to Namo. "The prosecutors needed some kind of evidence or witness. And there was none."

Namo held Lal's hand.

"I have to see Pinta before they exile him to *Kala Pani*!" he said.

"Why?" Namo looked at Lal. "Why would you want to see that criminal again, Sardar ji?"

"Maybe I will get something out of him about Ma and *Bapu ji*," Lal said with a sliver of hope in his voice. "He's not going to be tried for this again. So he might say something that could bring some closure for us."

"Okay, but I don't want you to go there alone," Namo said.

"My silly Namo! He's not in a position to do any harm to me," Lal said giving her a snug hug.

"Still, take Kaku along."

It took Lal more than a month to get approval to see Pinta just two days before his transportation to the cellular prison at Andaman Nicobar Islands.

A prison guard led him into a hall with a high ceiling. Pinta sat in a small chamber behind a window fitted with vertical iron bars.

The guard pointed to a stool for Lal to sit outside the window.

As soon as Lal settled on the stool, Pinta smiled. "I knew you'd come, Laloo!"

"How so?" Lal was baffled by his comment.

"I'm sure you're anxious to know what happened to them. I mean your Ma and old man."

"Yes, tell me. What did you do to them?"

"Oh, we got them onto the train," Pinta said in a casual tone.

"You got them on to the train? What train?" Lal jumped up from the stool.

"Calm down, Laloo, you can't catch a train that's long gone!"

"Long gone? What you mean, long gone," Lal yelled.

Pinta pointed his finger towards the ceiling. "The train that goes but never returns!" He puckered his lips and blew out his breath in a big puff towards Lal. "Up there! Poof!" he said with a fiendish smile.

Lal felt blood rushing to his head. His temples throbbed and his hands clenched into tight fists. "Did you kill them?" he asked trying to control his anger.

"O, you poor, little puppy!" Pinta said and made a clicking sound as if calling a dog.

With a lightning speed, Lal stretched his arms through the window bars and caught Pinta's arms, pulling him with a strong jerk. Pinta's face hit the iron bars with a thud. Before he could recover from the unexpected attack, Lal repeatedly hit his head against the window. The guard standing nearby turned his back and did not intervene.

Bewildered, Pinta yanked his body to free himself from Lal's hold and fell backward. His forehead was swollen with numerous vertical bumps and a streak of blood ran down his chin from his left nostril.

Lal pushed the stool away and turned to leave. The guard smiled and his lips moved as if saying, 'well done,' as he passed by him. He left the prison building more baffled and enraged. How could men like Pinta, after killing his own father and sister, sitting in a prison cell, taunt and make jokes like that, was beyond his imagination.

"What did he say, Sardar ji?" Kaku quickly got up from the grassy patch outside the prison building, when he saw Lal.

"Nothing, Kaku," Lal said. "You go home and let Namo know, I'll be back the day after tomorrow."

"Where should I tell her, you are going?"

"I'm going to Hakam's village."

Chapter 21

The bus lazily moved along the potholed narrow road through the desolate dry areas with thorny acacia trees and wild caper bushes. Lal looked out the broken window that rattled with every bump on the road. Gusts of hot wind blew on his face. The dried-out uprooted prickly weeds tumbling in the wind caught his attention.

Am I like these uprooted weeds of the desert that have lost their tether to the ground? As I have lost my tether to Ma and *Bapu ji*. Would I be tossing myself around like these windswept weeds? A wave of sadness spread through his body.

Would I see Ma's face ever again? When I was sad, she wept with me. I smiled and she laughed till her eyes watered. When I was weak, she gave me strength. When I was strong, she admired me. Ma's tiny body turned into a strong and stanch 'Tahli' tree, when she stood up to *Bapu ji* for me.

And *Bapu ji*! How could I ever fit into his shoes? How can anyone be like him? Harder than a rock yet softer than butter, honest and impartial and so generous! When the villagers call me Sardar ji, do they expect me to be like him? Will I be a disappointment to them?

Lal shuddered with the thought.

The bus dropped him at a makeshift bus stop that seemed like in the middle of nowhere. He headed to the dirt road leading to Hakam Singh's village, Gajanpur, about three miles away. The barren areas here and there were interspersed with stretches of green crops, a sign of irrigation by canals and water wells. Luscious fodder crops grew side by side with cotton plants. Fluffy cotton peeked through the cracked ridges of matured pods, ready to be picked. Prickly thistles grew in the empty spaces between the crops. *Would Bapu ji ever compare himself to a tumbleweed, as I did?* Lal wondered.

"No, he'd be a big shady Banyan tree. Never a prickly thistle, you fool!" the words came out loud. He looked around to see if anyone heard him talking to himself. There was no one, except a pair of squirrels chasing each other from one branch of a tree to another.

Dust lifted with each of his footsteps and dissipated into the thin hot air. The sun seemed to be in a hurry going down the horizon, but the dust-filled air was still hot. "Almost there," he said seeing the village at a little distance.

Tired and gloomed by the encounter he had with Pinta in the jail, Lal knocked at Hakam's door at dusk.

"What a surprise!" Hakam met him at the door with a concerned look, hidden behind a wide smile. "Is everything alright, Lal?" he asked, giving him a tight hug, almost lifting him off the ground.

"It's good to see you, Lal. How are Namo and Pali?" Harjit joined them with a similar expression of worry and joy because of his unexpected arrival.

"They're fine. I just wanted to see my brother and bhabhi ji!" Lal said, forcing his lips to part in a smile.

Baldev ran towards him shouting, "*Lal Chacha ji!*" and clung to his legs.

"You have grown so big, Baldev!" Lal picked him up.

Baldev squirmed out of his arms quickly, stood on the floor, and tiptoed, "Look, *Chacha ji*, I am sooo long!" He stretched his arms above his head. Everyone laughed.

"You *are* very big and tall Baldev!" Lal said and tried to tickle him before he ran away laughing and clapping.

"You can't catch me," Baldev said running around, while Lal chased him. Soon Baldev was busy with his toy cart that he started loading with make-believe fodder for the cattle.

The evening phased into a glittering starry night. They sat in the courtyard after dinner, talking. A gentle warm wind felt pleasant. The moonless sky glimmered. An incredible shower of meteorites made it look like, the sky will be starless if it went on for a while longer. The shooting star would begin with a tremendous glow like a little sun was falling down and disappeared into nothingness within a few seconds.

Did my parents disappear into a void, like these stars, without making a sound? Lal thought looking at the sky.

"Do you ever hear the shriek of a star severed from the sky that glows for a moment before reducing to nothingness? Gone forever?" Lal said.

Hakam looked at him, "What is it, Lal? What are you saying?"

"I'm carrying this burden on my chest that does not let me sleep. I want to scream and holler at the top of my voice, but I can't!"

Hakam got up from his cot and held Lal's shoulders, "Talk to me!" he said.

The silent moments weighed heavy on Lal.

"I went to see Pinta today. He almost confessed to me about Ma and *Bapu ji.*"

"He did?"

"Yes, but we cannot do a damn thing about it. The case is closed."

"People like him should be on the gallows," Hakam said.

"No gallows for him! Even after killing his own father and sister, also Daulat. He's going to Kala Pani."

"And they are sending young men to Kala Pani even for distributing pamphlets or writing poems against the atrocities of the British rulers!" Hakam said. "The hollowness of justice!"

"That's why I'm worried about you Hakam! I could not bear losing you."

"I'm not going anywhere."

"You are walking on the blade of a sword!"

"If my walking on the blade could blunt the sword of tyranny, it will be all the worthwhile."

"Okay, if not me, think of Baldev and Harjit. What will happen to them?" Lal said looking him in the eye.

"Have you forgotten the day we exchanged our turbans and became brothers? You are not any less to me than Baldev and Harjit. You are my brother."

"Then do not put your life in danger," Lal begged.

"Lal, have you ever seen the signs outside of the clubs and the hotels, *'Dogs and Indians not allowed!'* What can be more humiliating than this? You tell me, can you travel in the first-class compartment of a train, even if you have money to buy the ticket?"

"They have machine guns! And what do you have? Only a little stick in comparison. That's what you have! A tiny little twig to fight their killer weapons." Lal panted with the thought of lurking danger.

"Let's face it. There are about 70000 of them ruling over three hundred million of us. We do not need machineguns. What we need is, to wake up each one of us, from this several hundred years-long slumber of slavery."

Lal felt like he was hearing him for the first time.

"I dream of our children Baldev and Pali to be able to breathe in the fresh air of freedom." Hakam continued, "are you listening, Lal? We're treated worse than animals in our own home."

The night was more than half gone. The sky did not look like it had lost any stars. It still sparkled proudly and majestically

Part-II
The Exile

Chapter 22

The stage secretary announced his name. Hakam Singh entered through the side door. He took a deep breath and scanned the hall. It was almost full. He had not expected so many people but was pleased by it. The front seats were mostly taken by the peasants and laborers. The back half of the hall was occupied by young men, dressed like college students, wearing buttoned-up achkans, and blue or white turbans.

The hall buzzed with indistinct voices. Hakam cleared his throat. The hall went silent. He felt multiple pairs of eyes focused on him. This was not the first time he had addressed a large crowd, but this was the first time after Bhagat Singh's martyrdom, the leader of revolution, the beloved son of Punjab, who at the tender age of twenty-three had challenged the mighty British Raj in a way that sent shock waves throughout the streets of London, and the occupiers were petrified to the core.

"Today, we honor the martyrs who gave their lives for justice and liberty. We pledge to keep Bhagat Singh's legacy alive. The torch of revolution Sardar Bhagat Singh ignited with his blood is ours to keep burning," Hakam's earnest voice turned into rage as he spoke. "Until the reign of oppression is eradicated, until the yoke of slavery is removed from our necks, until we breathe the fresh air of freedom."

"We will never forget the wretched day of March 23rd, 1931, when Bhagat Singh along with Raj Guru and Sukhdev were hanged, a day before the set date of execution. Bhagat Singh and Sukhdev were 23 and Rajguru was only 22 years old. Their bodies were secretly taken out of the Lahore prison during the night and never handed over to their families."

"Bhagat Singh… *Zindabad.*" A young man in a light blue turban stood up waving his fist. People answered with shouts of, "Long live, Bhagat Singh. Long live, Rajguru, and Sukhdev."

The hall reverberated with their shouts. Hakam signaled them to sit down and continued, "No matter how many the British tyrants kill, there will be more of us, like the stars in the sky," his voice grew stronger and louder.

"I quote from Bhagat Singh, 'Revolution is an inalienable right of mankind. Freedom is an imperishable birthright of all.'

"Can we ever forget the Amritsar Jallianwala Bagh massacre when the light of the day was turned red with the blood of innocent people?" Hakam's voice echoed in the hall.

"Thousands of people of all religions, Sikhs, Hindus, and Muslims had gathered in the grounds of Jallianwala Bagh near the Golden Temple, in the holy city of Amritsar. They were celebrating our largest festival, Baisakhi Day. The British General, Reginald Dyer blocked the only exit with armored vehicles and a wall of armed soldiers. He ordered the soldiers to fire at the unarmed and unsuspecting crowd without any warning. He ordered them to load and reload the guns several times until their ammunition was exhausted."

"People had nowhere to go as the only exit was blocked by Dyer's army. When people fell on the ground, he ordered the soldiers to shoot at the ground level. When people ran to the right, he ordered them to shoot to the right. When people ran to the left, the rifles followed them to the left. Men who tried to climb the walls of the buildings were shot at the level of the walls. The soldiers were ordered to fire wherever the crowd was the thickest. Many fell into the water well while running, and drowned. Many jumped into the well to escape the bullets. At the end, the well was filled to the top with bodies."

Hakam shook with anger. His knuckles turned pale by tight fists, his eyes looked fiery red and he stopped for a moment. A commotion of angry voices filled the room.

"Earth-shattering screams deafened the sky," Hakam roared. "The celebratory grounds turned crimson by the blood spurting out of men women and children who had come to celebrate. The wounded lay in puddles of blood crying for help."

"At the end of that terrible day, more than a thousand innocent men, women, and children were massacred by General Dyer. He then, marched his soldiers out of the area leaving the dead and the moaning wounded behind."

The man in the blue turban stood up again, "Death to Dyer, the butcher of the innocent!" he yelled.

Waving their fists people shouted after him, "Death to Dyer!"

Hakam gestured him with a slight nod to sit down. The man complied immediately. Hakam kept his voice loud and steady.

"But, instead of condemning Dyer for the slaughter, here's what our own Gandhi wrote in his newspaper, Young India: *I would not punish or procure punishment even of General Dyer for his massacre, but I would not call it voluntarily doing injury to him to refuse to give him a pension, or to condemn his action in fitting language.*

"They mercilessly crush us with their machine guns. They shamelessly trample our dignity under their heels, and this is what Gandhi has to say?"

"Does Gandhi mean that the British can freely kill Indians while they peacefully celebrate their festivals? Does he not want the killer to be held accountable? On the other hand, he strongly condemned Bhagat Singh and other revolutionaries like us who want to remove the British shackles from India's neck."

"My farmer brothers," Hakam's throat choked with emotion, "we till the land, and pour our sweat into the fields in the sweltering heat of the summer. We work in pouring rain and the freezing cold. We cannot afford warm clothes for our children in winter. We scold them when they ask for more food. We make them work in the fields instead of sending them to school or letting them play, like children should. We are forced to steal away their childhood."

"When we harvest, the officials snatch away the fruit of our labor. And we are left with nothing."

"No more! We shall resist. If they try, we will fight back. Be it with swords or guns or bombs. If we are ready to die, we are ready to kill," the room resounded with Hakam's infuriated voice.

Clamoring shouts of 'Down with the Raj' went on for a while. Hakam continued with fervor.

"The British regard themselves as very refined, civilized people. But when they come to India, all their manners and civility are left behind in England. Their behavior towards us is cruel, worse than animals. This is our home, our land, our nation. They are the invaders who have been plundering our resources and sucking the very life out of our nation. They are the parasites that need to be crushed."

"We will unite and fight as one nation, one people. But I want to remind us about their devious 'divide and rule' strategy. There are innumerable examples

I can quote, but let me talk about the despicable incident of the city of Peshawar."

People sat with their eyes fixed on him.

"In Peshawar, Muslim Pathans were peacefully demonstrating in favor of Gandhi's Salt-Satyagrah, the Civil-Disobedience Movement. The British commanding officer Captain Ricket ordered the Garhwali regiment under Chandar Singh to fire at the unarmed crowd. Chandar Singh refused."

"This infuriated the British official so much that he instantly fired on the closest soldier, missing him but killed his horse instead and called for reinforcement. A British platoon in armored cars sped into the crowd crushing many people under its wheels like they were insects and not humans. The British troops fired indiscriminately into the crowd. They shot at the windows and at the rooftops at people who were not even part of the march. They killed hundreds and wounded many more. The brave Chandar Singh and 59 of his soldiers were court-martialed for defying the orders to kill innocent people."

"What a way to divide and rule, order Hindus to fire at the Muslims and Muslims to fire at the Sikhs!" Someone in the crowd yelled at the top of his voice followed by multiple voices of "Long live the Revolution!"

"Long live Chandar Singh!"

"Every year the number of martyrs jumps into hundreds, but we remain strapped under the rein of cruelty. Is the non-violence civil-disobedience working for us?"

People looked at each other. The room hummed with inaudible voices. Hakam looked around with a stern gaze and continued.

"Gandhi went on hunger strike in the prison and was released after promising to suspend his civil-disobedience movement. Bhagat Singh and associates went on hunger strike in Lahore jail and were mercilessly beaten and tortured. They were too weak to walk and were carried on stretchers to the court hearings. Jatin Das succumbed to death by hunger strike and cruel beating. Bhagat Singh, Rajguru, and Sukhdev were given a death sentence."

Hakam's eyes met with the man in the blue turban again and saw an avid passion in his gaze. He shouted, waving his fists, "Death to Imperialism! Long Live Revolution!"

"Gandhi went to London after ending his Civil-Disobedience and made a pact with Lord Irwin. What did he gain? Nothing! Not a thing for the nation."

"I ask you, why did Gandhi not negotiate sparing the life of Bhagat Singh and others? Also, why did he not ask for the release of Chandar Singh and other soldiers who had refused to fire at the unarmed crowd who were demonstrating in favor of his Salt Satyagrah?"

"Gandhi saved his own life!" Many people stood up. The mayhem of angry shouts buried Hakam's voice.

"Please, sit down. Sit down." Hakam waved his arms.

"Gandhi came back from London and the journalists asked him the obvious question. And his answer was, the Garhwali soldiers had taken an oath to obey government orders, and they broke their oath. As for Bhagat Singh and his associates, his explanation was that they were young men who had lost their way."

The crowd froze into silence.

"On the contrary, Bhagat Singh illuminated the dark alleys of oppression for others to find a way to freedom. The freedom from slavery; from humiliating insults; freedom to walk with your head held high."

"And the Garhwali soldiers, do you think, had taken the oath to murder unarmed people? According to Gandhi, the soldiers should have obeyed the orders and fired at the peaceful crowd killing them. What about his non-violence policy he preaches? Is he a hypocrite or contradicts himself whenever it suits him?"

"I'm not here to badmouth Gandhi. I'm here to tell you the tale of tragedy that keeps happening. We cannot make pacts with the oppressor. Gandhi ended the cause and now what? Wait till the British hands over the freedom to us?"

Uneasy silence reined the room. The man in the blue turban walked to Hakam and asked if he could say a few words.

"Definitely," Hakam smiled and stepped to the side.

"My name is Didar Singh," he said glancing over the crowd. "I am a student at National College Lahore and a member of Bhagat Singh's Naujawan Sabha."

"I appeal to you, let's take an oath to our motherland today that we will not give in to the brutalities of the British. We will not be brought down by their cruelties."

As the crowd shouted slogans, Didar stood tall and confident. His voice got angrier and louder.

"India is the Crown Jewel of the Raj. Do you think they will let it go easily? Their informers and moles are everywhere. Freedom is not free my friends! We pay for it with our lives so that our children are liberated from the fetters of slavery. People of India have to rise as one against the Imperial."

"Police!" someone yelled.

A British officer and two Indian policemen stormed into the room thumping their heavy boots on the floor. People ran haphazardly to getaway. The British officer went straight to the front of the hall yelling profanities towards Hakam and Didar.

"Run!" Hakam shouted at Didar.

With lightning speed, Hakam grabbed the officer's gun and pressed the trigger. The bullet whooshed by the officer, scraping off the skin from his arm. The officer startled by the unexpected attack fell backward. The gun slid from Hakam's hand and dropped below the stage. The two Indian sepoys overpowered him and pointed their guns at him. "Take him alive!" the officer commanded. They handcuffed him and put a hood over his head. They dragged him out of the hall and pushed him into a vehicle.

Chapter 23

Hakam Singh lay in a darkroom on a heap of paddy straw on the floor. He shivered in the long cold night. He had not closed his eyes even a wink, thinking about Harjit and Baldev. Will my son go to school tomorrow? Harjit must be worried. I told her I'd be home by evening. Someone must have told her by now. He stared at the dark ceiling. Government moles are everywhere. Hope, Didar escaped!

Hakam turned in the straw bed. He extended his arm and touched the rough cold brick wall. Is our future like this brick wall? Impenetrable! Bleak! Cold!

But, where am I? Hakam stared into the darkness. Is this the central jail, Lahore, where they hanged Bhagat Singh two years ago? The emptiness of the room did not answer. "Good, the pamphlets had been distributed before the meeting and people had stuffed them into their pockets. The more they know the better!" Hakam whispered conspiratorially. The room kept its vow of silence.

Dim light filtered through the crevices between the door and floor announcing the arrival of the morning. The piece of flatbread *roti* they had thrown into the room yesterday lay untouched by the door. A small pitcher of water lay nearby. Hakam took a few sips. It felt good on his dry throat.

O' the morning has arrived
With all its glory and vivacity
After defeating the dark of the night
The righteous winning over the wicked
And the benevolent conquest the malevolent!

Remembering the poem, Hakam's lips parted in a cynical smile. Shall we ever have our own glorious morning? The morning after the collapse of the imperial! Our own free morning!

Footsteps outside the room pulled him out of his daydreaming. The door opened with a loud creak. Two Indian sepoys handcuffed him without uttering a word. Hakam's heart thumped in his chest and his gait staggered as he walked between the two sepoys. They led him to a windowless dimly lit room. Soon a British officer stormed in. He had a white bandage on his right arm above the wrist.

Is this the same officer I grabbed the gun from? Hakam tried to guess from the bandaged arm. Everything had happened so fast that he did not get a chance to look at the officer's face before shooting, and then he was blindfolded immediately.

"The right arm. Trap his right arm!" the officer ordered. The sepoys looked at him as if they did not understand.

"Did you not hear me? Trap his arm!" the officer yelled.

The sepoys tied Hakam's arm between two wooden stumps exposing the area between the elbow and the wrist. He wanted to break away but knew there was no escape. The sepoys held him tight. Hakam's body shook.

"Now!" the officer howled.

I will not give you the satisfaction by screaming, you Feringhee bastard! Hakam held his breath and clenched his teeth.

With a heavy club, one of the sepoys struck his arm. Like the snapping of a tree branch, the bone in Hakam's forearm broke with a crackling sound.

Hakam tried not to, but loud screams left his throat one after the other, echoing in the room.

The officer waited for him to stop screaming and smiled, "I could have killed you on the spot that day, but it would have been an easy way out for you. Now you will remember me the rest of your life." His taunting smile widened. Then he laughed a hard-cruel laugh and left the room.

This is how they win! Why did I give him the satisfaction of my screams? No more screaming! No matter what! Hakam clenched his teeth and his left fist.

He was dragged back to his cell. His body felt like a ton of rock tied to it. His arm quickly swelled up with excruciating pain. Hakam moaned.

Later, an Indian doctor came accompanied by a sepoy. The doctor examined his arm pressing it with his fingers. Amongst Hakam's groans through the stick they gave him to bite on, he felt his way to the broken bone and brought the ends together, while the sepoy held him. The doctor secured it with a flat wooden splint and bound it tightly with rough heavy bandages to keep the bones from moving. He put Hakam's arm in a sling hanging from his neck.

"Here, these will help you for pain. Take one three times a day, with a sip of water." The doctor handed him tiny packets of brownish powder, tightly wrapped in old newspaper cuttings. "Keep your arm still. Even the slightest movement could shift the bones and your arm might be crippled for life."

In the evening a jamadar brought *roti* and lentil *dal* in a tin pannikin. He placed it by the door and left without saying a word. Hakam reached for it impatiently and broke a piece from the roti. Dipping it in dal he chewed slowly.

The doctor came back the next day and examined his arm. Afterward, he checked him twice a week. The swelling had gone down and the arm seemed to be healing. A deathly silence, extreme loneliness, and the cold room was Hakam's companion, all this time.

What might be happening at home? How are Harjit and Baldev? Why no one ever came to see me? Do they even know where I am? The questions sprang up in Hakam's mind nonstop.

Even Lal did not show up. He must be angry with me. Would he ever talk to me again?

Days passed. No noise, no visitors, no British officers, no sepoys, except for the jamadar who came in twice a day with *roti* and water and the doctor who treated his arm. Finally he removed the splint and Hakam was able to move his arm almost normally.

As the jamadar was leaving one day, after placing his food by the door, Hakam asked, "What is your name?"

"Beeru, sir, Beeru Singh," he said with humility.

"Been working here long?"

"Three years. Five mouths to feed. Otherwise, this is no place to work," Beeru lowered his voice to a whisper.

Hakam nodded.

The quality of food improved in the next few days. Beeru brought an orange one day and another day a banana along with *dal roti*.

"Your family comes every day, *Janab*. Sir!" he said to Hakam one day. "Your wife and son and your brother, they have been coming almost daily." Hakam jumped from the straw bed,

"What! They've been coming?"

"And lots of people have been gathering outside the prison," Beeru told him.

Hakam slept that night like nothing bothered him. The straw bed felt soft like clouds and the tiny dark room felt like a grand palace. He was not alone. His family was with him. The people of Punjab were with him.

Chapter 24

A pin-drop silence enveloped the courtroom. Hakam Singh, with his hands and feet in chains, stood next to his lawyer, Mr. Pande. Judge Meyers read the sentence:

"Hakam Singh, of the village Gajanpur, is sentenced to 14 years imprisonment for killing an innocent farmer and the attempted murder of a British police officer. He will be transported to the Cellular Jail, Kala Pani (Black Waters) at the Andaman Nicobar Islands. His property will be confiscated and auctioned off."

The silence in the room stirred for a moment. The judge continued, "Harboring rebellious views and making insidious speeches with the intent of harming government officials will be dealt with firmly and steadfastly. No leniency for the killers and the destroyers of peace."

As soon as the judge read the sentence, Hakam defiantly looked at the judge. With an unyielding gaze, he waved his chained fists in the air and shouted, *"Inquilab Zindabad!* Long Live Revolution!"

The courtroom vibrated with his roar. Taken aback, Judge Meyers yelled, "Get him out of here..." but his voice was buried under Hakam's bellowing voice.

Hundreds of people gathered outside the court replied in unison shouts of, *"Hakam Singh, Zindabad!* Long live Hakam Singh."

"British Raj, Murdabad!"

"Down with the British Raj."

The earth shook under their feet and the sky seemed about to shatter into a million pieces with the resounding cries of 'Long Live Hakam Singh. Down with the British Raj.'

Surrounded by the police, Hakam was quickly whisked away into a waiting vehicle. He barely had a glimpse of his son Baldev and wife Harjit standing in front of the crowd. Lal Singh and Namo stood next to them. Lal gestured

117

Hakam by touching his heart and holding Baldev's hand as if saying, "I will take care of him!" Hakam nodded.

Will I ever see them again? He felt his heart sinking as the van picked up speed and turned around the corner.

The next day, his lawyer, Mr. Pande, came to his cell asking him to sign a petition for mercy. Hakam shook his head,

"I'd rather die than beg for mercy. I want justice, not pity. And justice is not in their blood. I will fight till death for freedom from this iron-clad regime that rules by the gun."

Tears in his eyes, Mr. Pande embraced him, "I am so sorry. I failed you, son. It's beyond me where they got the witnesses for the farmer that doesn't exist."

"It was not you, Sir. It is an unjust system. Our day will come, someday!" Hakam said with a dream in his eyes and certainty in his voice.

******

The ship, cutting through the dark waters of the Bay of Bengal chugged towards the Andaman and Nicobar Islands. In the lowermost deck, Hakam Singh was confined in a metal cage with reinforced iron bars. It was like a round birdcage only bigger and stronger. The other three prisoners from Bengal, who like Hakam, had revolted against the British Raj, were confined inside cages too. The ship was on its way to deliver them to a prison where the inmates were dying of hunger, malaria, and exhaustion due to unbearable manual labor and physical punishment. Hardly anyone had returned from Kala Pani in one piece.

During the first two days, the ship moved on smoothly. On the third day, it started shaking violently from side-to-side. One of the cages lost its footing bolt and fell onto the floor rolling and smashing into the windowless walls of the dungeon-like deck. A little later the other cages started falling. Hakam shut his eyes tightly and clenched his teeth every time the cage smashed into the solid wall. No one came down to provide any food or water during the storm or to take them out to the bathroom facilities, only a few feet away. The ship docked at Port Blair on the morning of the sixth day.

About a dozen ship employees came down to the lower deck. One of them shouted covering his nose, "Filthy bastards!" The others covered their noses and grimaced. They took them out of the cages and chained them together. As they walked out of the ship, they were pushed into the shallow waters to clean up. Clothes drenched in saltwater they walked in a file towards the dreaded prison surrounded by the guards.

Hungry and tired to bones they entered the prison courtyard. One of the guards removed the chain, the others stood with their guns pointed at them.

Hakam looked at the massive three-story building over the edge of the sea. He had only heard about the notorious prison but could not have imagined its seven radiating wings like the arms of an enormous octopus ready to swallow you whole. A huge bell hung from a central watchtower. The air was hot and humid. Even though there were hundreds of prisoners inside, it was quiet as death. The eerie silence sent a dreadful shiver down Hakam's spine.

"Take off your clothes," one of the guards ordered. "Walk," he yelled, as soon as they removed their clothes, and were led towards separate prison cells.

A tall, hefty guard with a pointy mustache and another stocky man with fierce, blood-red eyes walked on either side of Hakam. As soon as Hakam entered the cell through a narrow metal door, they jumped on him knocking him down to the cement floor. They bombarded him with fists and profanities.

"If I ever see that defiant look again, I will gouge your eyes out. Do you understand?" the guard with blood-red eyes yelled while locking the cell door.

Naked and tired, Hakam sat on the cement floor. His body ached from the blows he received from the guards as a welcoming gift. The tiny prison cell was dark and damp. The floor was thickly coated with moss growing in the crevices. A small window was high up on the wall impossible to reach or look outside. There was no bed or blanket, no water, no toilet, other than two empty bowls, one meant for food, and the other probably meant for the toilet.

The guards came in the evening with a blanket, a pitcher of water, and a bowl of thin insipid gruel. The pointy-mustached guard held the gun close to Hakam's head while the other poured water into the bowl.

"Here," he said, pointing to the bowl of gruel and threw a long scratchy shirt at him, cursing and swearing. Hakam gulped down the tasteless porridge and slid his head and arms through the oversize shirt.

"You seem to be a troublemaker." The guard holding the gun glared at Hakam, "I think you need some jewelry." The other laughed.

They came back and shackled his ankles in crossbar fetters.

"Here're your tinkling bells!" the red-eyed guard said as he locked the ankle fetters. "Now dance." The pointy-mustached guard burst into laughter. The other joined in.

Hakam's lips parted in a sarcastic smile, *Stupid bastards*. He spread the blanket on the floor and slipped into a fitful sleep.

Hakam looked at Harjit sitting on the side bench of the lecture hall, where she always did during the geography period. As soon as the class ended, they rushed out of the room. "Meet me in the Rose Park, by the pond," he said. Harjit nodded, walking towards the women's bicycle shed.

Hakam picked up his bicycle from the men's shed and headed towards the Rose Park, about two miles from college. Waiting by the pond, he saw Harjit on the walkway, surrounded by the rose bushes, loaded with flowers of all the colors of the rainbow. Her pink duppata fluttered in the breeze. Her dark curly tresses played with her peach bronze cheeks with each step. She is not a girl from this earth...she's a fairy, from some other world. There is no other girl as beautiful!' Hakam thought.

They sat by the pond without saying a word to each other but at the same time said so much. The water birds, teals, and coots playfully swam and swirled in the pond and the sparrows chirping in the rose bushes said everything that needed to be said. Every now and then, looking into the depth of her onyx dark eyes, Hakam gently moved away the locks from her face that kept falling back over her cheek. She returned the look with her most endearing smile. And they just sat there, without a worry in the world. Nothing bothered them when they were together.

The clouds started gathering up in the sky. The gentle breeze turned into wind and the wind turned into blustery gusts. Soon it became a storm the strength of a hurricane. Suddenly the sky lit up as if a thousand suns had descended onto the earth and it erupted like a bomb explosion. Harjit was decimated in the blink of an eye. Hakam tried to reach her but she was reduced to a pile of ashes. A gut-wrenching scream erupted from the depth of his being that woke him up.

It took a while for him to realize that it was a dream and he was in a prison cell, thousands of miles away from home, the rose park, and from Harjit. His body shook like a withered autumn leaf. He felt an intense piercing pain in his left thigh. Nothing was visible in the dark but he felt like he had been stung by something. Intolerable excruciating pain in the thigh caused him to moan. How badly he wanted to be with Harjit and Baldev and hold them in his arms, never letting go. He felt he might die that night and never see them again. Disheartened and helpless, he cried like a child. Slowly, he slipped into unconsciousness.

"The dog is burning hot!" Hakam heard someone talking. One of the guards was trying to get him to sit up.

"Maybe he was stung by a scorpion. They keep coming back, no matter what we do."

"He'll survive. It's just a scorpion, not a cobra!" said the other.

Hakam could hear them but was unable to move or even open his eyes. The guards unshackled him and left when he could not respond to their orders. His thigh had swollen to almost double the size. He had a splitting headache and then everything went dark again.

Chapter 25

Hakam tried to open his eyes. Dim light filtered through the window and the rusty metal frame of the door. He did not know how many days or nights had passed, going in and out of consciousness. Feeling a little better he pulled himself up and sat leaning against the wall. His mouth felt dry and cracked like the floor of a dried-out lake. A small reddish earthen bowl filled with liquid lying by the door caught his eye. He reached for the bowl and drank it in one gulp. His mouth filled with a stale foul taste. How long the watery porridge had been lying there he did not know, but it sure was spoiled and tasted nasty.

Hakam remembered hearing the word 'scorpions.' He tried to look around the room, and there it was! A big black scorpion half-visible through the moss, sat in a crevice between the wall and the floor. *I must've been stung by this poisonous bug!* He had never seen this kind of black scorpions in his life. The ones he had seen were less than half the size and were yellowish in color, and he had never been stung by one before. I have to get rid of it, he thought.

The earthen bowl will shatter if he used to kill it. A shoe would have been the best weapon against this deadly little monster. He could not think of anything other than the long shirt he was wearing. He took it off and wrapped it around his fist in many layers. The scorpion had not moved and was still clearly visible near the crevice.

Hakam took a long breath and started punching the scorpion and crushed it with his fist. And lo, there was another one! "Son-of-a-bitch! Take this...and this and this." In a maniac rage he kept punching the scorpion even after it was nothing more than a little fleck of black slime. Crawling around the room in a fury, he pulled the moss out of the cracks and crevices but did not find any more. Out of breath, he leaned against the wall and closed his eyes. He felt weak and exhausted and was drenched in sweat. Though the swelling in his thigh had gone down, it was still painful at the site of the sting and was swollen like a hardball under the skin.

122

A little later he crawled near the door. It opened into a narrow verandah that seemed to run along the front of the rows of the prison cells. The arches of the verandah were also sealed by iron railings from the ceiling to the floor. At a little distance across a narrow grassy strip, there was a solid high wall without any doors or windows. This might be the back of the other wing of the prison, he thought.

"Isolation. Total isolation. That's what it is!" he mumbled.

The same two guards came into the cell and saw him sitting by the door, "*Ma Chode* is up. Motherfucker seems to have recovered," the guard with the pointy mustache sneered. "I thought I was going to feed him to the fish today," he chuckled.

"Not yet, but soon," said the other.

Weak and hungry and still aching all over, Hakam tried to sit up straight and pointed towards the dead scorpions. "I need medical help," he said.

The warder blatantly laughed at his face, "Oh, you killed your sons-in-law!"

"You dim-headed fools, these are your sons-in-law, not mine!" Hakam yelled.

"You are new here. And you have no idea what we are going to do to you, if you talk to us like this ever again," one of the guards said, kicking him in the face. Hakam doubled with pain and tried to cover his face with both hands. The other guard kicked him in the stomach. They threw the bowl of water at him that they were supposed to leave in the cell. "Here's your water. Drown in it."

Hakam felt his right eye swelling and soon he could not open it. Wet and hurting all over, he shivered and passed out again. How long he stayed in that state, he did not know, but when he woke up, his headache was gone and the swelling on his thigh had almost disappeared.

He looked around the room like a new person. He reminded himself of the struggle he and so many others were going through to get independence from the British, who came for business relations but had enslaved the whole nation by their cunning policies. *I cannot give up now, I will not let them kill me in this little death chamber!* He felt a sudden rush of strength and resolve. Sitting up straight he whispered, "*Inquilab... Zindabad! Long Live the Revolution!*" A faint smile appeared on his parched lips.

Chapter 26

Handcuffed and ankles in fetters that allowed only small steps like a three-year-old, Hakam Singh walked towards the courtyard, followed by a guard. The new prisoners lined up surrounded by the guards holding guns and bamboo truncheons. There were ten of them, recently exiled from Punjab and Bengal to this island prison. Hakam saw the outside of his cell for the first time since he had arrived. He could not clearly recall how many days he had been here because for a while he was not able to tell the difference between day and the night. He had no concept of how long he had slept or slipped into unconsciousness due to fever and scorpion poison.

Though weak and in chains, it felt good to be outside in the fresh air. A big Banyan tree nearby with its aerial roots supporting it like pillars and the birds flying in and out of the branches reminded him of his village, Gajanpur. In the center of the village, there was a Banyan tree with a brick platform built around it, where the elders gathered to discuss the affairs of the village or to play cards in the evening or just to sit and talk after a day's hard work in the fields. Children played hopscotch and *gulli danda* and *kotla shapaki* nearby, before their mothers called them in for supper. He felt like he just heard his mother calling, *Hakam, put that gulli danda away and come home. You've been playing too long.* That meant a call for his father too and they both walked home to the aroma of fresh *makki roti* and *saag,* loaded with butter and mango pickle on the side. His daydreaming about the days long gone along with his mother and father was shattered by a loud guttural shout,

"I am Andrew Parker, the superintendent of this place."

The jailor seemed to have appeared out of nowhere. He stood in the shade, under the Banyan tree, while the prisoners were standing in the sun.

"You will live here according to my rules and for your own good, you will follow them. If not, you will receive punishments you have never imagined."

He gnashed every word under his teeth before bellowing it out and his nostrils swelled up and down with each breath. The words came out like bullets to strike right into the prisoner's chest. He was like a wolf, baring teeth, growling and snarling, about to attack a puny poodle. His pasty white skin changed color from pale to red and back to pale, during the momentary pause between the sentences.

"See those gallows and poles? Look carefully!"

He pointed to the gallows and metal frames attached to the poles not far from where they stood. There was also an oil pressing mill, not far from the gallows.

The jailor continued, "So, here are the rules!"

"Rule number one: No talking to each other. Ever! Not a single word to be exchanged between the prisoners.

"Rule number two: Finish the task you are assigned. No rest or food until the work is completed.

"Rule three: No talking back to the warders or the jamadars or any employee of the prison.

"Rule number four: Do not ever think of escape. You will never get out of here alive. I will shoot you or the sharks will feast on you.

"Also, do not think even for a moment that you are political prisoners. You are nothing more than the scum of society."

While the jailor lectured them about prison manners, there was a young prisoner barely in his twenties, walking towards the mill followed by a guard. He was harnessed to the mill like a bullock and he started walking in circles, turning the wheel of the mill that extracted oil from mustard seeds. He was emaciated, almost a skeleton, and could hardly walk but was still going round and round nonstop.

There was another young prisoner being pushed and shoved by the jamadars. *Maybe they are taking him to the mill, to put two of them together and make it easier to turn the wheel.* Hakam thought. Instead, they turned towards the poles. He was ordered to remove his shirt and was bound to the frame facing the pole with his back exposed.

"Go!" the warder shouted.

The jamadar's hands and throat came into action, flogging, and counting "One two…three."

With each strike, the prisoner let out a piercing scream that could poke a hole into the sky above. Soon his screams turned into moans and the moans into complete silence, but the whole atmosphere shuddered with each flogging.

Blood oozed from his back and buttocks, trailing down the back of his knees and ankles. At the end of the flogging, they dragged his limp body towards his cell. A streak of blood followed his path. The jail superintendent pointed towards the man being dragged by the guards and said, "That's what happens when you disobey my orders…"

Hakam's eyes followed the prisoner. *Clearly, he wanted us to see the punishment being carried out. He wants to crush us! Our body and soul, both! I will not let him kill my spirit, no matter how cruel the punishment!* Hakam stood tall and defiant.

"Take a good look…" the jailor bellowed. A few moments later he turned abruptly walking towards a building on the other side of the banyan tree. As soon as the jailor was out of sight, the guards started poking the prisoners with gun barrels and truncheons, shouting, "Get moving."

******

The jamadars were ordinary criminals, murderers, rapists, and robbers who were incarcerated for life and were exiled to this island prison. But here they were promoted to the ranks of petty officers by the prison head. They inflicted boorish and vulgar violence against the prisoners. The political prisoners on the other hand were young, mostly college students in their twenties and some even younger. They were full of spirit and abhorrence for the brutal British Raj. The jailor Andrew Parker was determined to eradicate these enemies of the British Empire.

The jamadars led them into the dining hall and removed their handcuffs, leaving the ankle fetters on. They sat on the floor in a straight line against the wall. A number of prisoners were already there, sitting along the opposite wall. How long they had been in the prison was hard to know, but their skeletal figures were telling the untold story. They seemed to communicate with each other in a subtle sign language, Hakam noticed. Some of them nodded to the newcomers and smiled.

A few of the prisoners had a peculiar neck collar with a letter D written on a wooden plank hanging over the chest. *What does this D mean? Distinguished? Decorative, or does it mean Delightful?* Hakam chuckled, at the thought of his own joke. He wanted to ask someone, but it was against the rules to talk.

It was quiet in the room, other than the clanking sound of ladles in metal pots, and the thumping footsteps of the jamadars, serving food. They quickly distributed some kind of boiled leafy wild grass and watery porridge. This was the first time Hakam had seen the porridge in the daylight and saw tiny little maggots floating on the surface. He looked in horror towards the other prisoners pointing to the maggots. "Is this what we eat?"

The jamadar, who had not moved from there yet, hit him on the shoulder with the serving ladle, without a moment's hesitation. Porridge splashed over Hakam's face and clothes. He stood up in rage, "You motherfucker..." and raised his fist. But before he could knock the jamadar down, the other prisoners intervened and pulled Hakam away.

It's Pinta! Hakam looked at the jamadar in shock. Two vertical scars on his forehead confirmed, what Lal had told him. Pinta, who had murdered his own father and sister along with her lover and had abducted young girls into prostitution, had become a jamadar in this prison. The jailor had given him power over the political prisoners who were trying to free their nation from the clutches of slavery.

Did he recognize me? Hakam's heart almost jumped out of his chest. But Pinta could not have seen him during Lal's parent's trial that lasted only one day. Hakam along with a lot of other people had sat behind Pinta and his lawyer and had left the courtroom as soon as the judge announced the judgment.

Hakam wiped the porridge from his face with his shirt and sat down but could not eat or drink anything. Most of the prisoners tipped the bowl to drain the little worms from the surface and started eating, and some did not bother to remove the maggots. They ate like it was just a mechanical action. Hakam tried a few sips of salty boiled grass but did not touch the porridge.

Before they left the dining room, one of the warders came to him with a neck ring, a big letter D written on it. It did not take long for Hakam to understand, D means dangerous. That translated to even harsher treatment for prisoners like him, who still had some speck of spirit left in them. The warder locked it tight against his neck.

The following day Hakam was harnessed to the oil mill. He took a long breath and started turning round and round nonstop while a Jamadar fed the mill with fresh mustard seeds. A thin stream of oil flowed into the container placed below a drain at the end of a long gutter. As the mustard seeds were getting squeezed out of oil, strength was getting squeezed out of Hakam's arms and legs. Soon they were numb enough to not feel pain and he kept going. Suddenly he felt a sharp twinge on his back and heard a growl, "Why are you slowing down?" The guard had hit him with a leather whip. Tired to every fiber of his flesh at the end of the day, he limped towards the cell followed by a jamadar. He pushed Hakam into the cell as soon as they got to the door. Before Hakam could recover from the fall the guard was locking the door behind him and was out of sight.

Chapter 27

Hakam Singh was exiled to Kala Pani, and his property would be confiscated. The word spread quickly. The next day people started gathering at his house. Women tried to console the hysterically crying Harjit. Baldev sat by his mother, scared and helpless. He was unable to make any sense of what was happening. *They have arrested my father and sent him to a faraway place. The police are going to take away everything we own and we will be thrown out of our home. They're going to take our land also, all the mango and guava trees along with it! Why?* Baldev wanted to run away from all of this but he kept sitting by his mother staring at the floor.

He thought about the mustard fields bursting with bright yellow flowers and the sweet juicy sugarcane crops. He was waiting for the day they were going to start making *jaggery* and brown sugar. It was always a time of celebration when the juice was squeezed out of the canes, boiled and evaporated in huge cauldrons over a furnace, dug out in the ground near the sugarcane fields. The thickened juice was poured onto the wooden molds to make the *jaggery* cakes with added peanuts and a little bit of ginger, and lots of other spices. It was the most delicious treat he had ever tasted. The contractors from the city would come to buy it, still leaving behind enough for the whole year.

They will not let us make any jaggery cakes this year? Baldev tried to hold back tears.

The cow's calf was only about two months old and his mother-cow provided milk for the family. Baldev had named the calf 'Sheru' which means, 'like a lion.' Every day after school he played with him. He would run around holding fodder leaves in his hand and Sheru followed him everywhere.

Are they going to take away Sheru too? The thought made him feel sick and his stomach felt like turning inside out. He got up and ran towards the yard but threw up before he could reach the far side, away from people. Worried sick, Harjit rushed to him and held his forehead while he vomited. Another woman brought a glass of water and helped Baldev clean himself up. Feeling a little better, he held his mother's arm and walked back to the cot in the verandah where they had been sitting all morning.

Elderly Baba Budh Singh said, "Listen everyone, they might be here any minute, or they may come tomorrow. We have to try to save whatever we can!"

As people realized what he meant, there was quite a stir in the crowd. They quickly started packing clothes and kitchen utensils into sacks. They stacked pillows, quilts and sheets ready to be carried to the neighboring houses.

"Ram Singh, make a list of everything so we know which items were sent to which house," Baba ji said. "Joga Singh, you go to Hakam's farm immediately and relocate the buffaloes and oxen to your farm."

As the neighbors rushed to hide as much stuff as possible from forfeiture, Baldev sat by Harjit's side as if in a trance. He stared at people packing and whispering to each other. His eyes forgot to blink.

As soon as one of the neighbors went out of the door carrying a sack stuffed with pots and pans, they came, a British police officer and three Indian sepoys, in two vans.

"What the hell is going on in here?" the officer shouted furiously. He tapped the sacks filled with clothes and other household goods, with his baton.

"Get out of here, you thieves! I will arrest you all, for stealing government property."

Then he broke into a brisk laughter. The sepoys first giggled and then joined him in a hearty laugh too.

Holding his stomach, still laughing he bellowed, "Well done! You stupid hogs, well done! You made it easy for us. You packed it, and now you will load it for us into the vans."

"Get out of the house, all of you, except...you and you." He motioned the baton towards two young men. "Load the sacks."

Baldev looked at his mother as they were ordered out of the house. *Where will we go now? What will we eat? Where are we going to sleep at night?* He wanted to ask, but the words did not come out. His mother's face was expressionless and she did not look at him, even once. She was not crying anymore.

After everything was loaded into the vans, the sepoys put double locks on the front door. Baba Budh Singh took Baldev's hand, "Let's go home," he said to Harjit.

******

The mother and son spent the night at Baba ji's house, then another night, and another. A few days later there was an announcement in the village with the beat of a drum, "Hear, hear you all! Hakam Singh's property will be auctioned off next Saturday. Everyone is encouraged to participate in the auction. It will be sold to the highest bidder."

Harjit felt the ground slipping from under her feet when she heard it. "They already confiscated everything from our house and made us homeless. Now they are auctioning our land too? What are we going to do, Baba ji?"

"Listen, Harjit, you do not have to worry one bit. We're going to take care of everything. I'm sending for Lal Singh right now."

"You've always been a father to me, Baba ji, and Lal, a brother. What would I do without you two?" Baba ji took Harjit into his arms and kissed her head with fatherly love.

Lal Singh and Namo arrived the following day. Flood gates from Harjit's eyes suddenly loosened and tears gushed out in two streams, "What did my son do to them to deserve this? Why?" Harjit clung to Namo. Without saying a word Namo held her tight, wiping her own and Harjit's tears.

"They did not allow us to see him before he was exiled to Kala Pani. The only glimpse we all had of him was outside the courtroom when they took him away," Harjit said between sobs.

"I should've stayed here after the court decision, but we never imagined everything was going happen so fast," Lal said.

Harjit wiped her tear sodden face and sat quietly, all avoiding each other's eyes.

"Listen, Harjit," Lal said after a while, looking beyond the walls of the courtyard, with a sudden verve in his voice, "We will deal with whatever they throw at us. Be strong."

"We will spread the word that no one should participate in the auction. It worked in another village, I heard," Lal turned to Baba Ji.

"It might work. I will send the message out," Baba ji said.

The message was simple and clear and quickly spread by the word of mouth from house to house and from village to village. 'We will all gather at the site of the auction but no one would participate. No one will buy Hakam's land or the house or anything that belongs to his family. We will leave as soon as the auction begins.'

Lal and Namo left the next day to come back a day before the auction. "We will do everything to prevent the auction and get the land and the house back," Lal reassured Harjit, before leaving.

"I will bring Pali along," Namo said to Baldev.

"Promise!" Baldev's eyes widened and he clung to her.

"I promise," she said.

The day of the auction arrived much quicker than imagined. Men gathered at the village center. Sitting on the brick platform built around the Banyan tree, they talked in hushed voices. Some of them stood in small groups whispering and exhaling noisily. Children gathered around, curiously waiting for something unusual to happen.

"They're here! They're here…!" Children shouted as soon as they saw clouds of dust behind two jeeps, coming down the unpaved road. People looked towards the fast-approaching vehicles, nervously talking to each other.

The jeeps stopped extremely close to the gathering. Two Indian sepoys who accompanied the auctioneer and the British police inspector, took out the folding chairs from the vehicle and quickly unfolded them onto the ground. They set up a wobbly table and a chair for the auctioneer. The auctioneer placed his briefcase on the table and unsuccessfully tried to pull up his pants above his hanging belly. He breathed heavily and was already sweating in the morning breeze. Without looking at the crowd he retrieved some papers from the briefcase. With the back of his fleshy hand, he wiped the sweat from his forehead.

"Bidding will start with the house…" he cleared his throat. Baba ji got up to leave before he finished the sentence. Following Baba ji Lal Singh and the others started walking away from the auction site.

"Come back, all of you! Right now…!" the police inspector yelled.

They all kept walking. No one looked back.

"Come back, I say!" the British police officer shouted. "I will arrest all of you… Don't you hear me?"

No one seemed to have heard him. Soon they disappeared into the narrow village streets.

Only the children were left behind, giggling and pushing each other towards the officers. A little later they too started running after their fathers and elder brothers, except a few brave ones who stayed back. They looked amusingly at the police inspector and the plump auctioneer fretfully talking to each other in a language they did not understand. Finally, the white police inspector gestured to the sepoys to pack up. They folded the table and chairs and loaded them back into the vehicles. They left, as they had come. Children shouted clapping and laughing,

"They're leaving! They're leaving!" Some of them ran after them and gave up as the vehicles picked up speed.

The armed police were disarmed by the unarmed villagers. They all gathered again in the evening, this time, to celebrate the victory. "We will not give up. We will do the same if they come back," said Baba ji. People cheered and felt proud of defeating the authorities. But the fear still lingered, veiled by the outward celebrations.

The next day they gathered at Hakam's house and opened up a small entrance door in the back wall of the house. The front door lock was left in place. A few days later Namo and Lal came back with a cart full of household items for everyday needs. Harjit and Baldev moved back home with mixed feelings of joy, relief, and concern about the future.

That night Baldev wrote a long letter to his father but did not know what address to write on the envelope.

Chapter 28

Two prisoners sitting across from Hakam in the dining hall said something to him in the prison sign language. Within a few weeks, he had started understanding the communication between prisoners. He touched his head and heart, meaning 'wholeheartedly' and mouthed, "I am with you."

We are going on a hunger strike! The word spread in the room like a soundless wave, and a breath of approval was let out by almost everyone. They were sick of the humiliating and brutal punishment, maggot-filled food, and backbreaking manual labor with no proper medical treatment when needed.

The prisoners quickly gathered in a circle in the middle of the dining room. And that was against the rules. Jamadar Pinta shoved the prisoner nearest to him with a bamboo truncheon and yelled, "Line up against the wall right now or I will split your heads." Another jamadar holding a bucket of liquid food hastily dropped it onto the floor and ran towards them, "Get against the wall and sit down."

"We want to talk to the superintendent," one of the prisoners shouted as though the guards were deaf. He was a tall man with a body reduced almost to a skeleton. The hollows under his bony cheeks were deep, covered with a thin layer of skin. His eyeballs looked like they would fall out of the sockets any moment.

"Move against the wall before I hear anything you have to say," Jamadar Pinta yelled. No one moved.

"We will not talk to a criminal like you. Go tell the superintendent," the same prisoner shouted back as if he had been saving his voice to say this.

The superintendent rushed in furiously thumping his feet. "What the hell is going on in here? Sit down, all of you."

The prisoners stood unyielding to his shouts. But a wave of fright undoubtedly shook their posture. Hakam remembered the limp body of a prisoner being dragged after flogging. He was terrified. Trying to hide his fear he straightened his neck. "We will not move from here until you hear what we have to say." His own voice surprised him for he had not used it since he came to this prison.

"You have something to say?" The superintendent laughed.

Hakam looked at the man who had initiated the idea of the hunger strike, gesturing him to speak.

The man took a step forward, "Mr. Parker, we respectfully ask you to listen to our rightful demands." Recovering from the initial panic he looked straight at the superintendent.

"Number one: We will not eat maggot-infested food and boiled grass anymore. We want real food with real vegetables."

"Number two: We will not be harnessed to the oil mills like bullocks and treated like animals. Coir pounding and removing the coconut husks with bare hands is totally inhumane. You force us to continue even when the blood is oozing out of our fingertips. We will not do this harsh labor anymore."

"Three: Stop flogging and hanging us by the feet from the ceiling, just to squeeze the lifeforce out of us."

His voice grew stronger and his posture straighter as he spoke.

The superintendent and the jamadars looked at him in awe.

"We want proper toilet arrangements and other hygienic articles, toothbrushes, soap, and bathing facilities."

"Also, we want light in the cells and reading materials, magazines, newspapers, and books," he added.

"Most importantly Mr. Parker, we demand the restrictions on communicating with each other be lifted immediately!"

The prisoners spoke all at once. "Yes, yes! We want our demands fulfilled right away!" a chorus of jumbled voices followed.

The jailor glared at them. The prisoners, whom he did not even consider humans, were defying his orders.

"You *will* follow my orders and comply with whatever the jamadars command you to do." He looked at Pinta and the other jamadar standing next to him.

"Also, you *will* finish the task you are assigned. If not, no god will save you here or in hell if I decide to send you there," he spat each word scornfully. "So do not be foolish. Go back to your cells. Now!" he shouted.

The prisoners ignored him and started talking. They hugged and asked each other's names and what part of India they came from. They felt elated and strong. The prisoner, who had communicated the demands to the jailor, hugged Hakam. "I am Bikram," he said.

"I am Hakam Singh." Hakam picked Bikram up from the ground in excitement. The whole atmosphere became one of triumph and jubilation. They talked and laughed loudly. Soon the hall vibrated with the shouts of, *Inquilab... Zindabad!* Long Live the Revolution!

Their shouts seemed to be strong enough to pierce through the prison walls and spread with a force that could push back the waves of the ocean. Hakam picked up the bucket, one of the jamadars had dropped on the floor. He turned it upside down and stood on it, shouting at the top of his voice.

"Brothers, we will die with dignity instead of being killed in disgrace and humiliation at the dirty hands of these criminals. We will die for justice and we will die for freedom. We shall fast unto death." Hakam, though fairly new in the prison, quickly rose to inspire the others.

"We will support each other like the aerial roots of the Banyan tree that support it like pillars. We all have seen the tree in the courtyard, I believe." He looked at the prisoners nodding and smiling. "Our demand for freedom is the Banyan and we are the pillars supporting it."

The prisoners cheered. They quickly decided that the ones in better health will go on the hunger strike and the physically weak will refuse to do the labor of the oil pressing mill and coir pounding. They would not agree to anything less than the demands they had conveyed to the jailor.

Before they knew they were tackled by the guards who came running from all sides with bamboo truncheons and guns. They pushed and punched them and dragged them to their respective cells. The prisoners kept shouting,

"*British Raj... Murdabad!* Death to the Imperialism!"

They could not see each other anymore, but they heard each other shouting the slogans.

On the morning of the third day after the strike began, Hakam heard a lot of commotion in the neighboring cells. He looked toward the verandah, wondering about the noise when three guards entered his room. One of the hefty ones jumped onto his chest holding his arms and another sat on his thighs pinning him down to the floor. A third one tried to push a rubber tube into his nose. Hakam violently twisted and turned his body coughing and yelling at the top of his voice, "Get off of me. Son of a bitch!"

Hakam was able to push the tube out of his nose a few times. Then another ruffian jamadar entered the cell and pushed his head onto the floor holding it tight while the other pushed the tube down his nose. Hakam felt a sudden rush of cold in his stomach. They left the cell, yelling and cursing him.

Hakam felt helpless and defeated. Tears flowed from his eyes and mixed with the salty streak of blood dripping from his nose. He wiped his face with his shirt and sobbed silently. In the evening the same torturous procedure was carried out again.

The following day there were a lot of muted voices and uneasy footsteps on the verandah. A doctor and the jailor along with some other employees of the prison hurried towards one of the cells. Something serious was going on.

Hakam shouted, "Have you killed someone, you bloody bastards?" Banging his chains against the metal door he kept hollering. Prisoners from the other cells joined in shouting and clobbering their chains against the metal. But the chains and the metal doors were too strong for anyone to break. The prisoners could not do anything other than yell.

24-year-old Mahavir Singh was killed by force-feeding. Within a few days, two more prisoners died due to food pushed into their lungs instead of the stomach. The men who force-fed the prisoners were not professionals but petty officers told to insert the nasal tube and pour the milk through a funnel. In the name of keeping men alive by force-feeding, they had murdered them. The prisoners starved and never provided any milk when alive were killed by drowning their lungs in milk. Their bodies were weighed down with rocks and dumped into the sea.

The killings created uproar in the prison that the jailor could not control. The rest of the prisoners who had refused to work but were not on hunger strike also joined in, to fast unto death or until their demands were fulfilled. Parker tried to control the minds of the prisoners by keeping them locked up 24 hours a day in solitary confinement. He went into the cells individually telling each prisoner, that he was the only one killing himself. All the other prisoners had broken their fast and were eating healthy food.

"You don't want to die this painful death, do you?" Parker told them.

None of the prisoners believed him and the strike continued. Finally, the inspector general of prisons known to be an expert in breaking up hunger strikes was called in from Punjab. He went around the cells and ordered,

"Remove all the water pitchers from the cells. From now on the prisoners would be fed only once a day."

The guards rushed into each cell hollering and collecting the water containers.

"Now we will get you! We'll see how long you can keep your arrogance."

One of the guards said to Hakam while picking up the water jug from his cell, "You will beg for mercy in no time."

Hakam looked at him and thought, *how shamefully ignorant these people are!*

The new inspector general could not break them either. He did not want any more deaths because the prisoners were extremely frail, unable to move or talk. Some could not even open their eyes.

The news of the force-feeding murders had leaked out and spread throughout India like a forest fire. Shopkeepers closed their shops and employees walked out of their offices. The students and teachers abandoned their classrooms to protest the deaths of the political prisoners. The old and young filled the streets like swarms of locusts that would devour the foliage of the British Raj.

Finally, the jailor agreed to meet their demands. The prisoners unable to walk were carried out on stretchers into a common area in the balcony of the central tower. Though too weak to talk or walk, they felt stronger than ever to see each other. Real vegetables were served with the evening meals along with fresh *roti*.

The other demands were slowly being fulfilled. The prisoners could talk to each other freely and the cells were provided with oil-burning lamps. But the jamadars still ruled the prison. Zafar Khan was the head of them and Pinta next to him.

While the other prisoners were slowly coming back to health, Hakam was still weak and not gaining any weight. His hair was coming out in clusters and there were empty spots on his chin and the sides of his cheeks within his bushy beard. His gums bled and brushing was painful.

Chapter 29

"What? Denied again?" Harjit yelled as soon as she read the official letter. She trembled with rage and picked up the first thing lying nearby, that happened to be a brass plate, and angrily threw it across the verandah. It made a clanking sound as it hit the hard surface and bounced across the courtyard near the front door of the house. The neem tree stood silent, except a few frightened sparrows flying out of its branches.

For a while, she yelled and cursed the officials for denying the petition and then broke into a hysterical fit. Her uncontrollable screams sucked the strength out of her body and she slowly dropped onto the floor, sobbing and sniveling. It was the fourth time she had petitioned to visit her husband at the Andaman Islands Cellular Prison, and each time it was denied. Exhausted, she closed her eyes and lay there.

"What happened, Ma?" Baldev threw his book bag into a corner of the verandah and ran to her. "Why're you lying on the floor?" He shook her shoulder. Harjit opened her eyes and stared at him as if trying to recognize him.

"What's the matter, Ma?"

"O, Bal, I'm so sorry. You're back from school?"

"Yes, I'm back, but why are you lying on the floor?" He looked into her swollen eyes.

"You must be hungry. I made some *parathas* for you," Harjit said, barely audible. "It's wrapped in a *pona* in the kitchen."

"Don't worry about the *paratha*. First, tell me what happened. Why have you been crying?" he said helping her get up.

"No Baldev, I wasn't crying."

"I'm not a child anymore. I'm 14, soon to be 15. Even a child can tell if his mother has been crying!"

"I was upset."

"Why? What's wrong?"

"They've denied the petition. We cannot go to see your father."

"They denied it again! Motherfuckers!" Baldev blurted out. He had never said a bad word in front of his mother before, but she didn't seem to have heard him.

"We can't give up like this, Ma! You're going to get sick!" Baldev put his arms around her. Harjit sobbed again.

The roles switched. Baldev comforted her like a mother, while Harjit sobbed on her son's shoulder.

"We have to be strong! I'm sure we'll be able to see him soon," Baldev said holding her close.

"No, Bal. How can you know? Anything can happen in six months before we petition again. Everything is falling apart, Baldev. Everything!"

"Ma don't say that! Nothing is falling apart." Baldev tightened his embrace around her.

"It's been four years since they took him away and only one letter from him so far. They don't even allow the prisoners to write home. They could kill him and we wouldn't even know." Harjit was inconsolable.

"Ma, look at me!" Baldev took a step back and held her by the shoulders. "First of all, they are *not* going to kill him. Secondly, we are *not* going to wait another six months for the petition. We're going straight to the higher authorities."

"The higher authorities are all the same. They won't listen to us."

"We'll go through a lawyer this time. Ma, please look at me."

Harjit looked up. An unwavering gaze in Baldev's eyes reminded her of Hakam. *Like father like son, resolute...determined*! She suddenly realized Baldev was already taller than her. Smiling through the tears she whispered, "My son!" and hugged him tightly. *He's not a boy anymore, he's a young man.*

She wiped her eyes with her *duppatta* and kissed him on the forehead. Another realization! She had to tip-toe to reach his forehead.

"Okay, Ma, enough of the kisses, and no more crying! Let's eat." He held her hand walking to the kitchen, "I'm starving!"

"It used to be your father's favorite!" Harjit sighed. "Whenever I made these *Parathas,* he wouldn't stop eating. Wheat and chickpea flour kneaded together with minced onions and spices and shallow fried in butter over the hot griddle. He liked it with a lot of yogurt too."

"It's my favorite too!" Baldev added more yogurt to his plate.

He looks and acts so much like his father! Harjit thought.

"I think we should go to Rampur to see Lal *Chacha ji* and talk to him about hiring a lawyer. Day after tomorrow is half-day at school and then I have three more days off after that," Baldev said chewing a big bite of *paratha*.

"We can't bother him about this too, Bal! He's been helping us so much all these years."

"Okay, we won't bother him about this, but can we go anyway?"

"We could do that. We'll leave as soon as you come back from school."

"My friends are waiting to play *Kabaddi,* Ma. I'll be back soon," Baldev said, going out the door, "but promise, you won't cry anymore."

"I won't, but don't be late."

How are we going to pay for the lawyer? Harjit asked herself, as soon as Baldev left. "Ask father? No, never!" she answered her own question.

She recalled her father screaming, that's why people don't let their daughters out of the house! He dragged her into the back room. Put some kind of chains on her feet, until we decide what to do, he had yelled looking at her stepmother.

"I told you high school was more than enough. She was not going to become a judge by going to college." Harjit heard her stepmother.

"Now look what she has done! No wonder she's been throwing up all morning. How are we going to show our face in public?" Taking her husband's side she glared at Harjit.

I was a daughter who had brought shame upon the family. I had 'blemished his forehead with a black stain and trampled his turban in the dirt!' father had said. For them, I died the day I ran from home and married Hakam.

Harjit tried to remember her own mother's face but could only envision a shadowy grayness of a human figure.

How can a two and a half years old remember anything? That's how old I was when she died during childbirth. And the baby did not survive either.

"Would she too have hated Hakam because of his caste?" she murmured, looking towards the courtyard. The wind whooshing through the leaves of the neem tree, the birds chirping in its branches, or the brass plate still lying by the door did not seem to care or had any answer.

Fourteen years, and never a visit or even a letter from them! Maybe I didn't want them in my life any more than they did.

"What a sham of character! Father considered himself a devout Sikh. He even tried to preach the Sikh values to others. But didn't the Sikh Gurus abolish

141

all manacles of the caste system and taught the world – '*manas ki jaat sabhe eke pehchanbo*' – 'recognize all of mankind as a single caste of humanity.'"

Thoughts tossed her around like a little boat in a giant storm. She felt she was drowning and could not breathe. She shook her head to get the thoughts out of her mind. Sitting on the floor against the wall she wrapped her arms around her knees.

She remembered the very first day of college when she had noticed Hakam's momentary glance at her and was mesmerized. Friendship soon developed into adoration and unfathomable love.

"And we made a mistake!" she whispered. "But that was the best mistake of our lives..." Baldev's face emerged on the sky of her soul like a full moon and her heart filled with tender motherly love. Her face glowed and her eyes sparkled with gratitude. She folded her hands in prayer.

As she sat thinking about Hakam and Baldev, it occurred to her, *I still have my wedding necklace! It should be more than enough to pay a lawyer's fee.* A sliver of hope flickered.

During the raid, police had taken the bigger items and the things that had already been packed, while her jewelry was hidden inside a cavity in the brick wall of the back room. None of the sepoys had paid any attention to the walls of the house. She wiggled the loose brick side-to-side and pulled it out. There lay her jewelry in a red velvet pouch. Her hands shook while retrieving it. She had not seen it for many years. Now looking at it she was amazed how stunningly beautiful and intricate the design of the necklace was, with matching earrings. Strings of yellow gold studded with vibrant colored rubies, emeralds, and sapphires hung from a half-moon shaped choker. The longer strings with bigger gems in the middle gradually become smaller towards the sides and looked like an inverted pyramid. The broad choker also studded with diamonds and precious stones, shone in the dim light inside the room.

She quickly stepped out into the bright daylight and tenderly rolled her fingers over the gems. Holding the necklace against her chest she sighed. A sad smile spread over her face, remembering how Hakam had put the necklace around her neck on their wedding night. He had even tried the earrings on her ears by himself and had giggled while struggling to secure the posts behind her earlobes.

The more she wanted to forget, the more she remembered. She felt Hakam's warm breath on her neck. His strong hands softly and slowly rolled over her shoulders. She felt his fingertips gently caressing her breasts. A spontaneous sigh left her lips. She looked up and felt the touch of his lips over hers. A sudden flash of lightning passed through her body. Her eyes closed in a miraculous feeling of ecstasy and bliss. A passing sensation of harmony and peace swept over her. She sighed and sat in a dream-like state, clutching the necklace against her heart.

The next morning she took the necklace to a jeweler, while Baldev was at school. The goldsmith looked at the piece of jewelry, and she could see a shrewd smile on his face. He placed the necklace in the safe behind a small curtain and handed a few bills to her, "Ours is the only place that gives the best price for old jewelry like this," he said. She knew she had given away a piece of herself and Hakam for the price of dirt. A deep feeling of sadness seeped into her heart. She counted the money and left the shop, dragging her feet towards the lawyer, Mr. Pande's office.

Chapter 30

"Ready, Ma?" Baldev shouted from the doorway. He excitedly tossed the school bag against the wall and two books flew out.

"Respect your books! That's not how you treat them," Harjit scolded.

Baldev picked up the books and put them back. "Sorry!" he mumbled. "Okay, let's go!" He lifted the bag Harjit had already packed and slung it over his shoulder. By the time Harjit locked the door he was already halfway down the street.

Soon they were out of the village and onto the dirt path that connected the village to the main road. The bus stopped here only if someone was waiting to get on, or somebody had to get off. Soon a bus was approaching, "Here it comes!" Baldev's excitement spilled over.

"That's not our bus, this goes in the opposite direction. We are going towards Lahore," Harjit said.

The bus zoomed by, leaving behind a very disappointed Baldev and a big gust of wind. Their clothes fluttered. Harjit caught her *dupatta* before it flew away and securely wrapped it around her neck.

"Hope our bus comes soon. We have a long way to go." Baldev scratched the ground with the heel of his shoe. He squinted to the other side to see if their bus was coming.

"Rampur is not very far, Bal, and the daylight stays for a while after the sunset," Harjit said.

Baldev paced the roadside. His excitement was sagging with each passing minute. After what felt like forever, he saw a bus in the distance, "Is that our bus?" he shouted.

"That's the one," Harjit said.

The conductor swung open the door as the bus stopped. "Quick, quick," he hollered.

Baldev rushed towards it, Harjit right behind him. The bus sped along the narrow road towards Lahore. They sat quietly on the worn-out seats and their bodies lurched and bobbled on the bumpy road. He looked at his mother's somber face. *She looks so sad.* He tried to put the thought out of his mind and looked out the window.

Although their village was not far from Lahore, they hardly visited it. The last time they had gone to Lahore was during his father's trial, but not by bus. They had hired a horse-driven tonga. Lal Singh *Chacha ji* and two other men from the village sat in the front seat and he sat next to Harjit and Didar in the back. Baldev remembered.

Ma looked so sad that day also. So many people had gathered outside the courtroom. They shouted the slogans at the top of their voice when the police brought his father out. The police didn't let anyone go near him. They quickly pushed him into a van and drove away.

Baldev's eyes welled up. Didar was also arrested a few days later. We don't know where they took him, whether they sent him to Andaman like father or some other prison. Baldev wiped his eyes with his sleeve.

"What is it, Bal? What's the matter?" His mother touched his shoulder.

"Nothing!" he said without looking at her.

"Close the window. The wind is getting into your eyes."

"Yeah, it's the wind," he whispered, closing the window.

The bus entered the city limits. Soon the roadside was crowded with rickshaws, bicycles, trucks, and bullock carts. Dust flew and loud voices pierced the air. Everyone seemed to be in a hurry. Some briskly walked one way and the others rushed in the opposite direction. It looked like the city would be emptied out soon if people kept running like that.

The bus slowed to a crawl and Baldev opened the window again. A street hawker holding a bunch of bananas ran alongside the bus, "Sweet bananas only an *anna* for a dozen!" he hollered. By the time Harjit took out the money, the bus picked up speed. The hawker could not keep up and was quickly out of sight.

"I couldn't take out the money fast enough!" she said.

"That's okay, Ma."

"We'll buy some at the bus stand before getting on the next bus."

Crawling through the crowded road, the bus stopped at the central bus stand.

The conductor announced, "Passengers going to Amritsar and Jullundhar stay in the bus. We will stop here for fifteen minutes and new tickets will be issued." Both the driver and the conductor got off.

"That's great!" Baldev looked at the people getting off the bus. "We don't have to change."

"Let me get some fruit for Pali and Pash. I'll be right back." Harjit hurried down the bus.

"Don't be late, Ma. It's only 15 minutes!" Baldev shouted after her.

Harjit came back with some bananas and oranges. New passengers got in and the bus filled up. Twenty minutes passed, the driver and the conductor didn't show up. All the seats were taken and people stood in the aisle. Another twenty minutes passed. No sign of the driver and conductor. The afternoon sun shone towards the west, still raining down its summer fury. The bus felt like a crucible. People sweated and fanned themselves with their hands and small handkerchiefs. A baby cried in his mother's arms. She tried to cool him down by blowing on his face.

"Where are the driver and the conductor?" a man standing in the aisle said.

"Why aren't they starting? The bus's been full for a while."

"Do they think we are a bundle of mangoes tightly packed up in a box for ripening?" Someone shouted.

Others laughed.

"We will soon start rotting instead of ripening in this heat," another one joined in, followed by a bout of giggles and laughter.

The bus full of Hindus, Sikhs, and Muslims, was like one big family lodged in a small house trying to make the best of a very uncomfortable situation. Humor and frustration intermingled, creating an atmosphere that was amusing and tolerable.

Baldev keenly listened to the conversation with a constant smile on his sweaty face. *They all seem to be nice people.*

A man trying to get into the already stuffed bus announced, "They are at the *Dhabha* eatery."

"They are sitting in the shade eating chicken curry while we roast alive in this *tandoor*! Where are their work ethics?" A frustrated voice cut through the hot air.

"No work ethics these days! They grew wings and flew away!" A man standing near the front door of the bus abruptly opened his fists, mimicking as though two birds just took off, and made a "Shhhh…" sound through his teeth.

"Here they come!" the crowd heaved simultaneously. The driver went straight to his seat and started the engine.

"Everyone standing in the aisle get out of the bus," the conductor announced. A lot of commotion and whispering arose, that got louder.

"We've been waiting for so long and now you are telling us to get out?" a man from the back of the bus shouted.

"I want you people out of the bus right now."

No one moved.

"The bus is not going anywhere until the people in the aisle get out," the conductor announced again.

The driver turned off the engine and got out of the bus. A shouting match started between the sitting and the standing passengers.

"Do as the conductor says!" someone sitting on a seat yelled.

"You be quiet! They delayed the bus for hours while we waited in this hot oven and now, they want us out?" Angry voices came from all sides. The seated people wanted the standing persons out of the bus, and the standing people stood their ground. No one was ready to give in.

How can they turn on each other so quickly? Baldev was baffled.

"There will be one more bus after this, going to Jullundhar. Why don't you people take the seats there before that one also fills up," the driver stuck his head through the window and announced. People looked at each other and hurried out of the bus, pushing and shoving.

Hope the driver didn't lie to those people! Baldev scratched his back where the sweat was trickling and wiped his sweaty face with his sleeve.

The bus started moving and the air felt good.

The sun had just gone down the horizon when the bus dropped them at a place that seemed like in the middle of nowhere. Cotton fields stretched on both sides of the road and an unpaved dirt path ran between the fields.

"Where is Rampur?" Baldev looked around. "I don't see any houses anywhere!"

"Bal, we have to walk a little."

147

The air was hot and at a standstill. Baldev slung the bag on his shoulder. "Which road are we taking?" he said looking at Harjit with a jokey smile and started walking on the only path, there was.

"Very funny, Bal!" Harjit tried catching up with him. The dirt road gradually became narrower and lower than the surrounding fields. Overgrown cactus with the prickly pears and Gula bassi shrubs lined the path on both sides. The Gula bassi bushes with trumpet-shaped delicate pink flowers intermingled with the cacti with long sharp thorns.

How can the delicate and the thorny plants grow together? Baldev wanted to ask. It's like the bad and the good holding hands. He wiped the sweat trickling down his neck and kept walking. "I see some houses!" he shouted picking up speed.

"That's Rampur!" Harjit said letting out a long breath.

The river Beas flowed on the east side of the village. Rampur was situated much higher above the riverbank and water did not reach into the village even when flooded during the monsoons. However, it became dangerous in a different way. Many times cattle had fallen into the swollen river and been swept away. Children were strictly guarded against going near the river during that time. It surged rapidly forming treacherous whirlpools that could swallow a big buffalo in seconds.

During the drought however it was a different story. The river would shrink to a shallow rivulet, flowing lazily in the middle, leaving large dry sandy areas on the sides. Children played on the soft riverbed during this time of the year. They would glide from the top of the bank down to the sandy playgrounds. The older kids played cricket using sticks for the wickets and a ball made out of old rags rolled and tightly sewn together and they used homemade bats. The smaller children who were not allowed to participate in the game would just slide up and down from the bank to the riverbed or roll in the sand spreading their arms and legs like wings. The fun would not stop until their mothers hollered for them to come home. The children would return with half-torn clothes, strewn with sand and mud while their mothers yelled at them, swearing not to let them out of the house ever again. The next day, mothers as well as the children would forget the previous night's reprimand and wrist slaps. The mothers would get busy cooking and spinning the wheel and the children chased each other to the riverbank.

The monsoon had not yet arrived and the pond outside the village was shrunken to the center, leaving the edges dried and etched. Baldev and Harjit half circled around the pond towards Lal Singh's house, the only one with a *chaubara;* a room upstairs. The other houses were single-story and most of them were mud houses with thatched roofs. "I see Lal *Chacha ji's* house!" Baldev turned to Harjit.

She looked exhausted, struggling to pull herself forward. "You tired, Ma?"

"A little," she said.

Chapter 31

Pali looked towards the farm but did not see her father's horse by the bend, where she normally would have seen him. The whole village and the surrounding area were visible from the *chaubara*. Two people walking towards the village in the grayish evening light caught her eye. She squinted, is it Aunty Harjit and Baldev?

"Ma, Harjit Aunty and Baldev are coming!" she shouted running down the stairs and darted towards the front gate to meet them. Baldev also quickened his pace towards her. As Pali hugged him, his 14-year-old body almost froze. Subtly he tried to pull back, but Pali's strong tug was somehow mysteriously enticing. His face flushed.

"O, my sweet little girl!" Harjit squeezed Pali against her chest and landed multiple kisses on her dimpled cheeks.

"Come Baldev!" Pali wiggled out of Harjit's arms and took Baldev's hand pulling him through the courtyard. Namo stood in the doorway holding Pash in her arms.

"Ma, look!" Pali skipped along holding Baldev's arm.

"You've grown so tall Baldev!" Namo smiled at him.

Soon Lal Singh entered the courtyard. Pali ran to him. "Look, *Bapu ji*." She pushed Baldev towards him.

"When did you come?" Lal extended his arms toward Baldev. "Come give me a hug."

"They just came!" Pali answered for Baldev. Namo and Harjit met them halfway in the courtyard. "So nice to see you, Bhabi ji," Lal said.

"Baldev had a little break from school and we had not seen you all for a while," Harjit said.

"That's great, I'm so happy you decided to come." Lal patted Baldev's shoulder.

"I am happy too and so is Ma," Pali said chirping and hopping like a little sparrow.

Cheery talk and excitement filled the air. Namo told Kaku's wife, Fatima to make *masala chai* with cardamoms and cloves adding a piece of ginger. Namo and Harjit worked on making fresh roti, while Kaku selected the biggest rooster from the hen house to make chicken curry for dinner.

As they finished eating the evening turned into a windless, moonless, warm night. Suddenly an army of mighty mosquitoes attacked, making them run to the safety of mosquito nets. While the children fell asleep the adults sat in their cots surrounded by the mosquito nets and talked.

Pali's excitement did not let her fall asleep. Lying in her bed, she heard the adults talk, but hardly understood much of anything, other than when she heard her mother say, "Baldev and Pali would be a perfect couple when they grow up."

"That's what Hakam always said." Pali heard Harjit.

"Hakam and I promised when we exchanged our turbans that if we had a boy and a girl, we will marry them. And these two already seem inseparable."

Are they talking about Baldev and me? Are we going to get married when we grow up?

Pali pretended to be asleep.

The air cooled down and the mosquitoes tired of whirring around vanished into the night. Gentle breeze brought a sliver of the moon up into the sky. Pali didn't realize when she fell asleep.

It was bright daylight when she woke up. All the other cots were empty but Baldev was still sleeping, under the mosquito net.

"Wake up, Baldev, wake up!" she pulled his arm.

Baldev rubbed his eyes. "What is it Pali?"

"We have to go to the river," she said. "Get up."

"Isn't it too early?"

"No, it's not! This is when everybody goes there."

"Why?" Baldev tried to open his drowsy eyes.

"The sand gets too hot if you go late. That's why."

The morning was cool and breezy. Pali wanted to get to the river before everyone. They're going to ask, who is he? She smiled at the thought. She wanted to show him off.

"Okay, I'm up," he said getting out of the mosquito net.

"You get five minutes to get ready. Okay!" Pali gave him an ultimatum. She tied her shoes and anxiously waited for him.

"We'll be back soon, Ma!" Pali shouted running through the courtyard. Baldev followed.

Without hesitation she slid from the top of the riverbank onto the sand below, where a number of children had already gathered. They all stopped playing and stared at Baldev.

"Who is he?" Some of the boys around Baldev's age surrounded them. And then the girls came, giggling and admiringly looking at him.

"Oh, he's my uncle's son, Baldev," Pali said. "And these are my friends, Shindo and Raji and Jeena." Pali pointed to each of the girls. "And these are the boys," she didn't bother telling their names and kept looking at Baldev. Her doe like eyes shone with excitement. The other little children gathered there were not important for her to mention.

"Where does he live?" one of the boys asked. The circle of children got narrower as everyone tried to get close to Baldev.

"Far away, you have to change like four buses to get there," Pali said standing on her toes.

"Usually, you change the bus once," Baldev said, "but yesterday we didn't have to, because the same bus continued after stopping for a while at Lahore and Amritsar."

"You've seen Lahore?" A boy wearing a blue cotton shirt and pajamas asked. His eyes opened wide and mouth even wider.

"A few times." Baldev stood tall with his arms crossed against his chest.

"Wow, I can't believe this! My uncle's friend once told us that there is no city like Lahore." He moved even closer as if trying to get a glimpse of Lahore from Baldev's face. "So, what is it like?"

"Well, lots of tall buildings and shops and people frantically running—"

The boy seemed a little disappointed and interrupted him. "Well, Amritsar is like that too, lots of people and buildings."

"I believe most cities are similar in that sense," Baldev said.

"But Amritsar has the Golden Temple. There's nothing like that in the whole world," another boy, holding a ball made of tightly sewed rags, said.

"I've heard too, there's nothing like the Golden Temple anywhere," Baldev agreed with him.

"You want to play cricket with us?" a barefooted boy almost as tall as Baldev, in a half-torn shirt asked.

"Sure." Baldev nodded.

"He's the best cricket player!" Pali said, although she had never seen him play.

"You want to bowl or bat?" the boy in the blue shirt asked.

"I'll bat."

"Okay then," one of the boys handed him a bat that was slightly crooked near the upper end. "This is our best bat," he said, noticing Baldev staring at it.

They walked to the cricket field the boys had drawn in the sand and set up the wickets made out of sticks. Baldev stood in front of the wickets with the bat. The tall barefoot boy stood at the bowling crease, ready to pitch.

The bowler made a sound, "Huh," as he threw the ball. Baldev swung the bat hitting the ball and ran back and forth between the wickets. He made three runs before the boy in blue shirt threw the ball back. The boys shouted shaking hands.

The girls sat at a little distance watching them play. Pali noticed Baldev looking towards her every now and then. She waved at him and he waved back.

"I told you he's the best cricket player," Pali said. "I'm going to marry him when I grow up!" Pali whispered the secret with her hands cupped around her cheeks. The girls giggled.

"Really?" Jeena held her face in her palms. Her eyes widened and her lips stretched into an ear-to-ear smile. She pulled in a long breath and stared at Pali.

"Now, I'm like 12 and he is 14," Pali said, still keeping her hands around her mouth.

"My uncle's son is only seven years old," Shindo, a little younger than Pali, said. She puckered her brows and lips in disappointment.

"You don't marry your real uncle's son, silly!" Pali scolded her.

"Our fathers are not real brothers. They became brothers in college."

"How do you become brothers in college?" Raji asked.

"You switch your turbans with each other and say, 'we will be brothers forever.' And then you become brothers." Pali straightened her neck and held her head high with a beaming smile.

"My father never went to college. He didn't even go to school," Jeena said.

"When are you going to marry him?" Shindo asked.

"When his father comes back," Pali said, looking towards Baldev who was now bowling instead of batting.

"Come back from where?" Raji followed Pali's eyes looking at Baldev.

"Oh, I don't know much about it, but they say it is a very nice place. And it's really far away. It takes a long time to come back." The cheerful smile from Pali's face faded and she turned a little somber.

"Why did he go there?" Raji wanted to know all about the mysterious place.

"Pali, your mother wants you home." They heard Kaku calling from the ridge of the riverbank.

"Baldev, we have to go home," Pali shouted at the top of her voice.

"I can't leave in the middle of the game! You have to wait a little," Baldev hollered. "No, we have to leave right now!" she hollered back brushing off sand from her clothes.

"Why! What's the hurry?" Baldev stopped bowling.

"Ma wants us home! That's the hurry!" She walked towards the ridge and started climbing.

"Maybe we can play again tomorrow." Baldev handed the ball to one of the boys and ran, catching up with Pali.

"Slow down!" he tugged on the corner of her shirt causing her to slip and slide down towards the bottom of the ridge.

"Stop that!" she yelled. "I'm not going to marry you if you do that again!"

Baldev quickly bent down and caught her arm, stopping her from sliding further down.

"What? Marry who?"

"You!" she shouted angrily.

"Marry me?" Baldev's face turned crimson.

"What you saying, Pali?"

"You don't know anything." She rubbed her palms flicking off the sand from her hands and kept walking up the ridge, "I'm not going to tell you."

"I'm sorry! I didn't mean to hurt you!" Baldev said as soon as they got to the top of the riverbank.

"Where did you hear about us getting married?"

"Are you sorry for real?" She looked at him.

"Yes for real! I'm sorry for real," he looked into her eyes.

"Are you going to tell me now?"

"Ma and *Bapu ji* and your Ma were talking last night. They said we were like inseparable."

"They said that?" A grin beamed over Baldev's face, "but…"

"But what?" Pali looked at him.

"The only boys and girls our age I know, who got married had never gone to school. And they were mostly Mussalmans."

"Not now, silly, only when we grow up and finish school!" Pali slapped his arm.

"You know what! You're the prettiest girl there's ever been," Baldev did not seem shy anymore.

"I am?" Pali blushed for the first time and ran through the half-open gate towards the house.

******

Baldev stopped at the gate looking at the big house. The outer courtyard had a row of servants' rooms on one side and the sheds for the buffalos and horses on the other. The inner courtyard with a colorful brick floor was for the family gatherings. Red and yellow marigolds bloomed on either side of the verandah in rectangular patches and stairs to the *chaubara* ran from the verandah.

What a beautiful house! Baldev thought looking at the *chaubara*. Pali won't like our small house in the middle of the village. I will build her a big house when I grow up. Baldev smiled and heard Pali saying, "Why're you standing there? *Parothas* are ready, Ma says."

Chapter 32

The aroma of basmati rice slowly cooked in milk, until soft and mushy with a generous amount of brown sugar, filled the air. "Is the kheer ready, Namo?" Lal Singh called, as they patiently waited for the dessert. Namo handed them bowls of kheer while they sat on cots, talking.

"Any news about the petition?" Lal asked Harjit.

"It's a no," she said. The spoon full of kheer shook in her hand and she put it back into the bowl. A loud sigh followed.

"They denied again?" Lal Singh yelled. His voice and the cot shook with his loud outburst.

"How could they do that?" Lal felt the sweetness of the kheer turning bitter in his mouth and he placed the bowl on the ground. The evening suddenly turned darker.

"We are going to petition again, through a lawyer this time!" Baldev said.

"Seem like we have no choice. I'll talk to Pande, tomorrow." Lal looked at Harjit's shadowy silhouette in the gray evening.

"I already talked to Mr. Pande." Her hands trembled.

"Okay then, I will go and pay his fee."

"It's been taken care of. You don't need to worry about it," she said.

"How?" Lal asked.

"I had some jewelry I didn't need."

"What? You sold your jewelry?" Lal shouted for the second time this evening. He remembered when Hakam had taken him along to a reputed goldsmith in Lahore and showed him the drawings he had made himself. He wanted the goldsmith to create just one piece of the most exquisite necklace. *Only one piece!* he had told him, *like one life! Precious!*

"How will Hakam feel that his wife had to sell her jewelry to pay for the lawyer?" Lal's voice was mixed with hurt and anger.

"I don't want to burden you with this. You are already doing so much for us," Harjit said. "It is already done."

"Then it needs to be undone! Tomorrow, we are going to get the jewelry back. And that's final!" Lal got up and walked towards the outer courtyard.

******

As Lal Singh entered the shop the jeweler stood up, respectfully folding his hands. "What would you like to buy, Sardar ji?" he asked courteously.

"I'm here to buy back the necklace my sister-in-law sold to you two days ago." Lal recognized the necklace displayed in the showcase.

"No, Sardar ji, an item once sold cannot be returned. Done is done." The jeweler waved his hand gesturing him to leave.

"Here, I'm giving you more than what you paid her. Just return the necklace." Lal took out the money from his pocket.

"I didn't go to her house and ask for it. She came to my shop to sell it."

"Doesn't matter if you asked for it or not, here's your money."

"I'm not returning anything. Get out of my shop," the goldsmith yelled.

"I'm not going anywhere." Lal lowered his voice almost to a whisper, "I am politely asking you again to return it."

"I'm not returning anything. I'm politely asking you again to get out of my shop," he mocked Lal's voice.

"You son of a bitch," Lal caught him by the neck and landed his fist on his temple behind the left eye.

"Please...please, Sardar ji, don't hurt me!" The jeweler's short, rounded body trembled under Lal's six-foot stature.

"Don't hurt you? I'll split your head if you don't give it back right now!"

"But..." the goldsmith tried to say something.

"Do you think the necklace was only worth the money you gave her? It's not buying and selling; it is plain stealing." Lal pulled him closer and raised his fist to punch him again. "I won't let you get away with it, you thief!"

"Okay...okay!" The goldsmith tried to pull away.

"Okay, what?" Lal said without loosening his grip.

"I will give it back!"

"Now you're talking." Lal loosened grip on his neck.

The goldsmith took his time opening the showcase lock while Lal waited impatiently. "Can you give me a few more rupees, Sardar ji?" The goldsmith held the necklace in his hands and looked at Lal Singh.

"You have no shame!" Lal laughed in disgust and grabbed the necklace from his hands. "You don't want another punch, do you?" he said, throwing the bills at his face.

He wrapped the necklace in a handkerchief and stuffed it in his pocket. *Good, I didn't have to punch him twice*, he thought, walking to the bus stand.

He bought a newspaper from a stall before getting onto the bus. He had taught Namo to read Punjabi from a children's book and brought home a newspaper every time he went to the city. He planned reading and writing competitions between the mother and daughter but Namo was no match for Pali.

Namo said to him one day, "I've learned enough, Sardar ji, no more competitions. It's Pali you should concentrate on. She might go to college one day."

He took a seat and opened the paper full of news of arrests and unrest all over India. The atrocities of the Raj were getting severer as they relentlessly tried to crush the freedom movement. The news from Kala Pani revealed the inhumane treatment of prisoners who were falling like dead flies. The British had been unable to stop the newspapers from being published and the unrest spread throughout the country. Hitler of Germany was gaining strength and war loomed over the European skies.

Flipping through the pages he noticed the man sitting next to him constantly trying to take a peek at the newspaper. Lal instinctively tilted the paper towards him. The bus clunked along sluggishly, leaving behind a trail of thick black smoke. It stopped at Rampur late in the evening. *Harjit should not see the newspaper. Why worry her about the news from Kala Pani.* Lal gave the paper to the man sitting next to him. "Here," he said, getting off the bus.

A sudden twinge in his belly, the kind he had a few times in the past few months, made him recoil with pain. Namo had tried to talk him into seeing a doctor but he had been putting it off. He wrapped his arms around his stomach and bent down. The thought of walking two miles to get home petrified him.

To his surprise, Kaku stood there waiting with the horse.

"What are you up to, Kaku?" Lal asked trying a smile on his pain-ridden lips.

"Bibi ji was worried about you. She said you were not feeling well this morning."

Kaku gazed, "You don't look well, Sardar ji!"

"I'm alright. Let's go home." Lal took the reins from him and mounted the horse. He winced with pain. "Maybe it's a bit of indigestion. Hop on."

"You go, Sardar ji. I'll walk home."

"We'll talk on the way, just hop on." Lal stopped the horse close to Kaku.

"The cotton field on the far south side seemed almost ready two days ago," Lal Singh said.

"Yes, it is ready. Fatima and three other women along with their children are picking the cotton tomorrow. I believe four are enough for now," Kaku said. "We can hire more, later when the other fields are ready."

"What would I do without you, dear friend?" Lal said.

Kaku always knew what needed to be done at the farm. For generations, Kaku's family had worked at Lal Singh's home and the farm. His father Raheem had worked for Lal Singh's father Rattan Singh and his father had served Lal Singh's grandfather.

For generations Muslims, Sikh and Hindus lived side by side in Rampur as well as all over Punjab. Kaku (Kareem Khan), a Mussalman was not just a worker. His relationship with Lal was more as friends. People of the fertile land of Punjab, had culturally more in common, in spite of adhering to different religions. They were Punjabis first and Sikh, Hindu, or a Muslim later. Some of the villages consisted of mainly Muslim landowners and others had majority of Sikh landowners. The village Rampur consisted mainly of Sikhs.

Lal Singh felt the necklace in his pocket as he got off the horse. The pain was gone and he almost felt normal. "Never think about getting rid of this again, Bhabi ji!" He handed the necklace to Harjit.

Her eyes welled but her face lit up. She pressed the necklace against her chest. Silent tears flowed down her cheeks. Everyone watched quietly.

Pali looked at the necklace and her eyes opened to the widest. She had never seen anything like this before. It looked very different from her mother's jewelry.

"Don't cry, Aunty." Pali put her arms around Harjit.

"No one will ever take it away from you again," using Harjit's own duppatta, Pali wiped her tears.

"My sweet Pali." Harjit smiled through tears.

Lal had the same piercing pain again later and threw up. The village doctor diagnosed it indigestion and gave him digestive *chooran* to swallow it with warm water. "No heavy stuff like parotha," he warned.

Namo made *khichree,* equal amounts of rice, and split yellow lentils cooked together until soft and gooey. The whole family decided to have *khichree* for dinner. Everyone had it with a dollop of butter on the top except Lal Singh.

******

The next morning as the roosters crowed, Baldev got up, ready to go to the river, while Pali sat on her bed yawning, eyes half-closed.

"Let's go Pali, hurry up," Baldev said looking towards the gate.

"We don't have to go that early. What's the hurry?" Pali said getting out of the mosquito net.

"The sand gets too hot afterward. That's the hurry," Baldev chuckled. "You get five minutes to get ready."

Pali smiled.

Chapter 33

The night sky glimmered with a gentle glow of stars. Lying in the courtyard Baldev tossed and turned in his bed. A warm wind blew softly, causing the bedsheet corners to flail and flutter quietly around the cot.

Baldev looked towards his mother's bed, "Are you asleep, Ma?"

"No. What is it, Bal?" Harjit said sitting up in her bed.

"Six days till we leave." Baldev sat up in his bed too.

"Finally the day is here we've been waiting for."

"Will father recognize us?" Baldev's voice was a little raspy.

"Why not, Bal? I'm sure he too is anxiously waiting for us." Harjit looked up. The big dipper in the clear sky had rotated towards the west. The night was more than half-way gone.

"What if he doesn't?"

"He *will*! You are his son. How could he not recognize you?" Harjit walked to his cot and sat by his bedside. "Try to go back to sleep."

"I can't." Baldev cleared his throat.

"I know you are worried, but I assure you that he still loves you the same as the day you were born. Close your eyes and get some sleep." Harjit placed her hand over his eyes and stroked his hair with the other, as though he was a little baby. Baldev soon fell asleep breathing softly and peacefully.

She kissed his forehead gently and went back to her bed, waiting for the morning. Her eyes wide open she sat in her bed alone while the world slept. The anguish of loneliness deep in her breast, the pain of separation, and a fire of longing in her heart, she was like a lotus withering without water. Her soul had yearned to see Hakam's face for so long. She had wept more than the clouds had rained. She had sighed more than the wind had blustered. If the tears were pearls, she could have strung them into a string that could go around the whole earth. If the sighs were a little gust of wind, hers could have caused countless tornados. Finally, the day she had feverishly waited for was approaching and she was ecstatic and somber at the same time. The days were dreary and the nights restless. The clock ticked much slower.

The big dipper had disappeared behind the roof of the house and a glow was visible on the eastern sky when she dozed off.

******

Suitcases were packed and set aside. "You can put the purse by the suitcases now, Ma." Baldev smiled. She had taken out the official letter from the purse, folded, and put it back several times. She had counted the money again and again.

"Just making sure," Harjit said.

"Tomorrow's the day." Baldev looked at the suitcases. Harjit nodded looking beyond Baldev's face.

The villagers started pouring into their courtyard to say goodbye. Since the day the approval letter came, people were in a festive mood as if they were all going to see Hakam Singh. Kala Pani had been the topic of discussion wherever they met, under the Banyan tree or Nand Lal's shop or the *kabbadi* playground. They all talked over each other to show their closeness to Hakam. They told stories about their friendship and wanted to convey their messages to him.

The schoolteacher, Jiwan Singh also stopped by their house and brought a few books. "You can read during the journey," he said to Baldev. "Don't worry about missing school. I will help you catch up when you come back."

Baldev stuffed them into the already bulging suitcase. He retrieved a cardboard box from the shelf containing letters he had written to his father but never mailed. He had to use a step stool to reach the shelf when he started writing the letters but now, he could reach it without it. The letters were neatly stacked by the date. Father would like to read the letters, he thought. He pulled out a letter from the bottom of the box,

November 16, 1933

Dear Father,

    They came with the police and took all of our stuff. They put a lock on our house and Ma cried. We are staying at Baba Budh Singh's house. Then Lal uncle came and bought all the new stuff for the house and kitchen. They tell us not to worry about anything. I wish you were here.

Your son,

Baldev

December 21, 1933

Dear Father,

    It was a very exciting day today. They came in the morning in two vans. One white policeman and two Indian policemen came along with another fat man. They brought folding chairs and a table and wanted to sell our land. People from the surrounding villages had gathered under the Banyan tree. Baba ji had told everyone that no one should buy our land. When the fat man started saying the auction stuff, all the people got up and walked away. The white man yelled at them to come back, but no one did. So they could not sell our land and they went back in their vans and never came back. Later Lal uncle and Babaji and other men built another door at the back of our house and we moved back in. I miss you so much.

Your son,

Baldev

April 20, 1935

Dear Father,

    You'd be so happy. Our results were announced today and I won the first position in all subjects, arithmetic and history and geography, and Punjabi. I'm now in the seventh grade. Ma is very happy and proud of me. Wish you were here.

Your son,

Baldev

He kept looking at the letters. Many of them he stuffed in the suitcase without reading. A recent letter caught his eye.

June 29, 1937

Dear Father,

Ma and I went to see Lal uncle and the whole family. We took the bus from Gajanpur to Lahore and from there to Rampur. You remember the time we went to Lahore when I was little. On the way, we came up with a story about the backward running trees and the giant crocodile chasing them? It was a long time ago. Now I'm fourteen and I could not come up with any story but I missed you so much. We are planning to come to see you soon. Ma petitioned again, through a lawyer this time.

Pali and I went to the river to play. She is so very...

Baldev read the unfinished letter and blushed. He had started writing when they returned from Rampur but did not know how to tell his father about Pali. He stuffed all the letters in his suitcase. Only a day left to start their long journey to Andaman and Nicobar Islands.

Lal Singh and Namo came to see them off too and brought Pali and Pash along.

"I want to know everything when you come back," Pali said to him, "All about Hakam uncle and the ship and the place he lives."

"Okay, I will." Baldev held her hand.

"Promise?"

"I promise."

A plumpish man in a pantsuit holding a briefcase came in. Breathing heavily he looked around and fixed his gaze at Lal Singh.

"Who's he?" people mumbled.

Lal almost jumped from his seat, "Is everything alright, Mr. Pande?"

"There's a problem," he said in a low voice.

"I received this letter only in the morning and left immediately to inform you. They have changed the policy again." Mr. Pande was breathless.

"Here's the letter. They're not allowing relatives to visit. I'm so sorry, Sardar ji. I did my best..."

"Slow down Pande ji. It doesn't make sense. They're leaving tomorrow..."

164

A sudden vacuum engulfed the room. The wind stopped blowing and everyone forgot to breathe.

A moment later, people let out a noisy breath. Dumbfounded they looked at Mr. Pande who was heaving like he had just finished a wrestling match.

Harjit's legs gave in and she slumped onto the floor, looking pale.

"Get some water," Namo shouted.

"Ma…" Baldev dashed to her. "You okay, Ma?"

How could she be okay, when the ground from under her very feet had been snatched and she was falling into a bottomless abyss? How could she be okay, when she had lost all hope and her confidence in life? How could she be okay when the scab of her wound that had just started healing was prodded again with the tip of a knife!

Harjit slowly opened her eyes. "I'm okay, Bal." She looked at Baldev, her lips barely moved.

"It's all your fault." Jang Singh, Hakam's cousin, jumped on Pande knocking him down.

People quickly separated them and helped Pande up from the floor. A yelling match started, some blaming Pande and the others in his favor. Gritting his teeth Jang tried to charge at Pande again but men held him tight. He kept shouting his head off, "You think it's a funny joke? One day you come, 'O, here's the letter, you can visit him. When they are ready to leave, you come back with the letter, they can't see him."

"It's not his fault. He came as quickly as he could, to inform us," Joga Singh said.

"The lawyers are all leeches. They care only about the money they suck out of people's pockets."

"If he cared only about the money, he wouldn't have come here. His job was done!" Joga Singh shouted back.

"Stop this nonsense right now!" Lal Singh yelled.

Everyone hushed. But muted voices started immediately.

"I'm sure Mr. Pande did his best. Why blame him?" Jiwan Singh, the schoolteacher stepped forward. "This is not anybody's fault. This is the fault of our fate, the fault of our destiny. They are the masters and we the slaves: they tell us, 'die' and we die: they tell us, 'live' and we live: they tell us, 'crawl on your knees' and we bend down and crawl. We are the puppets and they play us the way they want. This is what living in slavery does to you, and then we blame each other and fight each other without thinking."

"True, very true!" Joga whispered.

"But some brave ones like Hakam make sacrifices to wake us up from the slumber and stop cleaning the tyrant's shoes with our tongue. They want us to stop crawling and start walking with our heads held up high."

People nodded.

"That's why Hakam's been exiled. That's why the dictator government hanged Bhagat Singh and Rajguru and Sukhdev."

Moments later, Jiwan Singh began singing the song, Bhagat Singh and his companions sang with so much passion that it had become the song of freedom, the song of martyrdom, they sang walking to the gallows,

"Dye my robes, the color of saffron, O, Mother India,"

"Paint my robes with the spirit of sacrifice,"

"Dying for freedom is better than a hundred lives in bondage."

Everyone joined in. *"Inquilab, Zindabad!"* he shouted at the end of the song. Long live the revolution.

"Inquilab, Zindabad!" people answered in one voice.

Chapter 34

Hakam moved closer to the door and took out the broken chunk of a mirror from his pocket one of the prisoners had given him during lunchtime. The mirror had been circulating among the prisoners for a while, but no one actually knew where it had come from. Carefully holding the irregular sharp edges, he looked into the mirror. A stifled scream came out of his throat. He pushed the mirror away as if he had touched red hot coal.

"This is not me. How could it be me?" He trembled with nauseating disgust. His face did not seem to belong to him. He felt the sides of his cheeks with his fingertips and pressed the empty spots within his beard. He rubbed his sunken eyes with the heels of his palms. He rolled his hands from his shriveled face down to his chest. His ribs felt like iron bars bulging out of his chest, separated from each other by furrows of stretched out skin. His hand suddenly dropped onto the hollow of his withered wrinkly belly. His eyes watered.

Harjit and Bal are not going to recognize me. Would Harjit be repulsed by my sight? Would Baldev run away instead of giving me a hug? He felt a sharp twinge in his heart. I'm like the stagnant water in a ditch, separated from the river of life, that flows and that renews and recharges. Cut off from my river of life, Harjit and Baldev, I lay in the prison ditch, torn and tattered, dying a torturously slow death. Hakam sat on the cold floor in a daze slowly shaking his head side to side.

They'll be here soon, both of them! The thought exalted him and pained him at the same time. Delight and anguish held hands, locked their fingers around him, and blurred his vision. How long had he ached to look into Harjit's eyes and tell her, he loved her with every speck of his being? How badly he had wanted to hold Baldev against his chest and tell him what a wonderful son he was. Finally, the day was approaching, and his feelings were so jumbled up.

With his index finger, he stroked the scar on his upper lip and pressed the hardened gums of his two front missing teeth. His already weakened teeth were broken by the jamadar Zafar Khan about two years ago. One day a young prisoner named Kaka was being beaten by Zafar Khan and Pinta while the others watched in silence. They repeatedly punched and kicked him, laughing and yelling while the boy rolled on the ground in a fetal position.

Hakam jumped on Zafar, "Is it a game for you? You bastard, son of a bitch…!"

Although Zafar was much stronger than the emaciated Hakam, the sudden attack knocked him to the ground. Pinta pulled Hakam from Zafar's top and they both started punching him in a maniac rage.

"Quench his thirst, Zafar!" Pinta yelled. A trough full of seawater was always kept at hand. Zafar held Hakam by the hair and dunked his head into the water until he gasped for breath. Pulled him out and dunked him again. The longer Hakam tried to hold his breath, the longer Zafar kept him underwater.

As Zafar's wrath was winding down and he was about to let him go, Pinta yelled, "Dunk him one more time!" Zafar hit Hakam's face on the edge of the trough before dunking him into the water. It did not make much of a sound to knock out his two upper front teeth. Soon the green seawater in the trough was colored red and Hakam left toothless with bloody swollen lips.

No action was taken against Zafar Khan and Pinta, but Hakam received ten lashes on his back for attacking a jamadar. Dr. Todd refused any treatment for the broken teeth or his painful infected right ear where the seawater had entered. Almost two years had gone by and his gums had hardened, the lip healed with a scar but the hearing in his right ear was gone.

Zafar was famous for his punishing techniques. He had been the head of a band of dacoits who terrorized several villages for years. They would come on horseback, brandishing guns, and shooting in the air to let the people know of their arrival. "Zafar is here…" the word would spread rapidly. People hurried in and out of their houses, collecting grain and money or whatever they could offer. Women and girls were sent into hiding. Even the slightest delay was not tolerated by the mighty Zafar Khan. The last person surely risked being shot dead, and it had happened in many villages. People trembled at Zafar's name until the day one of his own companions double-crossed him and informed the police about the day and the village they were going to attack. He was finally caught after a hefty gunfight that killed his horse and injured his leg. He was incarcerated for life in this prison. The British jailor's hate for the freedom fighters had promoted him to a jamadar to torture the political prisoners. He proudly talked about his brigandage days to the jamadars and guards.

Hakam wanted to look into the mirror again, but the piece of glass lying nearby felt like an enemy who had just defeated him. He closed his tired eyes and lay in the silence of his stone walled cage.

Walking under the azure sky, Harjit held his hand. A cool mist caressed their faces. The velvety soil under their feet cradled them softly and a mellow wind fluttered their saffron robes. They walked towards the gate where freedom resided with all its glory and grandeur. Baldev walked a few steps ahead of them looking back once in a while. Love flowed from the dimension of their soul to the heavens above and the earth below. 'The beauty of love never fades. It does not get disfigured by the broken teeth, the sunken eyes, the hollows of the cheeks. The splendor of love is not tarnished by the grayed eyebrows or the bulging ribs!' Hakam bent his head close to Harjit's face to hear her. He heard the voice of the earth and the whispers of the wind. He heard the golden rays of the sun speak to him. Love is eternal! Unending! Undying! Timeless! Harjit looked up at him and smiled.

Startled by the sound of galloping horses they looked back. Gigantic, beastly figures were catching up. The gate to freedom lay at a little distance in front of them. 'Run Baldev,' Hakam shouted. 'Take Harjit with you, and Pali and Namo! Run! Take everyone with you!' Hakam bent down and picked up a fistful of moist soil and hurled it at Baldev. 'Here, take it to freedom.' Baldev leaped up and his arms stretched beyond the sky. His body grew past the stars and he caught the earth in his hands along with all the humans and the animals, the mountains and the forests, and ran disappearing into the immensity of the gates of freedom.

Right that moment, one of the beasts caught up with Hakam.

He woke up with a jolt. Wiping his sweaty face he looked around the dark walls of the cell. "Does it mean I pass the torch of revolution to Baldev?" Wide awake he waited for morning.

Chapter 35

Hakam waited impatiently for the guard to unlock his cell door. "Today's the day! Who'll I hug first, Harjit or Baldev? Both of them together!" Tears of joy flooded his eyes and he laughed. A wave of incredible bliss raced through his body. With the slightest noise outside the cell, his gaze darted toward the door. He had been imagining what Duni Chand the guard, would say opening the door, *Ah Hakam, your family is here!* Or he'd say, *Ah Hakam, come out, your wife and son are here to see you!* And he'd run out of the prison cell and hold them in his arms. *How big would've Baldev grown by now? Maybe up to my shoulder, maybe even taller!* Hakam touched his shoulder and then slowly raised his hand above his head as if seeing Baldev grown taller than him.

The day turned into a shadowy evening and was quickly replaced by the night. Everything went silent. Hakam's mind though caught in an emotional typhoon did not let him rest. After a torturous sleepless night, he sprang to his feet as the guard inserted the key into the lock, next morning.

"Are they here?" Hakam dashed to the door.

Duni Chand looked at him as if seeing him for the first time, "Who?"

"My wife and son!" Hakam shouted excitedly.

The guard let out a curious laugh. "Have you lost your mind?"

"They were supposed to be here yesterday. They should be here by now…"

"You must be dreaming! Now hurry up and get out of here. I've other cells to open too." Duni Chand swiped his arm in the air gesturing Hakam to get out of the room.

Hakam felt his feet glued to the floor, unable to move. "I have the letter. Look, I have it here!" Hakam's hands trembled fiddling around the pocket to retrieve the letter.

"Look, I don't have time for this. Don't you know, no one is allowed here?" The guard frowned.

Hakam felt the room spinning. The guard standing by the door faded and reappeared and faded again in front of his eyes.

For the first time, Duni Chand lent a hand to prevent him from falling and helped him to slowly slide on to the floor, "You okay?" He looked at Hakam's skeletal figure from head to toe.

Hakam sat staring blankly at the wall. His lips quivered.

"What's wrong with him?" Duni Chand whispered to himself. He locked the door and left. He came back in the evening with a bowl of rice and found Hakam sitting in the same spot.

"Here, eat." He tapped his shoulder.

Hakam's lips moved, "Harjit!" Slowly he appeared to ease out of a daze and took the bowl from him but did not eat.

"I brought you Vaseline for your cracked heels that you've been asking for," the guard took a shiny aluminum tube from his pocket and put it by his side.

Hakam had requested medication for his cracked heels several times but got none. Past few days he had been walking on his toes so that his painful heels would not touch the ground. Hakam absentmindedly looked at his heels where the blood had dried in the cracks.

The next few days the dreaded Duni Chand, called 'Cheetah' behind his back, and who had wanted to *feed Hakam to the fish* when he first arrived in this prison, began showing a bit of kindness. Over the years his harshness had softened not only for Hakam but in general. He regularly brought food for Hakam and tried to make him eat but Hakam could not eat more than a bite or two. A few days later Duni Chand let him out of his cell and he wobbled to the dining hall to join the other prisoners. He could not recall their names and sat with an empty gaze looking nowhere.

The days became weeks and the weeks turned into months. No one told him why his wife and son didn't show up. A shadowy night had spread over his anguished heart that ached for a glimpse of the morning. Hakam lived and walked in a perpetual darkness. While the other prisoners read newspapers, discussed, and grumbled about politics, Hakam sat quietly through their heated arguments about the leaders, Gandhi, Nehru, and Mohammad Ali Jinnah.

Provincial elections were taking place in their homeland in a boiling cauldron of political and social chaos. The leaders distrusted each other and the newspapers were filled with stories of communal killings. Stark differences between the Indian National Congress headed by Nehru and the Muslim League, headed by Jinnah, had flared up an atmosphere of already existing communal hatred and divisiveness. They gave fiery speeches at huge gatherings.

Gandhi went around, wrapped in a homespun shawl and a half dhoti around his bony legs. A walking stick in his hand and young women on either side, his scrawny body reeled forward with a determined stride. The frame of his spectacles wobbled up and down on the bridge of his nose with every step. He went from place to place spreading the message of nonviolence and celibacy.

Whereas Gandhi was worshipped by many, he was equally despised by others. Scores of Hindus, Muslims, and Sikhs disagreed with him. They wanted a progressive India with modern technology and industries but Gandhi wanted to go back to the ancient way of life. He publicly scolded who so ever went against his wishes.

The prisoners of Kala Pani were also divided as the Gandhians, and the Muslim Leaguers and a few as high casts. There were other revolutionaries, like Hakam Singh and Bikram, who disagreed with Gandhi's shrewd tactics and Nehru and Jinnah's fire-spitting propaganda. They just wanted freedom for their motherland.

"Look at Gandhi's hypocrisy," Bikram said, "He calls the untouchables *Harijans*, meaning God's children. But when the British agreed to give them a separate quota of electorates for their social uplift, Gandhi threatened to go on a hunger strike unto death." Bikram shook his head, "why wouldn't Gandhi want uplifting of the downtrodden?"

"Maybe Gandhi is worried that if the untouchables were allowed education and other means of their uplift, no one would carry on the work of washing and cleaning the latrines. And no one would dispose the dead cattle or work with their hides," Chandar Sen answered.

"So, calling them 'Children of God' and keeping them working, as usual, is Gandhi's best conniving strategy. And he threatened the British with a hunger strike."

He turned to Hakam, "Am I not right, Hakam?"

Hakam did not move. Legs spread in front of him and hands resting in his lap, his gaze remained fixed somewhere beyond the wall. The prisoners waited a few seconds and resumed their loud conversation.

"Remember when we went on a hunger strike four years ago. Mahabir Singh and two others were murdered by nasal feeding tube unloading the food into their lungs instead of the stomach. And the jailor shamelessly ordered their bodies weighed down with rocks and tossed into the ocean?"

Another prisoner joined in. "What a horrendous torture!"

"How can we forget? It's because of the hunger strike we gained the right to talk to each other and read newspapers and know what's going on back home."

"How come Gandhi survives the hunger strike every time? Maybe they put some sugar or glucose in his water," Bikram said.

"Gandhi gave up everything for the sake of our country? He could have a life of luxury, but he chose poverty, while Nehru and Jinnah live in big mansions and wear silk," one of the Gandhians shouted.

Bikram turned his famished body towards the short-statured, equally emaciated Gandhian and bellowed, "No, no, no! It is us, and scores of others like us, who gave up everything for our country. And here in this hellish fire, we burn little by little, every day."

Others nodded.

"How was it morally right for Gandhi to tell the victims of the earthquake in Bihar that it was the result of their sins?" Bikram yelled, "Finally when he visited the area, where more than twenty thousand people had perished, he told the destitute victims that the earthquake was a chastisement for their sins of untouchability. If God brought the calamity due to the sin of untouchability, all the poor low caste should've been spared. Not a single one of them should have died," Bikram sneered.

"Why does Gandhi shove the dagger of religion into the throat of every problem, whether political, social, or even a natural disaster like the earthquake?" Chandar Sen asked.

The Gandhian walked away and sat down placing his food bowl in front of him. The rest of the prisoners continued until jamadar Pinta threatened to 'fluff' them up, the word used for flogging.

Chapter 36

Hakam absentmindedly took a bite of *roti* from his dented aluminum plate. His face shuddered as if he had bit into something bitter. He pushed the plate away and rested his head on the wall behind him. Eyes half-closed, mouth half-open, he stared across the room.

"Have a little bit more," Bikram sitting next to him said.

Hakam did not answer.

Ahmed quickly picked up Hakam's plate and gulped a large piece of *roti*.

Bikram snatched the plate away from Ahmad, "Have you no shame left?" he yelled.

"He wasn't going to eat it anyway!" Ahmad protested.

"And that gave you the right to steal his food?" Bikram shouted.

"His food goes waste every day, and we're all starving." Ahmad defiantly stood facing Bikram. Some of the other prisoners nodded in agreement.

"You're right. We're all starving," Bikram argued, "But we still are eating enough to keep us breathing. Hakam will die if we started stealing his food instead of helping him eat!"

"We're not responsible for him in any way," Ahmad shot back.

"If he is not going to eat, why can't we have it?" Kaka took Ahmad's side.

"What has happened to us? Have we forgotten who we are and what we stand for? We sacrificed our freedom for the freedom of our motherland. We pledged for unity, we sang the songs of martyrdom and sacrifice. Now, look at us!" Bikram's voice choked.

"Remember, how Hakam kept our spirits high during the brutal days of hunger strike?"

Chandar stepped in, "And you a thankless snake." He glared at Kaka, "how could *you* forget when he saved you from Zafar and got himself beaten mercilessly?"

"That's when they broke his teeth and almost drowned him to death."

Hakam sat unaffected looking nowhere.

"The Congress party won with a landslide!" Mohan hollered grabbing the newspaper as soon as jamadar Pinta threw it in the dining hall. The prisoners dashed towards him, "The Congress won?"

"What about the Muslim League? How many seats did they win?" Ahmad snatched the paper from Mohan. He read the headlines out loud, "Nehru's party won most of the seats leaving Jinnah's Muslim League in the dust!"

"*Ma chode* Nehru, motherfucker," Ahmad bellowed.

One of the Hindu prisoners caught Ahmad's shirt below the neck and twisted. "Now dare say one word and I'll strangle. First, you knocked down Mohan and now you are slandering Nehru?"

Within seconds the shouting between the prisoners turned into blows and punches knocking each other down. Bikram's pleas to calm them down got buried under the hollering and name-calling. The loud rumpus came to an end when the jamadars rushed into the room charging them with bamboo poles.

"Get to your cells right now!" Pinta shouted, indiscriminately hitting them. The prisoners ran like cattle towards their cells, Pinta right on their heels showering them with profanities and bamboo hits.

Hakam didn't move from the spot he had been sitting since morning, oblivious of the chaos around him. "Are you deaf? Didn't you hear the order?" Zafar struck Hakam with the bamboo pole. A stream of blood gushed down his forehead. Zafar pulled him by the arm and pushed him towards the door.

The guards ran around in a frenzy locking the prison cells. Guard Duni Chand saw Hakam bleeding and yelled at Zafar, "Why did you hit him?"

"He wouldn't comply with the orders," Zafar yelled back.

"Are you blind? Don't you see he is incapable of..." Duni Chand shouted locking Hakam's cell door. A little later he came with a bandage.

The next morning, handcuffed and feet in fetters, the prisoners lined up in the courtyard. Many had head wounds and black and blue marks on arms and legs due to last night's beatings. Superintendent Mr. Parker flanked by armed guards marched out of his quarters and stopped in front of the prisoners. He addressed them in his raspy deep voice, "You will be locked up in your cells for the next seven days and the daily ration will be cut into half. Anyone heard talking or making any kind of noise will be punished with thirty lashes." His doughy white face turned red from the muggy heat of the afternoon and he lowered his hat to block the sun from his eyes.

"Now herd them back to their damn cells!" he ordered the guards and hurried back to his quarters.

Prisoners started mumbling, "Thirty lashes? Even 15 could unstitch all the seams of your body and bleed you to death!"

"We're already starving and he wants to cut the food into half while the jamadars eat like pigs and get stronger to beat us up!"

The muttering went on until one of the guards yelled, "Shut your smutty mouths up. Get moving."

Walking towards their cells Bikram shouted, "*Soor da bacha,* Parker!"

"Son of a pig, Parker," the prisoners answered loudly. They continued chanting long after they were locked up.

After the end of the lockup week, they were let out into the dining hall. Bikram reached out to Ahmad, "Look, we cannot divide ourselves on the issue of Hindu, Muslim, or Sikh. We're here for the same goal. If we get together, we can force them to close down this hell hole and transport us to the mainland."

"And how are we supposed to do that?" Ahmad asked.

"Hunger strike."

"Have you lost your mind?" Ahmad stared at Bikram.

"No, I have not!" Bikram said, "rather I'm starting to think logically again. The week we spent locked up gave me a new perspective on the situation. If we go on a hunger strike, some of us might die. If we don't, all of us will die a death that will be slower and more painful," Bikram said. "Look, what they've done to him!" He pointed to Hakam. "He may still survive if the strike is successful and we are sent to our home states. We all may survive."

Mohan joined in, "We have our own state governments now. They should have some say into closing down this graveyard!"

"Let's do it!" Ahmad said and walked to a group of prisoners.

The word spread quickly. "So, when do we start?"

"In two days," Bikram's voice deep and determined, he shook hands with all the prisoners.

******

The whole country seemed to have held its breath on that hot summer day when the news spread, 'Another Hunger Strike at Kala Pani!' A frenzy of discussions began. In the cities and in the villages, at the bus and train stations and in the shops and the markets, wherever two or more people gathered, they asked, "Why again? What will happen this time?"

The ones, who could read, read the newspapers to the ones who could not. People, who had not paid much attention to it before, found themselves running to the newspaper stands lest it sold out before they got there.

The village of Gajanpur appeared to have woken up with a jolt. Men gathered under the Banyan tree, discussed and reasoned, and discussed more.

"Why are our boys killing themselves? Don't they know what happened last time? The last hunger strike killed three! Who knows how many will die this time? What about the ones already dying with dysentery and TB and malaria, every day! And the family gets a damn letter that their son died of natural causes. Aren't the tyrannical rulers butchering them, rather methodically, inch by inch starving them, viciously beating and punishing them? Hope Hakam's okay."

"Shh! Baldev is walking this way," Nand Lal said.

Every head turned. The crowd went silent. Baldev turned toward the men. His athletic gait was strong and confident as he walked in long strides. In a sky-blue *kurta pajama* and a maroon turban neatly tied on his head, he looked poised and self-assured. He had a book under his arm and a pencil in the front pocket of his *kurta*.

Baldev folded his hands in respect to the elderly as he approached them. Jang Singh, Hakam's cousin got up and gave him a hug, "What is my nephew up to today!"

"I'm on my way to Master Jiwan Singh to study," Baldev answered.

"But you are already at the top of your class, I hear!"

"Master ji said I should take advance algebra and geometry."

"Don't delay the boy, let him go," one of the elderly men said loudly when other men started talking to him.

As soon as Baldev was out of earshot, Jang said, "He looks just like Hakam. Walks like him too, long strides."

"Mother and son seem to be coping well with this unexpected blow of the hunger strike."

"What choice do they have?"

"Poor boy, I think he's wiping his eyes!" Jang Singh assumed by the movement of Baldev's arm, although he was at quite a distance now.

"Not easy to put up a brave face. Who knows what goes on inside his mind?"

The discussions went on uninterrupted long after Baldev was out of sight.

Part-III
The Departing Soul

Chapter 37

Unaware of the hunger strike chaos all over the country, Lal Singh left the hospital frail and exhausted. Over two months of treatment did not do him any good, his condition worsened instead. A lump in his belly was untreatable, the doctors told him, and they had done everything possible.

The midday sun shot red-hot rays like arrows towards the earth and turned the ground into a sizzling griddle. A gust of sweltering wind hit Lal Singh as he walked out of the hospital building, supported by Kaku, Namo walking right behind them.

A barefooted boy in rags holding a bundle of newspapers dashed towards them, *"Kala Pani Hartal,* Hunger Strike at Kala Pani," he waved the newspaper close to their faces.

"Get lost! Don't you see...?" Kaku yelled.

"No, wait! Buy the paper," Lal said. But as soon he saw him bouncing his shoeless feet on the hot ground unable to stand still, he told him to go into the shade under the nearby tree.

The boy ran towards the shade.

"Take me there, Kaku." Gathering all his strength, Lal walked to the tree. "What's your name?" he asked the boy.

"Mangu." The boy's curious eyes scanned him.

"Where's your father?"

"Home. Sick all the time." The boy scratched the ground with his grime-covered big toe. "Any brother or sisters?"

"Two sisters and a brother. All younger than me!"

"Give him some money," Lal said to Namo.

She took out a velvety pouch from the knapsack she carried. "How much, Sardar ji?" she asked opening the pouch.

Seeing the pouch full of bills the boy's eyeballs almost bulged out of sockets. "So much money!" he whispered.

Lal took four bills from the pouch and handed them to the boy, "Now run straight home and give it to your mother to buy shoes and clothes for all of you."

"My mother is dead. I buy food with newspaper money every day. This will buy us food for many more days." Mangu's eyes lit up. "I don't need shoes and I already have one more shirt at home."

Before Lal could say anything, the boy was running towards the food store.

"Bring the buggy here, Kaku," Namo said taking Lal's arm, supporting him.

"I'll be okay, Namo, you can let go of my arm." He tried to wiggle it out of her hands. "Why don't you get some mangoes for children while Kaku gets the buggy?" Lal Singh pointed to the fruit stand nearby.

"We have a mango tree at home, why buy from here?" Namo held on to Lal's arm.

"It'll take at least another two to three weeks for them to ripen. Kaku keeps me informed about everything, our crops and cattle, our house and horses and the dogs...everything." Lal laughed; a bout of coughing began instead. He crouched holding his chest.

"Oh, Sardar ji, what can I do?" Namo looked around, panicked.

The man at the fruit stand came running with a glass of water, spilling almost half of it on the way. "You okay, Sardar ji? Take a sip of water."

As Lal recovered, a tear left Namo's eye and stopped at the chin before falling on the ground. Lal patted her shoulder and tried a smile. "Can you get us some mangoes and pears?" he turned to the man from the fruit stall.

Kaku brought the buggy close to Lal Singh and helped him into it. "What happened?" He asked looking at Lal's face.

"I'm alright Kaku, let's go home!"

The shopkeeper came back with a big basket full of mangoes and pears. Namo handed him two bills.

"Only one," he said.

"Keep it," she told him getting into the buggy.

Every little bump on the narrow road made Lal Singh recoil with pain. Hot air struck their faces like thorny cactuses. The tar on the surface of the road melted into small black puddles of hot lava. An unbearable smell of tar hung in the air. The sun's anger seemed endless and the buggy inched forward like an unwilling beast.

How will Namo manage without me? And Pali and Pash...what will happen to them? Withered like an autumn leaf Lal Singh held on to the straphanger inside the buggy. Namo supported him on the other side.

How will she cope with it? Thoughts created a storm in his mind. "How long do I...?" he thought out loud.

"What is it, Sardar ji? How long what?" Namo looked at him appearing equally withered and pale.

"Nothing!" Lal Singh closed his eyes.

"Didn't you say something?"

"No!"

Namo took his hand into hers, pressed it against her forehead and then her lips.

Maybe, Hakam would be back by then! Lal Singh rested his head on the back of the seat. A sliver of hope peeped through the darkness of dejection and hopelessness. Suddenly he remembered about the newspaper boy, 'Hunger Strike at Kala Pani.' The words reverberated in his ears. Oh no! Hakam, don't do it...don't do it, Hakam! Lal Singh's lips quivered, his head moving side to side.

The distance to the village seemed to have stretched beyond measure. The road was barely wide enough for one vehicle at a time. The horses suddenly veered off the road and stopped abruptly, jolting Namo and Lal off their seats.

"Watch it, Kaku! Have you lost your mind?" Namo yelled. A big truck whooshed by after causing a near-fatal accident.

"I'm so sorry, Bibi ji. These damn truck drivers..." Kaku tried to bring the buggy back onto the road. His hands trembled holding the rein of the startled horses. "They behave like the road belongs only to them."

"Why didn't you move before the truck was too close?" Namo was not done with Kaku yet. "You almost killed us!"

"Namo be a little easy on him." Lal looked at apparently shaken up Kaku. "Let's stop in the shade for a moment and calm down the horses," he said, gently stroking Namo's shoulder.

The sun had gone down when they reached home.

Chapter 38

Pali woke up several times at night worrying about her father. Why didn't he get better in the hospital? Jeena's mother was very sick but she came back from the same hospital healthy and strong. But *Bapu ji* can't even walk. Now it was daylight and she did not want to get out of the bed. Taking off the sheet from her face she looked around. Sparrows chirping on the neem tree irritated her. She pulled the sheet back over her head.

The day before she had come up with the bellyache and her mother had let her stay home. Pali peeped through the corner of the sheet. The shadow of the *chaubara* over the courtyard announced the time to get ready for school. But how can I stay away from *Bapu ji* the whole day? What if he died while I am at school?

"You'll be late for school, Pali." She heard her mother.

"I don't want to go!" Pali tightened the sheet around her.

"You'll fall behind! Even yesterday you stayed home." Namo held her by the shoulders and lifted her up.

Pali defiantly fell back onto the bed. "I'm not going!" She folded her knees against her chest.

"You get up right this minute, or I'm telling your father."

He's going to take Ma's side, Pali thought. "Can you let me stay home one more day, Ma? Please!" Pali's tone changed from defiant to meek.

"Only, if your father says yes!" Namo said walking to Lal Singh's room. Pali followed and waited outside impatiently.

"Okay, one more day!" Namo told her coming out of the room. "And listen, you are going to stay home and study as many hours as you would have at school."

"Yes, Ma, I will!" Pali said and rushed to her father's bed hugging him tight until Lal Singh almost choked. "You're the best *Bapu ji* in the whole world!"

"My sweet *Shehzadi*...my princess..." Lal caressed her hair.

"Oh, you father and daughter, don't spoil her, Lal ji." Namo faked anger.

Around the midday, a street hawker came to the village selling bangles, toys, needles, threads, scarves, bras, and laces. He came every few months on his rickety bicycle which he could not ride because of loads of merchandise hanging from all sides. He walked his bike village to village announcing his arrival in a bellowing voice, "Red bangles, blue, yellow and green bangles! Come children come. Look what I have brought for you. Come and get your toys."

Women would gather around him and select bangles and bras and haggle for the price. Children whined pulling their mother's clothes for more toys.

Pali heard the hawker. "Oh, the bangle man is here, *Bapu ji!*" She excitedly looked at her father.

"Buy as many as you want, Pali," Lal Singh said with a weak smile.

She hurried out of the room. "Ma, I want new bangles," she hollered. But looking at her mother's sad face her excitement flew away.

"You already have lots of bangles."

"It's okay, Ma, I don't need to buy any more. Please, don't be sad!"

"O, Pali, your father is so sick..." Namo took her into her arms. They sat in the verandah holding each other.

A while later, Pali came back to Lal's room.

"Why's my *Shehzadi* looking sad?" he asked. "Didn't you buy the bangles?"

Pali shook her head. Tears rolled down her cheeks.

"Wipe those tears away and tell me what happened."

"I want you to get well first." She wiped her eyes with the back of her hand.

"Listen, I want you to buy the bangles you wanted today and when you grow up and get married I will buy you gold bracelets studded with diamonds," his voice was weak, breathing shallow.

"But the bangle man is already gone."

"Tell Kaku to go after him and bring him back."

"Really!" Pali ran out the door.

The street hawker came back to their house. Lal Singh said to Namo, "Buy all the bangles and toys from him."

"What?" Namo looked at him.

"Let Pali and Pash keep what they like and distribute the rest to the village children." Soon their courtyard was full of happy children and their mothers.

Pali looked admiringly at all the rainbow colors of glass bangles that tinkled when she moved her arms. She also added a pink comb and a mirror to her special possessions.

Chapter 39

Namo sat by her husband's bed sobbing, "What am I going to do without you? How will I raise the children by myself and manage the farm and the workers and crops…?"

Lal Singh wanted to say something but his voice failed. He wanted to hold her in his arms but had no strength. The love in his eyes spilled through tears. He had adored his wife all his life and had loved his children more than himself. But now he lay helpless, unable to move. Sadness spread over his face like the shadow of death. He could only manage to lightly press her hand as if asking for forgiveness.

The next morning, Namo walked to his bed. "I brought you some warm tea Lali," she said, mixing sugar in the cup.

"Where are you, Namo?" Lal stretched his hand in the air towards Namo's voice.

"I'm here Lal, right here, in front of you!" In horror, she saw the glow from Lal's eyes had vanished leaving a pair of stiffened pupils behind. She sat on his bed and lifted his hand to her face.

"Look, I'm here!" she whispered. She rolled his fingers over her face from forehead to her cheeks, from chin back to her forehead. His fingertips gazed at her face as though they had suddenly developed eyes.

"Have some tea," her voice trembled. She fed him with the spoon little by little. Soft rays from the rising sun filtered through the window creating a shadow on the wall, moving rhythmically side to side as Namo's hand moved from the cup to Lal's mouth and back to the cup. Unaware of the act being played between the rays and her shadow on the wall, she went on feeding her husband and knowing, *this might be the last time*.

"No more," he whispered.

At night Lal Singh went in and out of consciousness. His fingertips also turned stiff and cold. Sitting by his bedside all night, Namo watched him taking shallow breaths. He mumbled something she could not understand. "What is it

Lali?" She placed her ear close to his lips. Unresponsive he slipped back into a deep sleep. She looked at his face by the dim light of the kerosene oil lamp. The flame in the lamp flickered as the oil was running out. *I should have asked Kaku to fill it up last night,* she thought. The spark of life in Lal Singh's body also flickered like an empty wick. *God, please give him back to us. O, merciful God!* Hands folded, she pleaded.

"Merciful?" Her jaw tightened.

"No!" she said gritting her teeth.

"There's no mercy." Her grief turning into anger, she abruptly got up from Lal's bed and slammed her head into the wall. "Either you take me with you or come back from wherever you are! Do you hear me, Lal? Do you hear me?" she yelled.

Eyes turned into salty lakes flooding over her cheeks mixing with a streak of blood flowing from her forehead. She walked back to his bed and lifted his cold arm. A gut-wrenching scream left her lungs.

******

Lal hovered near the ceiling looking at his body lying on the bed. Feeling light like a feather he floated up and down in the room. "No pain!" he shouted. "Look, Namo, I can fly. I'm not hurting anymore. Please, Namo, stop crying!" He glided down to wrap his arms around her but his hands passed through her body like air. He tried going back into his body but it was too painful and he could not get through. Namo got up from the bed and angrily banged her head into the wall. He tried to stop her but it didn't work.

"O, please, Namo, don't hurt yourself. I'm right here with you!" he shouted at the top of his voice. "Why can't you hear me, Namo? Look I'm free of pain." He tried in vain to wipe her tears. He floated around her for a while not knowing how to comfort her.

"I'm coming, Ma!" Lal heard his mother calling. He flew through the brick wall like it was made of fog. That very moment he heard Namo's horrifying scream. He tried to look back but could not. Pulled by a whirlwind of rays of light he swam in the air above the village. He soared over the icy mountains and the green pastures. He fluttered above the thick forests and the dry deserts. Enchanted by the rippling sounds of the waterfalls and the bellowing roars of the ocean, he flew over them again and again. Feeling free and weightless, he whirred through the thundering clouds and passed over the erupting volcanos. Everything looked beautiful and vibrating with life. Enveloped in a cloak of blissful rays of light he hummed and laughed as he effortlessly swam through the cosmic nothingness. Not separated by time and space he felt being everywhere at the same time. He flew over his farm and saw Pali at the irrigation well. "No, Pali, no!" he whooshed by her.

Chapter 40

The news of Sardar Lal Singh's death spread like a forest fire. The whole village gathered at their house. A constant stream of men and women from the neighboring villages poured in.

The outer courtyard of the house was filled with men talking about his untimely passing. "What a tragedy..." They shook their heads in despair.

The women sitting in the inner courtyard wailed and moaned with their faces covered with their *duppatas*. Whenever a new group of women came in, they all stood up in a circle and wept beating their chest and thighs with both hands as was the custom. Then they clung to Namo one after the other and cried. Namo sat like a spectator, unaffected by the shrieks of the wailing women. Her gaze fixed somewhere beyond the walls of the house. Fate had cruelly stared at her and not a tear was left in her arid eyes.

"It's time!" said one of the elderly women. They helped Namo, more or less carried her to Lal Singh's body for the 'last look.' She tightly closed her eyes. This was not Lal and she did not want to see it.

******

"Who's going to show the flame?" someone in the crowd asked as they placed Lal Singh's body on the bier to carry it to the cremation grounds.

"It should be Pash, his son," another man answered.

Sardar Puran Singh, the longtime family friend shook his head. "This will be too hard on him. He is just a child, only seven or eight."

"But that is the custom! The son shows the flame to the cremation pyre." Many voices came at the same time. "No matter how old."

"What about Namo, his wife?" Puran Singh looked at the men.

"Who are we to change the tradition? A woman has never done it before."

"It has to be Pash!" A collective murmur of voices subdued the other viewpoints.

Four men carried the bier on their shoulders. The funeral procession consisting of hundreds of men and lamenting women followed. Puran Singh holding Pash's hand walked behind the bier.

After the body was transferred to the pyre, Puran Singh handed a torch to Pash. "Touch the flame to the wood, Son," he said.

Pash pulled his arm free and ran through the crowd screaming, "No!"

They brought him back and handed him the torch again. "I'll walk with you." Puran Singh held his hand and went around the pyre touching the flame on several places. The dry wood sprinkled with *Ghee,* flared up quickly. The sky filled up with flying embers from the spluttering wood and pushed the men away from the pyre.

******

Pali was lost in the crowd. No one noticed when she slipped out of the house. Confused and angry she ran through the empty streets of the village. Seeing no one out there she ran towards the family farm. Falling, getting up, she kept running and did not notice her bruised knees and elbows. She had gone to the farm countless times with her father. He would carry her on his shoulders when she was little and trotted like a horse that would make her laugh. Later she went on horseback and sometimes on foot.

She stopped by the irrigation well. This is where her father sitting on the *Diwan* under the mulberry tree, used to discuss and assign duties to the workers. The place that had always been filled with loud talking and laughter was silent. The workers had collected at her house, mourning their master's death.

Pali wanted to see her father sitting on the *Diwan*. She wanted to hear the voices that made the place buzzing with life. "Everything is dead now," she murmured. "Why am I alive, when *Bapu ji* is not?" She stepped onto the edge of the well. Looking down she saw her shadow deep in the well shimmering over the water surface. *That's where I should be!* She took a deep breath and closed her eyes.

"Jump!" A voice inside of her shouted and she flew. With a sudden pull from behind, she fell backward hitting her head on the ground. Writhing with blinding pain she held her head in both hands and screamed,

"Baapuu ji. Baapuu…ji…"

No one heard her cries. Realizing she had not fallen in the well she crawled towards the rim again. Screaming she started hitting her arms against the brick edge of the well until the glass bangles that her father swayed her to buy a few days ago, were broken. Blood trickled from several places painting her arms with obscure designs of red over her brownish skin. Exhausted, she lay there until the sun was near the horizon in the west. She looked around and began walking towards home. She saw fire burning in the distance. The air was filled with a peculiar smell of burning flesh. She ran as fast as her injured legs could carry her. A few times she wanted to look towards the blazing pyre but did not dare to.

Kaku met her near the outer gate of the house looking pale, his eyes swollen red. "Where've you been, Pali? We were worried sick!" His wife Fatima walked her to bed. She cleaned her wounds and waited until she fell asleep.

Pali's arms healed after a while. The bruises on her knees and elbows disappeared but a crater of sadness was left in her heart. The year was the summer of 1938 and that was also the end of her childhood.

Chapter 41

The night dissipated slowly wrapping the earth in a shroud of diffused glow that quickly changed into a sweltering summer day. The trees stood still as if in shock from yesterday's events. The stagnant air was filled with a peculiar ashy smell. The birds too seemed to have decided to stay in their nests and not a single crow was heard cawing in its nagging loud pitch. Everyone had left after the funeral except Namo's brother Banta Singh and his wife Jeeto. They stayed overnight.

Namo stood in the doorway as Banta and Jeeto were leaving the next morning. He turned to her saying, "I will take care of you, Namo." Her eyes slipped off his face gazing beyond the arches of the verandah behind him.

"I can even move here to manage your farm."

Banta stepped a little closer. "You know how bad the times are! Nothing is safe these days."

Still numb from her husband's death Namo was unable to think or say anything. A voice inside her screamed No! But she nodded yes.

Jeeto gave her a hug much tighter than usual, "Your brother and I will stay here to help you. Our boys are already grown and they don't need me around much," she said and turned to leave.

Once again Namo nodded without looking at her.

Halfway through the courtyard, Jeeto looked back and hollered, "We will be back in a few days." Banta looked at Namo's grief-stricken face and turned to catch up with Jeeto.

Namo's legs buckled and she sat on the floor watching them disappear behind the gate.

******

Night and the day played the chase game they have been playing forever. Namo felt weak as if she had been sick for months. Grief coiled around her like a serpent and every breath became a struggle. Dark circles appeared under her eyes and her cheeks suddenly pushed inwards. She was exhausted and lay on a cot in the verandah, with a bedsheet stretched from head to toe. Anger and helplessness tormented her. *I was a poor young girl, you gave me all the comforts of life; I was an orphan, you gave me a home; I was downtrodden and you lifted me to the peak of a mountain of respect; I lived in the servant quarters of my master, you sat me on the throne of your heart! And now you have left me to deal with the world on my own! Why, Lali... Why? I cannot do it... I can't, Lali!*

"Ma, Pali wouldn't play with me." Pash pulled the sheet from her face. She came out of a trance-like state and looked at Pash as if trying to recognize him. "Oh, I'm sorry, Pash, what did you say?"

"Nothing, Ma," he said looking at her and walked away.

Namo followed him to the kitchen and found Pali sitting on the floor in a corner. Not having the courage or the strength to look at Pali or say anything, she quietly sat next to her. Pash stood there for a moment and then he put his thumb into his mouth and sat next to them on the floor with his head resting on his mother's arm. He had stopped sucking his thumb many years ago but now eight years old he suddenly started to suck his thumb again. Namo noticed but did not intervene.

Kaku came into the kitchen followed by Fatima and found the three of them sitting in a corner. "Bibi ji, you cannot give up like this. You have to be strong for the sake of children..."

His eyes watered seeing Namo sitting on the floor in total resignation. He had spent most of his life serving them and was more a part of the family. He was devastated by Lal Singh's death too.

Fatima helped her up from the floor and walked her and the children upstairs to her room and came back to the kitchen to make dinner. The children ate a little bit that night, but Namo could not get anything down.

Banta Singh and Jeeto showed up a week later, leaving their two sons seventeen and fifteen behind. Namo had still not recovered from the shock. On one hand, she was appreciative of her brother and on the other their presence gave her an uneasy feeling.

In the past, the only time Banta had come to their house was to ask for money or grain, and every time Lal Singh helped him had given him a piece of advice too, "Banta Singh, do not come knocking on my door asking for help again. You have to work to support yourself and your family."

"Won't you be embarrassed if your brother-in-law was doing some kind of menial work?" Banta would laugh brazenly.

"No, not at all! Now go and don't come back," Lal Singh told him. But a few months later Banta was at their door again.

How are Banta and Jeeto going to help me now? They always came only to get money from us. The thought troubled her, but she could not do anything about it.

Once or twice a month Banta and Jeeto loaded the oxen-pulled cart with grain for their sons and went back to their village. It went on for a while and then Banta decided that the boys should move in with them too because it was very hard on him to go back and forth like this.

Now the whole family was in Rampur, occupying a major part of Lal Singh's big house.

Chapter 42

Namo collected the dry clothes from the line, tied between the pillar of the verandah on one side and a branch of the *neem* tree on the other. She folded the clothes and placed them in separate piles for each member of the family.

"Hey, Namo!" Jeeto hollered.

What was she doing in my room? Namo looked at her coming down the stairs.

"I think it'd be better if your brother takes the upstairs *chaubara* room," Jeeto said. "It will make things easier for him, you know…"

Did she say they wanted to move into my bedroom? Namo stopped folding the clothes.

"What you mean Jeeto? I don't understand," she asked with a baffled nervous look in her eyes.

"What I mean is that your brother can keep an eye on the farmworkers even when he is home. You can see most of the farm from there." Jeeto stood close to Namo, staring at her.

"I'm sure Lal did the same," Jeeto said briskly nodding her head.

They're already occupying most of the downstairs rooms. Now she wants to take over the upstairs chaubara too? "No, Jeeto, Banta should be going to the farm. How can he manage while sitting at home? Also, Sardar ji went around the farm twice a day," Namo said trying to sound firm, stressing the word *Sardar ji*, but inside she trembled like a leaf.

"And what were you doing upstairs in my room?"

Jeeto's eyebrows curled up close together and she glared at Namo, "Listen, your brother cannot walk to the farm, his knees hurt. And what was I doing upstairs? I live in this house too! Why can't I go into that room?" she said bringing her face close to Namo's.

Namo stepped back. The same fuming stare and the same hostile face she had seen as a young girl was in front of her again. Growing up without parents and trying to do all the house chores, Jeeto had slapped her for every little mistake. It was the same face she saw working as a maid at Lal's aunt's house when Jeeto came to take away her earnings. It was the face that had harassed her in her dreams. Namo had plucked this face out of her memory after marrying Sardar Lal Singh. Once again that face was there, so close, and she was shaken to the core.

I am Sardar Lal Singh's wife, Sardarni Nam Kaur. I'm the owner of this place. This is my house! I will not let her trounce over me again! A loud voice stirred her deep inside. Heart thumping in her chest she gathered the courage to confront Jeeto for the first time.

"He's running around with your boys all the time, wrestling and chasing each other and you say he cannot walk? Keeping an eye on the farm from the upstairs room is just a lame excuse." Namo's voice sounded tough but she shook inside.

"You think I'm lying?" Jeeto looked at her with bloodshot eyes. Her hands trembled.

"Don't ask me if you're lying or not. You know the truth." Namo's own loud voice surprised her. "And you listen to me I will not hear about you moving into the *chaubara* again." For the first time, Namo felt strong like a tigress.

"Banta can take the horse to the farm," she added.

"But the horse doesn't let him come near her, and how can he ride her?" Jeeto said, softening a little.

"I will tell Kaku to help him with the horse."

Jeeto mumbled inaudibly and walked away.

The *chaubara* room was like a shrine to Namo. She felt peaceful and safe here. The best moments of her life were spent in this room. Lal Singh had built it a year after they got married. He had hired the best mason and the finest woodcarver he could find in the area. He wanted to build the most magnificent *Chaubara* to match 'Namo's beauty,' as he would say.

The doors and the window shutters were carved with images of lotus flowers and dancing peacocks spaced by intricately designed rectangular wooden sections. The headboard and the wooden legs of the bed also boasted elaborate carvings. The room had tall windows in all its four walls with multicolor silk curtains hanging from the top.

The ceiling was the most spectacular part. It was studded with tiny little mirrors that mimicked twinkling stars in the light of the flickering flame of an oil-burning lamp at night. Lal Singh did not allow kerosene oil lamps in this room. Only an earthen lamp with *ghee*, clarified butter and a cotton wick could be brought in here.

Namo remembered when the *Chaubara* was being built. Lal Singh had told her not to go upstairs because he wanted to give her a surprise. The work went on for many months and finally, it was time to reveal the special gift he had for her.

That evening he blindfolded her with her *dupatta* and held her by the elbow to help her up the stairs while holding the lamp in the other hand. He put the lamp in the corner and the whole ceiling filled up with twinkling stars.

"Okay, Namo, take off the blindfolds," he said to her.

Her mouth opened in amazement by the astonishing sight inside the room. Her heart filled with utter admiration for her husband and she was speechless.

He bowed in front of her with his most inviting smiles and said, "I, Lal Singh, the Sardar of the village Rampur, hereby bring you all the stars of the sky. Open your arms and catch them…" And Namo had laughed and laughed until her eyes watered and her sides started to hurt.

What an irony, Namo thought. That time her sides were hurting with laughter and happiness and now she was hurting all over with grief. Thinking about the conversation she had with Jeeto, she felt like she had been stabbed and her heart bled with sorrow. *I will never give up the 'chaubara' to Banta and Jeeto. No matter what!*

Every fiber of her body suddenly felt tired and she sat down on the cot in the verandah, looking at the courtyard gate. She remembered the days when Lal Singh went out the gate on horseback to go around the farm each morning. She ran upstairs and waved at him from the window. He always looked back at the precise moment, and it was like magic. The magic of love!

Thoughts galloped in her mind, taking her in and out of the past, *I had never stepped inside of a school when I was little, even though I always wanted to. This is the room where you taught me how to read, Lal; this is the place where I learned to write my name; this is where you laughed and corrected me when I made a mistake. This is the place where your love lingers as a lasting gift.*

And Jeeto wants to move in this room? No, Never!

She did not realize how long she had been sitting on the cot and was almost startled by a gentle touch. "Ma, I'm hungry," Pash said, touching her shoulder.

They walked into the kitchen where Fatima was stressed-out cooking dinner for everyone. The teenage boys ate like horses. The food was never enough for them and their mother never thought about helping in the kitchen.

"Fatima, Jeeto will be helping you in the kitchen from now on," she told her, feeling a kind of strength she had not felt before.

"Pali go collect the eggs from the hen house. Be careful. Don't break any," she said.

Pali picked up a basket, "You want to come with me, Pash?"

"No!" Pash made a face at her.

"Why're you so grouchy all the time?" Pali shouldered him on her way out of the kitchen.

"Ma, she hit me," he shouted.

"Pali, don't do that to your brother," Namo said, but Pali was already out of earshot.

Namo buttered a *roti* Fatima had just made and gave it to Pash along with curried chickpeas and yogurt and sat by him while he ate.

Jeeto came into the kitchen. "Only this you've made so far?" she said, picking up all the *roti* from the container.

"Listen, Jeeto, you make the roti, starting tomorrow and Fatima will cook the vegetables," Namo said looking straight at her.

"Huh? What did you say?" Jeeto seemed to be caught off-guard.

"You heard me. Also, tell Banta that Kaku will help him with the horse tomorrow morning."

Every morning Kaku had fed and groomed the horse, while Lal Singh got ready for his round of the farm. They had both taken care of the horse since she was very young, and they had named her 'Bukky' after a legendary horse from the love story of 'Mirza and Sahiban.' They say, Mirza's horse Bukky was so fast that she didn't seem to gallop but flew with the wind. Lal and Kaku's Bukky was also one of a kind.

The next day Kaku fed Bukky as usual and saddled her for Banta. As soon as he tried to mount, Bukky jumped and Banta fell. Kaku tried to calm the horse and massaged her neck and asked him to try again. Bukky raised her front legs up in the air and he tumbled down hitting the ground with a thud.

Banta angrily picked up a thick bamboo truncheon and started beating the horse, cursing, "I'm going to kill you...you bitch of a horse..." and violently kept hitting her with all his strength.

"What the hell are you doing?" Kaku yelled trying to take the bamboo away from him but Banta was an unyielding maniac.

Bukky tried to break away but the rope tied to her foot was too strong. She jumped up and down in terror while Banta beat her like a mad man.

"Stop hitting her!" Kaku hollered, "Sardar ji would never do that to Bukky. Stop! Stop it!"

Banta's deaf ears did not hear and his cruel hands did not stop beating the horse.

Finally, Bukky jerked her body and yanked the wooden pole she was tied to, out of the ground. She ran out of the gate. Rope still attached to her foot; the pole dragged behind her.

"You son-of-a-bitch! Look what you have done!" Kaku had never been so angry.

Banta, already boiling, became even more enraged hearing a servant calling him names. He started beating Kaku with the same bamboo stick.

"You bastard, get out of here right now. I am the Sardar ji now. You listen to me," Banta cursed foaming from his mouth.

Namo and Fatima came running hearing the noise.

"Stop hitting him!" Namo yelled and tried to take the stick away from Banta.

"You stay away, Namo! Is this how the servants behave in this house? I'm going to teach this dog a lesson," he roared.

"Don't you dare touch him, ever again!" Namo yelled back at the top of her voice. Her intervention gave Kaku a chance to run away.

******

Kaku found Bukky near the well at the farm. She gave a mournful whinny as he approached. He combed her mane with his fingers trying to calm her down. Her back and shoulders were swollen where Banta had hit her. She looked at him as if asking, "Why?" Kaku also had black and blue marks on his arms and legs from Banta's wrath. Wrapping his arms around her neck, he cried like a little boy. His eyes flowed like the gutters after a flash storm. It took a while for both to calm down.

It was almost midday when Kaku said, "Let's go home, Bukky. We have to go back, for the sake of Namo Bibi ji and the children. We have to go back for Lal." Kaku patted her.

Since then Kaku's presence irritated Banta like a grain of sand in his eye and he glared at him with clenched fists any time he saw him.

Part-IV
The Homecoming

Chapter 43

A chill hung in the air. Autumn had arrived. The land of Punjab was warm during the day, but as soon as the sun went down, a nippy air crept in. The tepid wind of the day holding water vapors could no longer contain it and unloaded its weight at nightfall. In the morning, dew drops dripped from the trees and roof awnings in perfect harmony, momentarily glistening in the sun before falling onto the ground. People had started sleeping inside, but some who still dared to sleep out in the yard or the rooftops had their quilts soddened with dew. The beddings were left out to dry in the sun during the day to be soaked again the next night.

The autumn wind was calm but the people of Punjab were not. The prisoners at Kala Pani were on hunger strike again. As if a water dam broke its barriers, people rolled into the streets and flooded the gorges and the gullies. The air vibrated with their slogans,

'Kala Pani, Shut it down!'

'Right now…right now!'

The inmates of the mainland prisons also declared hunger strike in support of the Kala Pani prisoners. Schools and shops rarely opened. Offices shut their doors as soon as they heard the cries of demonstrators marching through the streets. More people would join at every corner and the crowds swelled to hundreds. Children, who hardly understood what was going on, holding their parents' hands, would yell at the top of their voices, "Right now…right now!"

Police on horseback would emerge out of nowhere, fitfully beating the crowd with truncheons. Blood dripping from their clothes, people would push through the streets and disperse. Many more would reassemble and march again repeating the process. This had become the norm of the day throughout the country. The village of Gajanpur was no different. Their very own Hakam Singh was at Kala Pani Prison and they wanted him home.

The news stunned everyone. 'The Kala Pani prisoners will be transferred to the mainland! They will be sent to their respective state prisons until their sentences are completed.' People celebrated with equally noisy processions.

"Baldev, wake up! Hurry, Bal!" Harjit pulled the quilt from Baldev's face. Out of breath, she shook him.

"What is it Ma?" Baldev sat up in the bed. "What's going on?" he asked looking at the beaming smile on her face.

"O, Bal, your father is coming home. He is! Really, Bal, he *is* coming home."

Baldev jumped out of the bed. "Really? Is that true?" He lifted her up and spun her around laughing and shouting.

Her legs dangled and her cheeks wet with happy tears, she yelled, "Put me down, Bal, I can't breathe!"

Baldev put her down. "When is he coming?"

"Your uncle Jang Singh stopped by. He said it's all over the news, but he didn't say anything about when." Harjit's lips changed from a smile to a solemn arc. Uncertainty crept in and she suddenly felt tired.

"Let's go to Baba Budh Singh's house and listen to the radio." Baldev pulled her by the arm and ran to the street. Harjit panted and puffed trying to keep up with him. Within minutes they were at Baba ji's house.

"I was about to send for you, Harjit. This is great news." Baba Budh Singh took them both in his arms with such enthusiasm that her doubts melted away. The news repeated itself again and again and her heart echoed *it's true! It's true.* Whosoever heard the news rushed to Baba ji's house to hear it firsthand because this was the only radio in the village. People hugged each other and celebrated till evening.

In the coming days, Harjit was lost in daydreaming. She talked to Hakam in her imagination and smiled. For the first time in years, she hummed while cooking and cleaning. Long forgotten love songs returned. Sweeping the backroom she noticed a layer of dust on the lid of the wooden *sandook.* She stopped. "My wedding dress is in the *sandook.*" She dusted the lid and lifted it up. The color of the silk *kameez, salwar,* and the hand-embroidered, red shawl was still vividly bright. She held the kameez against her body and wrapped the shawl around her shoulders. Thinking about the wedding night, she blushed.

It should be here somewhere. I know it is in the sandook. She frantically took out the rest of the clothes and there it was at the bottom, yellowed, worn-out piece of paper folded twice into a square. She opened it gently,

To my Harjit,
Directionless I wandered
In the dark of my being
Your one sweet glance
A million moons
Brightened the lane
Revealed the path

A lifeless pebble I lay
In the alleys of rock and clay
Your gentle touch
Your radiant smile
Awakened the grace
In the depth of my heart

Your tender embrace
Your soothing voice
My love…

Her eyes welled up. The words on the ragged paper flickered and she could not continue reading but repeated it from memory like it was yesterday. The very first poem Hakam wrote for her. "22 years ago," she whispered. She lifted it to her lips, then pressed it to her chest and sighed softly. Delicately folding the fragile paper, she wrapped it in her silk wedding *dupatta* and placed it back into the *sandook*.

"Hakam!" her lips moved. She sat staring beyond the walls of the house into the vastness of the sky; past the boundaries of the land and the ocean; passing through the ramparts of the Kala Pani Prison, she reached Hakam. His strong arms wrapped around her; she felt his tender kiss. Her head on his chest she heard the sound of his heartbeat while his fingers stroked her hair. Ecstatic bliss and contentment filled her body and soul. She smiled.

The house's shadow had lengthened halfway through the courtyard when she returned from daydreaming. She quickly stuffed the rest of the clothes in the *sandook*. *Baldev will be hungry when he gets back from school.* She hurried towards the kitchen.

******

The nights lengthened; the days shortened but waiting seemed endlessly stretched. The winter snuck in unannounced and bit toes and fingers if not covered. People talking to each other looked like little harmless dragons with their warm breath condensing and fuming in the cold air. The sun lost its warmth, unable to thaw the hardened ground that crunched under their feet.

Everyone at Gajanpur seemed restless. They had not forgotten the day Harjit and Baldev were given the green light to visit Hakam after years of petitioning only to be denied at the last moment.

"Not again!" People wrapped up in homespun cotton blankets talked to each other and shook their heads.

Finally an announcement: a group of the Kala Pani prisoners was sent to Bihar, and another to Calcutta. Once again optimism ran through the streets of Gajanpur. A spark of hope rekindled and Harjit and Baldev waited anxiously for Hakam's return.

Chapter 44

The yellow envelop shook in Harjit's hands. It was always a frightening experience to open a letter with the government stamp on it.

"It's okay, Ma, let me read it." Baldev quickly scanned it. "It says, *Bapu ji* was transferred to Lahore jail two months ago and will be released on Thursday, March 1st. It also says he will be arrested again if he engaged in any activities against the government."

"He's been in Lahore for two months?" Harjit's face flushed. "Monday, Tuesday, Wednes…four days!" she counted. Grabbing the letter from him she pressed it to her chest. "He *is* coming home." Ecstatic tears flowed.

"We will go to Lahore to pick him up." Baldev wrapped his arms around her.

"We will, Bali!" she said placing multiple kisses on his forehead and cheeks.

"Okay, okay, that's enough, Ma. No more kisses and no more tears."

"O, Bal, I'm so happy."

"I am happy too. I'll go tell Baba Budh Singh." Baldev dashed to the door.

"No, wait. We are not telling anyone until he comes home."

"Good, we'll give everyone a surprise, but can I go play with my friends?"

"Sure, we'll give the village a big surprise."

Baldev was out the door before she finished the sentence.

After Baldev left, Harjit opened the *sandook*. Several times she decided which clothes to wear on her way to Lahore and that many times she changed her mind. *He liked light yellow on me. No, it was pink he liked the most. Sure it was my pink dupatta he once wrote a poem about, sitting by the pond. Waterbirds were swimming with their ducklings and the sparrows chirped in the rose bushes. The poem was about, the ripples on the surface of the water and swaying of dupatta in the breeze…*

Lost in thoughts she looked into the mirror. The bygone years peeked through the grays of her temples. The wrinkles around the eyes told a story of forlorn days and desolate nights. *Would he too have changed, like I have?* She rolled her fingers over the wrinkles around her eyes, and felt the furrows on her forehead and sighed.

The day was not over when people started flocking to their house. Excitement filled the air as men and women filled their courtyard congratulating Harjit and promising to come back to see Hakam.

After everyone left, Baldev timidly confessed telling only one friend who did not keep the promise. "I'm sorry, Ma."

"Bal, it's alright. It rather felt good seeing everyone happy for us," Harjit said.

Thursday morning was still studded with fading stars and a glow in the east when Harjit woke up. She wore a printed *kameez* and a rose-colored *salwar* with a matching *dupatta.* Seeing her cheeks unexpectedly rosy in the mirror, she smiled.

"Ready, Bal? Let's go," she called out.

So much had happened since Hakam was exiled. Many springs and summers had gone by. Many babies had been born and a lot of older men and women had passed away, some of the younger ones too.

How am I going to tell him that his dearest friend and brother Lal, was gone at the prime of his life? How is he going to bear the pain of his death? As the bus rumbled along the rutted road, Harjit's thoughts mixed with excitement and worries ran faster than the bus.

Baldev saw her lips moving, "Did you say something, Ma?"

"No, nothing, Bal," she said. The rest of the way they sat quietly.

Waiting at the gate of Lahore jail was torturous. The two guards at the prison gate did not know anything about anyone named Hakam Singh. After hours of not knowing what to do or who to ask, they were tired and hungry.

This is the place where she'd had the last glimpse of him almost nine years ago, when he was whisked away into a waiting police van. Hundreds of people had gathered in his support. The air was filled with bellowing cries of, *Hakam Singh, Zindabad,* while the police tried to keep the crowd in control. Now, it was only the two of them, mother and son.

The prison gate partly opened and a scrawny figure walked out slowly. Her heart throbbing in hope, she looked towards the gate behind the man to see if Hakam would follow. The gate closed.

"Where is *Bapu ji*?" Baldev kicked the ground in disappointment. A layer of dust settled on his shoe.

"He'll be here soon, Bal. Be patient!" Harjit glanced at the man who had stopped midway looking down at the ground. *What is he doing? Seems like he doesn't know what to do.* The man shifted his weight from one leg to the other and kept staring at the ground.

"That is not him! Can't be Hakam! Is it?" Harjit ran towards the man. Baldev followed. "Hakam?" Harjit threw her arms around his bony shoulders.

For a split second Hakam's eyes lit up and his lips seemed to part in a faint smile. But suddenly as if a whirlwind extinguishing a flame, the sparkle from his eyes disappeared. His lower jaw drooped to the left and he was not there anymore. "Hakam…" a shriek came out of her throat. She hollered to Baldev who was staring at Hakam like a statue, "Bal, go, get a Tonga!"

******

The excitement evaporated like water drops on a hot griddle. An eerie silence spread over the village. People talked in hushed voices asking, "What did they do to him?"

"He used to be a spirited person, full of life."

"He's not the same Hakam."

"It's like they took his soul away."

People came to see him sitting in the courtyard, and left without a word. Many did not have the courage to knock on the door.

A collective feeling of loss enveloped the village. People scolded children making noise or laughing loudly. They stopped paying attention to their daily chores.

When the spring arrived dressing up the trees in new clothes, like newlywed brides, the leaves from Harjit's tree of hopes scattered, yellow, lifeless, with each gust of her sighs. When the sparrows filled the air with melodic singing and built their nests in the mulberry tree, Harjit's nest of sanity fell apart.

Hakam seemed to be floating in an endless dark void. She would hold his face in her palms and look into his empty eyes. "Where are you Hakam? Come back to me! Come back to your son." She caressed the scars on his forehead. She massaged his scalp with *ghee*, and fed him with her hands as to a child.

She tried to peek into the darkness hoping for a sliver of light. The more she tried, the more she was sucked into the abyss. Hopes turned into despair and the dream of celebrating his return faded away.

Within a few days, the people of Gajanpur went back to their ordinary lives performing their everyday mundane duties. Perhaps the warm spring sun had wiped the gloom off their faces. Gajanpur returned to normal again, but Harjit and Baldev were far from any feeling of being normal.

Chapter 45

Baldev saw Jang Singh by the door and went into the back room of the house. He had been avoiding people who wanted to talk to him about his father. After Jang left, Baldev went straight to the outer door, "I'll be back soon, Ma," he said without looking at her.

"Wait. Where are you going?" Harjit walked towards him.

"I said I'll be back soon," Baldev shouted. "Are you deaf?"

Harjit froze hearing angry rude words from her son. "Bal!" she gasped.

"What do you want from me, Ma?"

"I... I just want you to talk to your father. That's all," she said.

"You've been talking to him for months. Is it working? Tell me, Ma, is it working?" Baldev's voice staggered, eyes welled up and he ran out the door.

The summer sun was at its full fury. The brick platform under the Banyan tree, always packed with men talking over each other, and where the children played and laughed and argued, was deserted. The enormous tree, with its numerous aerial roots supporting its boughs like sturdy columns, seemed lonely and friendless. Not a single leaf stirred. Not a single bird chirped in its branches.

Baldev sped by the tree as if it were going to ask about his father. His stunted shadow ran in front of him bobbing up and down with each long stride. The hot air smacked his face. Once outside the village, he let out a loud scream. Suddenly he tripped over the edge of a rock protruding from the ground and fell facedown. Covered with a yellowish floury dust he pulled himself up. Blood spurted out of his nose and dripped through his fingers. Excruciating pain did little to stop him from running until he reached the water well in his fields.

Anger and turmoil smoldering in his heart for a long time erupted like a volcano. He kicked and screamed until he caught sight of Sheru, the bullock, he had brought up as his pet. The calf that followed him everywhere at the farm was now an adult bullock. Baldev clung to Sheru's neck and cried.

213

"You hear me, Sheru? Look what has happened! I've lost everything. I've lost everyone." Sheru was completely still. He did not move his ears or tail while the other cattle constantly whipped their tails and shifted their weight around.

"*Bapu ji* is not there anymore and Lal *Chacha ji* died a year ago." Sheru turned his head towards Baldev.

"You're asking about, Ma, Sheru? She's busy with *Bapu ji* day and night and maybe she doesn't even remember if I exist." Baldev loosened his grip from Sheru's neck and looked into his eyes.

"You know, Sheru, I hate when people come to our house and stare at *Bapu ji* like he's some kind of a strange animal. Sometimes I want to grab them by the neck and throw them out of the house. But I just go into the back room until they leave."

Sheru listened like a good friend, breathing slowly and softly. Once in a while, he quivered as if responding to Baldev's anguish, reassuring him that everything will be okay.

Feeling a little better, Baldev washed his hands and face in a puddle of water near the well from the previous night's irrigation of the maize crops. "Let me wash your neck, Sheru." He cupped some water in his hands and washed the dab of blood that had come from his nose.

"You're my best friend!" He patted him and sat reclined against his enormous body under the dense shade of the *Tahli* tree and dozed off.

Pali ran out and closed the gate behind her. "Stop, Pali, wait for me,"
Baldev shouted running after her. He pushed the panel of the gate but it was
too heavy. He pushed it again, nothing happened. "Open the gate, Pali!"

"Just jump over, don't be a wimp." Pali looked at him from the top of the
gate.

"I can't!" Baldev tried to climb but slipped back.

"Try again."

"It's too high and slippery."

Pali pulled him by the arm over the gate and he landed with a thud. "Let's
go!" she said and flew towards the river. Her golden wings gleamed in the
morning sun as she flapped them up and down.

"You can fly?" Baldev ran to keep up, but she was soon out of sight. He
reached the river out of breath but no sign of her. The river was swollen to the

top of the bank. The swiftly flowing current created numerous whirlpools where tree branches and a few animals swirled in a tumultuous cyclone.

"Where are you Pali?" He heard fluttering of the wings and saw Pali hovering over the whirlpool. She dove down like an eagle and picked up a struggling calf from the river and gently dropped it on the dry ground. She flew back to pick up another animal from the river and then another. Baldev looked at her in awe. Mouth and eyes wide open his gaze followed her. A little later she came down. Her wings wrapped around her waist, she stood in front of him like an angel.

"You...you have wings!" Baldev looked at her, wonderstruck.

"You have them too, Bal." A starry glint in her eyes, she softly touched his chest to calm his out of control heartbeat and flew away.

"Pali don't go..." he shouted and ran after her.

Baldev woke up panting. The shadows had lengthened and the *Tahli* shade had moved away exposing him to the setting sun. The other cattle had shifted along the movement of the shade, but Sheru had not moved an inch. "Get up, Sheru, move into the shade, buddy." Baldev jostled him gently. Sheru looked straight into Baldev's eyes as if to say, *Grow up Baldev...you are 16, not a child anymore!*

You're right Sheru, I'm a stupid crybaby. Baldev looked down in embarrassment. *Even Pali knows I'm a useless coward. What's wrong with me?*

"I am a pathetic coward," Baldev mumbled. Then he shouted at the top of his lungs, "Grow up, you fool. Grow up!" his resounding voice echoed through the surrounding fields. "Be a man...a man!" he screamed. A lone feathery cloud that had suddenly appeared in the sky seemed to have its integrity disrupted and quickly dissipated. Exhausted by the shouting and sweating, he sat down. The dream reappeared in front of his eyes. "The wings," he murmured. "Wow! What was that all about? It is *courage*, stupid!" He laughed. "Thank you, Pali."

The wind picked up. Clouds gathered and covered the leftover fiery redness of the setting sun. Thunder and lightning opened up the skies like a million spouts. Arms up in the air, Baldev closed his eyes and let the rainfall on his face. It felt soothing on his achy nose. Soon he was drenched head to toe. The first torrential rain of the monsoon washed away his bitterness like dust from dirty feet. He grinned. Walking home he looked at the village as if for the first time. The houses did not look too shabby. The air felt fresh and the platform around the Banyan tree was washed clean by the storm. The rain had stopped, but the gutters still spurted water into the street. He returned home feeling a new person.

"What happened?"

"The best thing happened, Ma!" he said, "Sorry I've been such an idiot."

Part-V
World War II

Chapter 46

Pali sat by the window, embroidering her *phulkari* shawl. Sunlight filtered through the windowpanes and imparted a golden hue to the red cotton fabric. A small straw basket filled with a rainbow of silk threads lay next to her. Every now and then she looked at the intricate geometric design slowly emerging on the fabric. Stich by stitch a vibrant motif was taking shape. In the end, the whole shawl would be covered with a garden of colors leaving hardly any gaps. She wrapped the half-done shawl around her shoulders. *It will look beautiful over my wedding duppatta.* Her mind's eye saw Baldev smiling at her. She smiled back. Her dreamy eyes closed spontaneously.

Rummaging through the basket she selected another skein of thread, "That's beautiful!" She threaded the needle. Most of the village girls learned to make *phulkaris* when they were ten or twelve but Pali had been busy at school. She remembered how her father wanted her to go to college. But she did not even want to go to school after he died, let alone going away to college. She hated everything and everybody after his death and school was at the top of the list.

She counted the warp and weft threads and kept working the shawl. While a colorful design developed on the fabric, her solemn thoughts weaved a grayish pattern of sadness in her heart. Her father's death and Hakam uncle's prison torture that left him an empty shell of a body, unable to recognize anyone, pained her immensely. Tears flowed. She folded the shawl and put it in the basket, but could not find any bin to stow away the melancholic thoughts besieging her mind. She looked out the window. The buffalos in the courtyard peacefully chewed the silage. Hens and rooster roamed nearby and were shooed by the buffalo tails. The white horse Bukky and the brown one, Lakha were not in the shed. Bukky had not let Banta ride or even come close to her since he had mercilessly beaten her. Lakha 'the brown horse' was good horse but nothing like Bukky. She was named after the legendary love story of Mirza and Sahiban's horse Bukky. As *Bapu ji* said, 'She's one of a kind!' And truly, she was.

Bapu ji too had a love story of his own. He saw Ma at someone's wedding and they say he was smitten at the first sight and starved himself until his parents agreed to his wedding to Ma.

"You were an amazing man, *Bapu ji*! And you loved Ma till the last breath. I hope Baldev is like you. I'm sure, he is!" Pali said under her breath. She felt a ripple of contentment in her heart.

The quiet mid-morning left Pali with her thoughts racing freely, some joyful, some sad, painful. Her mother had gone to the farm and Pash to school, while Jeeto sat under the *neem* tree combing her hair. Pali noticed she was using her mother's comb again, even though a new comb was bought for her.

Why's she obsessed with Ma's things? Do we really need them here? She wanted to go and tell her not to touch her Mother's things again, but she kept looking at her through the window. Why did Ma agree for them to move in with us? Pali felt a bad taste in her mouth. Instead of helping, they had become the problem. One good thing was that Jeeto's sons, Jagir and Joginder did not live with them anymore. They came and went as they pleased and were gone most of the time.

Pali closed the window and went into the courtyard.

"Did you finish your *phulkari*?" Jeeto asked in her usual uncouth loud voice.

"Not yet," Pali said.

"You're too lazy!" Jeeto waved her finger. "You'll never finish at this speed."

"It's none of your business!" Pali shot back.

"What did you say?" Jeeto's glare could have sliced Pali's face in two if she was any closer.

"I said what I said. It is not any of your business, Jeeto!" This was the first time she had dared to fight back. Anger shook Pali inside out.

"Now you're calling me by my name, instead of *Mami ji?* What a little bitch you are!" The cot shook with Jeeto's fat body.

"Your words describe *you*, Jeeto. Not me." Pali walked towards the house ignoring Jeeto's rants and raves.

"Bitches! Both, mother and daughter! If it were up to me, I'd smack their faces to pulp. Banta is a coward, not letting me do anything..." The twister of Jeeto's fury made the birds fly out of the neem tree.

Chapter 47

Baldev darted through the courtyard to the verandah where Harjit folded clothes.

"Guess what, Ma?" He grabbed the towel she was folding.

"What is it, Bal? You look so happy!" Harjit looked at his exuberant smile. "How's college?"

"I'm joining the army."

"What? The army?"

"Yes!" Baldev moved a little closer to her.

"Have you lost your mind?" She stepped back as if her son had turned into a thorny cactus.

"No, I actually found my mind! Do you know how many boys I know are enlisting? All of them!"

"Listen to me, Bal, this is your first year of college and your father just started turning around. And you want to…" Harjit panted like she was running up a hill.

"Haven't we been reading the newspaper? The Japanese have demolished village after village, town after town in Burma, killing everyone, even piercing babies with their bayonets. And they're on their way to India."

"Stop right there, I don't want any explanation." She tried to take the towel back from him.

"Ma, can't you listen for a moment?" He raised the towel above his head where Harjit could not reach. "Hitler is taking over all of Europe and he rounded up the Jews from their homes and transported them to no one knows where," Baldev said in a confident determined voice. "It's been going on for over three years now, almost four."

"And you want to join the army and fight on behalf of the British, whom we have fought all our lives and sacrificed everything?" she glowered.

"Ma, please listen!"

"What more is there to listen? How could you even think about it?" She turned towards the heap of folded clothes.

"You taught me about Guru Gobind Singh and the Sikh history even before I was walking. You taught me who the Saint Soldiers are, Ma. You told me how it is the moral duty of a Sikh to stand up against tyranny and protect the weak." Baldev held Harjit's arm, "Ma, please look at me."

"What about your father, who gave up everything for freedom from the British. Look what they did to him. Starved and beaten in the Kala Pani Prison for years until he completely lost his mind. Would he have let you go if he was...?" She turned to face away from him but Baldev held on to her arm.

"He would, Ma. I'm sure he would. Don't we believe in the hymns that instilled a spirit of being a saint and a soldier at the time of need?"

"It's true but things are different now." Harjit seemed to have been caught off-guard and turned to get her arm free.

"Remember when *Bapu ji* bought me a book about Jassa Singh Ahluwalia, and you used to read it to me? The Sikhs were persecuted for refusing to submit to the Mogul ruler's reign of terror, 'embrace Islam or be killed.' Thousands of Hindus were killed or converted to Islam. It was the Sikhs who resisted and came to help the weak. Their own houses were looted and destroyed and were forced into the jungle. The Sikhs practically lived on horseback those days." Baldev let her arm go and continued.

"That's when Nadir Shah of Persia invaded and unleashed a monstrous killing giant. For many days people of Delhi were massacred and looted. At the end of the murderous rampage, Nadir Shaw was returning with the famous 'peacock throne' that had taken seven years to build." Baldev's eyes sparkled. "His loot included the invaluable diamond *Koh-I-Noor*, the mountain of light and *Darya-I-Noor*, the ocean of light, that the Sikh Maharaja Ranjit Singh brought it back."

Harjit stood motionless, staring.

"While returning to Persia, he took with him hundreds of girls both Hindu and Muslim and young men as slaves including masons and builders and stonecutters. The booty was loaded on elephants, horses, and camels and he entered Punjab assuming his name was frightening enough to churn terror. No one, he thought, will ever dare to attack his army."

"And listen, Ma! That's when Jassa Singh Ahluwalia led the Sikhs out of the jungle to attack Nadir Shah. He was only twenty-one at that time. The Sikhs freed all the Hindu and Muslim girls and men slaves and sent them back to their families." Baldev's neck stiffened as if he was already a proud soldier of the Sikh army.

"He did not discriminate if the slaves were Hindus or Muslims, even though the Sikhs had been massacred by the Muslim rulers. He made sure the girls and men were taken safely to their families. That was the righteous war."

Harjit stomped her foot. Raising her arms above her head she yelled, "That's enough Bal! I will not let you jump into the fire started by someone else. This war has nothing to do with us and we will not be a part of it." A frown wrinkled her face. "Also, I don't need a history lesson from you!"

"But don't you think history might help a little that you seem to have forgotten! Ahmad Shah Abdali of Afghanistan raided India nine times and each time it was the Sikhs who dared to fight his enormous army." Baldev looked at Harjit with a winner's smile.

"Do you know where the Koh-I-Noor diamond is now? Maybe you don't." Harjit glared, "after Maharaja Ranjit Singh's death, the British shattered the Sikh Kingdom. They took his teenage son Dalip Singh to London along with the diamond and all the rich treasury of the Sikh empire. The young Dalip Singh was converted to Christianity and a part of the Koh-I-Noor was studded into the Queen's crown. And you want to give up everything for them?"

"But Ma…"

Harjit turned and walked towards the kitchen, "Not another word from you, Baldev Singh!" A little later pots and pans clanked in the kitchen as if being thrown around.

Baldev's excitement flew away leaving him like a windswept tree. They ate dinner quietly and went to bed earlier than usual. Unable to sleep Baldev got out of the bed and stealthily went out of the house. The full moon imparted a mystifying vividness to the trees and everything around. Walking aimlessly, he heard a nonstop hum of crickets that was unexpectedly harmonious and quite pleasant.

He looked up at the night sky. The irregular spots on the moon, he was told as a child, was the great grandmother sitting on a stool spinning the wheel. *And I actually believed it!* He chuckled. Looking at his blurry shadow in the moonlight he stopped. *My mind is not blurry like my shadow. I know what I need to do. Ma is doing her part and Bapu ji did his.*

"I will do mine." His voice floated over the tree silhouettes and bounced back softly. Taking long strides he walked home.

The morning did not seem any different than any others however the mother and son both felt different than when they had gone to bed. Baldev stood with an unwavering gaze, "I need your blessing, Ma." He bent down to touch her feet. Harjit knew no argument would convince him against enlisting. He was his father's son. Teary-eyed she patted his shoulders. She held his face in her palms feeling his beard, still soft and silky. She tip-toed to kiss his forehead but ended up below his right eye.

She held him by his upper arms and looked into his eyes, "Promise me, you will return home safely. Do you hear me? Do you hear me, Baldev...?" She broke down kissing his arms and hands.

"O, my sweet, little, worrisome Mother..." Baldev held her by the shoulders smiling and singing in his husky voice. His six-foot stature towered over her slender five-foot three physique. "Dear Mother...don't you worry, I will hurry, the enemy to bury..."

Harjit laughed and cried at the same time, "Like father like son! He too did the same comedy show when he wanted to get his way."

"Nothing can harm me when I have a mother like you? No more crying," he wiped her tears.

"How are we going to tell Pali?" Harjit let her arms drop to her sides.

"Bali will be back for Pali," Baldev sang. "O, dear Mother..." he picked her up and gave a swirl, as he always did when happy.

Chapter 48

My dearest Pali,

It's been a few months since I saw you, just before going to college. As always, we went to the river, but this was the first time neither Pash nor any of your friends were with us. It had not rained for a while and the water level in the river was low. The evening sun seemed to have drowned in the river and colored it fiery orange. The vibrant colors rippled rhythmically in the water as it flowed quietly and peacefully. The two of us stood by the bank watching a kind of slow dance of the gentle water waves. Distorted shadows of birds heaved up and down as they flew over the river. A calm cool breeze suggested the end of a burning hot summer.

I turned towards you, and there it was…the reflection of the sun on your face. You glowed like a goddess, the goddess of delicate love, the goddess of immeasurable strength. A split-second touch of our lips, a split-second jolt of electricity, and an everlasting sense of bliss! I remember the moment so well, Pali, it doesn't seem to be in the past but always in the present.

I know you are asking, why I'm leaving the comforts of life to join the army. Ma was taken aback too when I told her and you might as well, but we are the Sikhs of the Khalsa Nation that taught us to defend the weak and fight against injustice and cruelty. And why side with the British now whom we fought year after year for our freedom? It is because the Axis forces of the Japanese Imperial and Hitler of Germany will not be any better if the British lose the war. It is our moral duty to side with the allied forces at the time of crisis. I'm not alone Pali, thousands are joining the army and many are even younger than me.

You know Pali, what makes me laugh? It is Gandhi's statement in his newspaper, the 'Harijan' preaching the British. He says,

"… I hope you do not wish to enter into such an undignified competition with the Nazis. I venture to present you with a nobler and a braver way, worthy

of the bravest soldier. I want you to fight Nazism without arms... I would like you to lay down the arms you have as being useless for saving you or humanity. You will invite Herr Hitler and Signor Mussolini to take what they want of the countries you call your possessions. Let them take possession of your beautiful island, with your many beautiful buildings. You will give all these, but neither your souls nor your minds. If these gentlemen choose to occupy your homes, you will vacate them. If they do not give you free passage out, you will allow yourself, man, woman, and child, to be slaughtered, but you will refuse to owe allegiance to them."

So I am asking Gandhi, isn't that what Hitler is already doing? Slaughtering! To me Pali, it seems like the old man has lost his mind. Well, enough about Gandhi and his nonviolence nonsense! You know most of the time violence breaks out as soon as he leaves, after lecturing about nonviolence. We will do what is right. And the right thing at this time is to join the army against the Imperial of Japan and Hitler.

I might be gone for a while, but I want you to know, no matter how far I go, I will always hear the tinkle of your bangles. No matter how long I am gone, I will always feel the freshness of your breath. Your soft, spontaneous laughter will resonate in my ears to the depth of my heart. It is my promise to you Pali, that, I will be back.

Remember, 'Bali will be back for Pali.' Oh, I just saw you smile!
Yours always,
Baldev

******

"What is it, Ma? You're smiling!" Pali asked as Namo returned from the farm.

"The postman gave me this letter, must be from Gajanpur," Namo said.

"It's from Baldev." Pali eagerly went through the letter. The excitement quickly faded and the letter shook in her hands.

"What is it, Pali? What did he say?"

"Nothing!" Pali replied staring at the letter.

"Tell me what he wrote. Is everything okay?"

"I don't know."

"What don't you know? You just read the letter."

"Everything is fine, Ma."

"Doesn't seem like it. I can't read the letter but I can read the change on your face."

"Leave me alone."

"Listen, if you don't read it to me, I'll ask Pash. He'll be home soon."

"The letter is only for me. Pash is not supposed to read it."

"I know when something's bothering you, Pali." Namo spread her arms towards her.

"Baldev is joining the army." Pali walked into her mother's arms.

"Joining the army? Why? Why now?" Namo's lips quivered.

"Ma, he has promised me he'll come back safe. I believe him."

"Guns and bombs do not know the meaning of promise." Namo trembled, her face ashen with fear.

"He will come back," Pali said not sure if she was trying to comfort herself or her mother.

"I thought he'd become a doctor or a lawyer or some kind of big…and look what he's doing! We have to leave now to stop him."

"I'm not going anywhere. He'd be gone by the time we get to Gajanpur." Pali said. "Ma, Jeeto is coming this way. Don't tell her."

"I won't."

"Is something wrong?" Jeeto asked, switching her gaze between Pali and Namo.

"Nothing is wrong, Jeeto," Namo said. "Listen, Fatima is making *tandoori naan* today. Could you go and help her?"

Jeeto mumbled walking towards the kitchen.

Later that day Pali locked the letter in the *sandook,* and hid the keys in the *chaubara* at its usual place.

Chapter 49

Jeeto had been scheming to gain power over Namo since the day Lal Singh died, but the more she tried, the more Namo became stronger. Anger blazed on Jeeto's face because everything she tried so far had failed. Now Pali too had started telling her off.

Jeeto's thoughts spewed venom. Namo would still be a servant, cleaning other people's shit, if it wasn't for Lal Singh. She bewitched him by her charm and he married her. She became Sardarni Nam Kaur, the owner of half the village and I am still poor. She used to be afraid of me, now she orders me around. Jeeto gnashed her teeth.

She saw Banta coming through the gate and hollered, "Are you listening?"

"You haven't said anything, Jeeto. Have you?" Banta walked towards her.

"You never listen when I talk to you," Jeeto asserted.

"I just came home. Is something wrong, again?"

"Something is always wrong in this house."

"What happened? Tell me." Banta held her arm walking out the gate, so no one would hear them.

"You are not going to do anything even if I tell you," Jeeto sobbed.

"I always did whatever you wanted me to do."

"Look at Namo, she goes around on horseback and people stand with their hands folded showing respect to her. And I stay home. She wears beautiful clothes and I wear rags, she…"

"Wait, what're you saying? You're not wearing rags," Banta squinted. "I just bought you new clothes. The best I found in the shop."

"She used to be afraid of me," Jeeto sniveled, "now she orders me around, do this Jeeto! Do that Jeeto!" She twisted her lips mimicking Namo. "And have you seen the upstairs *chuabara*? It's not less than a queen's room in a palace! And I'm not allowed to even peek into it."

"So, what do you want me to do? This is her house."

"You can do a lot, but you're not doing it," Jeeto glowered.

"I stole so much from her already and she doesn't trust me anymore. Lucky, she has not thrown us out. She trusts Kaku more than me."

"You're a coward!" Jeeto brought her face close to him and whispered through her teeth. "If it were up to me, we could have become the owners of this place by now."

"You listen to me woman, I'm not a coward. And stop grumbling all the time." Banta shouldered her out of his way and went into the house.

"Coward…coward," she called after him.

"What a bitch!" he mumbled.

******

As the days passed Jeeto seemed calm but her inner ferocity knew no bounds. Every time she saw Pash, her chest tightened, how can I squish this little bug? He's the one standing between my sons and the property. If he is gone, all will be ours. She fancied. But Kaku, the son-of-a-bitch has too much power. Namo trusts him more than Banta. He should go first! "Good plan, Jeeto!" She chuckled. "No, Sardarni Jeet Kaur!" she corrected herself.

She slyly followed Pali to the river where she went for a walk almost daily. She followed Pash as he went to play with friends. She would go into the upstairs *chaubara,* when no one was home. She was convinced the keys to the *sandook* were hidden there and the letter that had clearly troubled the mother and daughter must be in the *sandook*. She wanted to know what the letter was about.

One day she found two keys in a cavity in the wall behind a mirror. "Aha! This mother and daughter don't know how clever I am." A wicked smile playing on her face she ran down the stairs to the *sandook* room. She had imagined owning the contents of this magnificent piece of furniture. She had caressed the intricate carvings on the panels of the *sandook* and now she held in her hand the keys to this secret treasure. The top of the *sandook* almost touched the ceiling. She dragged the three-step ladder and opened the front panels. The left side of the *sandook* was filled with velvet quilts, sheets, and pillows. There were stacks of silk and cotton fabrics.

She twisted a handle on the right and it opened up a chamber divided into an upper and a lower half with a trapdoor. In the upper chamber, there were numerous small lockers. "The jewelry must in these cubbyholes!" She tried the key to each locker, but it did not fit. She lifted the trapdoor from the lower chamber and was astounded by the sight. It was filled with silver bowls and tumblers and a stack of silver plates shining in the dim light of the room. Her heart stomping her chest she quickly removed two of each, plates, bowls, and tumblers. Delirious with joy she ran to her room and hid the silver under the bed.

She decided to try the smaller key one more time hoping to find jewelry. With a soft click, one of the lockers opened. It was mostly filled with bangles, some lace and ribbons, a picture of Baldev, smiling and the letter lay nearby. "Aha!" she picked up the letter. "I will ask Joginder to read it." she laughed. "Hope you never come back," she said scratching Baldev's picture with her nails and left it in the locker.

She went upstairs to return the keys. Her meaty legs wanted to give in at every step and she panted like a dog in summer. There must be more keys to the other lockers hidden here. She couldn't help thinking. Maybe some other day, she decided and placed the keys behind the mirror. She had barely made it downstairs when Pali walked in.

"You okay?" Pali asked. "You seem out of breath."

"Don't talk to me," Jeeto yelled walking to the hand pump.

"What's wrong with you?" Pali shook her head walking away.

Jeeto splashed cold water on her face at the hand pump mumbling profanities at Namo and Pali, "The bitches will soon know what I am capable of."

******

Jeeto anxiously waited for her son Joginder who did not show up for a while.

"Come with me, Jogu, I have to show you something." Jeeto held his arm walking out the gate as soon as he came into the house.

"Where're you going?" Jogu asked.

"Read this." she handed him the letter as they reached behind the courtyard wall.

"What is it, Ma?" he looked at the letter.

"Just read it."

He read the letter and smiled, "Baldev is gone, maybe forever."

"What you mean gone forever?" Jeeto's eyes sparkled.

"He's gone to war, been gone for a while." Joginder's perpetual smirk widened, "not many come back! Do they?"

"Great!" she hugged Joginder. "It's the best news. You can become the Sardar of this place."

"Let me keep the letter."

"What will you do with it?"

"You'll know." Joginder snapped his fingers.

Jeeto grinned inside out. "You're so clever, like me!"

Chapter 50

Dark clouds of war had enveloped the skies of the world. The thunder of bombs raining down, the rumble of fighter planes, and a frozen silence of the dead gave a ghastly feeling of mankind gone mad. The belly of the earth was strewn with deadly mines that would explode with the slightest touch, tearing apart the human body.

That's when Baldev left everything behind and plunged into the inferno of war. Young Sikh men from Punjab joined the army in hundreds of thousands. The Sikh soldiers had been in the fore front battling the aggressors throughout history. Again, the Sikhs made up a disproportionate number in the British Indian army. They saw this war as a *Dharamyudh* – the war of righteousness.

The train packed with hastily trained young soldiers headed towards Burma. A constant deafening sound of the engine, chhak chhak chhe…chhak chhak chhe, and an occasional bellowing whistle made the train sound like an enormous creature running for its life. Every burst of dark smoke spurting out of the beast seemed to be its last breath. The wooden seats in the third-class compartment of the train jerked and jolted side to side with every curve of the track. With hardly any room to move around, the soldiers sat with their shoulders pressing against each other. Small bundles of their belongings lay between their feet. They sang songs of gallantry and heroism and told jokes and laughed.

Baldev sat across from Captain Sundar Singh. Soldiers Jagtar and Kewal sat on his left and right side. Jagtar clapped to attract the soldier's attention, "Kewal, the comedian, will now entertain you with his slapstick jokes," he announced.

"Not now Jag," Kewal said.

Jagtar and Kewal were from the same village, had gone to the same school, and had played hockey and *Kabbadi* together. They joined the army the same day and now were on their way to war together.

"Come on, Kewal, I know you're itching to unload at least some of them," Jagtar insisted.

"You used to tell jokes to the trees when no one wanted to hear them."

The soldiers laughed.

"See, you don't need my jokes to laugh. Everyone is already laughing," Kewal said.

"Kewal... Kewal... Kewal..." the crowd chanted.

"Okay, just one!" Kewal shouted over the chanting.

"A man working away from home writes a letter to his wife." Kewal looked around the compartment. The soldiers nodded.

"My darling wifey," he writes. "I did not get paid this month. So instead of money, I'm sending one hundred kisses"

The soldiers giggled.

A few days later he received a letter from his wife. He opened it as quickly as his fingers allowed.

"My darling hubby," she wrote, "received your letter containing one hundred kisses instead of money. Here's how I used them,

I gave 17 kisses to the vegetable hawker.

Bitu's school fee was due. So I had to give 20 kisses to the school principal. The milkman was not satisfied with six. That bastard wanted ten more.

And let me tell you about the landlord. That son of a bitch wanted *huggies* along with all the 47 kisses, I had saved. Otherwise, he said, he'll double the rent..."

Boisterous laughter broke out. Many puckered their lips as if kissing.

"Where've you been hiding all this time Kewal?" Captain Sunder Singh said laughing.

******

The Japanese had driven the colonial armies out of Hong Kong, and Singapore which was regarded as Britain's invincible fortress. The British General Arthur Percival had surrendered and thousands of British and Indian Sikh and Gurkha soldiers became prisoners of war. Most of them were massacred by the Japanese. They were machinegunned and then dead or alive, doused in petrol and set on fire. The war had warped human life to the lowest of its dignity.

The Japanese army was unstoppable. It had quickly advanced into Burma. The remnants of the beat-up British Indian army under General William Slim had retreated to Imphal, India after losing most of its troops and transport. The surviving soldiers with oozing wounds, afflicted with malaria and dysentery reached Imphal in a pitiable condition.

At the same time, the American General Joseph Stilwell, nicknamed 'Vinegar Joe' due to his harsh personality and toughness, also walked 29 days with his troops through dense jungles and strong current streams, finally escaped to Imphal too.

By May of 1942, the Japanese occupied Burma completely and made the prisoners, as well as civilians, dig their own graves before gunning them down.

The conquest of Burma unleashed a mass exodus of civilians towards India. Thousands starved and perished on the way and thousands more succumbed to the disease. The allied morale was at its lowest ebb having lost to the Japanese Imperial.

This is the time when the train carrying Baldev and fellow soldiers was speeding towards Burma. On the way, Captain Sundar Singh told his troops stories of Sikh bravery. And there was no shortage of valor and gallantry in the realm of Sikhism.

"A Sikh never bows down his head, nor does he make compromises when in pain," Sundar Singh told them.

Baldev listened with eyes wide open and lips in a barely noticeable smile. Sundar Singh reminded him of Baba Budh Singh back home, the captain though was much younger.

While the Indian soldiers traveled in the third-class compartments, the British soldiers traveled in the compartments with sleeping berths and padded cushiony seats. They were served hot meals and cold drinks.

"Why the hell are we fighting for those who treat us like animals?" Kewal blurted out, while eating cold *roti* and *dal*. The compartment went dead silent. A hundred and fifty pairs of eyes darted towards his face.

"You're right, Kewal, why the hell are we fighting? Let me explain it to all of you." Captain Sundar Singh stood up, "We're not fighting for one person or one race or even one country. We are fighting for the truth. We are fighting for the righteous." The captain looked around the compartment. "At the moment, the British are the righteous, not the Imperial army of Japan or Hitler of Germany."

"Bole So Nihaal!" Baldev shouted the Sikh slogan.

"Sat Sri Akaal!" the soldiers answered, which means, 'Hail the True and the Timeless One.'

Baldev led the lyrics of the Sikh anthem written by the tenth Guru. The soldiers joined in.

Deh Shiva Barr Mohe Eehe, Grant me this boon, O God.

Shubh Karman te Kabh Hun Na Taron, May I never refrain from righteous deeds. *Na Daron Ar Saun Jab Jai Laron,* I fight without fear all foes in life's battles. *Nische Kar Apni Jeet Karon,* With determination I claim the victory.

Singing and waving their arms the soldiers were ready to fight and win. Baldev's voice heavy with determination bellowed the last verse of the anthem with even more intensity and passion.

"Jab Aav Ki Audh Nidhan Banai, (When this mortal life comes to end),

At Hee Ranh Mai Tab Jhujh Maroun, (May I die fighting with limitless courage).

While the train echoed the last line of the anthem, 'may I die fighting...' Baldev's inner voice revolted. I will *not die* fighting with limitless courage. I will *live* fighting with limitless courage! Baldev repeated to himself again and again.

Then he shouted, "We will *live* fighting with limitless courage. We will be victorious. We will not let the Japs get away..."

"We'll get each and every one of them..." Kewal cried as he rose from his seat.

They all stood up, tall, and proud. They shook hands and hugged each other. They talked loud and laughed wholeheartedly. They talked about their families and about the villages they came from. In an instant, they were like brothers, born to the same mother. Wearing the same kind of turbans and military uniforms they could be mistaken for a big brood of twins. Their voices rumbled as if in competition with the rumble of the engine. They all seemed to have made their tryst with destiny, heading to the same meeting place. They were the warrior brothers, the martial race of Guru Gobind Singh, who had sacrificed all, including his four sons fighting against the mighty armies of the brutal Moghul emperor, Aurangzeb, who wanted to convert the Hindu and Sikhs to Islam.

The sun had long gone down. The train ran through the dark, relentlessly hissing and jolting as if it were about to go off the track. After a while, it stopped at a station. The captain hurriedly got off.

To everyone's delight, several wicker baskets full of bananas and pears were loaded into the compartment. Next, even a bigger surprise came with *poorian* 'fried bread' and *sholai,* chickpeas cooked in tons of spices, green peppers, tomatoes, and onions until soft and mushy, raw onions and green chilies on the side. The compartment filled up with the aroma of freshly fried *poorian* and mango pickle. The captain came into the compartment smiling, "I've been trying it at every stop," he announced. Within minutes the train was on its way running and hissing.

"We have a big day tomorrow. I want you all to get a good night's sleep." He rested his head on the back of the seat and closed his eyes.

The compartment went silent for a few moments and then someone shouted, "Hey, Kewal, only a hundred kisses?"

A wave of chuckles arose that ended up in a chant, "One hundred kisses...one hundred kisses!"

"Quiet soldiers!" the captain yelled.

A pin-drop silence ensued.

Chapter 51

Pali saw Shindo walking through the half-open gate and ran to her. "When did you come back?" Excited to see her unexpectedly, she gave her a squeezing hug.

"A little while ago." Shindo held Pali tight in her arms. "I had to see my friend, before anything else. How are you?"

"I'm fine, and you?" Pali walked her towards the house, but seeing Jeeto in the verandah, staring at them, she changed her mind.

"Let's go. We'll sit by the river and talk." Pali held Shindo's arm and hurried towards the gate.

"Hey, where are you girls going?" Jeeto hollered.

"Don't look back," Pali said.

"Why not?" Shindo looked back over her shoulder. "Who is she?"

"I will tell you later. Let's get out of here first."

They sat by the riverbank looking down at the lazily flowing water. The wind was warm but not hot. The friends had not seen each other for over a year and a half. They had so much to talk about.

"Are you happy at your in-laws' house? Do they treat you well? How's your husband?" Pali asked in one breath looking at Shindo's healthy brownish cheeks.

"I am happy." Shindo intently looked at Pali. "Is something wrong? You look kind of pale, Pali."

"How's your husband?" Pali asked ignoring the question.

"He's good."

"Good? Just good? Not the best, a woman could have? Or the most wonderful man on the earth, or superb, etc.!" Pali laughed elbowing Shindo.

"Okay, He's great! He's the best! But I wish his sister was a little friendlier," Shindo said looking at the far side of the river, where the bank was almost at the water level.

"What's wrong with her?"

"A little jealous of me, I guess."

"Find a man and get her married off. It's the best way to get rid of her!" Pali chuckled.

"Good idea! Now tell me how's your Baldev doing? I mean the one totally smitten by you."

"He's gone to war," Pali sighed.

"What, gone to war? Why?"

"I wish I could tell you why," Pali said. "But he is coming back and I know it in my heart."

"It's war, Pali…"

Pali put her fingers on Shindo's lips before she could say anything more. "He *is* going to come back! No more discussion."

"I pray for his safe return."

"He *will* come back safe!" Pali said.

They sat facing the river with their legs dangling from the sandy bank.

"Remember we used to play on the dry riverbed when it had not rained for a while," Pali said. "We all used to slide down the bank one after the other. It was the best playground ever!" Pali's unblinking dreamy eyes drifted her into the past.

"I remember when you told us that you were going to marry Baldev when you grew up. We were all sitting on the sand watching him play cricket with the boys." Shindo laughed. "Jeena and Raji were with us too. I can still see you cupping your hands around your mouth and whispering the big secret." Shindo enacted the scene with her hands and winked.

"How can I forget?" Pali's laugh quickly changed into a sigh. "*Bapu ji* was still alive and Baldev's father had not been exiled to Kala Pani. They always talked about our wedding. Everything has changed now."

Shindo nodded, "But your love for Baldev is the same, and that's what matters the most."

"My love for Baldev has also changed," Pali said looking towards the treetops by the river.

"What are you saying Pali? I thought you…"

"It is stronger than ever!" Pali laughed looking at Shindo's startled face. "My love for Baldev keeps growing. I feel his presence day and night."

"Your Majnun will come back soon. In the meanwhile Layla, you take care of yourself." Shindo teasingly called her Layla and Baldev, Majnun, from a famous love story.

"Hey Shindo, come home," her younger sister called.

"Who was that woman at your house?" Shindo asked before leaving.

"I will tell you later. It's a long story."

"You want to stay a little longer, *Layla*, thinking about your *Majnun*?"

"Actually I do. It's so calm here. I could listen to the river for hours and not get tired."

"Don't get too absorbed in Majnun's thoughts." Shindo waved, leaving.

Pali looked at the low flowing water. Ripples on the water surface looked like heartbeats of the river. She felt her own heart beating with the rhythm of the rise and fall of the gentle waves. Does the river get lonely too? I believe it does. It has its own emotions. Sometimes it is swollen to the top and angry, engulfing everything in its way and sometimes calm and soothing, just like today.

She felt Baldev sitting next to her as they had sat facing the river, many times. Would you have gone to war if we were already married? She turned her head to the right as if Baldev was there for real. I know, you would have, because you are so true to your convictions. The answer came effortlessly. She wrapped her arms around her legs and rested her head on her knees.

Where they might have sent him? The whole world is like an inferno! Fearful thoughts clamored in her head. She felt the strength sucked out of her body. Would they train him to use a gun? Is he going to kill people? No, enemy soldiers! But the enemy soldiers too have their mothers and sisters and…and their own Pali, waiting for them. She felt a vacuum in her heart getting bigger with each breath. "Am I ever going to see you again, Bal?" she sobbed. "How will I live without you?"

'Have faith Pali!' She lifted her head from her knees and looked up. Did someone say that? But no one was around. Where did the voice come from? She stood up and looked back towards the village. Seeing no one, Pali smiled. Did Baldev just talked to me? Is it him telling me to have faith? She looked toward the sky, or could it be God telling me that nothing bad will happen to him? It felt like a beam of light came down and lifted the overcast of gloom from her heart. She turned towards the river again to take another look at the

water before heading home but decided to stay a few more minutes to savor the ecstatic moments the 'voice' had brought to her.

She closed her eyes. The time seemed to have jumped backward when she was a little girl, maybe four years old. Her arms open she ran towards Baldev who had just entered the gate followed by his Ma and *Bapu ji*. "Paleee!" The six years old Baldev ran across the courtyard like a bullet and took her in his arms. He tried to pick her up. "You're too big, Pali," he said and led her by the hand towards the house.

O, how I remember it like yesterday. Pali sighed. Our families used to visit each other so often, but things changed. Our mothers are so weighed down by the tragedies of life that they hardly think of anything other than dealing with the new problem with each new day.

"Hey Pali, what're you doing here? Sleeping?"

Pali opened her eyes. Joginder stood in front of her, arms crossed against his chest, legs two feet apart, and a sly smile on his face.

Startled, she stood up. "Oh, I was just resting," Pali said.

"Don't you have a place at home to rest? Or it's something else." Joginder's eyes fixed on Pali's face.

"I told you I was just sitting here. And what does it have to do with you anyway, Jogu." Pali turned to go home.

"Whoa...whoa, Pali, don't be so angry!" Jogu walked in front of her, blocking her way.

"Get out of my way!" she yelled.

"He's not coming back, Pali." Jogu's wicked smirk stretched to his ears.

"What are you talking about?" Taken aback Pali's brows wrinkled and she glowered at him.

"You know who I'm talking about. War is bad!" Jogu revealed a corner of Baldev's letter from his pocket.

"Where did you get that?" Pali's face turned ashen. "You have no right to any of my things." She extended her hand to get the letter from him.

"Finders keepers!" He pushed the letter back down into his pocket. "By the way, if he came back, with only one eye or half a leg or one arm blown away, what would you do? So sad!" Jogu said with a lusty stare, "you're so beautiful."

"Have you no shame, Jogu? You're my cousin!" She nervously twirled the corner of her *dupatta* around her index finger. Holding back tears she felt a knot building up in her throat.

"Cousins! So what? The Muslims marry their cousins all the time," he said taking a step towards her.

"Get out of my way right now! Or I will gouge your eyes out," sweet Pali suddenly roared like a lioness and waved her long-nailed paw close to Jogu's face.

"Angry bitch…" Shocked by Pali's response he stepped back. His smirk turned into a wicked frown.

"Angry tigress, you fool! And I will tear you apart," Pali snarled. "Is this how you pay for our generosity? Giving you a place to live and food to eat, and…and clothes to wear…ungrateful vipers."

"I know what you and Baldev did. He wrote it in this letter."

Jogu stammered sheepishly, "I will tell people."

"Go ahead. Climb a tree or go up on the roof and shout whatever you want, you hideous bastard! The village belongs to us, not you." The volcano of Pali's rage had erupted and could have charred his face if he had not stepped back. She turned and headed home. Taking quick steps and heart-pounding her chest she looked back, "You've made the biggest mistake of your life, Jogu," she shouted.

How did he get the letter? I'm sure I had locked it in the *sandook*. How dare he bully me like that? Her thoughts ran faster than her feet. As she entered the courtyard, she saw Jeeto leaving the house.

"Where've you been all this time, Palo?" Jeeto's smirk and a piercing stare infuriated Pali even more.

"Shut up Jeeto!" Pali ran into the house and went straight to the *chaubara*.

"What a bitch," Jeeto mumbled and went out of the house.

Pali found the keys to the *sandook* where they should have been, behind the mirror. *It must be Jeeto's doing,* she thought, stealing the letter and putting the keys back. "What if she stole all of Ma's jewelry?" Pali frantically retrieved the keys to the jewelry lockers from the tiny chambers carved into the wooden legs of the bed and ran downstairs to the *sandook* room. Panting, she opened the lockers one after the other and found all the jewelry in place. Nothing seemed to be missing. She heaved a sigh of relief.

Next, she opened her own locker. She found Baldev's picture crumpled up and held it against her heart. "Why Jeeto? Why did you destroy his picture?"

Although nothing seemed missing from the jewelry lockers, other than the letter, an uneasy feeling hovered over her mind. *I should tell Ma. Well, maybe, not yet.* She decided.

Jeeto was still out, who knows where. Pali went into her room. All the windows were close and a musty smell launched an attack on her nostrils. She stood by the door for a few moments to adjust her eyes to the dark and her nose to the mildewy smell. "This room used to be one of the best in our house after the *chaubara*, and now it is…"

Nothing seemed unusual other than some of Namo's clothes lying on her bed. Pali left the room still suspicious. "Wait, under the bed!" she murmured and went back into Jeeto's room. "Evil bitch!" Pali yelled, as she saw the sack with the silver plates, bowls and tumblers. She pushed the sack back under the bed and came out angry and bitter.

Pali anxiously waited for Namo. Every minute felt longer than an hour and extremely tiring. She went to the upstairs *chaubara* where she could see the irrigation well and beyond through the window, but no sign of Bukky or Namo. Frustrated she came downstairs and walked towards Shindo's house but soon realized that her whole family worked at the farm these days due to the harvest season. So Shindo won't be home either. She turned back home and saw Jeeto sitting in the verandah, adding to her anger. *When will all this be over?* She mumbled and went back upstairs, sobbing herself to sleep.

Chapter 52

Since the time Namo became suspicious about Banta stealing from the farm, she had taken things into her own hands and Kaku was a big help. In the beginning, people talked behind her back. Some made fun of her and some even scowled when she first held Bukky's reins and went around the farm looking over the crops and the irrigation and talked to the workers. Ignoring the rebuffing looks, she undauntedly managed it all and the crops were getting healthier and more profitable each year. Her generosity and appreciation for hard work had won the hearts of the workers and their families. "She has an even bigger heart than Lal Singh himself!" people said about her. "And she knows what to do." They greeted her with folded hands and admiring looks, as she approached them.

Namo came home in the evening and found Pali sleeping in the *chaubara*. She gently touched her shoulder, "You okay, Pali? You went to bed without eating anything." Pali opened her eyes and clung to Namo, "I've been waiting for you all day long."

"Is something wrong?" Namo looked into her swollen eyes.

"A lot is wrong, Ma! Everything's gone wrong." Pali broke into tears.

"Tell me what's going on." Namo sat on her bed and took Pali into her arms.

As Pali told her everything Namo's face constricted into angry furrows. Jogu's offensive behavior, the letter, Baldev's crunched up picture and the silver plates and tumblers that were still lying in Jeeto's room under the bed, was too much to bear.

"We'll take care of everything in the morning. Now let's go into the kitchen and eat something." Namo kissed her hair.

"I'm not hungry, Ma," she started crying again, "they wouldn't have dared if *Bapu ji* was alive."

"I miss him too, Pali. But I assure you that they'll have to pay for what they've done." Namo wiped Pali's tears and her own. "Let's go and eat. I haven't eaten all day either." Namo put her arms under Pali's shoulders and tried to pick her up. Unsuccessfully, though.

"I'm getting up, Ma. Seems like you forgot, I'm taller than you now." A little laugh escaped Pali's sad lips.

As they stepped out of the room, they noticed Jeeto running down the stairs.

"How long have you been spying on us, Jeeto?" Pali shouted after her. Jeeto didn't stop and went to her room.

"Listen, Jeeto, we'll talk about it in the morning. Obviously, Pali is very upset at what Jogu did," Namo said patiently walking to Jeeto's room.

"She's the one, throwing herself at him, not Joginder!" Jeeto shouted.

"Stop this nonsense! I don't want to hear anything from you right now. I told you we'll talk in the morning," Namo shouted. "Pali's not lying."

"And you say I am a liar?" Jeeto stood in the doorway blocking it with her ample physique.

"Yes, you are!" Pali answered instead of Namo.

******

Namo woke up to a loud furor of yelling and swearing. She looked down the window. To her horror, Banta was whipping Kaku with a lash used for the oxen.

"What did I do? Why're you beating me?" Doubling down in pain Kaku tried to run away.

"What did you do? I tell you what you did!" Banta ran after him raining down another batch of quick floggings. "That's what you get for stealing the silver and planting it into our room."

"Stop it, I didn't steal anything," Kaku begged running around the courtyard. "You can ask Namo Bibi ji. I never stole anything in my life."

"Do not bring her name on your dirty lips. How dare you try to sleep with her? I will kill you today, here and right now." Banta foamed baring his teeth like a ferocious beast.

Kaku fell on the ground exhausted, "I respect her more than my own mother and sister...how could I? Sardar ji, please..." he cried like a little boy.

"Jeeto saw you with her own eyes, you lowlife servant!" Banta looked at Jeeto standing in the doorway of her room. "And then you steal and put the blame on her to hide your own sins!"

"I… I spent my whole life serving this family… I could never…" Kaku had given up the struggle and lay on the ground whimpering while Banta blindly kicked him in the face.

"Stop!" Namo ran down the stairs and stood between the two. "I'm ashamed to call you my brother, you evil horrendous man, Bantu!" she bellowed. "Get out of my house right now. And take your wicked wife with you." She snatched the lash from him.

Eyes almost bulging out of the sockets, Banta stepped back. "I'm on your side Namo. This man, this filthy servant is trying to take advantage of all of us."

"I told you get out of my house and never show your face again, either of you," Namo shouted looking at Jeeto.

Like lightning, Jeeto ran and jumped on Namo knocking her down. "You are the one who'd be leaving, not us!" Jeeto punched Namo in the head.

"What're you doing Jeeto, stop it," Banta shouted, while Kaku bleeding from his nose and mouth got up from the ground and tried to pull Jeeto's blubbery body off of Namo.

Jeeto scuffled to free herself from Kaku's grip cursing and shouting at Banta, "You're taking her side? You gutless eunuch, have you ever done anything right?" She squirmed out of Kaku's hold and tried knocking Namo down again. "You can't even handle this puny little cat of a woman and you call yourself a man?"

"Get away from my mother, you filthy bitch!" Pointing a gun at Jeeto, Pali stood in the stairs. Boiling with anger, her face cherry-red and eyes bloodshot, she didn't look any less than the ferocious Hindu warrior goddess *Chandi,* who tears apart the evildoers, and who rides a lion and fights with eight arms. And Pali appeared to have transformed into just that, the warrior goddess *Chandi.*

The time seemed to have stopped. Everyone froze wherever they were. All eyes fixed on Pali.

"Pick up your stuff and get lost, both of you, before I kill this wicked woman." She furiously looked at Jeeto and Banta. Jeeto trembled. Her bulky body shook like a mild earthquake was happening under her feet.

"And tell Jogu, that I will blow his brains out if he comes near our village, let alone our house." Pali roared.

Banta took the stunned Jeeto by the arm and walked, partly dragging her towards their room.

"O, my God, Pali…" Namo ran to her. Gently taking the gun out of her shaking hands she helped her upstairs into the *Chaubara*.

A ferocious-looking warrior a minute ago now shook like a tiny delicate branch in a windstorm. Her lips quivered. Her eyes dry as a pebble in the desert and her face pallid as if painted with turmeric powder.

"It's okay, Pali! It is alright…" Namo helped her to the bed and held her tight.

"No, Ma, it is not." Pali sobbed without tears.

"Shhh…calm down, Pali. Take a deep breath." Namo kissed her forehead.

"I was going to kill her," Pali hid her face in Namo's chest.

"Listen, you did not kill anyone." Namo held her close

"Even the thought of a gun troubled me, and today I really wanted to kill her for what she did to you to me and to poor Kaku," Pali said nervously shaking her head,

"You saved me, Pali. You saved Kaku. Who knows what she'd have done!"

"If only *Bapu ji* was alive," Pali whimpered. Her dry eyes turning into a monsoon shower overflowed to her cheeks down to the neck.

"Let me tell you something. Your father was a gentle soul. He'd never hurt anyone. But do you know why he bought this gun?" Namo said wiping Pali's cheeks.

"Two brothers Pinta and Babbu lived in the nearby village. They bullied and terrorized the whole area and did the most horrible things to people. No one felt safe because of them."

Namo did not want to tell her the details about how they abducted young women and how they had killed their own sister.

"And one day they threatened your father too."

"They threatened *Bapu ji*? Why? Where are they now?"

"Don't worry Pali. They are not here anymore, and neither are their parents, who were good people though." Namo took a long deep breath.

"Your father believed in the spirit of a saint soldier, the spirit that was infused by Guru Gobind Singh into the Sikh consciousness. He taught us to be kind as well as fearless and ready to protect ourselves and the ones who are defenseless."

Pali nodded, "I know Ma. I know about the *Zafarnama,* the letter Guru Gobind Singh wrote to the Mughal Emperor, Aurangzeb, who had ordered the killing or converting the Hindus and the Sikhs into Islam. *Bapu ji* used to tell me the stories when I was little."

"Do you remember anything about it?" Namo asked.

"Yes, I remember a little bit of it." Pali closed her eyes, thinking. "It was a long letter written in Persian,

"Chun kaar az hmah heelte dar gujasht,

Halal ast burdan ba shamsheer dast!" Pali recited the lines.

"I believe you know the meaning of it too, that when all peaceful ways to redress the wrong have failed, it is only righteous to pick up the sword. However, they are forbidden to ever engage in a first attack for whatever reason." Namo kept massaging Pali's hands. "You're a brave girl, Pali. Never forget that."

"I know, Ma. *Bapu ji* used to say that too." Pali smiled her normal self.

"We tried everything for Jeeto and Banta, but the things kept getting worse. They'll be out today. And don't you worry about Jogu either."

"Why are some people so evil, Ma?" Pali sighed. Exhausted, she lay on the bed.

"Wish I could tell you, Pali. But don't forget, there are a lot more good people than the bad ones." Namo placed the gun back in a chamber hidden behind the bed. "Why don't you rest for a while?" Namo said closing the door behind her and went down the stairs.

The courtyard was filled with the villagers and workers. People poured in as they heard about it. Elderly Puran Singh comforted Kaku who was still bleeding from the nose. "You've been the most loyal person to Lal Singh's family," Puran Singh said handing a small towel to Kaku, "Here, wipe your face. Whatever happens, there's always a meaning hidden behind it that we don't understand at the time…"

"What meaning could be there, behind Lal Singh's death?" Kaku dabbed his face with the towel and broke down.

People talked to each other in whispers looking at Kaku and towards the *chaubara.*

"How dare this woman attack Namo Bibi ji!" one of the workers said out loud.

"They are no good. They should not be even here," another one said.

"Pali's a brave girl," Puran Singh said as Namo came down the stairs.

"She's fearless and daring. Look, how she handled the situation." Gopal Chand widened his eyes. "Otherwise who knows what Jeeto would have done to Namo Bibi ji."

Namo went straight to Banta and Jeeto, sitting in the room. "Do you need help packing?" she sneered.

"Forgive us Namo. I'll never do anything like this again." Banta stood up from the cot with folded hands.

"Pack up and leave right now. Otherwise, I'll have to ask someone to throw your stuff out," keeping her voice down Namo said firmly looking straight at him.

"You're my sister, Namo. I always wanted to help you…"

"I do not want to hear another word from you. I want you to get out of my house right now," Namo yelled. "And take this wicked woman of yours along."

Jeeto glared at Namo but did not move from the cot, "You cannot throw us out of the house like that…"

The very next moment, she looked towards the door and got up like a spring. She started packing and shaking with equal intensity.

What happened to her? Surprised by her sudden move, Namo looked back. Pali stood in the doorway, hands on her hips, glaring at Jeeto.

A little later Banta and Jeeto carrying bundles of clothes and nick-nacks left through the main gate of the house followed by many of the chattering sniggering villagers and workers.

"It is all your fault!" Jeeto yelled at Banta right when she stepped out of the gate.

"Shut up, you despicable woman!" Banta retorted. Balancing the bundle on his head he took a long stride out the gate.

Chapter 53

Baldev sat behind a thick veil of bushes. Kewal crouched next to him on the left. They had dug just enough flat ground in the steep Sinzweya hills to secure the Bren machine gun. The riflemen sat on either side in shallow trenches partly obscured by the underbrush.

The night jungle pulsated with buzzing insects. An owl's hoot sliced through the humming stillness followed by a shrill cry of a bird. Baldev rubbed his cheek squishing a mosquito. Kewal kept scratching the top of his wet boot.

"Kewal, take off your boot and see what's going on," Baldev whispered.

"What if they come when I'm removing my shoe?"

"I will handle it. Take off your shoe."

"It's a motherfucking leech!" Kewal winced twisting the slimy leech attached between his big and first toe.

"Must be from last night when we crossed that damn muddy stream," Baldev whispered. "I removed several from my legs as soon as we came ashore."

"I did too, but this one must've crawled into my shoe," Kewal muttered under his breath as he put the shoe back on.

They sat and waited. The wind picked up and the towering trees along the slope swayed side to side intermittently exposing a full moon overhead.

"They're here," Kewal murmured as the bushes moved slightly. Baldev tightened his grip on the trigger of the Bren and mouthed, "No, not yet."

The spot they occupied must be held they were told, even at the cost of their lives. Admin Box – the main administration and supply point in the Arakan region of Burma – was a small clearing, surrounded by steep and thickly wooded hills. In the center a slightly raised area, the 'Ammunition Hill' where hundreds of barrels of petrol and cases of ammunition stacked around it, lay in the open.

The Japanese had attacked the British General Messervy's headquarters at Launggyaung two miles northeast of Admin Box a week ago and all lines of communication had been cut. General Messervy pinned down by heavy fire on an isolated hill finally had managed to reach the Admin Box with only a few of his men. The Box with its ammunition hill had to be protected that was constantly pounded by the enemy fire.

"Baldev, here's a letter for my daughter," Kewal whispered. Scratching the back of his neck he looked at Baldev in the darkness. "Here," he said, taking a folded piece of paper out of the inner pocket of his flimsy jacket and extended it towards Baldev. "Tell my wife to give it to her only when she can read it by herself," Kewal's voice cracked.

"Are you out of your mind? Give it to her yourself, you idiot." Baldev felt his heart hammering his chest.

"What if I don't survive?"

"Don't ever say that! We're going to squish these scorpion Japs and go home."

"Something doesn't feel right!" Kewal let out a string of sighs.

"You're right, so much is not right and that's why we're here." Eyes wide open Baldev scanned the bushes in the dark.

"Do not forget how they massacred our doctors and the wounded soldiers in the dressing station last week," he added.

"I know. Those bloody Japs didn't even spare the Red Cross medical staff," he said, "even after ransacking and looting all the hospital equipment and supplies."

"How old is your daughter?" Baldev asked changing the subject.

"Three. She'll be three next month," Kewal said.

"She must be talking a lot now. The three-year-olds are like chatterboxes."

"Oh, she's like a little parrot, repeating everything we say."

"But do not teach her your dirty jokes, Kewal," Baldev chuckled.

"No...no, she'll never hear those from me," he said taking the letter out again.

"I'm not touching your silly letter. Give it to her yourself, Kewal," Baldev said tightening his grip on the Bren, "and don't forget to invite me to her wedding."

"What about you? You married?" Kewal asked.

"No, but I will, as soon as I go back."

Suddenly the sky lit up with a thunderous explosion. "They're here!" someone yelled.

Screeching cries, *"Tenno Heika Banzai"* – long live the emperor, filled the jungle and hundreds of figures stood up from behind the bushes.

"Bole So Nihal," Captain Sundar Singh roared. The Sikh soldiers responded with a resounding, *"Sat Sri Akaal,"* the shouts rang through the thicket of the jungle echoing through the hills. Baldev emptied the magazine of the Bren and saw many Japanese soldiers fall.

For a moment the jungle fell into an eerie silence. The wind seemed to have held its breath and stopped moving through the tree branches. Even the humming sound of insects could not be heard.

"They're waiting for reinforcements," Kewal whispered.

Baldev pressed Kewal's sweaty arm that meant not to move or talk.

Within a few moments, the Japanese sprang up from behind the thicket once again and charged throwing grenades and shooting rifles. The Sikh riflemen darted towards them roaring like hungry lions, shouting, *"Sat Sri Akaal."* – True and Supreme is the Timeless God.

The fight was hand to hand, bayonet to bayonet. The green of the bushes turned crimson with blood that glistened in the momentary flashes of guns and grenades. Blown up body parts hung from the tree branches.

Baldev held on to the Bren firing beyond the immediate battle area wherever a bush moved slightly.

"They're running," Kewal yelled.

"Cowards, leaving their dead behind," Baldev yelled back emptying another Bren magazine and stood up looking at the bodies mangled and twisted within the shattered tree branches.

"Stay down, Bal!" the captain yelled from a few feet behind him. "They might still be there."

Baldev crouched but a little later they were collecting the injured and the dead. Kewal bent on his knees and picked up Jagtar's body. His clothes drenched with Jagtar's blood as he walked down the hill and calmly laid him down with the others, in a long row of the dead soldiers. He sat there with his head on his knees until Baldev walked up to him and led him away from Jagtar's body.

"What am I going to tell his mother?" Kewal buried his face into Baldev's shoulder and broke down. "We were like brothers. I feel like my arm's been severed."

Baldev wrapped his arm around him and walked him towards the tent.

The next morning was eerily calm, no noisy swearing or screaming. But as the soldiers finished their midmorning meals, the short-lived silence was shattered by the Japanese mountain guns. They opened a hellish fire from the Hill point 315 on to the ammunition hill of the Admin Box. The blazing stacks of ammunition detonated with deafening bangs, whizzing off laterally, and cutting down anyone in its path. The petrol canisters started exploding and turned the area into an inferno. The men were getting killed by their own ammunition ignited by the enemy.

It seemed like the sun had dropped onto the earth and was shooting balls of fire in every direction. The fire squads desperately tried to contain the blaze but to no avail.

Confusion and chaos lasted the whole day. At the nightfall, the soldiers were ordered to take positions. The hill point 315 from where the Japanese had attacked was stormed with artillery along with the tanks of the 25th Dragoons. Captain Sundar Singh's war cry, *"Bole So Nihal"* thundered louder than the machine guns. A unanimous reply of *"Sat Sri Akaal"* reverberated through the jungle and once again the Japanese were driven off.

The morning arrived as gray and gloomy as it could be. The night defenders came down the hill far fewer in number than had gone up.

"Why're you limping, Kewal?" Baldev asked walking down the slope. "You hurt?"

"No!" Kewal replied without looking at Baldev. "I think it's the leech I pulled out that day. It's like an open sore. So irritating…"

"Must be the leech's head left embedded in the skin when you broke it away. Get it taken care of at the dressing station." Tired to the bones Baldev kept walking. His eyes closed as soon as he hit the makeshift bed.

"Dakotas!" a number of soldiers shouted simultaneously. The hills rumbled with the sound of C47 Dakota airplanes that suddenly appeared in the sky. A few minutes into the sleep Baldev was woken by the hubbub. Rubbing his eyes he joined the others. His tiredness vanished, looking at the tins of food and rations, medical supplies, bundles of letters and newspapers being dropped by the airplanes. Boxes of ammunition, shiny canisters of petrol for the Dragoon tanks, and fodder for the mules were also pushed out the open hatches of the planes.

All packages were bound to different colored parachutes. The sky brightened up with red, blue, orange, and green as if a rainbow had appeared out of nowhere. They watched in awe until all the parachutes floated slowly to the ground. A few of them hung on the trees. As soon as the Dakotas left, they collected the supplies and separated them by the color of the parachutes. The soldiers laughed and hugged each other as if they had won the biggest lottery.

Since the supply routes had been cut by the Japanese a while ago, the ration and water supply was dwindling quickly. The water was foul and the food scanty and stale. Medical supplies had been looted and the injured were getting weaker by the day, struggling with flies and maggots in the wounds. The airplanes came like angels from the sky.

With food in their stomachs and wounds tightly dressed due to the blessing of the Dakotas, the infantry took their positions on the slope at sundown as usual.

Day after day the Indian and British soldiers defended the perimeter of the Box. They rejoiced the victory and grieved the fallen. They counted the dead and supported the wounded down the hill. Day after day they pushed back the attackers, who returned each time with a vengeance. Every time the Japanese backed away, they left their dead behind, rotting.

David Williams, a young British soldier sat not far from Baldev on the steep slope. He slapped an insect from his thigh and mumbled, "What a horrible place!"

"You're right. We have to find a better place to fight the war, David," Baldev chuckled.

"Your king rules more than half the world. Maybe he could order the Japs to throw flowers at you instead of grenades?" Kewal said.

"Okay, he would, if you, the weird mystic Indians, magically turn the Japs into pretty girls." David giggled which soon became contagious.

The gap between the rulers and the ruled had narrowed as they defended the Box together. The Sikh soldiers had gained the admiration and respect of the British by their fearless service. They laughed and joked with each other as friends. They all had heard Commander William Slim's speech, to the 14th army,

"I have never met a despondent Sikh in the front line," he had said. "He will go on to his last breath, and die with the battle cry of *Khalsa ji ki jai*, as he falls, Victory to the Holy Brotherhood! The Sikhs, a remarkable people, with their ten prophets, five distinguishing marks, and their baptismal rite of water stirred with steel; a people who have made history, and will make it again."

Commander Slim had thus reminded the British soldiers to respect them as equals.

The constant spluttering of machine guns and explosion of grenades, the braying of injured mules, and shouts of fire squads had become as normal as breathing. Orders of "Stay Put" were followed strictly. There was no rest for the soldiers, whether they were British or Sikhs, whether Gurkhas or Rajputs. From the officers to the lowest orderlies, they all were in the same environment of these sweltering hilly jungles, where the razor-sharp bamboo leaves and spiny hedges mercilessly pierced and cut through their skin.

Before the night ended, deafening shouts of *banzai* pounded the jungle once again. Flashes of exploding grenades momentarily illuminated the jungle. Crackling trees, thick smoke, and dust obscured Baldev's view. He felt a grenade explode close by. The stench of burning flesh filled his nostrils.

A gut-wrenching scream from nearby pierced his eardrums.

"David! You okay?" he shouted but heard nothing back.

Baldev kept emptying out the Bren even though he was blinded by thick layers of dust and smoke.

"Magazine, Kewal!" he yelled and looked to his left but saw nothing other than darkness. "Hand me a magazine! Don't you hear me?" Baldev screamed. "Have you gone deaf…you idiot mother fuc…" Baldev retrieved the magazine from the bag himself.

It felt like an eternity until the flashes finally started dying down. Screaming gave way to hushed voices. It was almost daylight when the smoke dissipated and the dust settled. Slivers of sunlight pierced through the jungle exposing the rattled human bodies. The friends and foes lay together on the bloody ground. Some bodies lay touching hands with extended arms and some lay on top of each other, killed in hand-to-hand combat. There was no sign of enemy anywhere. They had fled again after a night of killing and being killed.

"Kewal…!" A squeal came out of Baldev's exhausted lungs. A big blob of flesh glistened where his head should have been.

"No…no, Kewal no…" Baldev howled as loud as his angry lungs could. He picked him up on his shoulders and started down the hill. Suddenly he felt a yank on his foot from behind and fell facedown. Kewal's body rolled down the hill and stopped in the bushes.

Baldev got up and looked at the wounded Japanese soldier lying on the ground who had pulled him by the ankle, tripping him. Baldev picked up a bayonet lying nearby and thrust it into his stomach with all his might. "That's what you get, you son of a bitch!" The Japanese soldier's body shuddered, eyes wide open, his head tilted to the side.

Screaming and howling, Baldev started down the hill. David lay a few feet down with his left leg blown off below the knee.

"I'm coming back for you David." Baldev kept going down the hill where Kewal's body lay in the bushes. He bent down and took out the letter from his bloody jacket and put it in his pocket.

"My promise to you Kewal, I'll get the letter to your daughter," he said and wiped his eyes with his bloody palms and headed back up the hill.

Looking at David's pale face he whispered, "You'll be okay, David." He took off his turban and tore it in half. His long black tresses that were covered in a bun under the turban spread out over his shoulders reaching down to his waist. He wrapped the stump of the leg with one half of the turban and made a sling with the other half to carry him.

His uniform torn and his shoes slippery with blood, Baldev carried David to the dressing area, crowded with rows of injured soldiers. Baldev laid David on the ground with the others. "Hang in there, buddy." He pressed David's hand and turned around.

Captain Sundar Singh, barely alive with both his arms blown off, lay unconscious on the ground. Baldev fell on his knees next to him. "What am I going to do without you?" He broke down. His screams blended with the squealing sounds of the wounded soldiers and dissipated into the jungle where the trees were equally wounded and torn apart and where the ground was saturated with blood. He touched Sundar Singh's feet out of respect and walked back dragging his legs that felt heavier than lead.

A little later during the day, the Dakotas dropped more food and medicine, but there were no roars of excitement this time. They stared with bloodshot eyes at the parachutes slowly settling onto the ground.

******

Baldev had been awake all night sitting in the shallow trench, straining his eyes towards the jungle for any movement. The shelling from the Japanese had gone down since the all-out suicide attack two days ago. They had flung themselves into the direct fire with shrill cries of *banzai*. Both sides suffered

256

heavy casualties but many more on the Japanese side. Kewal and Captain Sunder Singh along with many others succumbed to their wounds. Their bodies were placed in the pit dugout in a dried stream bed, along with many others.

Baldev walked down the hill after another night of defending the Box. He was surprised to see a pack of mules loaded with food supplies. "Where did these come from?" he asked.

"It's the Japanese food convoy," Tom, a lanky young soldier, excitedly told him. His bluish eyes sunken like little caves and high cheekbones covered with a thin layer of white skin with little fat underneath made him look famished, although there had been ample food supplies dropped by the Dakotas a few days ago. The Japanese fighter planes had been demolished by the Royal Air Force Spitfires and their supply lines were disrupted.

"Most of them are killed and the rest will starve to death, those little vipers!" Tom said with a wide smile. His eye-caves momentarily got deeper than before and the cheekbones even higher, like two tiny hills on his face. Swinging his arms back and forth he took long strides towards the mules and started unloading.

Last night was the first time in many days when the Japanese did not attack and Baldev did not empty out the Bren. Last night was the first time when the jungle seemed to rest too. No branches crackled and no trees caught fire. It was the first time when there were no dead or wounded soldiers to be carried down the hill.

Baldev passed by the dressing area where the injured and the ailing waited patiently and some impatiently. The wounded could not be taken out of the place since the Ngakyedauk Pass, the only way out, had been seized by the Japanese. David lay on a stretcher with the stump of his leg wrapped in bandages, eyes half-open.

"David!" Baldev said bending down close to his face. A weak smile appeared on David's pain whipped lips.

"You'll be running around before you know it, Dave," Baldev said, gently massaging his hands. "Can I get you anything, buddy?" David slowly shook his head. Baldev sat by him for a while and then walked towards the burial pit that was not far from the dressing area. "Why Kewal? Why did you not live for your daughter?" His lips quivered. A thin stream of tears from his tired eyes trickled down and a few pearly drops trapped in his beard glistened in the pitiless sun. Thinking about Captain Sunder Singh he felt like a young boy who had lost his hero. *"How will I get through this without you?"* A stifled sob came out as a hiccup.

The next day under the command of Major Sarabjit Singh the resounding Sikh war cry *"Sat Sri Akaal"* penetrated the jungle while they attacked and captured the Hill Point 1070 back from the Japanese. Stepping over the bodies scattered everywhere, they conquered the Sugar Loaf Hill the very next day. Starving Japanese fled leaving behind their dead and injured as usual. Finally, the month-long siege was over and the Ngakyedauk Pass was opened.

Major Sarabjit Singh looked at Baldev, "Well done, Corporal!" He shook hands with him and then held him in a brotherly embrace. The soldiers hugged each other. They laughed and cried with tears of joy. Soon they were on their way to Dimapur.

Chapter 54

The morning sun rays filtered through the branches of the *Neem* tree by the window, into the room. Waking up, Pali stretched with a loud yawn. She looked at the picture on the opposite wall, as she did every morning. The shadow of the tree branches danced around the picture taken during their engagement ceremony. The movement of the branches seemed to be playing a kind of hide-and-seek with the photo and the wall calendar nearby.

Baldev wore a burgundy turban and an off white Tafta *Achkan,* and she was wearing a rose color silk *Salwar Kameez* with an elaborately embroidered silk *duppatta.*

We look so happy here! He's more handsome than any prince would be. Pali smiled and stretched again. The very next moment a gush of sadness overshadowed the blissful moment.

Her eyes erupted like black clouds, pouring torrents of warm salty rain. "Baldev, please come back to me. Come back!" she was pleading with Baldev or maybe the all-merciful God, she did not know, but those were the words that came to her lips. With a peculiar ache and a yearning in her heart, she begged for Baldev's safe return from the war.

"No, I'm not going to cry!" she said, wiping her tears. "He is coming back. He promised he would."

She came out into the verandah and took a deep breath. Winter was almost over with a feeling of warmth in the air. A flock of sparrows jumping from one branch of the *Neem* tree to another chirped in a strident chorus. They seemed to be competing with a couple of crows sitting on the rim of the roof, constantly cawing in their annoying tones.

The day had started as usual, Kaku fed and groomed the horses, *Bukky* and *Laakha* and Fatima was in the kitchen churning milk for making butter and *Lassi.*

"Pali Bibi ji, what would you like to have this morning, tea, or some *Lassi?"* Fatima momentarily stopped churning, as Pali came into the kitchen.

"Tea today, Fatima," Pali said yawning again.

Why did the village people grumble when Fatima started working at their house? 'She's a *Musalman,*' they had said, and should not be working in our kitchen. If *Bapu ji* and Ma didn't mind if she was a *Musalman* or a Sikh or Hindu, then why should anybody else? People are so ignorant.

Fatima handed her a cup of steaming hot tea. "You make the best *masala* tea, Fatima," Pali said, taking a sip. She fanned the steam with her hand inhaling the aroma.

"Namo Bibi ji taught me how to make it." Hearing words of appreciation, Fatima raised her hand to her forehead in a 'thank you' gesture with a smile.

"I'm making *Missi Tandoori Roti* today, one of your favorites, Pali!"

"Good, thank you, Fatima!" Pali said walking out of the kitchen. Sparrows still jumped around in the branches as if today was the last day on the earth. They always look so happy! Pali smiled. The crows had flown away and a bunch of doves had landed in the courtyard calmly rummaging through the hay near the horse stalls.

Setting the teacup on a table in the verandah, she looked towards the sun with eyes closed. The softness of the sun felt good.

"You're up!" Namo said coming down the stairs from the *chaubara,* "You're getting so fond of tea lately, Pali."

"It's really good, Ma, you should try some." Pali extended the cup towards her.

"I used to make it for your father," she said taking a sip from the cup. "He was fond of it too." A sigh escaped Namo's lips.

Pali exhaled loudly as if Namo's sigh was contagious and made her do the same. "Don't be gone too long, Ma." She held Namo's arm like a little girl.

"I'll be home soon. I just need to check if the crops were watered properly last night. The plants are still young and delicate, you know," Namo said walking towards the courtyard. "Last time they did not do a good job."

Kaku saddled Bukky and held the stirrup as Namo settled onto the horseback. He followed her out the gate riding Laakha, the brown horse.

Pali stood in the verandah, drowned in thoughts. Baldev prefers *Lassi* over tea, and he certainly likes *Missi Tandoori Roti.* Do they give him proper food there?

Why is he not writing back to me? Is he hurt? Is he wasting away, lying helplessly in a hospital somewhere? She felt an invisible fist hit her in the chest.

Unable to keep standing she leaned against the table knocking the cup to the floor.

"Oh, oh!" She picked up the broken pieces and wiped the floor with a rag still lost in thoughts. *Baldev, please write back. Tell me, you couldn't get a paper to write on...or you didn't have time to write. Bal, please tell me you're okay, and you're not hurt.*

She felt a twinge in her stomach. Panicked, she hurried to her room and picked up Baldev's letter that had some numbers and letters in place of the address under his name.

'I cannot tell you where I am, but I will get your letter at the address on the back.' He had scribbled as if in a hurry and 'I love you more than anything in the world.'

What if the address is wrong and he never received any of my letters? Maybe the letter that Jeeto stole had the correct address. But he had not yet gone to the army when he wrote that letter. Spiraling in a tornado of dilemma, she ran back inside and picked up paper and pen.

I will keep writing to him until he writes back. And I'm going to write the longest letter anyone ever wrote. Slowly she felt strength coming back to her body. This time I will tell him everything that's happening here.

She filled page after page describing how Jeeto and Banta had been stealing from the farm and Jeeto had stolen his letter and gave it to her son Jagu. She wrote about Jagu's advances towards her and how he had tried to blackmail her with the letter. She described how she handled the situation like a lioness and made him run with his tail between his legs.

She filled more pages about how Jeeto had attacked Ma and she had to threaten her with a gun. She wrote how Banta had mercilessly beaten Kaku and Bukky, and finally, they got rid of Jeeto and Banta both. While things were calm after they left, there was too much chaos and turmoil outside. The Muslim Leaguers were telling the *Musalmans* that they will be better off if they got their own separate country. They were demanding to divide Punjab and make Pakistan out of it.

She wrote about how the newspapers were filled with rumors that all *Musalmans* will live in one place and the Sikhs at another. How was it possible?

How could they force people, whose lives were intertwined for hundreds of years, to leave their homes and go to some new place and start all over again?

So many protest marches in the streets were turning violent and many getting killed. Obviously, Gandhi's non-violence was just a name, not reality. It seemed like the leaders were creating more problems instead of solving them. She wrote.

She read the letter before stuffing it into an envelope. "I don't think I should write any of this rubbish to him. He's out somewhere in the war and here at home, they are talking about severing the limbs of the homeland. "How would he feel knowing all this?" Pali murmured. She tore all the pages and started again.

My dearest Baldev,

I'm waiting for the day you'll come home.

Without you, I'm like a statue, a soul-less walking and talking statue that fakes smiles and pretends to be living. Without you, Bal, I'm a sparrow whose wings are severed. But with you by my side, I'm an eagle, soaring above the skies.

You held my hand and taught me how to walk, when I was one year old and you, three and a half. Ma and Bapu ji always talked about how inseparable we were. Time flew faster than the blink of an eye and I suddenly felt shy looking at you, when you and aunty Harjit came to visit.

Bal, you were my savior when Bapu ji died. You gave me the strength and a reason to live.

A shadow of gloom darkened the skies of her soul, while the pen in her shaking fingers kept drawing words on the paper. Tears blurred her vision. She pressed her eyes with the base of her palms preventing the tears from falling onto the paper.

When will I hear your voice again, that sounds better than any music I've ever heard?

When will I see your smile again, that seeps into the heart making it throb with joy?

Do not forget the promise you made, 'Bali will be back for Pali.'

And here's my promise to you, Bal; I will wait for you in this life and every life I come to this earth.

Yours always, Pali.

Chapter 55

Hakam Singh sat in the shade of the mulberry tree in the yard. He tried to focus his eyes on Harjit through a perpetual veil of fog surrounding him. *She has kind eyes. Her voice is so soothing.* Thoughts stirred up a pleasant feeling inside him that he had not felt for a long time. *Why doesn't this fog go away?* He shook his head and blinked a few times. *She's a good person!*

Harjit set the plate on a small table by the cot and sat next to him. "Hakam," she broke a piece of *roti* and extended towards him. "Here, eat some," she said, as she had done every day for the last six years.

"I will, myself," Hakam gently pushed Harjit's hand away and broke a piece from the *roti*, dipped it in *dal*, and slowly brought it to his mouth.

"O, Hakam…" Her eyes welled up and she hugged him. With folded hands in prayer, she looked up, "Thank you, God, thank you!"

A wide smile playing on her face, her gaze followed Hakam's hand from the *roti* to *dal* and from *dal* to his mouth. She looked at him as he slowly chewed his food. She sat by him watching the simplest task being performed as if it was the biggest achievement of her life.

This was the first time in years, Hakam had spoken a word. And this was the first time he was trying to eat by himself. No matter how hard Harjit had tried, he would take one bite and forget to take the next one.

"No more," a little while later he said, looking towards her but not at her.

"That's okay," she said, taking the plate away.

"Do you know, Hakam, how happy I am?" She held both his hands and kissed them. Cupping his face in her palms she tenderly pulled him close to her face, "Hakam, please, look at me just once…please, look at me!"

Focusing his eyes on her face Hakam felt a flicker of light penetrating through the gray expanse around him. Suddenly a balmy soft jolt shook his head. For a split second his eyes met hers. "Harjit!" he whispered.

"Yes, Hakam, I'm Harjit, your Harjit," Tears flowing, she laughed and she sighed and laughed again. She sobbed and kissed his bony cheeks. "I am your Harjit," she said again and rested her head on his shoulder.

"I'll be right back," she hurried towards the inside of the house and brought a large photo in a wooden frame.

"Here, Hakam, look at this." She held the picture in front of him. "It's you, me, and Baldev, your son."

Hakam looked at her and then at the picture, but his gaze quickly slipped away and he started looking beyond her and the photo.

"Here's your son. It's Baldev!" Harjit held it in front of him, trying to get his attention back to the picture.

Why's this gray haze around me again? Hakam blinked and shook his head but could not focus. "Harjit," he whispered and slipped into a void again.

"Oh, Hakam, please come back…come back!" Harjit begged.

******

Hakam had plunged back into the vacuum of his existence. It was a week ago when he had called her by name. She craved to hear his voice again. She wanted him to look at her and ask how she was doing. She yearned for him to take her into his arms and tell her, 'you're tired, Harjit, sit for a while and rest!' She wanted to talk to him about their son.

What did I do to deserve this? She had asked again and again. What did I do wrong to be punished this way? My only son is in the midst of a ruthless war and my husband doesn't even know who I am. Is my life worth living? Gloomy thoughts constantly scraped the tender wounds of helplessness that became deeper and more painful with each passing day.

The anguish and heartache that had been smoldering in her chest for years broke the barriers one day and exploded into an inferno. The fire of agony erupting from inside engulfed her whole being. Flames of anger leaped around her and she screamed. She wanted to scorch the sky and reduce the earth to ashes. She wanted to burn the house and herself along with it. She screamed until her voice became hoarse and her throat ached. The flames of anger slowly drowned in the flood of tears and extinguished.

Sitting against the wall inside the locked room she did not know how long she had been there. She looked towards the door and did not see any light coming through the crevices.

"The sun has gone down," she murmured. "My God, Hakam must be hungry!" She collected her scattered self and walked out of the room. Hakam was sitting at the same spot where she had left him after the midday meal.

How can I give up on him? The father of my son, the love of my life! He's going to come back one day. Harjit washed her face at the hand pump and hurried to the kitchen to make dinner. Why did I lose myself like that? A sense of remorse caught up with her. "Get a hold on you, Harjit!" she scolded herself.

In the light of the hurricane lamp, she fed Hakam. He looked straight at her. His wide-open eyes focused on her face, he touched her cheeks below the eyes and shook his head. "Don't cry!" he said softly.

"O, Hakam, I'm not crying." She fell into his arms. Tears flowed like gutters after the first monsoon shower. Hakam held her tight in his arms wiping her tears. The night was cool and calm. The first rays of sunlight found them in a gentle embrace on the cot. The food lay untouched on the table.

She heard Hakam's voice, "Wake up, Harjit, its daylight," he gently shook her arm. Harjit as if in a trance clung to him and cried again. "Is it true? Tell me it's not a dream, Hakam."

As the days went by, Hakam's presence was more real and more soothing. *One day he'll be back to his real self,* Harjit felt a deep sense of contentment.

She thought about the first poem he wrote for her, while studying in college at Lahore. Will he remember? Should I show it to him?

Harjit dug out the yellowed paper carefully wrapped in her silk wedding *dupatta* from the bottom of the *sandook* once again. The last time she had taken it out was just before leaving for the Nicobar island prison where Hakam had been exiled. After years of wrestling with the system through lawyers, she and Baldev were granted permission to visit him that was revoked at the last moment. Heartbroken they were unable to do anything about it.

Harjit gently unfolded the old piece of paper and sat next to Hakam,

"Do you remember this?" With a prayer in her heart, she looked at him.

To my Harjit,
Directionless I wandered
In the dark of my being
Hakam read the first two lines and looked at her.
"Go on," she nodded.

Your one sweet glance
A million moons
Brightened the lane
Revealed the path
A lifeless pebble I lay
In the alleys of rock and clay
Your gentle touch
Your radiant smile
Awakened the grace
In the depth of my heart

Your tender embrace
Your soothing voice
Filled my empty shell
With a song of ardor love
And wings to fly away,
From the land of despair,

After reading each stanza Hakam looked into her eyes. At the end of the poem, tears trickled down his cheeks. Wiping them with her *dupatta* she wrapped her arms around him. Hakam kissed her temples, where the grey had taken over the dark hair. He kissed the palms of her hardened hands, "Harjit!" he whispered.

Chapter 56

"Ma..."

"Coming, Bal!" Harjit hurried out into the courtyard. Not an insect stirred in the moonless night. The mulberry tree stood motionless, barely visible. A dog barked on the other side of the village and then another joined in. Is it Baldev walking home? Are the dogs barking at him? But why would he be on the opposite side of the village, in the middle of the night?

She peered towards the closed front door and waited as if Baldev was going to knock at any moment. The dogs stopped barking and the night went silent again. She opened the door and stared into the darkness hoping for a miracle that did not happen.

She pressed her chest with both hands, "Was it a dream? It felt so real!" She stumbled through the courtyard into the house.

The night seemed to have frozen at one spot, in never-ending darkness. She felt an intense emptiness inside, "O, Baldev, my son," she sighed.

The more she tried to fall asleep, the more she was wide awake. The bed felt hard and rutted under her body. After tossing and turning for a while she got out of bed and walked to the adjacent room. She lit a kerosene lamp and fumbled for paper and pen in the drawer. In the dim flickering light, she wrote another letter to her son.

My dearest son,

I wait every day for your letter. Write back to me, Bal! I want to know you're all right.

If you cannot write a long letter, just write one word, only one word, 'Ma' and I will know you're okay. I'm dying to hear from you.

In my previous letter, I wrote to you about your father. He's getting so much better. Would you believe he now recognizes almost everyone in the village?

He smiles and calls me by my name. Do you know what happened yesterday? I was peeling potatoes and he sat by me. After a while, he picked up a knife and started cutting the potatoes for me. Isn't it amazing! Your father is coming back, Bal!

I remember the day you were born, like yesterday. You rose like a little sun on the sky of my soul and my world brightened the moment I held you in my arms.

I laughed and cried with happiness when you said 'Ma' for the very first time. I'm dying to hear your voice again!

Come back home, Son. I am waiting for you. Pali is waiting for you. The whole village waits for you. There is so much more I want to tell you.

Nothing feels good without you, son!

Love you more than anything in the world – you are my world, Baldev!

Your loving Ma.

Harjit closed the letter. Wiped her eyes and blew out the lamp before going to the bedroom.

The room was filled with sunlight when she woke up. Hakam's bed was empty. She found him standing in the verandah staring at a fast-moving lone cloud about to cover the sun.

"I'm sorry, Hakam, I overslept." She held his hand.

Hakam's lips stretched into a soft smile, "It is alright. You need rest." Pressing her gently against his chest, he looked into her eyes.

An ecstatic wave ran through Harjit's body. "O, Hakam, I waited so long for these words!" She clung to him as if they had met after eons of time. The cloud had dissipated before it came in front of the sun. Harjit felt brightness inside out. With an unusual ease in her heart, she walked to the kitchen.

The coming days were calm, and the nights quiet but Baldev's absence rumbled the silence of her sleepless nights. How badly she wanted him to come home.

As Hakam was getting better, she noticed him gaping at the family photo again and again. *He's going to ask about Baldev. What will I tell him?*

A few days later, Hakam, holding the picture asked in a barely audible voice, "Where is Baldev?" He squinted and the vertical lines on his forehead looked like three deep furrows.

"He…he…he's at college!" Harjit stuttered.

She could not sleep that night. A mixture of fear, remorse, and helplessness engulfed her peace of mind. She closed her eyes trying to fall asleep but the words, *He's at college,* kept hammering her conscience. She felt her body tremor with guilt. How badly she had wanted him to remember his son! Her heart ached to talk about Baldev to him. She wanted to tell him about his engagement to Pali. But she had lied the moment Hakam asked about him.

She looked towards Hakam's bed next to hers and quietly went out into the courtyard. The night was cool and a little windy but Harjit's body felt smoldering with guilt of lying. She filled a glass of water from the pitcher kept in the verandah and took a sip. It felt good on her dry lips.

How could I tell him that Baldev is gone to war, fighting for the British? Father and son on the opposite sides! What can I do? She looked up at the sky, as if the stars of the moonless night had any answers. Is lying better at this moment? How can I shock him again by pouring out the truth? But he has to know the truth. The father has the right to know where his son is. She pondered. I will tell him as soon as he recovers a little more. She felt a burden lifted from her chest and came back into the room where Hakam slept peacefully.

Chapter 57

Every day men gathered by the brick platform under the Banyan tree in the afternoons as did their fathers and their grandfathers before them. They discussed the rain and the drought. They discussed how the crops were growing and whose oxen were better at plowing.

They talked about who had gotten sick or was in poor health and which young man was growing up into a shining star of *Kabbadi* or Cricket. The discussion was often about whose son or daughter was polite and obedient and who was spoiled or getting into bad company. They talked as if everything in the village was everyone's business.

They also discussed politics and the news. One person read the newspaper and the others listened. The newspapers these days were mostly filled with war stories. The whole world had been thrown into one big firestorm. They talked about the men who had gone to war and who had come back wounded. They flocked to the family that received the bad news and grieved with them, which was happening more and more these days.

They used bad words for the Japanese and cursed Hitler. Some blamed the British. "Japan wants to dominate Asia and the whole of Pacific." Jagat Singh, the high school history teacher, who most of the time volunteered to read, folded the newspaper and slapped it on the brick floor of the platform.

"You're right, Jagat, we know how quickly they invaded and conquered Malaya, Singapore, and many other countries." Teg shared his knowledge about the war. He had his own newspaper tucked under his armpit. "They killed thousands of POWs including our own Sikh and Rajput soldiers along with the British, when they conquered Burma."

"With Burma gone, it won't be long till they invade India." Jagat picked up the folded newspaper and slammed it back down. "The Japanese soldiers are merciless bastards."

"When you are a soldier, you have to be merciless. If you don't kill, they will kill you," Kirpa Singh said rolling his good hand over his gray beard. He never talked how he had lost his left hand. The only thing villagers knew about him was that he had fought in France a place they heard was very far away, on behalf of the British Army, about 25 years ago. Very few men had returned and the ones who did had lost one organ or the other and some never fully recovered to being normal.

"Our own Baldev is fighting along with the allied forces, maybe somewhere in the Burmese jungles or maybe in Europe or Africa, no one knows," Jagat said.

Baba Budh Singh folded his hands in prayer, "*Waheguru, Waheguru.*" The worry lines on his face suddenly appeared deeper than usual. Many joined him praying for Baldev's wellbeing.

"Sometimes I think something must be wrong with the stars of India. When we look at history, the invaders came one after the other killing and looting. They had some kind of fascination with India." Jagat stood up holding the newspaper.

"It was the land of gold and precious stones, loaded with treasures of spices and healing herbs, and exotic foods. India, the captivating land of tigers and elephants and peacocks…" Jagat Singh's eyes fixed somewhere far away as if reciting a mythical tale.

"And so many glorious temples," Nand Lal, the shopkeeper barged in.

"One bloodthirsty invasion after another," Jagat continued without paying attention to Nand Lal.

"First was Alexander, the great. He was called 'great' just because he attacked other countries and killed people?" Jagat looked at men asking for an answer. "Then came the Turks. Do you know, Mehmud of Ghazni invaded India seventeen times in 25 years and left with an enormous amount of wealth every time? He raided this part of Punjab, where we sit today, every year, and looted the harvest of this fertile land. He plundered the wealth and deities made of pure gold from temples and left them in ruins while building magnificent palaces and mosques back in Ghazni."

"I am sure he was not able to carry any of the palaces or mosques with him to the next world when he died," Baba Budh Singh said. "Greed is the biggest foe of mankind. They kill not realizing that everything will be left here when they die."

"True, very true…" mumbling voices filled the air. People looked at each other, "Everything is left here when you die," someone in the crowd said out loud.

Jagat went on to narrate the story of Babar, the king of Kabul, how he had invaded India through the Khyber Pass and founded the Mughal dynasty in the sixteenth century. "The Mughal emperors ruled with the sword in an effort to convert the Indian population into Islam. Then the Emperor Aurangzeb, sixth in the Mughal dynasty, occupied the throne of Delhi after killing his four brothers and imprisoning his own father, Shah Jahan. Aurangzeb was a religious fanatic and insisted conversion of Hindus and Sikhs into Muslim faith."

Teg Singh jumped in, "The Sikhs were the most persecuted people in his regime. He publicly beheaded our Guru Teg Bahadur who tried to protect the Hindus from forced conversion. It was Guru Gobind Singh who created the Khalsa Panth, an army of Saint Soldiers, to resist the brutality of Aurangzeb. He taught us to turn from sparrows into hawks in the face of tyranny."

"What's with Jang? He's running, coming this way!" someone in the crowd shouted.

Many heads turned.

"Hakam recognized me! He knew who I am." Jang was breathless with excitement and partly from running, "I'm coming from his house."

Did he really…? Are you sure about it…? Is it possible after so long? People bombarded him with questions one after the other.

"I stopped by his house a few days ago and he did not recognize or talk to me," Ashraf Ali said gaping at Jang.

"Why would I lie?" Jang's enthusiasm dwindled and his temper rose with all the skeptical stares. "Go and see for yourselves."

Everyone looked at Baba Budh Singh, expecting only he would know if that was true.

"He is finally turning around after years of tormenting agony. My only request to all of you is that do not start flocking to his house. It might be too much for him," Baba ji told them. "Let's give him some more time."

They nodded and talked in low voices. A loud sigh of relief spread through the crowd.

"He used to be one of the most brilliant men I have known!" Hardev said loud enough for everyone to hear.

"And look what they did to him!" another man sitting close to him said even louder.

"They don't call it 'slavery' for nothing, my friend!" Hardev tightly shut his eyes as if the word *slavery* had poked its nailed fingers into his eyes.

"The British have been sucking the very soul out of India's body for more than two hundred years."

"People never stopped revolting, though."

"But they brutally suppressed every revolt, executing and exiling who so ever tried to lift his head up."

"Who can forget Kartar Singh and Bhagat Singh, who were hanged in Lahore jail at the age of only 19 and 23?"

A jumbled clatter of many voices stirred up the hot afternoon air under the Banyan.

"Shame on them, who are joining the army and fighting on behalf of the British," Nand Lal, the shopkeeper opened his mouth and a whole hell broke out.

"How dare you criticize our boys who are sacrificing their lives for the good of every human, including you?" Jagat shouted.

Another person yelled back in favor of the shopkeeper. "They're traitors, siding with the occupiers!"

"We side with the righteous and at this moment, Japan is the aggressor and so is Hitler."

Sides were picked quickly, some in favor of the Army and some against. Shouting and yelling went on for a while and then the shopkeeper pushed someone off the brick platform. Reacting to this another person punched him in the face. A pushing and punching match started under the old Banyan. Children playing *Gulli Danda* nearby stopped and looked towards their elders.

Baba Budh Singh stood up, "Everyone, sit down!" he shouted. "Sit down, I say!"

A silence followed, so deep that even a leaf falling on the ground might sound like a stone hitting metal. People settled back on the platform some breathless and some exhaling loudly. Everyone's eyes fixed on Baba ji, they waited.

"First of all, a person must understand the need of the time," Baba ji's eyes scanned the crowd. "Our forefathers have lived here in harmony during good as well as bad times. We survived all the invasions and the wars because we worked as one unit, one people, regardless of being a Hindu, Sikh, or a *Musalman*." Baba ji's angry tone changed into a calm and soft voice, rather quickly, that was more like him.

His gentle way of helping people and resolving disputes had given him a fatherly temperament that everyone called him *Baba ji*. His flowing white beard and a neatly worn white turban gave him an impressive persona that people listened when he talked.

"The need of the time now is to side with the allied forces and push the Japanese out of Burma. We'll deal with the British later," Baba ji gave his suggestion and most of the heads nodded in agreement.

Yes. Yes, that makes sense. A loud murmur mingled with a few that did not seem to agree with it.

The wind appeared to have suddenly remembered to start blowing. The Banyan leaves swayed gently like a synchronized slow dance, fanning the men sitting in the shade and talking over each other.

"Look at the irony of the situation, father gave up everything including his sanity, fighting against the Raj and the son has gone to war to die for the Raj..."

"Do not use the word *die* for Baldev ever again!" someone scolded. "We pray for Baldev's safe return."

"Does Hakam know that Baldev joined the army?"

"Hope, he doesn't fall back into the same state when he finds out."

They talked until their children called them for supper.

The next day they were sitting under the Banyan and talking again as if nothing happened yesterday.

Chapter 58

The makeshift burial grounds in the sands of a dried-out stream bed lay a few yards away from the Admin Box. It looked like a lifeless ghastly forest of crosses made out of sticks, sticking out of the ground.

The British, the Sikhs, Rajputs, and the *Musalmans* were all buried at the same place. Born a white and raised a privileged ruling class lay next to a brown or dark-skinned poor Indian farmer. The men who tended to the mules and the officers, who commanded the Battalions, lay in the same pit.

The Sikhs and the Rajputs, who cremated their dead and the ashes were ceremoniously taken to a body of flowing water, were hastily buried in one shallow grave along with the British and the *Musalmans*. The crosses were haphazardly made for most of them regardless of their customs or religion. They had been so different in life but were so similar in death.

Baldev gazed towards the burial grounds. With the eye of his mind, he saw Captain Sundar Singh standing tall and strong like a *Peepal* tree with arms crossed on his chest and a proud smile on his face. And then his lips moved. Baldev blinked.

Did he say you'll be alright Baldev? How did he know, I feel lost without him?

Standing next to the Captain, Robert from Coventry, England, appeared to wave at him. "Robert?" Baldev murmured and rubbed his eyes.

Jagtar's face with just a hint of mustache and beard looked a little distorted with a peculiar grin. He was one of the youngest soldiers and had just started growing beard.

Baldev turned around and felt as if Kewal mouthed something to him.

"I know, Kewal, I'll get the letter to Roopi, I promise," Baldev whispered.

Did he just tell me his daughter's name? I haven't even looked at the letter yet. Did he say Roopi? Baldev felt his heart sink into his stomach and his legs shook like feathers in the wind.

"Baldev!" Major Sarabjit Singh shouted and covered his nose with a piece of rag again. Snapping out of a dream-like state Baldev ran towards the Major.

"Are you lost? Hurry up, help loading the jeeps," the major yelled.

The air was filled with an unbearable stench. Bloated bodies of Japanese soldiers scattered on the slopes were exploding one after the other, shooting out dirty red slush with a horrendous smell.

Everyone ran around loading the jeeps and mules, panting and shouting to quickly get out of the wretched place.

Clouds of dust arose every time a small airplane landed or departed on the freshly repaired airstrip. Wounded soldiers moaned louder than usual when loaded onto the airplanes. Many with shattered limbs and burned skin wrapped in bandages howled at the top of their lungs with the slightest movement. Some, too frail to move or even moan, still wearing forest green uniforms stiffened with dried blood lay on gurneys, quietly waiting for their turn. Flies swarmed around their lips and noses and bloody clothes.

Tightly packed into the jeeps, the defenders of the Admin Box were finally ready for departure from the hellish grounds that had been under siege by the Japanese. The mulers fed the mules and loaded them with supplies for a long journey back.

"We're on our way to Dimapur," Major Sarabjit Singh told Baldev as they got into the jeep.

Baldev nodded. Reaching into the inner pocket of his shirt he felt the letter and pressed it against his chest. "Kewal! No, Roopi!" he murmured.

The agony of leaving their friends and comrades behind, buried in shallow graves, hampered triumph of getting out alive.

Baldev looked back towards the burial ground once again through the dust cloud created by the wheels. Buddies, who he trained with, who he ate with, talked and laughed with lay unceremoniously buried in the sands of a dried-out stream.

Where would the bodies end up when the monsoon downpours gush through the stream? Will the wild animals dig them out before the rains? Vultures were already hovering around while the Japanese dead were exploding.

A sickening feeling overtook Baldev. The jeep jolted along the rough road and he closed his eyes.

As the caravan reached the Ngakyedauk Pass, Jack, one of the British soldiers riding two jeeps ahead of them started chanting, "Okeydoke... Okeydoke!"

"Here comes the savior!" Willy, sitting next to him, shouted in between the chant.

"What's Okeydoke?" Baldev asked.

"They've nicknamed the Ngakyedauk Pass as the *Okeydoke* pass," the major said. "Maybe, it's easier to say okey-doke."

"And call it the *savior*, the only way out of the Japanese stench," Baldev added.

"The knight in shining armor..." Someone in the same jeep sang louder than the deafening sound of the Dragoon tanks.

Laughter broke out in the caravan. Loud voices singing, 'knight in shining armor' filled the jungle air. Baldev and the major joined in. The dusty rough road, full of ditches and wide crevices being compared to a *knight in shining armor*, made everyone laugh and clap.

"Wait a minute!" Major Sarabjit elbowed Baldev, "We're the knights in shining armor, saving the Lady Burma."

The chorus changed to "Save Lady Burma..." while the jeeps tugged along the bumpy road of Ngakyedauk Pass.

"Didn't the Dakotas drop some letters along with the supplies? I remember seeing something looking like bundles of letters," Baldev asked the major.

"Yes, there were some bundles of letters, but we never had time to open them." The major leaned back and stared towards the jungle on his side of the road.

"Hope they distribute them when we get to Dimapur." Baldev's eyes followed major's gaze into the jungle, where the Japanese might be hiding and attack any moment.

"We sure will do that," major said.

Pali and Ma might think I'm already dead. Baldev suddenly felt lonely and miserable. He had not thought of home since they were dropped at the Admin box. Twenty-four hours of earsplitting artillery fire and hand-to-hand gun battles, shouting and running, collecting bodies, and shrill cries of the injured, had not let him think of anything other than fight and survive.

He rubbed his palms over his thighs as if straightening the wrinkles from his dirty uniform pants. He looked at his grime-covered hands and filthy nails.

His beard felt rough and unkempt. There had never been time to bother about cleanliness at the Admin box.

Pali would be repulsed by my sight. Ma might not even recognize me. Baldev felt lost.

Hope Bapu ji recovers to his real self.

Baldev wanted to take a long bath and change into clean clothes. He thought about wearing a burgundy turban and an off-white silk *achkan* that he wore during his engagement ceremony to Pali. He imagined himself sitting next to her.

Shouts of banzai and crackling sound of guns snapped him out of his reverie. They jumped out and took cover behind the jeeps. Baldev blindly fired into the jungle from where the shots were coming. The ambush lasted a few minutes and they heard the groans of the wounded Japanese. Two British and four Indian soldiers were badly wounded. The caravan continued. Soon they were airlifted to Dimapur, while the main body of the division was flown to Imphal.

Chapter 59

Baldev excitedly opened the dusty bundle of letters tied with a string of jute twine, as soon as it was delivered. He picked up the first letter from the top. It was from Ma.

His eyes moved quickly over the paper, left to right.

I wait every day for your letter... Tell me you are not hurt...your father is getting better.

"*Bapu ji*'s getting better!" He jumped with joy and continued reading.

My world brightened the moment I held you in my arms... I'm dying to hear you say Ma!

Baldev felt a knot forming in his throat.

I'm dying to hear your voice too, Ma. I'm okay, I'm not hurt. Poor Ma, she's so worried! I will write back to her right away.

Baldev picked up the next letter from the top of the bundle.

"Pali!" Baldev opened the envelope tearing it from the side.

Without you, Bal, I'm a sparrow whose wings are severed. But with you by my side, I'm an eagle soaring above the skies...

He held the letter tight with his shaky fingers and his heart raced faster than the Spitfire fighter jets.

You held my hand and taught me how to walk, when I was about one year old and you, three and half...

Time flew faster than the blink of an eye and I suddenly felt shy looking at you...

A peculiar wave of ecstasy ran through his body as he read the lines. He felt his heart skip beats.

Bal, you were my savior when Bapu ji died. You gave me the strength and reason to live.

You are my strength and reason to live, Pali! Baldev pressed the letter to his heart. Then read it again,

When will I hear your voice again, that sounds better than any music I've ever heard?
When will I see your smile again, that seeps into the heart making it throb with joy?
Do not forget the promise you made, 'Bali will be back for Pali.'
And here's my promise to you, Bal, I will wait for you in this life and every life I come to this earth.

Baldev overflowed with emotions as he finished reading. "I *will* keep my promise, Pali, in this life and every life I come to this earth." He kissed the letter, held it to his chest, kissed it again as if he did not know what else to do.

Tenderly folding it he placed the letter in his pocket. He felt a kind of loving warmth in his heart as he walked to the supply store to pick up a few sheets of paper and envelopes.

The soldiers had a few days off after the trenches were dug and they waited for further orders. They stood in groups laughing and joking with each other.

"Writing a letter to your *Heer*, Baldev?" Gurjit Singh a soldier from the Punjab Regiment said with a kind of mischievous smile, when he saw him buying paper and envelops. His playful expression quickly changed, realizing that he had joked with his senior about the tragic love story of Heer and Ranjha. "Sergeant, Sir, I didn't mean to…" he stuttered.

"No problem at all," Baldev said to him and hurried towards his tent.
Pali, my dearest,
He wrote. He instinctively held the end of the pen in his teeth and looked up. The tent fabric fluttered in the wind. The voices coming from outside got louder.

Received your beautiful letter, he wrote the next line and paused again. He wanted to pour his love into the letter.

"Here's another letter for you, Sergeant. It just came today." Orderly Mangat Ram handed him a yellowish envelope.

"Wow! Sergeant, you already have a big bundle of letters here," he said looking at the unopened stack in front of Baldev.

The new letter was also from Pali.

My heart knows you're alive, Bal! She had written.

There are so many rumors floating in the village. Even Ma has started believing them. 'He'd have written back if everything was okay,' she says and cries hugging me. I hate her when she does that.

"I'm alive! Do you hear me, Pali? I'm alive!" Baldev said nervously shaking his head.

I told her a few days ago that I will hang myself from the ceiling if she asked me again to consider a man in the nearby village, Ratowal.

Baldev's face ashen, "Oh, Pali, don't even think of doing anything stupid…" He felt the strength squeezed out of his body. The letter shook in his hands. The words started floating on the paper as he read on. He blinked several times to focus.

I do not talk to anyone anymore, Bal. Gina and Shindo and most of the other girls are living at their in-laws' houses.

"Pali!" Baldev exhaled and tried to swallow the knot in his throat.

Only the river is my friend these days. The waves seem to know the tale of my agony. Ma and Kaku keep an eye on me and try to cheer me up – nothing cheers me anymore, Bal!

Write back. Please write back! Yours and only yours,

Pali

Baldev's body quivered with panic and he frantically scribbled on the paper,

I'm alive and well, Pali. I know in my heart; we'll be together soon. There is nothing in the world that will keep us apart. You take care of yourself. I will write you a really long letter in a few days.

I miss you so much! Yours and only yours,

Baldev

He licked the envelop flap and sealed it. As he walked to the makeshift post office the sirens went off, which meant redeployment. They had been informed the night before about it but they did not know where they were going to go.

Baldev quickly scribbled on the outside of the sealed envelope.

Tell my Ma and Bapu ji at Gajanpur that I'm okay. He dropped the letter in the out-going mail basket and ran back to pick up his rucksack.

The soldiers rushed towards the lorries and loaded them with ammunition and rations. Within seconds the infantry was marching again.

"We're going to Kohima, Sergeant Baldev," Major Sarabjit Singh said as he got onto the jeep. Baldev nodded.

"Are you alright Baldev?" the major asked looking intently at him.

"Thank you, Sir, I'm alright," Baldev said, eyes focused far away. The words from Pali's letter were hammering him nonstop. *I will hang myself from the ceiling if she asked me again to consider...*

"Sir, I'm really fine, Sir!" Baldev said, realizing that Sarabjit Singh was still looking at him.

"Okay, Sergeant, if you say so. But do not hesitate to ask if you need any help."

"Yes, Major!" Baldev forced a smile.

I will be back, Pali! Baldev assured Pali in his mind, while the jeep lurched forward along the hectic mountain road with its numerous twists and turns.

Since their arrival at Dimapur, they had been digging trenches and fox holes around the town. Last night they were told to keep their rucksacks ready to move on seconds' notice.

General Slim had expected the Japanese to attack Dimapur, the main supply center, and a gateway to India in the state of Nagaland. It was the main staging post for the allied force and the fall of Dimapur would be disastrous.

Documents found on a dead Japanese officer from the battle of Sangshak revealed that a whole division of Mutaguchi's army was moving towards Kohima, and from there they planned to 'March to Delhi.'

"The Japs crossed the Chindwin River," the Major said gazing left and right. "We hear the river crossing is quite treacherous. And you know, what's funny?" he said looking at Baldev's somber face.

"What is funny, Major?" Baldev tried to smile at the unexpected comments.

"They were traveling with hundreds of oxen for food," the major cringed. "But most of them got sick and died. That's what the reports say."

Baldev balked at the idea of killing and eating bullocks that are used in the fields for tilling the soil to grow food crops. He thought of his pet bullock Sheru, who grew up with him and was his buddy from childhood, still the best plower at fourteen.

"That means we'll be facing desperate hungry Japs," Baldev said.

"We're going to join the soldiers defending Kohima. They're hugely outnumbered by the Japanese army," Sarabjit Singh said.

"We'll put the hungry Japs out of their misery and go home." Baldev suddenly felt homesick.

The infantry caravan marched towards Kohima. The road snaked upward through the mountains surrounded by dense jungle. A steep peak on one side of the road and an equally steep drop on the other, made it unstable and dangerous.

Suddenly the caravan came to an abrupt halt followed by loud voices. Baldev stretched his neck to see what was going on but an elbow-bend in the road and dense vegetation blocked his view. The major ran towards the front. Baldev followed.

A lorry loaded with ammunition had struck a tree bough hanging overhead and was dangerously balanced at the bend in the road. The soldiers were trying to push the lorry back onto the road.

The jungle was steamy hot due to a so-called mango shower (early monsoon) the day before and the midday sun was shining furiously. The sappers at the front finally pushed the lorry back onto the road and the caravan continued towards Kohima along the Manipur road.

Chapter 60

"Japs!" the major yelled and lurched backward. A red stream of blood sprang up from his chest like a fountain.

"Get down!" Baldev screamed.

They flattened to the ground wildly firing towards the jungle.

An ammunition lorry took a direct hit launching explosives in every direction. Within minutes the trees were engulfed in flames and the jungle crackled amidst the howling of humans killing each other.

A little later the Japanese disappeared into the jungle. Baldev sat with dry vacant eyes staring at Sarabjit Singh's lifeless body. Captain Smith touched Baldev on the shoulder, "Sergeant!" he said. Baldev got up to help remove and bury the bodies.

"We'll continue up," the captain said looking towards Kohima about two miles up on the mountain.

"Baldev get the company ready." He quickly turned to talk to the other soldiers.

They walked through the thick jungle at night and joined the troops at Kohima. The garrison consisted of a handful of Sikhs, a few Assam Rifles along with some Royal West Kent soldiers.

The town of Kohima, situated at five thousand feet in the mountains, was once a peaceful place spread on several hill ridges with cottages and beautiful gardens. The Deputy Commissioner's bungalow with its flower beds and tennis court stood on the hillside, and the British Club House was around the bend of the road. The Field Supply Depot (FSD) and Daily Issue Store (DIS) were situated on smaller hills along with several huts and bashas full of supplies and bread ovens. These ridges were overlooked by densely wooded peaks higher than ten thousand feet.

They dug out slit trenches as quickly as they could and waited. The Japanese army fifteen thousand strong surrounded the town, outnumbering the British Indian forces by ten to one.

A day later, hordes of Japanese army charged towards the FSD and DIS centers, shooting and screaming.

"Hold fire!" Captain Smith yelled.

But as soon as the Japanese were about fifteen yards away, "Fire!" he yelled and bodies started falling over each other. The numbers though were on the Japanese side and many overran the trenches reaching the supply bashas and the nearby bakery.

"Cover me!" Before the captain could say anything, a sapper from the West Kent dashed towards the basha huts. Baldev joined him along with a few more sappers and set fire to the bashas made of bamboo shoots and thatched roofs.

The Japanese trying to fight their way out through the flames were met with showers of artillery and Bren guns. Falling like flies, some of them still had their mouths full of bread.

"Do not be so foolish," Smith yelled as Baldev and others came back grinning ear-to-ear.

The next day mortar fire rained down continuously. After a bitter bloody battle, the Japanese broke through the lines and seized the FSD and DIS ridges along with the drinking water sources.

Desperately Smith ordered them to retreat to the tennis courts of the deputy commissioner's bungalow under the cover of Bren guns. The Japanese had dug the trenches close by on the other side of the court.

Every night the combat turned to a stalemate after the grounds were strewn with dead and wounded men, covered in dust, pools of blood, and clouds of flies. Defenders and attackers lay in the slit trenches only a few yards apart.

Three days of hurling grenades at each other became a lethal game. The Japanese continued with their onslaught and the British Indians refused to give in. Grenades fell with a thud and exploded with a deafening blast. A big chunk of hard clay fell into Baldev's trench, hitting him in the forehead. A piercing shriek came out of his throat and complete darkness engulfed him.

Pali flapped her golden wings and glided over the massive bars of the gate. She looked down. Baldev sat on the ground with his head between his knees.

"C'mon Bal, jump!" she hollered. "Don't you hear me, Bal? Jump, I said." She hovered above the gate flailing her wings gently.

"I can't." Baldev looked up. "You keep going, Pali." He wiped his eyes and bent his head into his knees again.

"I am not going anywhere without you. You have to jump over the gate," she insisted.

"My wings broke, Pali. I can't fly anymore," Baldev said without looking at her.

"That's why you have to jump." She flew down and nudged him. "Try harder, Bal...try again." She pulled him by the arm.

Baldev felt a splitting headache and a heavyweight on his chest. Someone stepped over his chest and jumped to the next trench. Then another person jumped over him. *The Japs! They think I'm dead. They're running into our territory.* Exploding artillery bombs and loud noise of gunfire was deafening. A wave of terror passed through his achy body. He felt for his gun. It lay next to him in the trench. He picked it upholding it tight. Moments later another Japanese soldier jumped into his trench. Collecting all his strength he thrust the bayonet into his unsuspecting enemy's neck.

The Japanese soldier fell into the trench. His startled eyes wide open and blood gushed out of his mouth while the battle continued outside.

This part of the tennis court had been taken over by the Japanese. Baldev stayed down in the trench with the dead man all day long and then crawled across the tennis court to the other side at night.

Pali! Pali! His mind kept repeating like a mantra. Baldev slid into a trench as soon as he reached the other side. Someone lay there in the dark, moaning in pain.

"Gurnam?" Baldev recognized his voice.

"Huhn, huhn...my shoulder," Gurnam groaned in a barely audible voice.

Baldev tapped his shoulders in the dark. The left side seemed okay. Feeling Gurnam's right shoulder, his hand dipped into a pool of sticky blood. "Oh!" Baldev mumbled. He rubbed his hand on his pants, but could not wipe off all the thick gluey blood.

Not knowing what to do, he stayed in the trench lying next to him. A hellish fire continued nonstop for the tiny strip of land in the tennis court. Relentless Japanese attacks were being met with unyielding intensity. The road to Kohima had been severed by the Japanese and the allied forces were stuck at Jotsoma. No relief was in sight.

Too feeble to fire back, Baldev lay quietly in the trench. The pain in his forehead felt like sawing his head into two. The water canteen lying next to him was empty. He inverted the bottle over his mouth and shook it up and down. A few drops fell onto his cracked dry tongue.

Gurnam had not moved or groaned for a while. Baldev pressed his fingers into his neck below the ear to feel his pulse. *He's alive!* He heaved a sigh of relief.

A little later Baldev tried firing his gun but it was out of ammunition. He picked up Gurnam's Sten and found it empty too.

They had run out of ammunition and food. The water source was under Japanese control. A lot of the rations and water-filled tire tubes dropped by the Dakotas, fell to the enemy side because the perimeter of the garrison was extremely small.

Hundreds had been killed on each side and no way of collecting the rotting bodies. The wounded lying in the trenches were getting wounded again. The medics trying to help them were getting killed too.

Lying in the muddy trench, Baldev tried to stay awake. A dull thud startled him. He was horrified to see a grenade that somehow did not explode. With lightning speed, he picked it up and threw it back towards the Japanese trenches, only a few yards away. The sky lit up with the explosion and bloody body parts flew out of the trench.

Panting heavily Baldev fell back into the trench and closed his eyes. He had not eaten for three days. Whether he fell asleep or simply fainted due to exhaustion, he woke up to the thundering clouds midst the thunder of bomb explosions. Rain poured down in buckets. Baldev opened his mouth swallowing the rainwater.

The trench quickly started filling up and soon it was like a shallow pond. How will I keep Gurnam's head above water if it keeps raining? He worried.

But the rain stopped suddenly as it had started. Baldev tried to check Gurnam's pulse again but could not feel it with his trembling hands. "Stay alive!" he whispered.

Chapter 61

The relief units stuck for several weeks at Jotsoma and Zuzba, finally pushed their way towards Kohima, fighting through the knife-edge ridges and dense jungle. They drove the Grant Tanks over the steep muddy mountain terrain and pushed them through the deep gullies.

The Indian unit from the 1st Punjab Regiment followed by the Royal Berkshires arrived before daybreak. The tanks fired pointblank at the Japanese bunkers. Hurricane fighter-bombers flew dangerously low to precisely strike the Japanese positions, which were extremely close to the allied garrison.

Undeterred, the Japanese kept coming back in waves into the direct fire, shouting their heads off. After over two months of bloody artillery and hand to hand bayonet attacks, the Japanese were beaten back. The tide was finally turned and they were stamped out of the garrison.

Ambulances sped towards Kohima and the wounded were quickly being loaded.

"I need help here!" Baldev hollered.

Two of the medics ran towards him and looked in the trench. Without a word, they ran toward the next trench.

"Where're you going?" Baldev yelled, "Come back. Don't you see he's hurt bad?" Baldev hobbled after them.

One of the medics shook his head, "We're taking only the injured at the moment."

"He's injured too," Baldev said.

"We will come for the bodies later," the other medic added.

"He's not dead," Baldev shouted.

"Looks like you are hurt too. Go to one of the trucks and get checked," the medic said looking at Baldev's blood-soaked muddy clothes.

"I'm okay, but you have to take care of Gurnam," Baldev yelled over the gut-wrenching chorus of groans that seemed to have suddenly developed after the ear-splitting noise of guns and mortars stopped.

"He's dead, and I don't want you to die here, too." the other medic yelled back and kept going towards the next trench.

"No, he's not." Stepping over the blood-spattered ground, Baldev limped along.

"Look, I'm sorry! He is dead! And right now, we're trying to save the ones that can still be saved." The medic turned quickly.

Baldev's legs shook.

A man stepped out of the trench. He had his hand wrapped in a bandage he might have made by tearing his uniform.

"You're alive, Baldev!" He stared at him like he saw a ghost, "they said you were gone."

"Robert?" Baldev turned to him. "I was. But I'm back." He looked at his hand, "you're hurt. Hope it's not too bad."

"It hurts like hell," Robert said. "They said you were dead, what happened?"

"It's a long story. You look so different with your long beard. I almost did not recognize you."

"No shaving for weeks." Robert flinched with pain pressing his bandaged hand to his chest. One of the Medics directed him towards the ambulance.

"Please take another look at my friend, he might still be alive," Baldev begged.

"Listen, we're sorry he is not. And you don't want to collapse here either."

Baldev turned towards where the surviving soldiers were gathering. He barely avoided stepping on a man on the ground, "Here's another wounded man!" he hollered to the medics who had moved further down looking for the injured.

It was a young Japanese soldier with his shin bones exposed and the left foot severed. He looked at Baldev with a begging expression. He pushed his fist towards his chest like a dagger, whispering something Baldev did not understand. His gesture suggested, he was asking him to kill him.

For the first time, Baldev looked at him as a human whose family might be waiting for him at home. The hatred for the Japs turned into compassion. He sat by his side and held his hand.

"I'm not going to kill you," Baldev said and waited for the medics. "I'm going to get you help." Baldev cringed as he saw the severed foot lying nearby with the shoe still on.

"The medics are coming," Baldev said pressing his cold hand.

The Japanese soldier wrinkled his forehead and mouthed something.

"They'll be here soon," Baldev said.

The Japanese soldier kept shaking his head side to side. He jerked his fist towards his chest again and again.

The medics rushed towards the soldier. "It's a Jap!" the medic yelled.

"It's a man!" Baldev yelled back.

"You go on soldier. Do not worry about him." The medic held Baldev by the arm and pointed to where the surviving soldiers had gathered.

Baldev staggered towards them. Tears flowed onto his mud-caked beard.

The soldiers sat where the deputy commissioner's bungalow once stood. He sat by the chimney, the only part of the bungalow left standing.

They were all emaciated beyond recognition, wearing filthy uniforms and torn shoes. Most of them could hardly walk or talk. The British soldiers had grown all different shades of beards and mustaches, golden, some brownish, and some with a reddish tinge. They had survived months of sleepless nights, hunger, and constant blasts while their comrades were blown to pieces.

The hill town of Kohima that was once famous for its beautiful terraced gardens and grassy knolls with flower beds was littered with rotting body parts, exploded bomb shards, and ammunition cartridges. The charred limbless tree stumps stood like ghosts. Rags of white parachutes hung from the leafless trees.

The songbirds that once nested in the gardens and hopped around from branch to branch were nowhere to be found. Instead, the vultures circled the skies above.

"Is that you Baldev?" Bachan Singh looked at his shriveled, ashen-grey face, squinting. He had reached Kohima with the 1st Punjab relief unit.

"Bachan..." Baldev murmured and his head lurched to the side.

"Baldev, Baldev. Stay with me!" Bachan Singh picked him up on his shoulders and carried him to a waiting ambulance.

Chapter 62

Harjit browned the chopped onions in butter along with some garlic and ginger and added the Brinjal slices into the pot. She stirred it with a wooden spoon and added garam masala and turmeric powder. The air filled up with the aroma of Brinjal cooked in butter and spices. Hakam would be home soon she thought and started making roti for dinner.

One of these days he is going to ask about Baldev. What would I tell him? Lie again? No, I would tell him the truth, no matter what the consequences. The lie she had told Hakam about Baldev being at college, was weighing her down like a heavy rock was bound to her chest.

"I will tell him today after dinner," Harjit decided. "Hope people at the Banyan don't say anything. Baba Budh Singh has been reminding them all the time."

Hakam walked in no sooner than the words left her mouth, "You're home!" She forced a startled smile.

"I left the farm a bit early and didn't stop at the Banyan today," Hakam said.

"You have to take it easy," she said. "Let Zahid do the farm work."

"He does most of the work. I just like spending time at the farm." Hakam held her hand.

After years of combating the demons of torture at Kala Pani Prison, Hakam had slowly returned to his normal self. He had started going to the farm, helping with the crops and cattle. He spent time at Baba Budh Singh listening to the radio. He sat with the villagers under the Banyan for a while on his way home from the farm.

Hakam walked straight to the verandah and sat with the newspaper.

"You look tired. I'll make you some tea." Harjit went to the kitchen thinking, *why's he so obsessed with the newspapers?*

Looking at the water boiling in the pot she felt as if the guilt of lying was boiling inside her and scalding her whole being. Does he know I lied to him?

Thoughts hammered her conscience. I have to tell the truth! If not now, when? She poured the tea through a strainer into the cup and took it to Hakam. "I have to tell you something, Hakam," she said placing the cup of steaming tea on the stool. She sat by him shaking inside and out.

Hakam lifted his eyes from the newspaper. "What is it, Harjit?" he said looking at her panicky, tense face. "Is something wrong?"

"I'm so, so sorry. I lied to you, Hakam, I lied!" She covered her face with quivering hands and sobbed.

Hakam folded the newspaper and put it aside. "Calm down, Harjit, it can't be that bad."

"I wanted to tell you so many times, but…"

"Come, come here." Hakam gently pulled her towards him, "Tell me, Harjit!" he held her close.

"Bal is not at college, I lied!" she hid her face in his chest. "You were just recovering from the ordeal and I did not want to shock you. He joined the army and he's gone to war," her sobs got louder.

"Stop crying, Harjit." He held her face and looked into her eyes, "I know. I've known it for a while now."

"You knew?" Harjit looked at him, startled, "since when? How did you find out?"

"I've overheard men talking by the Banyan tree, although they won't say anything when I am there." Hakam forced a smile. "Also, he did not come home on the weekends, or even during the summer break. And the newspapers are filled with war stories." Hakam pointed to the newspaper.

"Then why didn't you say anything to me?"

"I thought you would tell me when you're ready. I know you were trying to protect me, Harjit." Hakam held her tighter in his arms.

"O, Hakam, I worry about him, day and night. Not a single letter from him since he left." Harjit sobbed again.

"I'm worried about him too. I only remember him as a little boy." He wiped her tears.

"How badly I want to see him a grown man."

"He is so much like you, Hakam! He talks like you and he walks like you," Harjit gazed at his face unblinking, "he even likes the same food…"

Talking about Baldev, her face lit up with a beaming smile and she instinctively straightened her neck in a proud gesture.

"And you know what he does, when he's happy? He lifts me up from the ground and twirls around. My feet dangle and I beg him to put me down and he laughs and sings, just like you used to do when we were young."

"Ha...ha...ha..." Hakam Singh laughed heartily for the first time in years.

"Is he stubborn like me too?" He asked with a twinkle in his eyes.

"No, he's not as stubborn as you are!" Harjit jovially smacked his arm and ran towards the courtyard.

Hakam followed, laughing. She went around the *Neem* tree once and ran back towards the verandah. Hakam caught up with her and held her by the corner of her *duppata*.

"Here you are!"

Harjit turned and her *duppata* was left in Hakam's hands while she ran and stopped by the *Neem* tree laughing and panting. Hakam was out of breath too when he got there. He held her close and kissed her eyes and her forehead, her cheeks, and her lips.

"You've become a teenager again!" Harjit tried pushing him away.

"We are both teenagers again!" Hakam said, wrapping her *duppata* around her shoulders. They stood by the tree in a gentle embrace.

"Can't wait for the day when our son will come home." Harjit let out a loud sigh.

"He *will* come back home, Harjit." Hakam looked towards the sky as if praying to the unseen.

"I know in my heart he is okay and will be back soon." Harjit rested her head on his shoulder.

The sun had gone down. The farmers were returning home with their cattle and women in the kitchen making *dal* and *roti*. The village streets were filled with joyful shrieks of children playing and chasing each other homeward.

"Let me make some *kheer* today. You like it! You and Bal both like it," Harjit said walking to the kitchen.

"Isn't it a bit late to make *kheer*? Won't it take a long time to cook the rice and sugar in milk until it thickens to almost a cream?" Hakam followed her to the kitchen.

"But that's your favorite," she said, putting a pot of milk on the fire and added rice and sugar to it. Sitting on the low stool she constantly stirred it with a ladle.

A soft knock made them look towards the door.

"Who could it be, at this hour?" Harjit walked to the door.

Pali stood next to Namo.

"Hakam, look who's here!" she shouted with excitement.

"Is this our daughter, our little girl Pali?" Hakam looked at the tall 18-year-old girl in disbelief and took her into his arms and then hugged Namo.

"Come in, come in," he held Pali's arm walking them into the house.

"You must hungry. I made some Brinjal *sabji* and *kheer* would be ready soon." Harjit kissed Pali's forehead again and again, "My sweet, Pali."

They sat on their cots after dinner and talked about the farm and crops and how everyone they knew was doing.

"Why did Lal Singh leave us so soon?" Hakam's eyes welled up.

"Only God knows," Namo sighed.

"Who can understand His mysterious ways?" Harjit joined in. They sat quietly for a while. But the gloomy overcast was brightened by Baldev's letter.

"He wrote back." Pali took out the letter from her bag.

"He's alive!" Harjit kissed the letter and pressed it to her chest.

Hakam took the letter from her, "My son!" he whispered.

Chapter 63

While the British Indian army and the allied forces fought the war on various fronts, in Europe, Africa, and Asia, a different kind of explosive war brewed in the political arena of the Indian leadership.

Sensing the vulnerability of the Raj, Gandhi announced *puran sawaraj,* complete independence from the British.

Shouts of "Quit India" reverberated in the streets. Unprecedented violence broke out and mocked Gandhi's non-violence mantra.

The British police and the army retaliated brutally, killing thousands of civilians, while hundreds of thousands were arrested along with Nehru and Gandhi.

Meanwhile, Jinnah called for a separate nation for the Muslims and went around giving fiery speeches at huge gatherings. He wanted a sovereign land, called Pakistan, separate from Gandhi's hostile, infidel Hindu India.

In a Hindu nation, everyone will live in peace, Gandhi urged. India will be divided over his dead body, he said.

In a Hindu nation, Muslims will be treated worse than slaves, was Jinnah's reply.

The distrust between the leaders trickled down to the ordinary people all over the country and hostility flared up towards each other. Everyday lectures and rallies in the cities were intensifying the demand for a separate homeland for Muslims that spiraled down into the villages too. The village of Gajanpur was not any different. Men still gathered under the Banyan and talked for hours. They talked about Jinnah demanding Pakistan for the Muslims, and Gandhi opposing it.

Where would they make Pakistan, where only the *Musalmans* are going to live? Don't in every village and every town, Hindus, Sikhs, and Muslims all live together? The village people wondered.

One of these days, hundreds of flyers ended up in the village streets. Stacks of flyers secured under chunks of broken bricks and rocks were also found at the Banyan platform, where men gathered every afternoon.

Children played with them as make-believe money. Some acted as buyers and the others as shopkeepers. They sold pretend goods made of broken terracotta chips and fragrant *neem* tree branches and big banyan leaves. They hollered, 'come…come…buy the best oxen and cows and clothes.' The buyers haggled for the price. They laughed and yelled at each other.

Some of the children carefully folded the flyers and took them home, while the others tore them to pieces and the wind scattered them all around.

Baba Budh Singh picked up one of the flyers and read it out loud,

'Pakistan *Zindabad*!'

The Muslim Homeland, *Zindabad*!

The Land of the Pure, *Zindabad*!

With our lives, we will get Pakistan!

"What is going on?" Baba ji shook his head in disappointment, "Our boys are still not back from the war and our leaders are bent upon dividing the country!"

"So, what's wrong in asking for Pakistan?" Abdul Rahman asked, narrowing his eyes, he looked a bit puzzled.

"Don't you see, Abdul? It says, 'The Muslim Homeland,' where only the *Musalmans* will live, no Sikh or Hindu." Baba Budh Singh rolled his finger over the writing of the flyer.

"The leaders have no idea about the villages, how we live, and how we grow our crops and raise our children," Hardev Singh said waving the flyer above his head, "Why divide the country?"

"They don't know or they just don't want to know, that we, the villagers depend on each other. Our lives are intertwined, may it be a Sikh, Hindu or a *Musalman*." Baba ji's white beard swayed in the breeze as he spanned his gaze at men from one side of the platform to the other.

Many of them nodded while someone said loud enough for everyone to hear, "Baba ji is right. Our lives are connected to each other like nails attached to the fingertips."

Ajmal, Abdul Rahman's brother spoke even louder, looking at his brother, "It's not about dividing the people. It is only the change of name, I believe."

Abdul nodded in agreement. He picked up the flyers and began distributing to the men, regardless of the fact that most of the men could not read.

Soon everyone had a flyer in his hand, whether he was a farmer or the schoolteacher, whether he was a carpenter or the blacksmith. Men, who could not read, stared at the green paper as if the words were going to speak up and make some sense for them.

On his way to the farm, Hakam Singh stopped by, as he did every day, "What is going on?" he asked, looking at the flyers in their hands.

Abdul handed him one.

"*Divide and rule*, the British policy!" Frustration written all over his face, Hakam said, "It worked for them before, it is working for them now." He handed the flyer back to Abdul.

"Come, sit for a while, Hakam," Baba ji said, moving a little to the side to make room for him.

"It's all right, Baba ji, I should get going." He turned and continued towards his fields.

"He knows what he's talking about. Gandhi and Jinnah are at each other's throat, pressing harder with every passing moment," Baba ji said, "both rigid and inflexible, Jinnah and Gandhi. The war of words goes on even when Gandhi is in prison."

"He gets special treatment in the prison. They let him out even if he gets a runny nose, while many others die from mistreatment and disease," Jang Singh said.

Men argued and opposed each other. They discussed and agreed with each other. They were like foes at one level and friends at another.

"Look here, Gandhi is released from prison!" Hardev joined them with a newspaper under his arm. He opened it and rose above his head showing the picture of Gandhi on the front page. "I bet you, he will now go around spreading his message of non-violence that hardly ever prevents any violence."

"What about the rest of the thousands of prisoners? When would they be released?" A loud voice came from the far side of the platform.

"Who knows when they will be released? Every time they arrest Gandhi, he is released after a while and the others rot in prison for years." Hardev's forehead wrinkled into two deep furrows between the eyes.

"Has anyone ever wondered why Jinnah is never arrested?" Karam Chand, the shopkeeper sitting next to Baba ji said, "They've been arresting people even for shouting a slogan and Jinnah's speeches are fiery as hell."

"Maybe he's favored by the British," a man sitting behind Hardev took a gibe at Jinnah.

"His speeches are not fiery as hell, and he's not favored by the British!" Ajmal stood up and shouted, "It is Nehru and Gandhi, whom the British favor."

"O, I hear the Viceroy sent you a letter saying that Nehru was their favorite son. Is that true, Ajmal?" Karam Chand stood up laughing. Others joined in a hearty laugh at Karam Chand's witty joke.

"How dare you insult us like this!" Abdul dashed towards Karam Chand and knocked him to the ground.

Ajmal joined his brother and kicked Karam Chand, "You mock us. That's another reason for getting a separate homeland."

Hardev threw away the newspaper and pulled Abdul's arm, twisting it backward, "You think you can beat up anyone and not pay for it? I will turn your bastard bones into gravel if you ever try it again."

Other people overpowered Ajmal who kept shouting and kicking and held him tightly.

Soon the Muslims of the village were on one side and the Sikhs and Hindus on the other, growling at each other. They shouted obscenities and clawed at each other's old wounds.

Children stopped playing and stood like immovable little pillars, staring at their elders with popping eyes and open mouths. The buffalos, drinking water at the nearby pond, turned their heads towards the Banyan. Water still dripping from their lips they fixed their gaze at the brawling men.

"Stop it! All of you," Baba Budh Singh yelled at the top of his voice.

A sudden silence prevailed. Men stepped away from each other and looked at Baba ji. But the short-lived silence was crushed under the exchange of hot words that started instantly.

"Hakam was right when he talked about *divide and rule* policy." Baba ji stood up on the platform. "Hakam is right," Baba ji repeated.

Hakam's name acted like a calming balm on the angry voices and the atmosphere went quiet once again.

"All of you know that leaders don't know much about our village life. Has any of them ever come here to see you or talk to you?" Baba ji was out of breath whether due to old age or maybe because of what had just happened.

"Then why should we fight each other because of their hot-headedness?"

Muffled voices replaced the angry shouts and most of them nodded in agreement.

"I want you all to go home now and we'll thrash out any of the doubts or complaints you have about this tomorrow."

Hardev took Baba ji's hand helping him down the platform. A seed of distrust and enmity was sown into the hearts of the people of Gajanpur.

Chapter 64

Hearing hushed voices and soft footsteps, Baldev tried to open his eyes. *Where am I?* He blinked several times and looked around. Soon the hushed voices were not hushed anymore. He could hear loud grunts and groans of the wounded and quick footsteps of the doctors and nurses.

Where am I? Is it a hospital? Baldev tried to sit up and noticed a needle in his right arm connected to a bottle hanging by a metal stand. Liquid trickled from the bottle drop by drop, through a tube to the needle in his arm. *Glucose drip?* His whole body felt heavy as lead but no sharp pain anywhere.

I'm alive! Tears of joy trickled down his cheeks. He wiped them with the back of his hand. For a while he laid still, staring at the ceiling. A feeling of soothing calmness in his heart blocked the harrowing sounds of soldiers moaning in pain.

A man lay quietly to his right, with a drip bottle hanging from the same metal stand. Baldev stretched his neck to look at him. The man's right hand wrapped in bandages rested on his chest. Blood seeping through the white bandage had made an irregular red smudge on it. A few flies hovered around the red spot.

The long corridor was filled with rows of wounded men, some lying quietly and some loudly groaning. The air was heavy with the smell of 'Dettol' and medicines. Some areas of the hall were curtained off, where most of the activity seemed to be occurring. Doctors and nurses went in and out of these isolated cells constantly.

Baldev closed his eyes and tried to rest. *Is that Robert lying to my right?* A voice inside him whispered. He lifted his head and stared at the man. The reddish beard confirmed the doubt. "It *is* Robert, the West Kent soldier!" Baldev murmured.

"Hey, Robert!" he called out.

"Robert!" he called again, a little louder than before. The man laid motionless, pale, eyes closed shut.

302

Baldev looked at his bandaged hand. It looked kind of odd. It seemed like the bandage was wrapped around three of his fingers with tips slightly visible but no sign of thumb and the forefinger. *Did he lose part of his hand?* Baldev shuddered with the thought of amputation.

"Robert!" Again no answer.

Baldev looked at his own hands. He opened and closed his palms several times as if making sure all ten fingers were still there. He moved his toes under the sheet and pulled his knees towards his chest. *I'm okay!* He heaved a loud sigh of relief. A weak smile stretched across his face.

He rolled his hand over his face and stroked his lips and beard with his fingers. His long hair was tied in a bun. He looked to the sides for his turban but did not see it.

He was wearing a long bluish shirt instead of his tattered bloody uniform.

No underwear. Embarrassed he tried to tuck the sheet tightly around him.

"You're awake!" A nurse in a white uniform seemed to have appeared out of nowhere.

"You look good, Sergeant," she smiled.

Good, I tucked the sheet around me before she came. Baldev managed a smile.

"You won't need the drip anymore." She pressed a cotton swab at the site of the needle and pulled it out.

"Here, hold the swab down for a little while," she told him, removing the drip bottle from the stand.

Baldev pressed the cotton swab with his fingers and bent his arm to prevent any bleeding. He sat in his bed looking at Robert who had not moved so far. His chest was rising and falling steadily and evenly.

The nurse checked the level of the liquid in Robert's drip bottle and nodded. She gently lifted his bandaged hand where the blood had seeped through and murmured something that Baldev could not hear.

"Is he alright?" Baldev asked.

"Yes, he is," she said and quickly walked towards one of the partitioned off chambers of the hospital ward.

Does he know he has lost his thumb and the forefinger, the most important part of his hand? Baldev felt a twinge in his heart.

He's alive! The thought came as a consoling reassurance, and he will go back to his family. Baldev thought about the thousands of soldiers whose bodies could not even be buried or cremated.

"I should write home as soon as possible," he mumbled. "My rucksack!"

He looked around but did not see it anywhere. All the letters were in there. He tried to remember the last time he carried it with him but nothing came to mind.

Oh, no, Kewal's letter was in there too. How will I get it to his daughter? A wave of sadness overpowered the triumph of being unhurt and alive. Baldev suddenly felt weak.

"You look well, Sergeant Baldev!" Lieutenant Bachan Singh walked to his bed. "You scared the hell out of me back there," Bachan Singh said shaking hands with him.

"Did we win?" Baldev remembered the battle like it happened in a dream.

"Yes, we did! We defeated them at Kohima and Imphal, both," Bachan Singh said with a glimmer of pride in his eyes. "We destroyed them completely, and it's all due to brave soldiers like you, Baldev."

"Sir? No sir, I... I'm..." Baldev grappled for words.

"It's all right," Bachan Singh patted his shoulder, "You held firm against an army ten times bigger."

Baldev wanted to ask him about his rucksack stuffed with letters that he did not get a chance to read, but felt a little silly and childish.

"Kewal sat next to me when he was hit," he said, instead of asking about his bag. "And I could do nothing about it."

"Kewal from Mangatpur?" Bachan Singh's eyes widened with shock, "Killed?" he asked, stepping a little closer to Baldev's bed.

Baldev nodded.

"There was another soldier, Jagtar from the same village," Bachan Singh said.

"Him too. They were both killed at the Admin Box at Arakan." Baldev leaned his head down and shook it side to side as if he himself did not believe it.

"You knew them?" he asked the lieutenant.

"Yes, their village is near mine, only about three miles away."

"I had made a promise to Kewal that I... I will..." Baldev's eyes watered. Unable to speak, he turned his face away from Bachan Singh.

"What promise Baldev? Tell me." Bachan Singh's sturdy features turned soft and gentle. He tenderly held Baldev by the shoulder.

Baldev looked at him, wiping his eyes, "He wrote a letter to his little girl and wanted me to give it to her if he didn't survive. We were both working the Bren, he assisting me with the ammo."

"At the Admin Box battle?" Bachan Singh asked, listening with full attention.

"Yes, and I angrily told him to shut up and not say anything about not surviving. I told him to get the letter to her himself." While looking to the far side of the hospital ward Baldev continued,

"We made the Japs run with their tails between their legs every night, and every time they left their dead and the injured behind. But they kept coming back, again and again, more furiously. I was firing nonstop and Kewal was next to me, handing me the ammo belts. The next thing I know, his head was blown off." Baldev unsuccessfully tried to suppress a sob.

"I carried his body down the hill and took the letter from his pocket. That's when I promised to get it to his daughter."

"I know how hard it is to lose your companion, your army brother. But why are you so worried about the letter?" Bachan Singh asked.

"I had stuffed all the letters from home that I didn't get a chance to read, along with Kewal's letter in my rucksack and carried them from Dimapur to Kohima. Now I don't know what happened to it," Baldev said.

"I don't know what he wanted to tell his little girl." A loud sob erupted from his throat which Baldev could not suppress anymore. "He was a good man." Baldev rested his head on his knees.

"I doubt if we will be able to find the letter, but I tell you, Baldev, you go to his village when you go home. Talk to his wife and daughter," Bachan Singh said. "Tell them how brave he was. Tell them how he loved them. Tell them, the whole country is going to be proud of him."

Teary-eyed, Baldev looked up and nodded.

"He made us laugh by telling jokes. When we all felt murky and miserable, he was the one making everyone laugh." An instant smile spread over Baldev's gloomy face. "He carried the injured to the medics with utmost compassion and care. He was like a brother to all."

"These're the things you can talk to his daughter and wife about him. Tell the little girl about her father's courage and his kindness, as you would your own child."

Baldev's momentary smile had disappeared, but the tears persisted.

"Let me tell you something, Baldev. The Colonel is very much impressed with how you handled every situation with fearless valor," Bachan Singh said patting his shoulder. "I will recommend your promotion."

Baldev looked at Bachan Singh with his mouth slightly open and his arms wrapped around his knees.

Bachan Singh shook his shoulder rather vigorously. "We want you to rest a few days and then we will hurl the rest of the Japanese out of Burma, dead or alive."

"Yes, we will!" Baldev's voice suddenly was filled with solid determination. "We *will*, Lieutenant…Sir!"

Chapter 65

A column of armored trucks, Lee-Grant tanks, open jeeps, and lorries stretching for miles, rolled over the roadless passages of Chin Hills towards Irrawaddy Valley.

After defeating the Japanese at Imphal and Kohima, General Slim's forces were on their way towards central Burma and from there on to Rangoon, over 600 miles to the south.

The men were in great morale. With a few days rest and good nutrition they were fit and ready. A kind of heroic confidence emanated from their faces.

"Here we come, Rangoon!" Lieutenant Bachan Singh seemed to be in seventh heaven. He shouted and smiled at Baldev riding with him. Dressed in a brand new, still a little stiff uniform, Baldev rolled his palms over his neatly tied turban and smiled back, "Let's fling them out of Burma."

"General Slim wants us to get there before the monsoons. During the rainy season, the roads and the rivers become one indistinguishable big body of water," Bachan Singh said looking up at the cloudless blue sky.

Baldev nodded and instinctively looked up following Bachan Singh's gaze.

"At the moment, speed is everything to get to Rangoon." The lieutenant repeated General Messervy's words, he had said to his officers, "Speed is all-important, and risk must be accepted to obtain it. Every day is precious." Bachan Singh stretched his neck trying to look down the road beyond the jeeps.

"Yes sir!" Baldev said as the jungle vegetation slowly moved backward on the winding dusty passage. *Aren't we moving too slowly?* Baldev squirmed as if it would make the jeep go a little faster.

The caravan trekked along at a steady pace. The rumble and clattering noise of the tanks and armored trucks echoed through the hills. *Wish there was less noise and more speed.* Baldev adjusted himself in his seat again.

"I wonder whatever happened to the Americans?" Baldev suddenly seemed to have remembered. "We never saw them after Field Marshal Mountbatten gave us all a hearty pep talk."

"They've been building a road from India to China through the mountains, a supply road, they say." Bachan Singh shared his tad of knowledge about the American General Stilwell's road. "A very treacherous job, I heard," he added.

"But we've been getting supplies through parachutes. Isn't it more feasible than making a whole new road across the jungle-covered mountains with peaks and canyons?" Baldev asked looking sideways at the peak on one side and a steep fall on the other.

"It's the generals who make decisions. We follow orders," Bachan Singh said, "although, we make the immediate decisions when we lead our company during the battle."

Baldev nodded touching the new logo on his uniform and said, "That's right, Lieut...

"Oh, no, the jeep...the jeep..." Baldev stood up and shouted, "It went down!"

Suddenly a collective gasp froze the caravan with a jolt.

Three vehicles ahead of Baldev, a jeep slipped off the unpaved narrow passage and disappeared from view. Men ran to the spot where the jeep had gone down.

It was precariously balanced on a narrow cliff with hardly any trees on it. The trench below the cliff could measure hundreds of feet deep.

The driver and the soldier in the jeep looked panic-frozen. Soldiers stood by the edge of the road looking equally baffled as what to do.

"That's Jack! He was with me for a while when Kewal died at the Admin Box," Baldev whispered to the lieutenant as if the jeep would fall if he spoke any louder, "and the other I don't think I've seen before."

"Baldev, take off your turban!" Lieutenant Bachan Singh ordered, hurriedly unwinding his own. "We'll need two more. The cliff seems to be about twenty feet down," he said making a tight knot between the two turbans that made about a 30-foot long sturdy rope.

Gurjit Singh and Ram Singh took off their turbans and bound them together into a second 30-foot long cord.

"We'll have to pull both of them up exactly at the same time," the lieutenant said in a hushed voice.

Three men held one end of each of the turbans and lowered the other end down to the jeep.

"Hold tight." Bachan Singh looked down at the jeep. "Hold tight!" he said again as the cords reached the jeep.

The soldiers sat panic-stricken, afraid to move their hands to grab the turban ropes hanging close to their faces.

"This is the only way to get you out. The jeep is not going to hold much longer."

Bachan Singh shouted, "Grab the cords!"

"Pull at three," he told Baldev and the men holding the other ends.

"One... Two..."

The soldiers clenching their jaws grasped the rope.

"Cling to it with your life...

"Three," he shouted.

"Pull...pull...pull..." Bachan Singh bellowed. Many joined in. shouting and cheering.

The moment the men were lifted off the jeep, it went tumbling down the cliff, banging against the steep rocky wall of the mountain.

"Hang on..."

Baldev's hair fell to his shoulders as he sat on the ground with his feet firmly planted against the bushes on the edge of the road, pulling the rope with all his strength. Two men behind him stood in the middle of the road pulling the turban rope.

Gurjit sat next to Baldev with his feet also planted against the bushes, assisted by Ram Singh and another soldier who stood in the road pulling the other man clinging to the rope.

A chorus of 'pull,' 'hang on,' 'almost there,' echoed in the hills. They sweated and groaned and pulled the rope as if their own life depended on it.

As soon as the men reached the road level, they collapsed onto the ground face down. Arms still stretched above their heads; they lay still for a while heaving loudly.

The jungle-covered mountain reverberated with shouts of joy, "Yeh..." and they clapped and laughed and hugged each other.

The jeep looked like a mangled toy lying at the bottom of the trench partly obscured by the brush.

Both men pulled out of the jaws of death looked like in a trance, unable to speak.

Eyes wide open they seemed to see nothing, hear nothing. Their pants tattered at the knees by the friction against the rocks on the slope. Blood oozed from the scraped skin.

"Jack!" Baldev patted his shoulder.

"Baldev!" His lips barely moved. "Thank you," he whispered. Tears flowed down his cheeks that he did not try to wipe.

"Thank you!" the other man said staring at Baldev's long hair stretching down to his waist. "I'm Andrew." He weakly stretched his arm for a handshake.

"I'm Baldev." He gently took Andrew's quivering palm.

Bachan Singh untied the knot and handed Baldev's turban to him.

"Thank you for wearing those." Jack pointed to the turban. "They saved our lives."

"It's a gift from our Guru." Baldev smiled, tying his hair into *Joorha* (bun) on his head.

"You can do a little better job at your *Joorha,* Baldev." Bachan Singh laughed, "I think you tie it too loose."

"I know, Ma always said that to me," A grin played over Baldev's face, "We all removed our turbans but only my hair flung open."

"Well, it's always good to listen to your Ma," Bachan Singh teased.

"I will when I go back. I will listen to her, I promise," Baldev winked, laughing heartily.

They escorted the rescued men to one of the trucks and the caravan continued towards the Chindwin River.

Chapter 66

The Bengal Miner and sappers who traveled at the head of the convoy were already building a floating Bailey bridge across the Chindwin River when the rest of the caravan reached there.

The engineers worked at near lightning speed, putting together the premanufactured, wooden, and steel truss spans that were carried by trucks, from Dimapur.

The tanks and mules, the ammo loaded lorries and the trucks, the soldiers and the officers, all waited for the completion of the bridge.

The Japanese had left their posts and moved further down towards the Irrawaddy Valley. That's what the reports said.

Everyone was in good spirits. They talked and laughed, making fun of each other. Some of them opened their rucksacks and read letters from home. They ate biscuits and drank hot tea. Some chewed gum and smoked cigarettes.

Bothered by the cigarette smoke, Baldev went strolling by the riverbank and found Jack sitting alone with his back against a rock. Arms crossed over his chest and hands tightly dug into his armpits, he listlessly stared at the bridge.

"How's it going, Jack?" Baldev settled himself next to him.

"A near-death experience," Jack tried a smile. "I'm still numb."

"Anyone would be, after what you went through. Even I am kind of numb," Baldev said.

"I'd rather die fighting the Japs than be killed by a stupid accident."

"Well, I'd say, we fight the Japs but not get killed," Baldev said spanning the vastness of the river where the army engineers were rushing to put the bridge sections together.

"That's the best strategy, but doesn't always work in war," Jack looked straight at Baldev, "Look how many of our army brothers we've lost."

"There's no harm in hoping, though." Baldev nodded with an unsure smile.

"Uh-huh, no harm in hoping," Jack's voice was almost a whisper. "It would be a long floating bridge." Changing the subject he looked towards the river.

"Maybe more than a thousand feet across, I guess," Baldev said. "Quite a tricky job they're doing."

"And it has to be… What the hell is that…?" Jack shouted.

Suddenly the sky rumbled with Zeros, the Japanese fighter planes, strafing at the partially built bridge. A noisy chaos erupted and a portion of the bridge fell into the river. The anti-aircraft gunners frantically fired at the low flying Zeros.

Men shouted and lay flat on the ground. Some hid under the vehicles and others froze wherever they were by the unexpected attack.

"One going down!" Baldev yelled.

One of the fighter planes fell into the river with a fiery splash and another, smoke billowing from its tail, crashed on the other side of the river. Flames rising from the carnage set the nearby trees on fire.

"One escaped! … One got away!" someone shouted.

For a while no one moved, waiting to see if the Zeros were coming back. Slowly everyone got to their feet looking at four bodies being brought out from the bridge area.

Soon the work on the bridge resumed even faster than before.

The convoy crossed the river a few hours later and headed south towards central Burma.

******

"Another river? Not again!" Baldev scanned the flatlands that looked entirely different from the jungle-covered mountains they had left behind.

"Yes, we've to cross yet another river, believe it or not," Bachan Singh said as the jeep sped along the crude dusty road.

"Didn't they use up all the bridge construction spans at Chindwin?" Baldev asked.

"They did. We'll see what they come up with this river. At this time of the year, hopefully, it will not be very deep."

Once again, they waited by the Irrawaddy River's bank while the engineers struggled with collecting and making clumsy boats out of whatever stuff that could float. General Slim ordered them to collect boats from all the surrounding villages.

Finally, the Tank Brigade and the Motorized Infantry Brigades crossed Irrawaddy and secured bridgeheads on the other side of the river. For weeks the worn-out and leaky pontoon boats, ferries, and assault boats, ceaselessly carried the equipment and supplies, the men, and the mules across the river.

The tanks and infantry began to advance towards the historic town of Mandalay.

"Look, Lieutenant, look!" Baldev pointed to the hill. "I believe, this is the Buddhist holy place, they speak of."

About a thousand feet high, Mandalay Hill was located on the northeast side of the Mandalay city. The skyline crowned by multiple Pagodas and Temples dominated the view.

"Incredible view!" Bachan Singh said looking at the magnificent pagodas. "But this is where the Japanese have a stronghold and also in the Fort Dufferin, down in the city."

"Hope, they don't destroy these beautiful temples."

"The Gurkha Battalion has already reached there," the lieutenant said, "we're going to join them to flush out the Japs from the Pagodas before they try to destroy them."

As soon as they reached the base of the hill, Lieutenant General Rees spoke through a megaphone, "There will be no bombing on the pagodas. We will not destroy any of the temples," he announced looking up at the hill.

"Charge!" he yelled.

"Bole So Nihal!" Bachan Singh shouted running up the hill.

An echo of 'Sat Sri Akal' resonated in the air. Baldev and other soldiers right behind him. The Sikh and Gurkha battalion ran up the winding stairs firing at the hill.

A rain of fire came down from the Japanese guns and bodies started falling left and right. The Japanese bodies rolled down the stairs.

The battle continued all night, intermittently stopping for a few moments and coming back with even more fury. At the daybreak, firing suddenly stopped.

"I think they're done," Bachan Singh whispered to Baldev.

There were bodies on the stairs, in front of the temple doors and pagodas. Stepping over the bodies they looked for the Japanese.

The Gurkha leader walked up to Bachan Singh, "I believe, they are in the bunkers, below the pagodas," he said, "there are several tunnels also underneath."

"That's what I believe too," Bachan Singh said and stood still for a moment. Everyone looked at him, waiting for orders.

Glaring at the heavy doors that lead down into the bunkers, Bachan Singh ordered, "Get a few petrol drums!"

Many Gurkha and Sikh soldiers ran down the hill and came back carrying drums filled with petrol.

"Break the doors!" he yelled.

Within minutes the steel doors were busted with anti-tank projectiles and reduced to heaps of scrapped metal.

"We'll flush them out of their rat holes," he said.

One by one the drums were rolled down the cellar stairs and ignited with incendiary tracer bullets.

Shouts of 'Banzai,' thumping sounds of running men and the smell of burning flesh filled the air. Many trying to escape through the tunnels were gunned down by the soldiers, at the base of the hill. The Gurkhas stood by the broken doors with their Kukri knives, ready to thrust into the escaping Japanese.

The Mandalay Hill was conquered. They stood on the summit looking down at the city of Mandalay that once was the capital of Burma before Rangoon. It lay in ghastly ruins. Most of the buildings with blown-off roofs and dilapidated walls witnessed the devastation of war. After clearing the enemy out of Mandalay Hill, the attention was directed towards Fort Dufferin in the center of the city.

Surrounded by a 30-foot wide red brick wall, and a 20-foot deep moat on four sides, Fort Dufferin was practically impassable. The palace of the old Burmese King Mindon with its multiple stupendous buildings lay inside the citadel.

The fortress had been under Japanese control for over three years. Now the garrison was under attack by the British Indian forces.

The Sikh and the Gurkha infantry troops marching behind the tanks and Howitzers reached the fort in the heart of the city.

Tanks firing pointblank and the 100-pound howitzer shells could hardly put any dent in the impenetrable 30-foot wide walls.

"Stay back, away from the tank!" Bachan Singh shouted at Baldev.

"Yes, Sir." Baldev took a few steps back behind the tank.

A moment later the tank shuddered with a loud bang and shrapnels flew like little missiles in all directions.

The Japanese machine guns from behind the fort walls had knocked out the tank.

Men behind the tanks spontaneously hit the ground and lay flat while two more tanks were destroyed one after the other.

"How did you know?" Baldev asked with a horrified look on his face.

"I didn't! You were a bit too close to the tank, that's all," Bachan Singh said.

The more the howitzers pounded the fort, the more the Japanese held tight behind the garrison. The siege went on for days without any significant breach in the walls that were thicker than the width of city streets.

It was like a drill, repeated day after day. The Howitzers and tanks banged their heads against the unyielding fort walls and Thunderbolts bombed the inner compound of the fort, while the infantrymen waited for a breach, keeping their guns close to their bodies. Deafening noise of tanks and exploding bombs, fiery dust flying in all directions, and men shouting at the top of their voices created unparalleled mayhem.

"B25... Look, the B25s!" Baldev shouted. Everyone looked up. Low flying bombers roared directly above the citadel.

"Retreat! Retreat!" Bachan Singh yelled.

The soldiers ran as far from the fort walls as possible.

The earth rumbled by the 2000-pound demolition bombs dropped onto the fort walls by the American planes. The bombers were gone before anyone realized what had happened. Flames and thick smoke rising from inside the Citadel, clouds of dust along with men shouting their heads off, took time to settle down.

For a long while, nothing moved as if everything had died inside and out of the fort. Slowly the soldiers started getting up from the ground.

"They did it! Look!" Baldev hollered, looking at a huge gap in the wall.

Sikh and Gurkha battalions rushed in with guns and bayonets expecting a hand-to-hand battle.

"They're gone, no one's here," someone shouted.

"They're here," Bachan Singh stumbled upon a heap of dead Japanese. "It looks like a mass suicide."

"They'd rather kill themselves than be taken prisoners," Baldev said looking at bodies scattered all over the place.

Shouts of victory echoed. The flag was quickly hoisted above the ruins of the palace that was once a marvel of sumptuous beauty and luxury. Smoke rose from the smoldering buildings unable to hide the display of death and destruction.

Suddenly two Japanese soldiers walked out from behind the shattered palace, waving a tiny white flag.

Everyone looked dumbfounded by the unexpected sight.

"Disarm them, Baldev," Bachan Singh ordered.

As soon as Baldev walked closer, one of them took out a grenade from his pocket.

Boom...boom...boom! Many guns fired at the same time before he could pull the pin from the grenade.

Baldev stood stunned, staring at the Japanese bodies riddled with bullet holes, bleeding, and still twitching.

I could've been lying here too, blown apart by the grenade. The thought shook Baldev to the core. What is it that pulls me out of the jaws of death time and time again? Baldev walked back as if under a magic spell.

They scoured the area going through the completely obliterated palace buildings looking for any signs of life.

"Get here, quick," Bachan Singh shouted.

Many soldiers ran towards him.

Five skeletal human figures in flimsy loin clothes huddled against the wall in one of the badly damaged buildings. The others lay on the floor bayoneted in the chest and some killed by the falling debris.

They looked bewildered on seeing the Sikh and Gurkha troops inside the fort.

"The Japs are gone," Bachan Singh told them, "we've come to get you out of here," he said glancing at the soldiers surrounding them.

Sores all over the body and badly starved, they were hardly able to move.

"They tried to kill us all before leaving," barely audible, one of them pointed to the bayoneted prisoners.

"Then the building collapsed," he told them.

Three years of malnutrition and no medical help had taken its toll. They were carried out of the fort to the hospital.

Chapter 67

The capture of Rangoon, the capital city, ended the war in Burma in hot month of June. The harbor destroyed by the Japanese was quickly repaired and the river did its part, washing the dead to the sea.

Most of the allied forces moved towards Singapore. Some of the soldiers along with Baldev and Bachan Singh were deployed in Rangoon mainly to keep law and order in the city. A largescale looting and civilian killing had been going on during the Japanese occupation.

Baldev and Bachan Singh walked to their camp after swapping with the night duty soldiers.

"Any letters from home?" Bachan Singh asked.

"One. A brief letter from Ma, waiting for me to come home and she wrote something about the unrest of Muslim League going village to village spreading the demand for Pakistan," Baldev told him.

"That I've also heard is causing tension between the Congress and Muslim leaders, who are at each other's throat most of the time anyway."

"You're right, they will never agree on anything."

"Forget about the leaders." Bachan Singh looked at Baldev with a teasing smile, "any letter from her? Pali you said, her name is?"

"One from her too, since we've been in Rangoon. But the bundle of letters was lost at Kohima that I never had a chance to open, along with Kewal's letter."

Both sighed.

Suddenly the street became chaotic with people running and shouting. Two gangs had collided again, killing each other and the bystanders, looting shops and people. It had become a norm of life for a long time in Rangoon.

They ran towards the troubled area and met up with a few other soldiers. The gangsters disappeared leaving a dead man behind.

"The war with the Japanese is over, but it doesn't seem to be over for us." Baldev squeezed his pained eyes looking at the man lying face down in the street, "When is this killing going to stop?"

Since morning, three different parts of the city had been attacked, two dead and many injured.

A little later the police arrived, writing reports and moving bodies to the morgue.

"Hey, Baldev!" Hearing his name, Baldev looked back.

"You're Andrew I believe." Baldev recognized the man they had rescued along with Jack, from the fallen jeep.

"Yes, yes. I'm Andrew," he said giving Baldev a bear hug, "So good to see you."

"Good to see you too, Andrew. How's it going?" Baldev asked.

"Going good! Still alive!" he said, shaking hands with Bachan Singh.

"Yes, we are…still alive!" Baldev slowly nodded as if trying to convince himself after being close to death so many times. "How's Jack?" he asked.

"He didn't make it," Andrew replied.

"What you mean he didn't make it?" Baldev did not want to believe what he had heard. "He was killed at Meiktila."

"Oh, no," Sadness walloped Baldev's heart and he sighed loudly.

"You know what? He killed six Japs before falling," Andrew said proudly stretching his neck. "I'm sure he'd be in for the Victoria Cross."

The parents lost their son and the siblings lost their brother, what good is the Victoria Cross going to do? Baldev wanted to say.

"These are the men I was telling you about, the Sikhs," Andrew turned to his companion who was curiously staring at their turbans and beard, "The men with the turbans," Andrew said.

"You guys are on the night shift?" Baldev asked.

"Yes, we'll be roaming around the rubble of the shattered buildings and pretending to be in the flowerbeds of a manicured garden." Andrew's companion chuckled.

"Pretending helps, keeps our sanity!" Bachan Singh said.

They all chuckled. Nodding their heads they went on their ways.

The sun had gone down and people were hurrying home. Most of the shops were already locked and the streets were quickly emptying out.

"What about you, Lieutenant, you haven't said anything about your family?" Walking back to the camp, Baldev asked.

Bachan Singh's steps slowed as if he was suddenly very tired.

"You okay, Bachan?" Baldev asked holding his shoulder.

"It still pains to talk about her, Channi, my wife," he said.

"What about her?" Baldev asked, "What happened?"

Bachan Singh was quiet for a while, as if trying to find words.

"It's been five years now," he managed to say, "our unit was moving off to Africa and I went home to say goodbye."

Baldev held Bachan's shaking hand and waited.

"Both, Channi and Ma were like flying on the clouds with enthusiasm. They cooked my favorite meals and did all sorts of rituals to protect me from bad omen…" Bachan Singh took a long pause.

"Channi tied a thread amulet around my wrist that she said will protect me in the battle. It will also keep *yama,* the god of death away from me. She wholeheartedly believed it, I'm sure."

"So it did its job. You are alive," Baldev said.

"But little did I know about bad omens!" Bachan sighed. "At night she woke up with intense pain in her belly, that wouldn't go away with home remedies. Early morning we hired a *tonga* and left for the city hospital, over twenty miles away."

"Let's sit for a while." Baldev listening with all awareness led him to the steps of a closed shop.

"A little while later she stopped groaning."

Baldev pressed Bachan's hand, "I am so sorry!"

"I saw a truck coming from behind and I got out of the *tonga* to stop it, so we could reach the hospital faster. She was still breathing when we reached the hospital but a little too late." Bachan Singh buried his head into his knees. A muted sob escaped his throat.

"What did the doctors say?"

"They said her appendix burst open and poisoned her whole body."

"Appendix? What is it?"

"Appendix they said is a tiny finger-like structure that totally serves no purpose in the body, but it can get infected and burst open."

"I am so sorry!" Baldev wrapped his arm around his shoulder. "It's all God's will. What else can we say?"

"That's what they say, but," Bachan Singh said shaking his head. "I saw her touch the side of her belly a few times during the day while she ran around in excitement, cooking, and doing all those rituals which we had never believed in before that day. It did not occur to me to ask her about it and she never mentioned anything either. I have beaten myself up so many times that if we had taken her to the hospital early, she would still be alive." Bachan Singh took a deep breath looking around as if he was hoping to get a glimpse of Channi.

"But, I tell you Baldev, I fought in the deserts of Egypt and Libya. I killed the enemy in hand-to-hand battles. I flattened their convoys, showering them with bullets and threw grenades at them, blowing them into pieces. You fight and fight and you kill like a maniac and your superiors say, 'Well done, soldier!' While your own heart bleeds drip by drip, eroding your soul away, turning you into a dreary soulless killing machine, and this I believe is not God's will. How could this all be God's will?"

Baldev listened silently, not knowing what to say. They sat quietly for a while.

"Let's go, Bal," Bachan Singh said getting up, "I heard we'll be going home soon," he said changing the subject. "The war is over. The Japanese are beaten and we are still alive." He pressed Baldev's hand, appearing strong, as he always did with a perpetual smile on his lips. No one could ever guess the agony of his heart.

"Let's go," Baldev repeated after him getting up from the steps of the locked shop.

Part-VI
The Splintered Waters

Chapter 68

He's walking beside me but feels like so far away. What happened? Pali felt a twinge in her heart as they walked along the riverbank hardly saying a word to each other. He was so close when he was thousands of miles away, and now the distance of only a few inches feels like a million miles. Pali was consumed by emotions. She felt the strength being squeezed out of her legs and every step became heavier than before. Does he not love me anymore?

"You alright Pali?" Baldev looked at her, slowing down.

"Hunh?" Pali startled.

"You tired?"

"No, I... I'm not tired." Pali came out of a daze. *How badly I wanted him to say something and I was not even listening when he talked. Maybe, it's only me not acting normal, not him.*

"You haven't said anything." Baldev stopped walking and held her hand.

"The river missed you," Pali said looking beyond the other side of the river where the bank was not much higher than the water level. A few young cow grazers played in the shallow river laughing and splashing at each other while the cows drank and sauntered in the water.

"Only the river?" Baldev said with a slightly slanted smile on his lips.

"I talked to the river about you, every day." Pali covered her face with her hands. "Nothing was the same without you, not even the river."

"I missed you too, Pali. That's why I came to see you first before going to Gajanpur."

"Tell me how it was over there?" she asked intently looking at his face. The suppleness from his face seemed to have disappeared and his features looked hardened. He wore his turban a little lower on the right side of his forehead, but a part of a scar was still visible. "I want to know everything. Did you eat well? Did you have good sleeping quarters and beds? How's the land over there? Is it flat like ours or do they have hills and mountains? Do they have rivers like this?"

Baldev stood like a statue holding her hand in his battle toughened palms, looking beyond her face.

"I will tell you everything one day, Pali." Baldev sucked in a long breath and exhaled slowly. "But for now the only thing I can say is that you were with me all the time. I felt your presence during the day and I dreamt about you in my sleep." He looked into Pali's eyes for the first time since he came back. "A few more months and we'll be together forever. In the meanwhile tell me how your days passed and what did you do?"

"I wrote to you every week, Bal! In every letter, I told you how the things here were and how the crops were growing and how the river overflowed last year and a big portion of the bank fell into it and was washed away along with many uprooted trees." Pali pointed to a gap in the bank a few yards away.

"Every day I waited to hear from you, but never did. A gloomy whirlwind carried me back and forth between the river and home. And then Ma stopped my walks and wouldn't let me leave the outer gate of the courtyard." Pali tried to bury a sob, unsuccessfully. She felt her throat tightening and she gasped. "When all hopes were gone your letter came as my savior. I don't know what I would have done if I didn't get that letter."

She looked up at Baldev and wanted to rest her head on his shoulder but at the last moment shyness took over and she looked down at her feet. The sandy soil eagerly drank the teardrops falling from her eyes, drip…drip.

"Pali, look at me, no more tears." Baldev took her face into his hands. "See? I'm here!" He wiped her tears with his fingers and held her against his chest.

Pressing her tear-wetted cheeks against his shirt, she wrapped her arms around him, "Okay, no more tears," she whispered. A feeling of calmness softened her taut muscles. Her head softly moved up and down over his chest by his unhurried breathing movements. She felt the rhythm of his heart, *dhak dhak…dhak dhak…dhak dhak*, merging with her own heart rhythm and a wave of an incredible stillness descended over her body. A heavenly cloud showered her with its bounty of ecstatic joy. Time seemed to have stopped until she heard Baldev's soothing voice,

"Pali, look!" Several parrots were coming in and out of a hollow in the tree trunk. They jumped from one branch to another brightening the whole atmosphere. Their bright green feathers and red beaks stood out against the brownish tree trunk. They tweeted and nodded and gleefully extended their necks back and forth. They flapped their wings and rubbed their beak against each other. The parrots seemed to be singing and dancing to the cadence of flickering tree leaves.

"They're so beautiful!" Pali smiled.

"Yes, they are, but nothing in the world is even close to my Pali's magical beauty." Baldev held her hand against his lips. "It seems like they're celebrating something," he added.

"Maybe it's a wedding," Pali said.

"Are you two love birds coming home or going to fly away?" Pash hollered in his newly acquired raspy teenage voice, "Ma's been waiting for an hour. The food's getting cold, she says."

"My naughty, little brother!" Pali gently punched him when he came closer.

Baldev wrapped his arm around him, "You're growing so fast, Pash!" Baldev said looking at the tiny soft hair on his upper lip and chin. "Okay, let's go, little brother-in-law!"

Pash squirmed out of his arm hold and sped homeward, "Now hurry home, you two," he said like a grown man whose responsibility was to watch over his sister.

"Did you read my letters, Bal?" walking homeward Pali asked.

"I did, no no, I could not. I was able to read only two from you and one from Ma." Baldev almost stuttered.

"You read only two?"

"The bundle was lost before I could open it, I'm sorry."

"Lost? How?"

"I was hurt and evacuated to a hospital. My rucksack was left somewhere in the muddy trench and that area was overrun by the enemy."

"Oh, no, you were hurt?" Pali felt her heart flutter out of her chest. Her steps froze. She looked at him as if for the first time. "How did you get hurt, Bal? Tell me, I want to know everything!" She extended her arm towards the scar visible on his forehead.

Baldev turned his head away before she could reach the scar, "Not to worry, Pali. A few days in the hospital and I was up and running again." He laughed and mimicked running at the same spot, arms bent, moving back and forth and feet jumping up and down.

"How did you get hurt, Bal?" She held his arm stopping him from his comic display, "Tell me what happened!"

327

A serious look arose on Baldev's face as he looked into her eyes, "Your love pulled me out of the jaws of death, again and again, Pali," his voice turned somber, "I believe it deep in my heart!" His eyes closed momentarily as if in a meditative state. "Many of my companions did not make it."

Her gaze fixed on his forehead scar; Pali knew that she loved him more than she could ever tell him. How did I live without him all these years? No, it was not living. It was just inhaling the air in and breathing it out, day after day. Pali sighed, a sigh that was not out of desperation and gloom but more like a sigh of relief, a sigh of contentment.

Chapter 69

The bus crawled along the one-lane, narrow, rutted road while its engine groaned and whined like an unwilling participant. The metal frames of the broken windows rattled as the bus bounced up and down on the potholed road. Spongy cushions had been ripped out of most of the seats and the wooden planks underneath were exposed.

Only five other passengers were traveling on the bus besides Baldev. A young couple sat towards the front of the bus, three rows behind the driver's seat. Their shy smiles and whispers into each other's ears drew a pretty good picture of them being newly wedded. The girl, barely in her teens still wore the *churha*, the red wedding bangles around her wrists. Her unmatching green *duppata* and red *salwar* and the man's orange turban, with one end left hanging by the ear, suggested they were simple village people with little formal schooling.

The other men in the bus sat far from each other, maybe on the seats still holding remnants of the cushiony stuff. They stared at the couple from time to time and quickly moved their gaze away as if afraid of being caught red-handed, stealing something. The bus driver also peeked at them every now and then through the rearview mirror.

A few more months, Pali and I will be married, Baldev smiled. But I will buy her a jeep to travel. He looked out the window, seeing Pali with his mind's eyes. There's no one like her, he thought. The very next moment his body shuddered with the thought that Pali would have done something drastic if he had not returned. Her desperate letter had said it all. He whispered to an unseen savior, 'thank you!' She's okay.

Baldev did not know how and what to tell her when she asked him about what they ate and where they slept and if the land was flat or hilly and if there were any rivers like 'our river.' She wanted to know all about the time he was away but he stood like a statue, not knowing what to tell her.

How could I tell her that we ate tasteless dry biscuits from our rucksacks and slept in the blood-soaked muddy trenches? We fought in dense mountain jungles where the knife-sharp bamboo leaves cut through the skin and enemy bullets flew all around us? How could I explain to her that we stepped over the bodies of our comrades and kept fighting while the wounded howled in pain? That I had spent one whole day in the enemy's trench pretending to be dead. So many of my friends sitting only inches from me were blown to pieces and the air was filled with the nauseating smell of burning flesh. How could I even find the words to tell her that I had to carry my best friend's headless body on my shoulders to lay him with the others, in the pit of a dried-out riverbed?

Baldev shook his head to force out the harrowing memories, in vain. Every fiber of his core felt raw and bleeding to its end. Every breath smelled like charred flesh. His heart wanted to quit after every beat and he squirmed in his seat uncomfortably. He fiddled and tried to fix his turban that did not need fixing.

The newlyweds laughed loudly at something only they knew about, but it snapped Baldev out of his agonizing thoughts. All eyes darted towards the couple. The woman looked back at the passengers and shyly covered her face with her *duppata*. The man said something in her ear again and she giggled. Baldev smiled imagining his own life with Pali.

In the next village, the couple got off the bus, taking with them the lively cheerful atmosphere they had created. A dull dreary whimpering of the engine and a few quietly sitting men were left behind.

Within a few miles, the bus stopped again and a group of about fifteen men got in. As soon as they settled in their seats, one of them shouted,

"Pakistan *Zindabad,* long live Pakistan!"

"With our lives, we'll get Pakistan!" the others in the group answered.

The bus driver, a *Musalman*, also joined them. Shouting *Zindabad,* and kept driving.

The bus reverberated with their shouts while they threateningly stared at the other four men on the bus, all Sikhs including Baldev. They looked at each other with a troubled expression.

Baldev's initial reaction was to confront them but decided against it. Gajanpur was only a few miles away and he just wanted to go home.

The bus stopped by the dirt road leading to Gajanpur. Baldev walked to the other three men nervously looking at the gangsters shouting slogans, "Why don't you get down here and wait for another bus," he said to them.

The men nodded and got off the bus.

As soon as they stepped out, one of the men hung his head out the window and shouted, "This is how we will get our Pakistan, by throwing the infidels out." The others laughed and clapped as the bus sped away.

"This is unbelievable! How can they threaten us like this?" Baldev was furious. "I have never seen anything like this."

"It keeps happening more and more whenever they are in the majority." One of the men said looking at Baldev, "You've been away for a while, it seems."

"Yes, four years," Baldev said, "in Burma."

"In the army?" the man asked.

Baldev nodded, "Fought the Japanese."

"You must be very lucky! Three men from my village joined the army and none returned."

"I *am* lucky, I guess."

"Go home. Your woman must be waiting for you," one of them said patting Baldev's shoulder.

"I'm not married yet, but will be soon." Baldev started walking towards Gajanpur anxious to get home as quickly as possible.

The village seemed to have changed. Some parts of it were almost unrecognizable. The pond had receded leaving dry parched soil behind. The wild *Gulabassi* shrubs with large, pink, trumpet-shaped flowers that once grew on the edges of the pond were nowhere to be found. Many of the mud houses had brick rooms added on the front and some that were already built with bricks had added a *chaubara,* an upstairs room to the homes.

The Banyan tree umbrella had grown bigger with more stumpy aerial roots supporting it like pillars. The only thing that did not change was the men sitting on the platform under the tree and the children playing nearby.

"That must be him!" One of the children looked at Baldev carrying a large suitcase, "they said he was coming today."

The children stopped playing, "Look, he's here!" they shouted as if they had always known him well and ran towards him. Baldev patted some of the children on the shoulders and some on their cheeks, although could not recognize most of them. They surrounded him and walked with him towards the men under the Banyan.

The men excitedly shook hands and hugged him. Some of them had tears of joy, as if he was their own son. They greeted him as if he was the whole Gajanpur's son.

"Finally the family is together!"

"Life has tested them really hard."

"It is the *kismet*, we're born with…"

"No one can change your *kismet*. It *is* what it is!" Men talked to each other, as Baldev turned towards home.

"I will carry it, *Chacha ji*," one of the older boys took the suitcase from Baldev.

A child about six years old, who had been shouting, 'He's here,' at the top of voice, asked, "Who is he?"

"I don't know!" the child next to him, who was still shouting, answered, and cheerfully hopped and skipped around Baldev walking home with him.

The courtyard was already full of people and many more poured in. One by one they took Baldev in an embrace and congratulated his parents.

Baba Budh Singh announced, "Let us celebrate that the madness of war is over and our brave son is finally home. Tea and *Laddoo* for everyone." He took out two ten-rupee bills from his pocket said to Zahid, "go buy all the *Laddoo* the sweet shop has and hurry back."

Whosoever heard about Baldev and *Laddoos,* came running. The farmers and the shopkeepers, the blacksmiths, and the carpenters, the Sikhs, Hindus, and the *Musalmans* of Gajanpur were all in a festive mood.

Soon a big cauldron of water was boiling on the fire pit for making tea. Some of the women helped with the tea and some went to their homes and came back with cups and tumblers enough for everyone gathered in the courtyard. A few others made their own group talking and laughing. They scolded their children playing nearby when they got too noisy while they themselves talked over each other loudly.

Finally, Baba Budh Singh told everyone to go home, "Let the man spend some time with his parents now. See how patiently they're waiting?" he said, looking at Hakam and Harjit.

People left promising to come see him again and some invited him to visit them. The courtyard emptied quickly and the noise dissipated.

As soon as the last person left, the son and the parents rushed towards each other. They met in the courtyard by the *neem* tree. The three of them stood silently in a tight embrace. No sniffling, no tears, no sighs, just an embrace that could reveal the agony and the triumphs of a lifetime without uttering a single word.

Chapter 70

Pali on his mind and a spade on his shoulder, Baldev walked around the cotton fields, checking for any leaks in the irrigation channels. A soft breeze blew under the late afternoon sun that was rather warm and soothing. The young cotton plants reaching up to Baldev's knees waved in the gentle wind.

He collected more mud around a small section of the channel that looked a bit weak and thumped the ridge with his spade to pack the soil tightly around it. Pleased with the repair, he walked to the far end of the field. It looked fully irrigated. He changed the flow of the water to the next field and walked back towards the main water channel.

Lost in thoughts about Pali, an ecstatic smile spread over his face and ran through his body as a pleasant electric current.

"Three more weeks, I'll be a married man!"

The words of a long-forgotten song suddenly appeared as if written in the air and he sang,

"My heart sings
The joy of being alive,
My soul enjoys
The splendor of the sky…"
He struggled to recall the rest of the lines but nothing came to mind.
"The dazzling beauty of Pali
The delight of my eyes…"

He made up the next lines and laughed, "What an ugly singer I am! Pali would laugh her head off hearing me sing."

Even the crows sing better than you, I'm sure she'd say.

"Hope nobody heard me sing." He laughed and looked around. No one was there except him, the crops and the cattle under the trees.

The empty space where Sheru used to be fastened to the pole, gawked at him. A feeling of loss took over his heart, "He waited for me to come home. The other oxen of Sheru's age in the village were long gone."

Baldev recalled Sheru lying on the ground unable to lift his head or even open his eyes. He sat by him patting his skeletal body that used to be muscular and strong. He rested his head on Sheru's neck and cried. Sheru opened his eyes and even tried to lift his head as if he was telling him not to cry. A few minutes later he took his last breath while Baldev caressed his neck.

Baldev stood for a while at the spot where Sheru had been, a month and a half ago. A gasping sigh escaped his lungs. He walked over to the younger pair of oxen and added more fodder to their feeding trough. "Looking good and strong," he patted both of them.

"Baldev! Sardar ji!" Zahid called walking towards him.

"You don't have to call me Sardar ji, Zahid," Baldev said when he came closer.

"For me, you were Sardar ji even when you were a little boy," Zahid said, "Why don't you go home now. I'll take care of the rest of the fields and feed the cattle."

"It's okay, Zahid, I'm not tired."

"Go home. You're getting married in a few days. Eat a lot and rest a lot and take good care of yourself." Zahid gestured with his hands like he was eating and tilted his neck to mimic resting.

"Okay, Zahid, okay, I'm leaving." Baldev laughed and headed homeward.

A group of people stood by the outer boundary of the village, in a hot discussion with Jang Singh and Nand Lal the shopkeeper. Baldev heard Jang Singh yell, "Get out of here if you don't want to get hurt."

Baldev held Jang Singh's arm and walked him away from the group. "What's going on, Jang *Chacha ji*? Who are these people?"

"I don't know where they came from. I hear they're conspiring with the Muslims against us," Jang said. "These mobsters are telling them to drive us out of our village or convert us to Islam if we want to stay here."

"How dare they come to our village and incite violence? This is the land of our forefathers." Remembering the bus incident, two months ago, Baldev felt his stomach overturning in his belly. "For generations, we have lived here and tilled this land, grown crops, and raised our cattle."

Baldev walked up to the men, "Look, you have no business in our village. Better you leave right now."

"We don't want any trouble here." Jang Singh followed close behind him.

"O, you're the recently returned soldier, these dwarfies talk about." A burly man wearing a long green shirt that reached below the knees and a white *shalwar*, scanned Baldev's tall robust frame.

"Who are you calling dwarfies?" Nand Lal, the shopkeeper, looked like all the blood from his face had been wrung out. His Gandhi cap wobbled along with his quivering lips. He joined his hands together in a tight fist to stop shaking.

"Tell your Bapu Gandhi to hide you in his armpits and save your pathetic, spineless bodies. This place is going to become Pakistan soon." One of them defiantly stepped towards Nand Lal.

"He has no time for them! He's busy…very busy, with his own grand-niece Manu," the man in green shirt said. "She is 17, fresh, and tender." A hideous look on his face accompanied a wicked laugh.

"And they call him Mahatma, a great soul, while he sleeps with naked young girls!" Another man from the group shouted. "And Manu is not the only one. There are plenty of 'Manus' for him." He made a slurping sound with his lips, "Oh, and they're all young. Mouthwatering!"

"Everyone knows that he's the 'Mahatma.' He puts his celibacy to the hardest test," Nand Lal said. His words were drowned in loud sadistic laughter.

"So, this old scrawny looking *mahatma* of yours is testing these young girls for his celibacy?" the man in green mocked and laughter broke out again.

Baldev had heard and read about Gandhi's self-restraint experiments, having naked young girls sleeping next to him, and was disgusted by it. Some of Gandhi's close associates had left his ashram because of this sinful behavior, but most of his followers did not seem to mind or pay attention to it.

For preaching the highest moral values to young men and women at the ashram, Gandhi persuaded them to take baths together and sleep near each other without having sexual desires. They were harshly punished if any of them broke the rule. When he rebuked his own son for having sex with his wife, he revolted by getting drunk and going to the whore house.

Gandhi segregated the married couples and forbade them to be alone with each other. "Take a cold bath…" he told them, if they felt the urge, while he himself slept and bathed with his young doctor Sushila Nayar, the sister of his secretary Pyarelal Nayar. "I keep my eyes tightly shut while she bathes," Gandhi had said when asked by a journalist.

"I can tell from the sound that she uses soap." Baldev remembered the news articles and cringed.

"What about Jinnah, hunh?" Karam Chand joined with a voice loud enough for everyone to hear, "He wants a Pakistan, the land of the pure, but has he ever gone to a mosque or read the Quran himself. He drinks whiskey and eats pork and never fasts on Eid. Do you call this the rule of Allah?"

"Look at the puny man talking! We were the kings of this land and ruled your people for hundreds of years and now these midgets want to rule us?"

"You people used to be Hindus at one point. Your elders were cowards who converted to Islam to save their skin. They were circumcised, and cow flesh thrust down their throats while their penises were still dripping blood." Jang Singh trembled with rage. "It was the Sikh gurus who resisted the tyranny of the Mughal Empire."

"And some brave Hindus," Karam Chand added.

"It is time to do it again, to bring back the reign of Allah on this land," the man in green shouted.

"Pakistan *Zindabad*!" the mobsters bellowed.

"Muslim League, *Zindabad*!"

"Get out of our village before we split your heads open!" Baldev shouted.

"Don't worry, we'll be back soon to split yours," the man in green said, moving away. The rest of the group followed.

"The Sikhs are fools following Nehru's tail. He is going to betray you as soon as the British leave," he shouted over his shoulder.

"What the hell just happened?" Baldev looked at Jang Singh's worried face. "These men seem vicious!"

"Why did Gandhi and Nehru agree to divide the country in the first place?" Jang Singh shook his head. "Is it the same Gandhi who said, Pakistan will be created over his dead body?"

"He's a hypocrite! Neither Nehru nor Gandhi wanted to share an inch of power with Jinnah," Baldev said. "That's another reason he wants a separate country, Pakistan."

"They're brainwashing these ignorant people in the name of Allah."

"Yes, they are. And it is very dangerous."

Chapter 71

Uncertainty and fear had gripped the villagers. Every day, news of killings and looting flowed in. Hundreds of goons laced with spears, machetes, and swords, rambled in the towns.

On one hand the British were preparing to leave India after hundreds of years of a heartless reign and brutal suppression of freedom seekers, on the other, uncontrollable killing sprees were wildly spreading from the cities into the villages. While the leaders squabbled about gaining power, they blindly ignored the grisly situation that had gripped the whole of Punjab. The cobra of communal fanaticism slithered and ferociously spread its poison into the hearts of people who once lived together.

In the midst of a man-gone-mad atmosphere, Hakam and Harjit were planning their son's wedding. Hakam looked at Harjit's worry-stricken face, "Shouldn't we postpone the wedding until this madness cools down a little?"

"What are you saying, Sardar ji?" Harjit looked at him as if she misheard, "I've been waiting for my daughter-in-law for so long."

"I am waiting for her too. But look what's happening, all around us."

"What about Baldev? He's so excited, counting the days to his wedding."

"I don't want to disappoint him either." Hakam Singh rubbed his white beard with unsteady hands. "Herds of fanatic men roam around, attacking even the wedding parties."

"I just want to bring my daughter home," Harjit said. "Why don't we just the three of us go to Rampur and have the ceremony done?" She looked into his eyes expecting a yes. "We don't have to take with us the horse buggies and clamoring band music."

"Okay, we'll talk to Baldev tonight," Hakam said walking out the door, "I'll be at Baba Budh Singh's."

******

The jeep carrying the wedding party consisting only of Baldev, Hakam, Harjit, and Baba Budh Singh stopped in front of Sardar Lal Singh's spacious house at Rampur, just before the sunset.

The late Sardar Lal Singh's only daughter was getting married without any festivities. Nothing looked like a normal wedding where not only Rampur but several neighboring villages would have been a part of the several days of elegant celebrations.

No decorations or bamboo torches brightened the courtyard and no cooks ran around shouting at the younger cooks. No chickens were getting plucked and cleaned, or mutton being cooked in gigantic caldrons. There was no aroma of sweet fried *gulab jaman* or *laddoo* in the air.

There were no special tents with colorful beds, set up in the village grounds for the groom's party, as would have been for a customary wedding. The groom's party would have consisted of hundreds of men on horse-driven buggies, camels, even elephants going to the bride's house. There would have been several men hired to take care of the horses, feeding and grooming them. But Baldev's wedding party consisted only of four people who came in a single jeep parked in the outer courtyard and it did not need any special treatment or a servant to attend to its needs.

Also, there were no young women, dressed in gaudy clothes and glittering jewelry, singing and joking with the groom and the groom's men, which was the most amusing custom of a wedding. The bride's friends and cousins would ask the groom to sing for them or tell a joke. If he was not able to do any of this, or if his song or the joke did not appeal to the girls, which was almost always the case, he'd have to pay money to them. The girls and the groom's men would haggle until the girls agreed to the amount or if some elderly women intervened.

This was the time when the eyes would meet and strangers wouldn't seem to be strangers anymore. This was the time when hearts would be thrown into tumultuous beats and many of the love stories would begin and end in tragedy, and maybe a few lucky ones would end in triumph.

But in Baldev's groom's party of only four, there were no strangers. They ate dinner and slept as one family. The next morning at the wedding ceremony *Anand Karaj* was performed according to the Sikh tradition. Baldev dressed in a white and gold *Achken*, and a maroon turban, holding the ceremonial sword, stood in front of the Sikh holy book, Guru Granth Sahib.

Namo walked Pali down the stairs of the *chaubara*, dressed in red silk *Shalwar Kameez* and an embroidered see-through silk *duppata* that veiled her face halfway up to her nose. Baldev looked at her as she stood next to him. *She is stunning,* he thought. A barely visible smile appeared on his face like a ripple over the waters of a calm lake on a windless day.

If the circumstances were not so hostile, we'd have had a big beautiful wedding. Baldev felt a twinge mixed with helplessness and regret. But remembering Pali's response, 'big weddings may be important to others, not to me,' she had said. A kind of solace came over his heart. The smile on his face broadened a little, like a gentle gust of wind created a slightly bigger wave over the waters of the lake. *She's so thoughtful and caring!*

As they stood next to each other, *Granthi,* the Sikh priest read the wedding hymns. After each hymn, the couple bowed and walked around the holy book. Four hymns and four times circling the Guru Granth Sahib completed the wedding ceremony. Finally, the *Granthi* sang the hymn of completion, *Vivah Hoa Mere Babula,* 'Oh father, my wedding ceremony is complete.' Then he explained the significance of *Anand Karaj.* "It binds a man and a woman in a spiritual union. From now on you are as one soul in two bodies," he said.

Namo and Harjit sobbed quietly during the ceremony, one with grief of her daughter leaving and the other out of utter joy of having her son married and taking her daughter-in-law home.

"We'll be leaving soon," Hakam Singh said to Namo, "we should get home before the sun sets."

Namo nodded through the tears.

Chapter 72

Harjit opened the *sandook* and took out the clothes one by one. The necklace lay at the bottom of the *sandook*. It would've gone if Lal Singh had not bought it back from the pawnshop. She softly pulled it out of the velvet pouch with the reverence of something sacred.

She touched the necklace to her lips and whispered, "Be good to my daughter!" She caressed the intricate design with her fingertips and rewrapped it. "Pali deserves you." She held the necklace close to her chest one last time and walked out of the room.

"Bal, this is for Pali," she handed the necklace to Baldev. "Your father gave it to me on our wedding night."

"But this is yours, Ma. *Bapu ji* gave it to you."

"Now it's yours. You give it to Pali."

"She already has a lot of jewelry."

"I know, but this is special. Your father imagined the design and a reputed goldsmith molded it in gold." Harjit's lips moved, but her mind seemed to have traveled somewhere back to the past. Her eyes closed momentarily in an ecstatic sensation.

"And you know what? Pali's father rescued it from the talons of a greedy pawnshop vulture."

"I knew all about it, even though I was just a boy." Baldev looked at his mother, "Those dreadful days, how can we forget!"

"Your father is a great man, Bal! His love, unconditional. His sacrifices, wholehearted." A warm uplifting feeling filled her heart and she smiled. "And Pali's father, your Lal *Chacha ji*, was a great soul too."

"He supported us when *Bapu ji* was away. Maybe God needed him more than we did," Baldev said, as if he suddenly realized the mysteries of life.

"Maybe, he *was* needed more in the heavens."

"Your sacrifices are not any less, Ma." Baldev wrapped his arms around her. Her head barely reaching his shoulder, she tiptoed to kiss his cheek.

"Here," Baldev bent bringing his face close to her, laughing softly, "my sweet, little mother…"

The unfathomable mother-son love, a profound silence of the evening, and a deep-seated calmness in their hearts was like all the goodness of heaven had come down to this piece of the earth.

"Okay, Ma, we'll keep this necklace in the family, for our coming generations. Pali will give it to our son and our daughter-in-law to our grandson." Baldev laughed picking up Harjit and swirling around.

"Stop it, Bal! Put me down. You're going to crush the necklace."

The very next moment her voice softened like melting butter, "Go, Pali's waiting for you, Son."

Chapter 73

Men did not gather under the Banyan anymore. Since Jagat Singh was murdered while attending to his fields. No one went alone to their farms after dark. Hordes of *goondas* shouting Muslim League slogans had pounced on the unwary non-Muslims at numerous places including the cities of Lahore and Rawalpindi. Even Amritsar, the city of Golden Temple was involved in killing sprees where the Sikh and Hindus had retaliated, killing the Muslims.

The winter this year seemed to have skipped the spring season and directly replaced by a burning hot summer. The spring when everything comes to life, when the trees dress themselves in new robes of tender leaves and the roses and jasmines spread their fragrance into the air, appeared not to have happened. Spring is the time when sparrows knit their nests from sheaths of grass. Chirping and jumping, they announce the arrival of spring, the season of romance, the season of tender love. This is when the sky brightens with colorful flying kites and the air fills up with laughter of children running after them.

But in the year of 1947, the season of romance had become the season of death and disasters. Instead of wedding processions, there were processions of the dead carried to the cremation grounds. Instead of singing love songs, there were cries of wailing wives and mothers. Instead of bonfires for the *Lohri* festival, there were flames of funeral pyres. And the leaders Nehru and Jinnah were too busy squabbling for power in the so-called independent Hindustan and Pakistan.

This is when Baldev said to Pali one evening placing his hands on her shoulders, "I haven't fulfilled any of the promises I made." His words came out heavy and glum-soaked. His eyes looked somber and stressed and the smile on his face was nowhere to be found.

"What promises, Bal?" Pali asked.

"Remember, I always promised you that we will travel to so many places after we got married. I told you that we'll spend the hot summer of Punjab plains in the pleasant mountain town of Murree with its beautiful hills and cool waterfalls. Let alone Murree, we couldn't even go to Lahore to watch a film in the Rattan Theater."

"Bal, I'm not looking to go anywhere. I'm happy being here with you and Ma and *Bapu ji*."

"Four years in the war when death was all around me, I dreamed of a joyous life of peace and comfort. I wanted to take you to the amazing Shalimar Gardens and have a picnic, just the two of us, and then go shopping at the Anarkali Bazaar." Standing by the verandah, Baldev looked at Pali with guilt-filled stares, "I wanted the two of us to go to the Golden Temple too. It's just all this horrible insanity…"

"It's okay, Bal. We don't need to go now. Murree is not going anywhere and neither are we." Pali held Baldev's hand to her cheek, resting her face on his palm. "You don't have to feel bad about it."

"You know the other thing that keeps me awake? The promise I made to Kewal when he died that I will deliver his letter to his little girl, but I lost it along with yours and Ma's letters when I was injured. After the war when I went to their village, she ran towards me, Papu ji… Papu ji! The little girl mistook me for her father."

"O, poor Roopi, she wouldn't have any real memories of her father!" Pali lifted her face from his palm sighing. "And Mindo, her mother, how would she cope with her husband's death."

"When I was leaving, Roopi clung to my neck and wouldn't let go. I promised that I will come back soon. And I'm carrying this pang of guilt with me day and night."

"Why don't we bring them here, Bal? They're just the two of them, mother and daughter." Pali suggested. "Don't you think they'll be safer here, with us?"

"I will talk to Ma and *Bapu ji* today." Baldev felt a burden being lifted from his chest. "My promise to take you to Murree stands. We will go there soon." Baldev pressed his palms to her cheeks looking into her pearly, dark eyes. Pali smiled.

Baldev held her close to his chest. His fingers combed her hair and his dreamy eyes imagined the two of them strolling in the Shalimar Gardens. His lips touched hers.

******

Baldev woke up early. A few stars still shone on the western horizon while a yellowish hue started appearing towards the east. He stood in the courtyard listening to the noiseless morning.

"You should've waked me up, Bal." Pali wrapped her arms around him from behind.

"You're up, Pali." Baldev turned and gave her a gentle squeeze.

"I'll make some *parothas* while you get ready," Pali said walking to the kitchen.

Baldev felt like he was going on an important mission. He had checked the oil and water in the jeep the night before because it had not been driven since the wedding, many months ago. He started the engine and checked the petrol. Everything looked good.

Hakam and Harjit joined him in the courtyard, "Joga Singh is going with you," Hakam said placing his hand on Baldev's shoulder. "It's not safe to travel alone these days. He'll be here any minute."

"But *Bapu ji* we shouldn't give him any trouble. I'll be back soon with Roopi and her mother."

"What trouble are you talking about, my brave nephew?" Joga Singh, entering the doorway had obviously heard him. "Haven't you heard, one is just one and two ones make eleven?" Joga Singh had a jovial chuckle that they all joined in.

Baldev started the jeep and glanced back before driving out of the gate. Pali stood by the verandah next to Harjit. Baldev felt a sinking sensation in his heart. He tried to smile in vain. His lips felt tightly stuck together.

Hakam Singh walked with the jeep as it slowly inched out of the courtyard. "Be careful," he said, "there are ruthless people everywhere."

"Not to worry, *Bapu ji*. We'll be back tomorrow or the day after, at the most," he said over the rattle of the engine, but his voice quivered. He wanted to go back and take Pali and Harjit into his arms one more time. Instead, he pressed his foot on the pedal and the jeep picked up speed.

"Slow down, Baldev, we have to stop by my house," Joga Singh said pressing his foot at the floor of the jeep as if trying to apply the brakes.

"What for, *Chacha ji*? You already have a change of clothes in the bag."

"I need to pick up something."

"What something?" Baldev asked turning toward his house on the other side of the village. As the jeep stopped in front of his house Joga Singh hurried in and came out holding a gun.

"Whoa...what is that?" Baldev called out.

"Exactly what it looks like. You never know when you might need it, these days." Joga Singh placed the gun carefully on the floor of the jeep. "I didn't bring it with me to your house because Hakam is very much against any kind of weapons."

"But do you know how to fire a shot?"

"No, I don't. But you do. You've been in the army."

"Can you drive the jeep then?" Baldev laughed.

"How could I learn to drive? This is the only jeep in all the surrounding villages and only you know how to drive."

"Well, I just hope I don't have to drive and shoot at the same time." Baldev couldn't decide whether to be angry or laugh at the almost comical yet serious situation.

The jeep sped on the dirt road leaving clouds of dust in its wake. Gajanpur was quickly out of sight.

"What's the rush, Bal?" Joga Singh yelled over the noisy engine as his body rocked side to side. "Have pity on my old bones."

"You're not old *Chacha ji*! You're only in your 50s." Baldev chuckled, slowing down.

"And you think Fifties is not old? You'll know when you reach my age."

The two-mile dirt road ended at the paved main road and the ride became a little less bumpy.

Hot August air smacked their faces as the jeep tires rolled on the potholed road, speckled with patches of sun melted black tar and gravel. Cotton and sugarcane crops interspersed by the tender lush crops of maize spread to the horizon on both sides. Not a single cloud was in the sky and the sun pierced its merciless rays into the earth like spears.

An unsettling feeling bothered Baldev since they had left home. Faces of Pali, Harjit, and Hakam kept flashing through his mind.

Without saying much he kept driving.

"Why's my nephew so quiet?" Joga Singh said holding on to the metal bar supporting the canvas canopy of the jeep.

"I'm not quiet," Baldev said, but the tumultuous thoughts kept tormenting him inside.

How can I tell him that I feel like my soul is left behind at Gajanpur? How can I shake off an ominous feeling from my heart? Will I see Pali, Ma, and Bapu ji ever again? But I must keep the promise I made to Kewal.

Baldev nodded instinctively and blinked several times as if to evade the dreadful inkling that overshadowed his mind.

"We'll get to Lahore, maybe in another hour and Kewal's village is not very far from there," Baldev said and abruptly pressed his foot on the accelerator. The jeep jerked forward as if a lazy bullock was suddenly whipped to go faster. Rings of black smoke shot out of the exhaust pipe dissipating into the equally hot air of the summer day.

"Take it easy, Bal! What's the hurry?" Joga Singh's neck lurched backward and he held his turban with both hands.

"Sorry, *Chacha ji!*"

"You've been driving good for a while. What suddenly happened to you?"

"Nothing, maybe I just wasn't thinking."

Baldev said apologetically, "I swear to have pity on your old bones from now on." Baldev forced a smile, slowing down.

"Who're you calling old bones? Hah!" Joga Singh laughed. Flexing his arm he showed off his biceps, "I am strong as a horse. See!"

"What the hell is that?" Baldev shouted, looking at the charred crops on the sides of the road.

"Whoa…whoa, it's still smoldering. Looks like it happened not long ago." Joga Singh shouted even louder forgetting all about his biceps.

Baldev accelerated the jeep to full speed towards the city, ignoring Joga Singh's old bones.

Lahore was like a ghost town. All the shops were closed. No sign of hawkers selling fruit and peanuts and soda bottles. No tongas or man pulled rickshaws were on the road. Dark smoke billowed from the inner-city buildings. The main road passing through the city was empty.

The vibrant city of Lahore Baldev knew, looked dead. Half burnt buildings stood like huge carcasses. Baldev slowed down looking at the burnt vehicles with bodies still inside. The place was littered with the possessions of people fleeing. Turbans and *duppattas*, shoes and suitcases, walking sticks, and baby clothes rolled around in the gusty wind.

"What on earth happened here?" Joga Singh's mouth open and eyeballs looking like about to explode, he yelled, "Let's get out of here. Quick!"

Just as the words left his mouth a mob appeared from the corner and flooded the street. They ran towards them shouting, "Kill the *kafirs*!"

Baldev slammed his foot like a hammer on the accelerator, tightly holding on to the steering wheel.

The crowd hurled all sorts of weapons, sticks, rocks, spears, axes at them as the jeep sped away. A rock landed on the back seat and a spear hung through the canopy of the jeep close to Joga Singh's head.

"Pick up the gun, *Chacha ji*!" Baldev shouted.

"What?"

"Scare them with the gun!"

Joga Singh picked up the gun from the floor of the jeep and raised it towards the crowd, "I will blast your heads off, you sons of bitches!" he roared.

The mob already lagging behind started to disperse.

"These *Ma chod,* mother fucking, Musla marauders…" Joga Singh kept bellowing long after they were out of the area. Baldev slowed down.

"Well done, *Chacha ji*!" he said.

"You're the one who got us out of there, Bal. They wanted to kill us," Joga Singh threw the gun on the floor and yelled at the same pitch he had been swearing at the mob, "Oh no, you're hurt!"

"I'm fine."

"Look." Joga Singh pointed to his shoulder.

"I didn't even feel it." Baldev looked at the streak of blood coming down his arm, "Too much excitement, I guess."

"You call it excitement?" Joga Singh squinted puckering his eyebrows together, "well, I'm not very fond of this kind of excitement."

Chapter 74

How are they going to slit open the heart of Punjab and slice it into two pieces? What will happen to the five rivers whose waters run through the veins of this land? The questions were on everyone's mind.

The land of Punjab where the Sikhs, Hindus, and the Muslims at one point lived side by side in harmony had been thrown into a killing frenzy.

Sitting in Baba Budh Singh's spacious courtyard under the Mulberry tree, Hakam said to Baba ji, "I am extremely worried. Baldev's been gone for three days now." His forehead skewed into wrinkles, looking like a crumpled-up rag.

"Have faith, Hakam. He's a responsible man and Joga Singh is with him." Baba Budh Singh's snowy, white, long beard quivered.

"This is not the kind of independence we fought for, all our lives." Hakam let out a long noisy sigh. "We hear so many villages completely burned and people butchered like sheep."

"I believe it started last year when Jinnah announced in Calcutta, that they will get Pakistan by 'Direct Action,' and Suhrawardy's fiery speech, 'bloodshed is not evil if done for a noble cause...'" Baba ji shook his already wobbly head in utter disgust. "The ignorant people take it as a signal to start killing non-Muslims to achieve Pakistan and are getting killed in retaliation."

"I believe Gandhi and Nehru caved in, assuming it will stop the killings by accepting Pakistan. Instead, it aroused more butchery epidemic that flowed over into Punjab." Hakam got up to leave. "But the irony is, they are letting Jinnah divide the country but not letting him share the power with them as he initially wanted."

Baba ji placed his hands on his knees and stood up. An *unh* sound escaped his lips, "Oh these joints! We have to have a plan to defend ourselves. Our village could be attacked too," Baba ji said walked him to the door. "I will send out the message for all to gather in the school tomorrow."

Hakam Singh left Baba ji's house with troubling thoughts. "Baldev, come home, son!" He folded his hands and his eyes closed for a moment in a prayer.

"Any news from Bal?" Harjit and Pali both ran towards him, as he stepped in.

"We have to keep faith. He will come back soon," Hakam said. The words sounded fickle, empty.

"I told him to go and bring Roopi and her mother," Pali sobbed.

"He will come home, Pali. He will." Fighting back her own tears Harjit took her in her arms.

Chapter 75

"We could both be dead by now if you hadn't flaunted the gun at those Muslas. They didn't know you can't shoot." Baldev laughed. "You made them run with their tails between their legs."

Joga Singh chuckled slapping his thigh.

A few miles later Baldev stopped the jeep.

"Let me show you how to shoot. We might have to use it for real." Baldev picked up the gun. "Where are the bullets?"

"The bullets?" Joga Singh's whole body looked like a big question mark.

"That means we don't have any," Baldev shook his head in total disappointment. "Let's just hope we don't get into a situation where we need it." He placed the gun in the jeep and threw a piece of tarpaulin over it.

They continued through the jagged road that seemed to be intentionally busted at several places. The air smelled of burnt crops.

How will we get through Lahore on our way back when the mother and daughter will also be with us? That mob in Lahore meant to kill. Unsettling thoughts occupied Baldev's mind while he maneuvered the jeep on the rutted road.

"Isn't that Khanpur, your friend's village?" Joga Singh pointed to a village at a little distance off the road.

"That's the one." Baldev steered the jeep on to the dirt pathway toward the village.

"Something doesn't seem right!" He gasped at the vultures circling the sky above. A chilling wave of terror passed down his spine. The village was deserted, the streets empty.

A pack of wild dogs snarled at each other fighting for what appeared to be a human leg. The dogs ran away as the jeep came closer, leaving behind the half-eaten bloody flesh.

"What the hell is that?" Joga Singh's jaw dropped to the ground and his gasping breath shot upward.

Horrified to the core Baldev stopped the jeep near the entrance of a narrow street. "It won't go any further," he said. "Kewal's house is at the end of the street."

"Listen, Bal, there's no one here. It's better to get out now."

"I'm not leaving without checking Kewal's house." Baldev rushed through the street.

"But…" Joga Singh caught up with Baldev

The walls of the two-room house stood undamaged. A few rags and kitchen utensils lay scattered in the courtyard. The house looked ransacked. No sign of mother and daughter.

Baldev stood dumbfounded. "Anyone here?" His voice choked.

"Roopi! Mindo!" he called again. No response.

"We have to leave right now!" Joga Singh shouted. "No one's here other than the vultures and dogs."

"Roopi!" Baldev called, much louder this time.

"Are you coming or want our bodies eaten up by vultures?" Joga Singh angrily pulled Baldev by the arm out of the house.

I am so sorry, Kewal. I could not keep my promise. Baldev looked back at the house. An uninvited tear accompanied a deep sigh.

Joga Singh rushed through the street taking long strides, Baldev right behind him.

"The Muslas!" Joga Singh stopped in his tracks.

Two young men stood by the jeep. One of them got in the driver seat, pretending to be driving with both hands on the wheel.

"Get away from the jeep!" Baldev yelled.

The man in the driver's seat quickly got down.

"What are you doing here?" Baldev approached them.

"We live here." They looked at their turbans like they had never seen Sikhs before. "What are *you* doing here? Don't you know what happened here?" the young man, who was earlier in the driver seat, said, looking around as if something unexpected could crop up any moment.

"Where did you come from?" the other man asked.

"What happened here? Tell me." Baldev ignored his question.

"The Baluchi tribesmen attacked our village two days ago."

"There were Muslim League killers too," the other man added.

"Attacked?" Joga Singh shrieked.

"My Abbu, my father found out a day before the attack and helped our Sikh and Hindu neighbors to go to a safe place."

"What safe place?"

"We helped them load their bullock carts in the middle of the night and they went towards Amritsar."

"The attackers say this village is going to be in Pakistan and no Sikh or Hindu could live here anymore."

"They all left?" Baldev asked looking back towards Kewal's house.

"Some old people did not want to leave and they stayed."

"Where are they now?" Joga Singh moved a little closer to them.

The young men looked at each other.

"… My Abbu begged them not to kill the old people, but they threatened him too," one of them said after a long pause.

"They also stole everything from the Sikh houses."

"They said they will come back to kill us too if we tried to hide anyone."

"Tell your father, we are very thankful to him." Baldev patted them both on the shoulders.

"Get in, *Chacha ji*!" Baldev hopped into the jeep and turned it towards Gajanpur. "Let's get out of here."

Thinking about fighting dogs and circling vultures, Baldev felt his stomach turning inside out. The scene of burnt buildings and murderous gangs roaming the city of Lahore flashed on his mind and he wanted to get home as quickly as possible.

They had gone no more than ten miles when the road was blocked by a mob of hundreds of men, brandishing weapons.

"We have to turn back." Baldev reversed the jeep and sped eastward towards Amritsar.

"Motherfuckers!" Joga Singh's voice trembled.

"It's happening what we were afraid of!" Baldev kept driving in the opposite direction from home. "Punjab is severed into two."

"Where are we going?"

"I don't know, just away from these rabid killers."

After a few miles, the road was jammed with buses, cars, jeeps, bullock carts, tractors, and horse-driven buggies going towards Amritsar. Many walked carrying suitcases and holding their children's hands.

Soon there were more vehicles behind them. Row after row of carts overloaded with people, inched along the narrow road under the sweltering afternoon sun. The earth seemed to have turned into a hot griddle, searing people on the shadeless road.

After a while caravan came to a standstill.

"Why aren't we moving?" Joga Singh got off the jeep. "Water! They're drawing water from a well." Rolling his tongue over his dry lips he walked towards the well.

"Wait, *Chacha ji!*" Baldev shouted.

"I will bring some for you too," Joga Singh shouted back over his shoulder.

A few minutes later agonizing screams and wailing reached the back of the caravan like a thunderous cloud had exploded.

"Do not drink the water!" A man hollered at the top of his lungs above the chaotic noise. "The well is poisoned." He waved his arms in the air running back towards the caravan, "do not drink it!" the man shouted.

Poisoned? Did I hear it right? Baldev left the jeep and ran to the front of the caravan, looking for Joga Singh. He found him walking back towards the jeep with a noticeable wobble in his stride. "*Chacha ji!*" Baldev looked at him in horror. "Did you drink the water?"

Without answering, Joga Singh got into the jeep. Resting his head on the back of the seat, he closed his eyes. His face looked ashen and his breathing faster than normal. Baldev shook his shoulder, "Fight it, *Chacha ji*…don't give up…fight it!"

The caravan started crawling again on the road that seemed to be never-ending. Baldev stretched his neck looking beyond the caravan and saw nothing other than rows of carts and other vehicles.

In the last two hours, they had moved no more than half a mile. It looked like rows of giant snails in motion.

Joga Singh's breathing was becoming much labored and he started wheezing. A streak of foam flowed down from the right side of his mouth.

"No…no…no, wake up, *Chacha ji*, wake up!"

No answer.

Baldev turned off the engine and walked to the passenger side. "*Chacha ji… Chacha ji!*" He shook him.

"Keep moving or we will all be buried here," a man in the car behind him, loaded with crying children and women struggling to comfort them, stuck his head out the window and shouted.

Baldev looked at the man and started the jeep without uttering a word.

A little while later, Joga Singh was gone and so were many others. Children, men, women, young and old had succumbed to the poison in the water. Baldev helplessly looked on.

The day ended into a night not any less tragic. The caravan stopped moving. People were leaving their dead on the roadside. Baldev recoiled at the thought of vultures and dogs devouring the human bodies.

A man tried to take the body of his child from the mother's arms but she would not let go.

"Take care of the children who are alive!" he yelled.

"No, no my baby..." She sat in the cart holding him tight. Two other children sat by her like little statues.

"Let go!"

"My baby, my son," the wailing mother refused to give up.

Baldev walked to the man, "Let her hold him for a while," he said, gently touching the man's elbow.

The man nodded. A muffled screech came out of his throat, "He turned two only a few days ago." the man sobbed.

Baldev could not find the words that could dribble a few drops of water on the flames of grief the parents were burning in. He only touched his shoulders that moved up and down by his sobs.

I will never leave Chacha ji here! What will I tell his family, how he died? Coming back to the jeep Baldev shivered with the thought. *Why did I agree to bring him along?* He looked at Joga Singh's motionless body under the gloomy light of a half-moon. His head still rested on the back of the seat and hands in his lap. *Be honest, Bal! Weren't you happy that he was coming with you?* Baldev scolded himself.

What might be happening at Gajanpur? What if our village was attacked too! Pali, Ma, Bapu ji, how will they survive? Baldev squirmed in his seat. The thought shook him to the core.

He wanted to turn around and go back to Gajanpur. The empty gun lying under the tarpaulin and the images of killer mobs persuaded him to keep going with the flow for the time being.

The caravan began to move again. The daylight revealed more death and destruction on the roadside while the caravan stretched into miles.

"Get up right now, Ma, or I will leave you here!" An old woman sat on the roadside and a man with a child perched on his shoulders, tried to pull her by the arm. His wife, carrying a baby in her arms and a girl about seven, stood close by.

"I cannot walk anymore. Go ahead leave me here if you want," the old woman said.

The girl left her mother's side and sat on the ground too, "I want to stay with grandma. I cannot walk either," she cried.

"I say get up!" the man shouted. He angrily put the child he was carrying down and slapped his mother and daughter both. All three children started crying.

His wife held his arm, "Have you lost your mind?" she yelled.

"You stay out of this," he yelled back.

People of the caravan stared at them and kept crawling at the snail pace.

Baldev stopped the jeep. He looked at Joga Singh's lifeless body, "I am so sorry, *Chacha ji!*" he whispered and carried him to the roadside. His eyes were dry but his heart cried a sea of tears.

Baldev held the old woman's hand and led her to the jeep along with all the three children and their mother. The man walked alongside.

Baldev turned his head to take one last look at Joga Singh.

Chapter 76

The one-room school was crammed with people. They all seemed eager to unload their emotions and give their opinion.

It was the first time in anyone's memory that they had gathered at a place other than under the Banyan. It was also the first time when no Muslims were part of the discussions.

The atmosphere of the gathering was nothing like at the Banyan where they would laugh and joke and exchange the news of the day. Here they were talking to each other in whispers and sighs. The room hummed with their hushed voices.

"Mountbatten announced the independence two days ago and we still don't know if our village is going to be in Hindustan or Pakistan."

"You call it independence? It is total devastation."

"We're not leaving our homes and farms whether it is India or Pak."

"They cannot drive us out of our homes."

The pandemonium of voices dropped when Master Jiwan Singh got up shouting, "We will not let them take what is ours and what came from our forefathers." His gaze swayed from one nodding head to another. His face red and voice filled with anger, he continued, "this is our land and our farms and our homes. They cannot snatch it from us."

"We will fight for what is ours," Hardev Singh shouted.

Hakam Singh and Baba Budh Singh stood by the wall quietly. Listening.

"We cannot fight them with bare hands. They have weapons," someone in the crowd said.

"We've been collecting weapons too. We have two guns and more than a hundred rounds at home," Teg Singh told them.

"You have guns?" Nand Lal, the shopkeeper sprang to his feet as if a hot griddle was suddenly placed under his buttocks. "Good…good!" He sat back with a kind of satisfaction.

"But we are only about 150 able-bodied men who could fight. The rest are our elders, women, and children. The Leaguers, I'm told, attack in thousands," Karam Chand said, "and they all have weapons."

"We have to collect everything, swords, spears, knives, sickles, axes, daggers, clubs, I mean everything," Hardev standing next to his elder brother Teg announced. "We should also collect stones and bricks as many as possible on the roofs as well as in our courtyards," he added.

"Baba ji. Baba ji!" Baba Budh Singh's 13-year-old grandson darted into the room out of breath, "They said our village is in Pakistan. I heard it on the radio."

The room fell dead silent for a moment and then a jumble of voices sprang up, some audible and angry, some hushed and frightened. A few of the men stood up and some kept sitting as if afraid to move.

We are the majority landowners in the village. It cannot go to Pakistan...

We own the land and the shops...

The *Muslas* have been working for us...

The Muslim Leaguers and their new National Guards don't care if it is Pakistan or not, they just want to kill or convert all Sikhs and Hindus.

"Sit down for a moment, all of you," waving his arms up and down Teg shouted, "this is what I say to you, our Gurus gave their lives and sacrificed their families to protect the dignity of Sikh turbans and Hindu *janau,* the sacred thread. We will protect it with our lives."

After a few moments of heavy silence, Baba Budh Singh said, "Listen, everyone! Go home now and do whatever you need to do to prepare. Also, keep the jewelry and cash handy, if any. In case..."

People hurriedly walked out of the room and sped homeward, as if they just heard their homes were on fire.

"Now run along," Baba ji told his grandson, "I'll be home soon."

Walking out of the schoolyard, Hakam Singh turned to Baba ji, "We don't have anything to match those throngs of goons," he whispered.

"You're right, we don't have much to fight with." Baba ji walked slowly putting his 80-year-old feet, one step in front of the other.

At a little distance, a young man in rags limped towards the village. His hair disheveled on his shoulders and turban haphazardly wrapped around his neck with one end trailing on the ground seemed to be struggling to keep his balance.

"Who is he?" they both said simultaneously.

The boy collapsed as he came closer. He looked barely 14 or 15 years old. He had one shoe on and the other foot without the shoe bled between the toes.

"Oh, no, get some water, Hakam!" Baba ji sat on the ground taking the boy's head in his lap. "Come on, Son, wake up." He gently patted his cheeks.

Hakam ran back into the school and filled a glass of water from the hand pump.

"Here, put a few drops on his lips, Baba ji." Hakam sat down rubbing the boy's palms.

Baba ji dipped his fingers in water and touched onto his lips. Then he sprinkled a little water on his face.

The boy moaned and moved his head side to side. His eyelids flickered and limbs flailed on the ground.

"That's my boy! Wake up, wake up," Hakam Singh said while Baba ji put a few more drops of water onto his lips. The boy tried to open his eyes.

Suddenly, he got up with a gut-wrenching scream and pushed Baba ji away. "No...no," and tried to run but fell before taking another step and kept screaming.

"Calm down, Son, calm down!" Hakam Singh wrapped his arms tightly around him. The boy stopped struggling and he opened his eyes. A sudden calmness appeared on his face as he looked at Hakam and Baba ji.

They sat quietly while the boy calmed down and stopped trembling.

"What is your name?" still holding the boy, Hakam asked.

"Gurdeep," he said after a few moments of silence.

"Where do you live?"

"Basali." The boy looked around, fixing his gaze on the sugarcane field.

"Basali? That's about 25 miles from here, maybe more." Baba ji looked at his bloody toes. "Here, drink some water."

The boy emptied the glass in a gulp.

"Your family?" Hakam Singh asked.

The boy shook his head.

"How long you've been walking?"

"Don't know," he murmured.

"Can you walk? I'm sure you're hungry."

The boy nodded and awkwardly wrapped his turban on his head. The three of them walked to Hakam Singh's house.

Chapter 77

The caravan reached Atari, a small town at the border between the newly created Pakistan and India. Baldev was astounded to see a river of people trying to cross into Pakistan just as the Sikhs and Hindus were leaving their homes behind and crossing into India. Only a few days ago it was one country, one state of Punjab and one people. Now they belonged to two different countries, not by choice but due to the stubbornness of their leaders.

"What have they done to us?" Baldev said under his breath. Pictures of Mohammad Ali Jinnah, Nehru and Gandhi and the Viceroy Mountbatten flashed across his mind. "Do they even know what kind of calamity they have created?"

"Keep moving, keep moving," a man from a group of Sikhs standing at the border hollered. His flowing snowy white beard and white turban reminded Baldev of Baba Budh Singh back home.

"There's a refugee camp, two miles from here to the right. You will see it when you get there." He threw a packet of biscuits at the children in the jeep. The children devoured the biscuits like hungry cubs. The youngest child about three years old choked on the biscuit and coughed violently.

"Water, water!" looking around, the mother shouted. Baba Budh Singh look-alike man came with a large ladle of water. "You have a small pot?" he asked. Baldev shook his head. "We don't have anything. Only ourselves!"

The man tried giving water to the child directly from the ladle, who was already out of the coughing bout. The child took a small sip and gave out a joyful shriek. Everyone smiled forgetting their ordeal for the moment. All the children took turns drinking water from the ladle and laughed like there was nothing bad happening in the world.

The mother extended the leftover packet of biscuits towards Baldev.

"Keep it for the children," he told her.

"Have some, please!" She held the packet close to him.

Baldev took one. Munching on the biscuit he looked at the petrol gauge. It was down to nothing. *Hope it gets us to the camp,* he thought staring at it. He had not paid any attention to the petrol gauge since he left home.

About half a mile from the camp, the jeep stalled.

"Everyone walk to the camp," Baldev said.

The two older children started hopping and skipping towards the crowded camp as if they were going to a funfair. The grandmother tried to keep pace with them. "Slow down!" she hollered pulling the boy's arm towards her.

"Keep close!" she shouted at the girl who was already a few yards ahead of her. The girl stopped and waited for her to catch up. The mother carried the youngest child who tried to squirm out of her arms, but she held him tight.

Baldev and the children's father, Sukha Singh, pushed the jeep to the camp.

The children, who a minute ago were chirping and laughing, stood motionless as they reached the camp as if their innocent minds had sensed it was not a funfair after all.

The place was jampacked with people. Thousands of men women and children walked around looking bewildered and petrified. Some sat on the ground under the torching sun, fanning themselves with the ends of turbans and dupattas and some aimlessly wandered around. There were a few tents but were filled over the capacity.

In spite of the place being overcrowded, a deathly silence hung in the atmosphere. The gloomy faces of people looked like an unknown power had sucked out not only their physical strength but also their wits. Here and there a baby cried sounding like a sick kitten interrupting the eerie silence.

"You take care of your family," Baldev said to Sukha Singh, "I have to go and get some petrol for the jeep."

"How can I ever repay you? You saved my family." Wiping his eyes Sukha Singh gave Baldev an emotional embrace. "I will keep an eye on your jeep while you're gone," he added.

Baldev patted the children's heads and walked to the road going towards Amritsar filled with bullock carts going in the opposite direction towards Pakistan. The carts were loaded with suitcases and sacks filled to the limit. Some had hay for the animals, but the people looked equally bewildered as the people in the refugee camp.

After about three miles of walk, an old, rusty petrol station came in to view. Baldev, tired to his bones, heaved a sigh of relief.

"I need some petrol," Baldev said to the attendant.

"We don't have any."

"You don't?"

"No, we don't have any. I just told you."

"I don't need much, just enough to get to Amritsar," Baldev said in a very docile tone.

"We don't have any. Even if we did, how are you going to carry it? In your fists?"

"I'll buy a canister too. I'm sure you have a canister," Baldev said looking at a stack of canisters lying nearby.

"All right, you can buy a canister but no petrol."

"You are a Hindu brother and I am going to pay whatever the cost is. Then why do you have to lie?" Baldev said in a way as if he was talking about a proposal they were both going to work on.

"You're calling me a liar? I wouldn't sell it to you even if I had any," the attendant said looking at Baldev's gold *karra* on his wrist that Pali's mother had given him at his wedding.

Disappointed and tired Baldev turned to leave. Before he was gone far, a police vehicle turned to the petrol station and the attendant filled up the tank.

He's afraid of the authority or has some respect for them. No matter how angry Baldev was, this thought gave him some hope.

He had decided not to wear his uniform again when he returned from the war because it reminded him of his army brothers whose bodies he had to carry on his shoulders. It reminded him of the friends who were sitting next to him one minute and were blown to pieces the next moment. It reminded him of the days spent in flooded trenches and the screams of injured soldiers.

Although he never wanted to wear it again, he could not convince himself to throw it away either. It still lay packed in a bundle in the jeep under the seat.

Walking back to the camp he tried to remember the days he had been on the road. "Is it the third day or maybe the fourth?" he whispered to himself. An empty stomach and torturous journey had taken its toll on him. Joga Singh's pointless death had thrown him into lingering grief.

As he dragged his heavy lead laden feet towards the camp he heard a truck approaching from behind. Baldev waved at the truck to stop.

The truck stopped with a screech rather too close to him.

The driver wearing a blue turban shouted over the rumble of the truck, "Hop in!"

His companion, a young Hindu man opened the door for Baldev and he got into the truck.

"You okay, young man?" The middle-aged driver looked at Baldev's melancholic tired face. "Where're you heading to?"

"The camp," Baldev replied.

"You have family at the camp? How long you've been there? Where did you come from?" the driver bombarded him with questions in one breath.

"My family is at Gajanpur. I had come to look for my friend's family. They might be here at the camp." Baldev did not have the strength or the need to tell him the whole story.

"We are taking food to the refugee camp," the driver told him. Baldev's empty stomach growled at the name of the food. He had not eaten anything since he left home other than the tiny biscuit.

"You must be very hungry," the driver said. "Your stomach is louder than a thunder."

"I'm okay," Baldev lied.

"The food is in the back." The driver stopped the truck. "Billu, get some food for him," he told his companion.

"No, I'm okay. Really, I'm not hungry!" Baldev lied again. "The food is for the refugees."

"You look like a refugee to me too. You need to eat."

Billu brought a roti and potato *bhurji* from the back of the truck and handed it to Baldev. The compartment filled up with a spicy aroma. Baldev savored each bite of roti, as they sped towards the camp.

People swarmed towards the truck before it even stopped. Baldev helped the two to distribute the food as fast as possible. But the number of hands with spread fingers was too great to handle. People who sat in silence a little while ago were suddenly yelling and pushing each other. Out of thousands, only a handful were able to get food before it ran out.

"There's another truck coming soon with a lot more food," the driver shouted and started the truck. The crowd stumbled out of the way as it sped towards Amritsar. The sun was setting and a few clouds floated in the sky bringing some relief from the heat.

After the truck left, Baldev went looking for Roopi and her mother, who he guessed could be at the camp. Walking through the crowd, he shouted, "Anyone here from Khanpur? Anyone from Khanpur?"

Not long after, two men came running towards him. "We are from Khanpur!" both said simultaneously staring at Baldev.

"Is Kewal's family, his daughter, and wife here?" Baldev's face lit up with hope. "I am his friend, Baldev." He extended his hand to shake.

Instead of shaking his hand, they both looked at each other with a horrific look on their face.

"What is it?" Baldev sensed something terrible.

"They both drank from the well," the taller man who still had a tiny crumb of roti stuck in his beard said with a long sigh.

Baldev felt a spear was thrust into his chest. "Both of them?"

"We lost so many of our people." The other man shook his head as if trying to shake out some hideous memory from his mind.

Saddened and frustrated Baldev walked back, and found the family he had carried in his jeep nearby. The children ran up to him.

"Did you see my father?" the girl asked.

"Where did he go?" Baldev was confused by the question.

"He went to get food from the truck," the mother said.

"There he is!" the children shouted as they saw him walking towards them.

"I could not even get close to the truck," Sukha Singh said like a defeated soldier and sat on the ground in a kind of resignation. "How am I going to feed them?"

"There will be another truck soon, they told me," Baldev said to him. "Let me see what I can do." He took out his army uniform from under the seat and wore the pants over his *churidar*, seeing no place for privacy. He took off his white dirty shirt and put on the army shirt tucking it into his pants. Next, he tied his turban without a mirror. Suddenly he looked transformed into a man with authority. Remembering the petrol pump attendant staring at his gold *karra* he took it off and put it in his pocket.

"You're in the army?" The father sprang up from the ground astonished at Baldev's unexpected transformation.

"I was," Baldev said. "Not anymore. Listen, I need to go get petrol for the jeep. Why don't you wait near the truck entrance?"

Sukha Singh nodded.

Baldev walked out of the camp with renewed confidence although he was worried sick about his wife and parents back home.

The attendant saluted as Baldev entered the petrol station. He walked straight to the canisters and picked one.

"Here, fill it up," he said to the attendant.

"Yes, Sahib." The attendant filled up the canister without even looking at his face.

Baldev took out a bill and handed it to the attendant. The attendant seemed a little baffled as he handed him the change.

Chapter 78

"You want to tell me what happened, Son?" Hakam Singh said to Gurdeep.

"They killed everyone," the boy blurted out impatiently.

"Who killed everyone?" Hakam almost jumped off the cot.

"The *Muslas!* They came in the afternoon. Thousands of them." The boy started talking as if he was overflowing to tell it to someone. "They all had guns and spears and machetes."

"Where were you at that time?" Hakam asked.

"I... I was by the pond."

"Didn't they see you?"

"Don't know. I hid in the *gulabassi* bushes. There was a man and a little boy walking on the other side of the pond where there was no *gulabassi*," he said looking towards the door and took a deep breath. "They cut off the man's head and then hung the boy in the air with a spear stuck in his back."

Hakam gasped. The boy kept talking. He seemed eager to tell what had happened.

"Most of them ran toward the houses, yelling 'Allahu' and some stayed by the pond. They smashed a bullock-cart and made a fire. They kept putting more wood onto it. Many more arrived by carts and donkeys and tongas."

His face blank and eyes dry like black marbles, the boy's lips moved like a mechanized human toy.

"A little while later, I saw them dragging the women by the hair and feet and gathered them by the fire. Some of them holding babies were also brought there."

"What about the village men?" Hakam asked.

"I didn't see any men. They brought only the women. I saw my Ma and my sister and my brother's wife among them. She held my baby nephew. They beat all of them and tore their clothes off. They threw all the clothes into the fire."

366

"What? Your Ma and your…" Hakam felt his whole body spasm into painful knots.

"They burnt their clothes?"

Gurdeep nodded, "They snatched my nephew and threw him into the fire."

Hakam felt sick to his stomach.

"My mother tried to pull him out and they stabbed her. She didn't move anymore. Two other women with babies tried to run and their babies were thrown in the fire too. They were all screaming. I stuffed my turban into my mouth."

Hakam Singh stood up from the cot as if he could not bear to hear it anymore. The boy also stood up and kept talking as if he could not hold it inside of himself, any longer.

"They brought a Tonga and harnessed some of the old women to it in place of the horse. They did not have any clothes on. Many men climbed onto Tonga and ordered them to go around the pond while they laughed and whipped them. One woman fell and they stabbed her and cut the harness from her neck."

Hakam stood like a statue, listening to the boy spewing out words like corn popping out of a cauldron. He seemed in a hurry to tell everything.

"I bit hard on my turban and closed my eyes when they passed near the *gulabassi* bushes. When they reached back to the fire the *Muslas* started slashing their faces and they cut their breasts with machetes. They killed all the older women."

The boy stopped for a few moments and shook his head as if shaking out all the emotional feelings.

"My sister and the other girls were screaming and a *Musla* thrust a spear into one of the women's throat and she fell. They stopped screaming."

Hakam's hair stood on ends. How could humans be that cruel?

"And then they bound my sister and the other girls with ropes."

"Where was your father?"

"He was home when I took the buffalo to the pond to drink water. I hid when the *Muslas* came."

"And your brother was home too?"

The boy nodded and continued.

"The *Muslas* loaded the carts and donkeys with *sandooks* and all the other things from the houses and then I saw flames. The houses were burning. They tied my sister and my brother's wife and the other girls behind the carts and left. They did not give them any clothes to wear. They took our horses and the cattle too."

Hakam's hands spontaneously tensed into fists and his jaw tightened. He felt his bones cracking with rage. The boy did not seem to pay any attention to him and kept narrating the story as if reading from a book.

"When they were gone, I went home. My father and brother were tied to the tree with an iron chain in the courtyard. They were burnt. They were dead."

The boy looked at Hakam with desert-dry eyes. His face was vacant, and he swerved slightly side to side.

"*Bapu ji*, Ma says food is ready. Shall I bring it here?" Pali asked coming into the room.

"Shindi, Shindi...my sister..." the boy shouted as he saw Pali and collapsed on the floor. His eyes rolled back into the sockets.

"Oh, no..." Pali screamed.

"Go get water, Pali."

The boy regained consciousness but was impossible to console. He kept wailing, "Ma... *Bapu ji*..."

"What happened?" Harjit rushed in looking at the boy, then Hakam.

Hakam stood astounded not knowing what to do. A moment ago, the boy talked nonstop narrating a ghastly heinous story like it was only a dream, like nothing about it was real and now he was inconsolable and fainting.

"His whole family," Hakam mouthed and gestured as slitting the throat.

Harjit's questioning eyes almost bulged out of the sockets and she gasped for air.

"Gurdeep, open your eyes, Son." She sat on the floor.

Taking him in her arms, she rocked back and forth. "We'll take care of you...we will take care of you, Son."

The boy calmed down after a while. His shrieks slowly turned in to sobs.

"It's okay, it's all right," Harjit whispered in his ear.

The boy panted as if he had been running for miles.

"Look at me, Son. You can call me Ma. Here's your *Bapu ji* and sister." The boy looked at them one by one, sobbing and sighing.

Pali held his hand, "You're just like my little brother, Gurdeep. Everything will be okay."

Chapter 79

The fertile province of Punjab, the land of five rivers was torn into a Pakistani Punjab and an Indian Punjab. With the stroke of a pen on the map, a man who had never visited India had decided the fate of the people he knew nothing about. Cyril Radcliffe, a barrister from London, was flown in by the British to carve out a new country of Pakistan out of India.

Sitting behind a desk in a room, he stared at the map spread on a table and drew a zig-zag line on it, slashing the chest of Punjab into two parts. And those two parts writhed in pain like an animal whose belly was ripped open. What was just a line on a map was in fact a dagger thrust into the throats of millions of Punjabi people.

While Nehru and Jinnah celebrated and gave speeches about the newly acquired freedom from the British, the people who once lived side by side soaked the soil with each other's blood.

Hakam and Baba ji sat in the courtyard worrying their wits out, about humanity gone mad. Their village, Gajanpur was now part of Pakistan.

"It's hard to sleep at night, after what Gurdeep told us, and it's happening everywhere." Hakam's sleepless eyes looked swollen under his graying eyebrows.

Baba ji nodded, letting out a long breath. "This hellish fire is devouring the last bit of any goodness left intact."

"This is not independence this is annihilation of our very existence!" Hakam's face tightened as he tried to hold back his anger.

Baba ji held Hakam's trembling arm. "Take Harjit and Pali away for a little while, I suggest. Stay away a few days, until the situation settles down."

The sun had gone down but the mid-August evening was still bright. The birds had returned to their nests and children to their mothers. Smoke arose from the *tandoor* as Harjit added more wood to it, while Pali made the dough for *tandoory naan*. Gurdeep sat by Pali watching her kneading the wheat flour.

Although they could not hear Hakam and Baba ji, they looked at their worried faces every now and then.

"Where can we go Baba ji? This is our home. This is where we were born."

"Go to Rampur. Namo will be happy to see Pali and all of you."

"How can we leave without Baldev?"

"Not to worry about him, Hakam, I am here," Baba ji said. "You know the villages beyond Attari including Rampur have gone to India. It should be safe there."

"I know, but it's hard to believe that the whole Baar area became Pakistan, where we are the majority, and we own the land and we've been growing crops for generations."

"I'm baffled too, how could they give Nankana Sahib to Pakistan, the birthplace of Guru Nanak the founder of our Sikh faith?" Baba ji got up from the cot rubbing his palms together. "Listen Hakam, it's better to be safe than... Look what the boy told you."

"You're right, Baba ji."

"We have to talk to others too. We won't be able to fight against the army of butchers," Baba ji said hurrying out the door.

"Why did Baba ji leave abruptly like that? I thought he was having dinner with us," Harjit asked Hakam.

"I think we should go to Rampur for a few days until things get a little better," Hakam said ignoring Harjit's question.

"Okay, we can go when Bal comes back." Harjit looked towards the outside door.

"No, Harjit, we're leaving as soon as you pack a few clothes and jewelry in a bag. Tell Pali and Gurdeep to get ready."

"What are you talking about, Hakam? How can we leave now? It is going to be dark soon."

"Don't worry about the dark. It might be safer at night." The words seemed to be in a rush to leave his mouth, quicker than Hakam's lips could manage.

"I'm not leaving without my son. Do you hear me, Sardar ji?"

"We leave now!" Hakam yelled swinging his fist and aggressively stepped towards her. "You don't know what they do to the women."

Harjit stepped back shocked by his uncharacteristic sudden outburst. "What's happened to you Hakam?" she yelled back.

Pali and Gurdeep standing by the kitchen door stared at him equally baffled.

An absolute silence spread like an invisible wave in the courtyard. It seemed like the earth fell into a void. No sound, no wind, and no movement of any kind.

Taken aback by his own torrent of anger, Hakam felt weak. His legs shook uncontrollably and he sat on the cot.

"It's okay Hakam. We will do whatever you say." Harjit sat by him squeezing his hand.

The earth seemed back in its orbit. The usual evening sounds and noises of the village penetrated the silence and everything looked back to normal. But Hakam's mind did not. It silently screamed in anguish and dread of what Gurdeep had told him. He wanted to hide Harjit and Pali in his wings and fly somewhere far away. Instead, he said to Harjit, "I'm sorry. I shouldn't have yelled like that. It's just what's been going on around us."

"It's okay," Harjit said caressing his shoulders. They sat quietly for a while.

"Come here, Pali," Hakam's voice came out as if unsure of himself.

The three hugged, while Gurdeep stood by the kitchen like his feet were frozen to the floor.

"Come here, Son." Harjit's gesture to Gudeep was a bit louder than her voice, "You're part of this family now. Never think you're alone," she said including him in the group hug.

"We don't have to leave right now, Harjit. We can wait a few days till Baldev gets back." Hakam squeezed them all in his arms.

"Food is almost ready *Bapu ji*," Pali said.

Her voice was buried in hollering noises coming from the other side of the village.

"Sardar ji! Sardar ji!" Zahid came running. "They're attacking!" he yelled. "Bibi ji, please, run!" He looked like he had seen a ghost. His face red and mouth foaming at the corners, he kept shouting, "run, run..."

Harjit jumped up from the cot and ran in. She took out the brick from the inner room wall and retrieved the jewelry pouch. Pulling Pali by the arm she nudged Hakam to get up. He still sat on the cot looking bewildered.

"Let's go!" she yelled. Suddenly the roles seemed to have switched. Hakam, who a few minutes earlier wanted to leave right away, could not move as if his body was glued to the cot. Harjit, who did not want to leave until Baldev came home, yelled at Hakam to get up and move.

Screaming and yelling in the village became louder.

"To the sugarcane fields!" Harjit shouted pushing them out the door. They ran to the limit of their strength. Gurdeep and Zahid ran on either side of Hakam holding his arms.

"I will take care of your house and cattle, Sardar ji, till you come back!" Zahid said through tears. "They're not true Muslims. They're just cruel killers."

"I know, Zahid!" Hakam panted. "True Muslims are like you!" he said as they reached the sugarcane field.

"I am so sorry, Bibi ji." Zahid touched Harjit's feet in respect, "never imagined this could happen."

"Take care of yourself, Zahid. God willing we will come back soon," Harjit's voice quivered.

"May Allah protect you," Tears flowing, Zahid turned back.

They rushed through the sugarcane crop. The long sharp leaves left their arms and legs with cuts and abrasions.

"Here, we sit here!" Harjit whispered. They sat on the dry rough ground surrounded by the tall plants.

Hakam's breath slowly returned to normal.

Gurdeep sobbed silently. Pali pressed his hand that said more than assuring words.

Hearing the crunching sounds of dry leaves nearby, they held their breath. An infant cried not very far from where they sat. The very next moment, his voice was muted as if something was stuck in his throat. Hushing sounds continued for a while.

"I think, it is Nand Lal's family," Harjit whispered. "His grandson is about a month old." Hakam nodded.

Screaming and howling went on in the village that seemed to last forever. Then the dark night lit up with the rising flames. "The village is burning!" Hakam sighed.

Gurdeep squealed trying to stuff his mouth with the end of his turban and hid his face between his knees.

After a while, Nand Lal whispered through the sugarcanes, "Is it Hakam?"

"Yes," Hakam whispered back.

Nand Lal along with his son, daughter-in-law, and the baby grandson moved near Hakam and the two families sat motionless.

"I have to check on Baba ji," Hakam said to Harjit, as an orange hue appeared on the eastern horizon. "The *Muslas* I believe are gone."

"Wait a little longer. The houses are still burning." Harjit held Hakam's elbow. "Shhh!" Harjit tightened her grip on his elbow and put her finger on her lips.

A rustling sound came from the nearby cotton field. Two men came out like shadows and started walking towards the village.

"It's Master Jiwan Singh and Hardev." Hakam looked through the sugarcanes. First rays of dusty light struggled to penetrate the thick smokey air.

Master Jiwan Singh stopped in front of the sugarcane field, "Is anyone in there?" he asked in a barely audible voice.

"It's us, Hakam and Nand's family," Hakam's voice shook.

"I should go with them, see if there are any survivors in the village," Hakam said to Harjit.

"I will go with you." Nand Lal got up from the ground.

"We'll be back soon," Hakam said, as he and Nand came out of the field.

The four men walked cautiously towards the village, looking back and forth as if the devil of death would jump upon them any moment.

The houses smoldered. The streets littered with body parts of young and old. Battered bodies of naked women lay in the courtyards with severed breasts and limbs. Their guts hung out of their bellies. Half burnt bodies of their men hung from the trees.

Nand Lal's legs gave in and he lurched to one side and then to the other and managed to slowly fall to the ground. The very next moment he was throwing up.

"I'm okay. I'm okay!" he said, as he recovered from vomiting, "It is just unbearable..."

"Go back, Nand. You don't have to come with us," Jiwan Singh told him. "Don't tell them what you saw," he said as Nand Lal turned to go back.

They found Baba ji's body in the courtyard. One of his eyeballs hung out of the socket and the other was smashed in. His white turban and his severed legs lay nearby. His arms lay twisted in an unnatural position, still attached to his body.

"Baba ji!" Hakam screamed. His foot slipped on a pool of blood and he fell on Baba ji's mutilated body.

The roof of the house had collapsed and the neem tree was still burning with his son and teenage grandson tied to it. Melted body fat and seared blood dripping from the charred bodies collected under the scorched tree. There was no sign of his daughter-in-law.

The ghastly scene was excruciating. Humanity had died that day and Satan woke up with vicious demons that engulfed the last bit of compassion.

The village where they were born and played as boys; where they had worked in their fields and raised their families; and where so many of them had sacrificed their lives fighting for independence from the British. And this was the independence they received. The village they so loved, was burnt to ashes along with its people.

"We have to get out of here." Jiwan Singh helped Hakam up and they returned to the sugarcane field.

"Let's go," Hakam barely said the words. Harjit looked at him and without asking a question she gestured the others to get up. She felt the jewelry pouch in the inside pocket of her long shirt and walked out of the sugarcanes followed by Pali, Gurdeep, and Nand Lal's family.

Once outside, Hakam pointed to the west where the train station was supposed to be about fifteen miles away. The group started walking quietly. The sun arose with a vengeance. The scorched earth smelled of blood and smoke.

More people joined them on the way from nearby villages and a caravan of tired hungry people kept walking.

Chapter 80

The train station was a scene of chaos. People shouted and tried to get into the already stuffed bogies. People sat on the roof of the train. There were people in the doorways. Some dangled by the windows with no place to rest their feet on.

The survivors of the Gajanpur massacre ran towards the train but no place to set their feet. Jiwan tried to struggle his way in but was pushed out.

"Where do you come from?" one of the men in the train asked no one in particular.

"Gajanpur!" Hakam Singh and Jiwan answered simultaneously. The train left with a screech puffing out dark smoke.

The platform quickly filled up with thousands of Sikhs and Hindus, leaving their homes and thriving crops and cattle behind, in the newly created Pakistan, to seek shelter in India.

"Buy the tickets for the next train, that'll be coming soon," they were told. Muslim police roamed the station.

Pushing and shoving, people herded towards the ticket window.

"Four to Amritsar." Hakam Singh extended two bills towards the ticket master when his turn came.

"It takes ten bills per person," the ticket master said staring at Pali, standing nearby with Harjit and Gurdeep.

Hakam put his hand in his pocket and pulled out all the bills he had. "Here," he said. "20 more." The ticket master counted the bills.

"It took only two bills for four tickets, before." Hakam's voice was filled with helplessness as he put his hand back in his empty pocket.

"Hurry up!" Someone pushed him from behind.

"Twenty more or get out of the line," the ticket master yelled.

"Here, take these." Harjit walked to the window with a pair of gold bangles.

"These might only be worth ten bills. I'm sure you have more," the ticket master said without taking his eyes off of Pali.

Harjit's eyes popped open. "Each one of these is over a hundred."

"You want to get to Amritsar or not?" the ticket master yelled. "There are other people behind you."

"If you don't want to spend the money, let the others get the tickets." A man tried to shove them out of the line.

"Take these." Harjit slammed two more bangles on the ticket window.

"Now get out of here," the ticket master yelled handing them four tickets. Two policemen standing behind him laughed and patted his shoulder. "Well done!"

Another train came already filled to capacity. A river of people ran towards it before it came to a stop.

Men tried pushing women and children into the train and themselves clung to the doors and windows.

Gurdeep pulled Pali by the arm and pushed through the crowd followed by Harjit. Hakam tightly gripped the metal bar and clung to the door, along with Jiwan and Hardev.

"Where's Nand Lal?" Hakam looked around.

"Oh, no!" Hardev said as he saw him standing on the platform along with his family away from the crowd.

People standing in the ticket window ran to the train too and pushed their families without tickets into the packed compartments.

The train picked up speed without ever coming to a complete stop.

Suddenly the cracking sound of pewww...pewww, boom...boom ripped through the air and men clinging to the doors and windows started falling like rocks on to the platform. The Muslim police fired at the train without warning. Ear-splitting screams and howling created mayhem unparalleled to any. The train ran faster than ever and was quickly past the platform.

"Hakam..." Harjit screamed and pushed through the crowd towards the door as Hakam's bullet strewn body fell to the ground followed by Hardev. People held Harjit's arms as she tried to jump after Hakam.

"Let me go!" she yelled fighting off people holding her.

Injured men kept falling from the roof as the train picked up speed. Soon the fallen people were out of sight, as the train moved along a curve.

"Come back, Ma!" Pali held Harjit's arm and walked her towards the middle of the compartment. People made way for them as they passed by.

Chapter 81

It was late in the evening Baldev drove back to the Pakistan border at Atari. The road was still jammed with unending rows of bullock carts carrying uprooted people. Driving to the opposite direction through ditches and spiny bushes, the two-mile distance from camp to the border took hours.

The Sikh volunteers were still there, guiding the refugees to the camp, as they did when Baldev had arrived there in the morning.

Large earthen pots filled with water lay by the roadside with ladles hanging around the rim. Volunteers walked around distributing water and biscuits to the refugees.

Two of the volunteers hurried towards him, "Good, you're here!" One of them, a tall man with a long graying beard excitedly shouted loud enough to be heard by the others and shook Baldev's hand.

Baldev, puzzled by his remarks, looked at him and then at the other man.

"We've been waiting for the army for so long and they sent just one person?" the other man with a carelessly tied blue turban and tired dry lips said giving an equally puzzled look to Baldev.

"I'm not sent by anyone," Baldev said. "I'm trying to get home."

"Home?"

"Yes, my family is back in Gajanpur."

"You're not the army?" They stared at his uniform.

"No. I left the army when I came back from Burma."

"So you're not in the army anymore?" the man wearing the blue turban asked again with disappointment written all over his face.

"No, I am not."

"You fought in Burma?"

Baldev nodded.

"Thousands of our young men gave their lives fighting on behalf of the British and this is how they repaid us," the man with the gray beard said looking at the river of refugees pouring into Indian Punjab. He raised his arms above his head and reflexively brought them down slapping the sides of his thighs.

"They snatched the very ground from under our feet."

"Did you say your family is in Gajanpur?" The blue-turbaned man seemed to have suddenly remembered.

"Yes."

"Most of the villages in the Baar area, we hear, have already been emptied out in the last few days," he said.

"Emptied out?" Baldev remembered Khanpur's empty streets and wild dogs. A sharp electric jolt shook him. "But I have to find my family."

"Your family might have survived but you won't if you go into Pakistan now."

"What's going on?" An older man walked towards them.

"Baba ji, you go rest for a while. You've been on your feet all day," the volunteer said to him.

Baldev recognized Baba Budh Singh lookalike man. He touched his feet to show respect.

"He's not the army," the volunteer said.

"He wants to go to Gajanpur," the other volunteer pitched in.

"His family is there, he says."

They talked about Baldev as if he was not there.

I have downright disappointed them. A feeling of guilt enveloped him. *I have draped myself with a lie!* Baldev felt the uniform cutting through his skin.

Baba ji looked at him straining his eyes. "Didn't you come with your family this morning?"

"I picked up that family on the way. The children and women were unable to walk," Baldev told him.

Baba ji patted Baldev's back. "Listen, Son, you wait here or even better at Amritsar train station."

"Most of the people from that area are coming by train, I hear." The blue-turbaned volunteer agreed with Baba ji's suggestion.

Baldev nodded and reversed the jeep towards Amritsar. *I will keep the uniform on for the time being.* He unsuccessfully tried to straighten a wrinkle from his uniform pants.

******

378

Baldev walked a few steps towards the train station and looked back. He stood motionless for a few moments, and then went back to the jeep. He retrieved the gun from under the tarpaulin and looked at it as if he had seen it for the first time. *What good is a gun without the bullets?* The thought convinced him to put it back. The very next moment he changed his mind, *a gun without bullets is better than bullets without the gun.* He took it out from under the tarpaulin again, slung it over his shoulder, and hurried to the railway station.

The train station was flooded with thousands of people. It looked like an anthill had been knocked off and millions of ants were wandering around aimlessly. People made way for him as he passed through the crowd. "The army!" He heard them whisper.

The platform was full of Muslims waiting for a train to Pakistan. They looked bewildered and hungry and tired. Children clung to their mothers. Men stood by the *sandooks* and suitcases and their other belongings.

Baldev walked to the opposite platform where the trains from Pakistan were supposed to be coming. The crowd parted to let him pass through as he went up the stairs and across the bridge to the other side.

This platform was equally crowded with people waiting for their family members. They looked scared and talked to each other in hushed voices as if an unspeakable catastrophe loomed over their heads.

How am I going to find them? Baldev's head was spinning with exhaustion and trepidation. He noticed a group of people inquisitively looking at him. They whispered to each other and some of them walked up to him.

"Why are we letting them go while they killed thousands of our people?" One of them pointed to the Muslim crowd on the other platform.

"They massacred the whole train that came here yesterday," another man said. His face turned red and the veins in his neck inflated like taut ropes as if he was trying to suppress his anger, "only the dead bodies reached here."

"And the ones, who escaped death, came in filthy torn bloody clothes and nothing else."

Baldev's gaze slipped from one face to another while he heard the horrific account of killings. A pained look appeared on his face.

"Our army is protecting them and their army joined the marauders to kill our people."

Dazed by the comments he did not know how to respond. He just listened as if he was contemplating how to solve the problem.

"I bet you're here to protect them," one of the men, who had not uttered a word so far, said stepping a little closer.

"Listen, I am here just like you, looking for my family," Baldev told them.

"Your family is in Pakistan?"

"Yes, I'm hoping they are alive and get here by the next train."

Suddenly ear-splitting screams came from the other side. A group of Sikhs and Hindus wielding swords ran onto the platform attacking the Muslims waiting for the train.

Baldev ran up onto the bridge between the platforms, "Get away from those people," he roared, brandishing the gun.

People looked up. Baldev stood on the bridge like a giant who would crush anyone who dared to step forward.

"Army!" someone shouted.

"Get out of here!" Baldev roared again, even louder, this time, "or I will bust your heads!" The attackers started dispersing.

At the same time, a train stopped and people pushed their children and women into the compartments. Within a minute the train was gone leaving behind a few dead and a blood-stained platform.

Baldev looked down at the other crowd where people had been complaining to him just a minute ago. All the turbaned heads were turned upward staring at him. He felt their angry looks burning holes through his body. *They can crush my head in a split second.* Baldev felt his heart jumping out of his chest.

He put the gun onto the floor of the bridge. Gathering all the grit in his being he stood tall and strong like a tree. He raised his arms and bellowed at the top of his lungs, "Listen, brothers, our Gurus taught us never to attack the unarmed or the weak."

Suddenly there was pin-drop silence. Feeling more confident he continued, "I pray to you, if we let them go unharmed, our families will come home unharmed too."

The very next moment, several people shouted,

"Where were you yesterday when a train full of bodies arrived from Pakistan?"

"They slaughtered thousands of our people in Pakistan and you let them go?"

The voices got buried under the thunderous rumble of an approaching train. Smoke and steam along with two high pitched whistles of the train filled the atmosphere.

Forgetting about Baldev they all ran towards the train. "They're alive! They're alive…"

People hanging by the doors and windows started jumping onto the platform before the train came to a complete stop. As soon as the wheels screeched to a halt, people rolled out of the doors like potatoes spilling out of knocked over gunny sacks. Some jumped down from the roof and some helped others to get down.

People from the train as well as people from the platform ran around calling the names of their family members. They laughed and cried and hugged as they found each other.

Baldev ran down the bridge shouting, "Anyone from Gajanpur? … Anyone from Gajanpur?"

Many people he did not know hugged him and told him they didn't know anyone. Some shook hands with him looking at his uniform.

Baldev kept shouting through the noisy chaos.

"Did you say Gajanpur?" a man asked.

Baldev nodded eagerly.

"There were a few of them, but couldn't get on to the train."

"They couldn't get on to the train?"

"There was no room."

"You sure they were from Gajanpur?"

"Yes, there were quite a few."

Before Baldev could ask him anymore the man was surrounded by his family and walked to the exit.

Baldev along with many other disappointed people stayed, waiting for the next train.

Chapter 82

Where are we? How far is Amritsar? Pali felt lost and terrified. *Baldev doesn't know where we are. How will he find us?* Her body pulsated with muted sobs.

The wooden seats of the third-class compartment of the train were jampacked. The space in-between the seats and the aisles were crammed with people standing shoulder to shoulder. They swayed side to side as one unit with the movement of the train. A few of the men, who had escaped the police shooting, still clung to the door. No room for them to move inside. Even the toilets were packed with the fleeing destitute. The compartment was hot like a *tandoor* and smelled of sweat and urine.

The thriving farmers and landlords of the Baar area of Punjab, who fed the masses of India, were running for their lives, hungry and penniless. Village after village was plundered and people slaughtered like sheep. Prosperous a few days ago, paupers today, they were stuck in the train that chugged along slowly and reluctantly, as if unsure where it would end up.

Pali wiped her eyes and looked at Harjit sitting on the floor next to her, with her knees against her chest. She had not opened her eyes since Hakam Singh fell off the train. She looked pale as if the blood had been squeezed out of her body.

Pali turned her head to the left. Gurdeep sat with his chin resting on his fists. His unblinking gaze was fixed straight ahead, perhaps looking nowhere. He had not spoken a word since they left home. The crowd had pushed them towards the middle of the compartment after Hakam fell and Harjit had tried to jump after him. People had squeezed close together to make room for them. The three of them sat on the floor in-between the seats, Pali in the middle and Harjit, and Gurdeep on either side of her.

The compartment was quiet other than the monotonous chug-chug of the engine and spontaneous sighs leaving people's lips. They stood still as if still numb from the police firing at the refugees and men falling like rocks, while the train kept going.

How long have we been on the train? Pali tried to remember. *Was it yesterday or the day before?* She felt her brain had frozen and her heart was going to stop beating. The screams she had held back, were about to explode inside of her. Blood rose to her head and she felt her eyeballs about to rupture. Trying to control herself she rubbed her forehead and closed her eyes.

"Why's the train slowing down?" someone said.

People looked at each other.

Soon the train came to a complete halt.

Deathly silence overtook the compartment. Not even a sigh escaped. People forgot to breathe. They stared at each other without blinking. People stood dumbfounded as if a tempest was buried underneath the stillness.

The momentary silence suddenly broke by mumbling voices rising from every corner of the compartment.

"What's going on?"

"Why is the train stopping?"

"What station is this?"

Hearing the voices Pali opened her eyes and tried to look outside. Sitting on the floor, the only thing she could see was legs. She looked to the other side. More legs. Her vision was completely blocked by the people standing in front of the windows and every inch of the compartment.

"Is it Lahore station or are we already at Amritsar?" A man, wearing a long, white shirt with mud stains all over and a yellow turban torn to rags, asked looking at the people by the windows.

"There's no platform," someone near the left side window said.

"What about the other side?" a man standing in the middle of the aisle asked.

"No platform on this side either, only the sugarcane fields."

"Why would the train stop in the middle of nowhere?"

"It's been moving awfully slow from the very beginning."

"Maybe something's wrong with the engine."

People talked in hushed voices drenched in fear of some impending danger.

"I have a bad feeling about this," a young woman said to the man she stood next to. Her voice breaking up and eyes wide open, she wiped the sweat from her forehead. Her dark peach color *kameez* and an ornately embroidered *dupatta* looked almost new and pricy. The woman seemed to be around Pali's age.

"Don't say that!" the man wearing equally nice clothes said.

"Something's wrong. Otherwise, why would they stop the train in the middle of nowhere?" She held his arm by the elbow. Her lips quivered as the color from her face evaporated.

"Stop talking like that!" the man wrapped his arm around her. "Everything will be fine," he said bringing his face close to hers. The woman rested her head on his shoulder.

The couple stood not far from where Pali sat on the floor. She looked at them and could not keep her eyes off of them. She looked at her own clothes. Light green silk *kameez* and yellow *dupatta* with intricate green embroidery that matched with the color of the *kameez. One of my favorites!* A smile disappeared before it came to her lips. The muddy stains on her clothes reminded her of hiding in the sugarcane fields and the rising flames and screams from the village.

Looking at the couple consoling each other, she felt a razor-sharp twinge in her heart. How badly she wanted Baldev to hold her and comfort her. *Where are you, Bal?* She fought to bury the anguished scream that eventually came out as a loud sigh.

"Ma ji!" Pali shook Harjit's shoulder.

Harjit's eyes flickered.

"Wake up, Ma!" she shook her a little harder.

"What is it Pali?" Gurdeep asked as if he had come out of a daze.

"Ma won't wake up," Pali said and shook her again.

Harjit struggled to open her eyes. She looked at Pali and then at Gurdeep.

"You're awake!" Pali said, rubbing Harjit's hand. The taut lines of anxiety on her face eased. She heaved a sigh of relief. But the very next moment the panic returned as she heard people talking about the train in subdued voices.

"The train is not moving anymore, Ma." Pali turned pale again.

Harjit looked around and seemed to have become aware of the surroundings. She put her arm around Pali and reached out to pat Gurdeep's knee. "We'll be okay!" she said.

The already blistering hot compartment became even hotter. Loud thudding sounds and shouting started coming from the back of the train. They all turned their head towards the noise.

"They're attacking the back compartments!" Men clinging to the door shouted and tried to push in. "They're swinging swords and machetes."

People pulled the men into the compartment over their shoulders like logs, as there was hardly any room to put their feet on the floor.

"Shut the door!" a man standing at a little distance from the door yelled. He was a tall, well-built man with a neatly tied turban and rolled up beard under his chin, as do the Sikh soldiers in the army. He wore a white shirt tucked into the khaki pants with big side pockets.

A few of the men near the door stood on each other's thighs to make room for closing the door and then pushed their backs against it.

"Close all the windows," the man wearing the khaki pants ordered and pushed himself through the crowd towards the door. "Let the women and children move to the center." There was a bit of authority in his voice.

Pali and Harjit stood up from the floor to make more room around them as the women from the periphery of the compartment moved towards the middle.

"Anyone have any machetes or knives?" he shouted as soon as he reached next to the door. "Any size is good, big or small."

A few reached for their belongings pushing through a jumble of legs and arms and torsos to retrieve knives and machetes. They passed them from one person to the next in a chain action, handing them over to the men near the doors and windows of the compartment.

"Wrap your turbans or whatever clothes you can get, tightly around your hands and arms," he commanded. The man had taken the leadership role and people listened to him.

Pali looked at him without blinking, *is this man really going to save us?* She wondered.

"Gurdeep." She touched his turban and then pointed towards the man. Gurdeep took off his turban and handed over to the person standing next to him, who passed it on to the next and finally to a man near the door. Many other men standing far from the door took off their turbans and gave to the ones near the doors and windows. Older women offered their heavy cotton *dupattas* to the men preparing to fight the mob.

"We will snatch their swords and use them against whosoever tries to get in," the leader shouted.

As they stood ready to strike back, a deeply tense silence ensued. Everyone's eyes were fixed on the leader who stood tall and confident with a fierce sternness in his gaze. Pali looked at him with admiration. *If Baldev was here he'd done the same.* Her neck reflexively straightened as if she was looking at an older version of Baldev. A loud bang on the door hurled her back to the present and her body shuddered with fear. She tucked her head into her knees.

The attackers were outside the compartment banging on the door and the windows, yelling obscenities.

"We will fight to the last breath," the leader bellowed.

"We will fight…" the men answered in unison, wielding little knives. Most of the men swung their rag wrapped fists in the air. Courage won over the fear and they were ready to face the assailants.

"Bole So Nihal!" the leader roared.

"Sat Sri Akal!" Everyone including the women and children, young and old, answered at the top of their lungs. The compartment reverberated with the Sikh war cry.

One of the windows shattered and the glass flew into the compartment. A group of attackers tried to get in but were pushed back by the men stabbing their hands with knives. In the meanwhile, the mob kept banging on the door with iron rods, swords, and axes. The men in the train stood ready to strike back.

Finally, the door gave out and a throng of attackers tried to push in.

The leader snatched the sword from one of the unsuspecting attackers with lightning speed. Many layers of the tightly wrapped rags worked like a shield against the sword blade when he yanked it away. He turned around with such force that the head of the man was severed with one stroke and landed a few feet away from the train, shooting a fountain of blood on the way.

Encouraged by this, many others snatched axes and swords from the enemy. Very quickly the tables were turned and the attackers were now being attacked.

Finally, the assailants gave up on this compartment and ran to the other parts of the train leaving a few of their dead behind and many injured lying on the ground.

The men fought off the enemy with unparalleled courage. Many of them received injuries to their hands and arms while grabbing the weapons from the aggressors, but none too serious. The danger had been averted, for the time being, it seemed. But shrilly screams and howling continued in the adjacent compartments.

"Look!" someone near the door shouted. A man was dragging a young woman by the arm while she struggled to free herself.

The leader took the ax from a man nearby and hurled it at the kidnapper. It struck him at the shoulder severing his arm from the body and he fell flat on the ground with a sky-reaching howl.

The girl ran back towards the train. The leader and the other men helped her into the compartment.

The young woman was inconsolable. "They killed my little brother. They killed him…"

She screamed and kept wailing. "He tried to save me and they killed him."

"Help her towards the center with the other women," the leader said.

"They killed my father too…"

The woman immediately took to comforting her. They hugged her and wiped her tears. She lay in one of the older woman's lap, limp and exhausted. Pali sat next to her holding her hand.

"Sardar ji tell us your name," a man standing next to the leader asked as things settled down a little.

"Bachan Singh," he said looking around the compartment.

"Bachan Singh, *zindabad*!" someone in the crowd shouted.

"Long live Bachan Singh!" the compartment resounded with the shouts.

"Listen, everyone, we're not completely out of the woods yet," Bachan Singh hollered between the shouts. "They might come back any moment and we must not slack off."

The compartment went silent for no more than a moment when the shouts, "Get away from the train!" resonated in the air. Men on horsebacks seemed to have appeared out of nowhere and shot their rifles into the air, yelling at the assailants. The mob started running away. Many of them were shot while running.

"The army!"

"Indian army!"

"They all have rifles!"

People near the windows excitedly cried out.

The horsemen went back and forth a few times along the train. Soon the train gave a worn-out whistle and started moving.

As the train picked up speed a horseman galloped along and tossed a young woman into the compartment, he obviously had rescued from the attackers.

"Take care of her!" he shouted.

Chapter 83

Restlessly walking back and forth on the platform, the words, *there were people from Gajanpur but the train was too full for them to get in,* kept drumming his ears.

"That's what he had said, I'm sure," Baldev stopped walking for a moment and looked in the direction the train from Pakistan was supposed to come.

The platform had filled up with people, again to the limit. He felt an invisible bond with them. They were all like him, eagerly waiting for their families. Some of them stood motionless like statues and some ambled around aimlessly.

Hours went by and no sign of the train. "It should've been here by now," Baldev mumbled. "But there are no fixed times for trains these days," he answered himself.

Late afternoon the sky suddenly ripped open with thunderous lightning and pouring rain. People huddled under the tin roof that covered only a small portion of the platform near the bridge. Baldev along with many others stood in the rain-soaked to the skin. The slanting rain had not spared even the ones under the tin roof, except a few standing at the back.

The rain stopped after a while and a weak evening sun reluctantly peeped out of the clouds. For a moment it played peek-a-boo with the clouds and slowly disappeared down the western horizon. People started leaving at nightfall and the train station looked abandoned. Only a few stayed back, walking around in their soggy clothes.

Around midnight, a speck of light appeared on the Pakistan side of the train tracks and quickly grew bigger and brighter. A feeble chug-chug noise of the approaching train came a little later.

"The train! It's here!" many shouted.

The train let out a howling whistle before reaching the platform.

"Something's wrong!" Baldev shouted. "There's no one on the roof or clinging to the doors." He ran towards the train, as did many others.

Baldev entered the nearest compartment. A few bodies lay by the door. Blood mixed with the rainwater dripped onto the platform. People had huddled in the center, many lying on top of each other. No one moved.

"You are in Amritsar. You're safe now," Baldev hollered.

People slowly started moving from under the heap of flesh and bones.

"It's okay, you can come out now," Baldev called. His voice breaking and his heart hammering his chest he looked for Pali and his parents. No sign of them. He helped many of the wounded off the train.

A woman stood in the doorway of the next compartment holding a severed head in her arms. "They killed my son," she howled. Someone recognized her and ran to help her down the train.

Earsplitting screaming of the survivors and the relatives of the dead shook the ground under their feet. Many people from the surrounding communities rushed to the train station. Baldev went from compartment to compartment, asking, "Anyone from Gajanpur? Anyone seen a man name Hakam Singh?" No one seemed to know anything.

Suddenly he bumped into a man near one of the compartments. Without paying attention to him, he kept going, "Anyone from Gajanpur!"

The man ran after him. "Baldev! Baldev!" he shouted.

Baldev turned his head, "Bachan Singh?" He hurried back towards him, "You? Here?" He stared at him. "I can't believe it!" he said.

The unexpected encounter of the friends sparked a moment of triumph amidst the gloom and grief of the situation. They held each other in a tight embrace and laughed. They had fought together against the Japanese in Burma under the British Indian army. They had stayed back at Rangoon to keep order and peace in the city, after the war had ended but had lost contact after coming back home.

"Were you on this train too?" Bachan Singh asked.

"No, I'm looking for my family. I hope they didn't take this train," Baldev said.

"I hope so too. They attacked us in hordes," Bachan Singh said. "If the army had not arrived, we might have all been killed."

"What about your family, Bachan?" Baldev asked but then remembered that his wife had died before the war and he had two grown children.

"Both my daughters are married and live at Patiala. That's where I'm heading to."

Baldev nodded. "Good. They're safe."

The train had almost emptied out by now and the platform swarmed with people.

Through the tumultuous shouting and screaming, both went around looking for Baldev's family. "Anyone from Gajanpur?" Baldev shouted over the deafening noise, again and again. "Anyone from Gajanpur?"

******

"Ma ji, it's Bal. I heard him!" Holding Harjit's arm Pali pushed through the crowd. "Come, quick." She nudged Gurdeep.

"Bal!" Pali hollered and waved her arms in the air. "Take care of Ma," she said to Gurdeep and ran towards Baldev who had turned in the opposite direction.

Pushing through the dense crowd her *dupatta* got caught in people's belongings and gunnysacks. For a while, she kept freeing it but later she let it go. Her hair disheveled and her *dupatta* lost, she flailed her arms in the air, "Baldev! I'm here!"

Seeing a young woman, without the headcover, frantically trying to run through the crowd, people pushed against each other to make room for her to keep going.

"Baldev!" out of breath, she kept hollering.

"Did someone call my name?" Baldev turned his head, "Did I hear Pali?"

"Someone is calling you!" Bachan Singh shook Baldev's shoulder.

"I'm here, Pali... I'm here!" Baldev rammed through the crowd towards the voice.

The next minute, Pali was in his arms sobbing hysterically. Soon after, Harjit caught up with them. His already damp shirt became drenched with their downpour of tears.

Gurdeep stood motionless staring at them. "He's Gurdeep, my brother." Pali took his arm. Baldev looked at the boy curiously and squeezed him to his chest along with Pali and Harjit.

"Where's *Bapu ji?*" Baldev asked, but the look on Harjit and Pali's face told the untellable tale.

"I'm sorry Baldev." Bachan Singh patted his shoulder.

Pali saw Bachan Singh standing next to Baldev and gasped, "You saved us! He saved the whole compartment." She turned to Baldev. "You know him?"

"We fought the Japanese together, in Burma," Bachan Singh said.

Baldev stood astounded for a while. "Thank you!" his voice quivered as he gave Bachan a heartfelt hug.

Chapter 84

While the trains reached the platform filled with bodies and people wailed, Nehru's speech blared on the radio, "Long years ago, we made a tryst with destiny; and now the time comes when we shall redeem our pledge, not wholly or in full measure, but very substantially. At the stroke of the midnight hour, when the world sleeps, India will awake to life and freedom…"

"Did he say India will wake to life and freedom? Many people yelled as if Nehru could hear them. What freedom? He calls it life. What 'life' does he talk about? It is death, not life."

The radio continued, "Before the birth of freedom we have endured all the pains of labor…"

What pains did he endure?

Gandhi, Nehru, Jinnah, all bastards…

"Freedom and power bring responsibility. That responsibility rests upon this assembly, a sovereign body representing the sovereign people of India."

Suddenly the electric power was turned off at the train station, and the radio went silent.